Praise for Steph Mullin and Nicole Mabry

"This thriller keeps the shocks coming right up to the climactic end."
Lisa Gardner

"A fast-paced thrill ride, with dark twists and clever plotting that had me up way past my bedtime – and triple-checking the locks before I could finally fall asleep!"
Andrea Bartz

"A very original take on the serial killer theme with plenty of jaw-dropping moments."
Alex Pine

"A fresh, inventive take on the thriller. Brilliant and deliciously dark, it'll keep you enthralled until the very last page!"
Jeneva Rose

"Mesmerizing and chilling, *The Family Tree* simmers with tension. Expertly paced, it will keep you turning the pages right up to the stunning conclusion."
Daniela Petrova

"From the first page I was hooked. One word captures it all: Unputdownable."
Pamela Crane

"Pacy, compellingly creepy and, at times, blackly funny."
Sharon Dempsey

"Chilling from page one, this twisted and twisty thriller is sure to keep you up at night – either because you can't stop reading, or because you're too afraid to sleep."
Megan Collins

Steph Mullin is a creative director and Nicole Mabry works in the photography department for a television network. They met as co-workers in New York City in 2012, discovering a shared passion for writing and true crime. After Steph relocated to Charlotte, North Carolina in 2018, they continued to collaborate creatively. Separated by five states, they spend countless hours scheming via FaceTime and editing each other's typos in real time on Google Docs.

Nicole lives in Queens, New York, and is also the author of *Past This Point*, an award-winning apocalyptic women's fiction novel. *When She Disappeared* is the duo's second crime novel.

Also by Steph Mullin and Nicole Mabry

The Family Tree

WHEN
SHE
DISAPPEARED

STEPH MULLIN
NICOLE MABRY

avon.

Published by AVON
A division of HarperCollins*Publishers* Ltd
1 London Bridge Street
London SE1 9GF

www.harpercollins.co.uk

HarperCollins*Publishers*
1st Floor, Watermarque Building, Ringsend Road
Dublin 4, Ireland

A Paperback Original 2022
2

First published in Great Britain by HarperCollins*Publishers* 2022

A catalogue copy of this book is available from the British Library.

ISBN: 978-0-00-846127-0

This novel is entirely a work of fiction. The names, characters and incidents portrayed in it are the work of the author's imagination. Any resemblance to actual persons, living or dead, events or localities is entirely coincidental.

Typeset in Sabon LT Std by Palimpsest Book Production Limited,
Falkirk, Stirlingshire

Printed and Bound in the UK using 100%
Renewable Electricity at CPI Group (UK) Ltd

MIX
Paper from
responsible sources
FSC
www.fsc.org
FSC™ C007454

This book is produced from independently certified FSC™ paper to ensure responsible forest management.
For more information visit: www.harpercollins.co.uk/green

From Steph:
To my Aunt Chris Gerace-Johnson, for always
inspiring me to be brave and go after my dreams.

From Nicole:
For Rachael Ann, our brown-eyed girl,
our love for you will never end.

INTO THIN AIR: Season 9 Episode 903

'Whatever Happened to Jessie Germaine?'

Original Air Date: 10/10/2004

On May 26, 2004, Jessie Germaine went to school, turned in her final History project and cheered at a rally. Sometime that evening, she rode her bike into the forest and disappeared . . . Into Thin Air.

PROLOGUE

June 7th, 2019

~Fledgling hawks soar to peaking crests
Behind the canopy you'll find your quest
Jump the path at Lightning Tree
Journey west to rocks stacked three
Travel along the whispering creek
Pass the falls for what you seek.
Hawks fly high for the final test
We'll pass the torch at Senior Nest~

'You don't have to do this, Lenny. No one will give you a hard time if you jump from the lower rock. You're one of our best football players; the team is screwed if you get hurt! They'll understand.'

Lenny stood next to Farrah on the rocky ledge some thirty feet above the pool of water, its dark blue surface rippling tauntingly as the late-day sunlight bounced off it. His classmates were all in their underwear, but he couldn't bring himself to remove his oversized t-shirt. He'd hit six foot seven that year and topped the scales at over three hundred pounds. Surrounded by his much

3

shorter and smaller friends, his confidence waned, even with his popularity as the best defensive end in the state. But he refused to be left behind during this crucial moment. His class had been counting down to their final day of junior year, and they had finally made it. He was determined to join in as the exiting senior class ushered his own class into senior-hood in this secret hazing ritual Lenny now faced. He'd heard whispers of a traditional passing of the torch for years, but no one had ever spilled what they had to do. Not until they'd arrived at their destination.

Lenny eyed the water warily, weighing his options. If he walked away, he would surely be the class laughing-stock until the day he graduated. But if he jumped, well . . . he was bigger than everyone else. No one knew how deep the swimming hole was in this secret spot. Hell, they didn't even know it existed until those notes showed up in their lockers just that morning, giving them clues on how to get there. The thrill of the unknown had been exciting at the time, but now . . .

Everyone else had already jumped; the dare they were all required to complete for this transition of power and gain access to the coolest, most secluded party-spot in town for all of senior year. The cove next to the rock upon which he now stood was already decked out with coolers, a fire-pit and old lawn chairs, ready for a party at a moment's notice. It was one of the most epic places Lenny had ever seen, and he dreaded the idea of being excluded for failing the test.

'Really, Lenny, it's OK. You don't have to do it,' Farrah said kindly. She had waited with him at the end of the line. They'd been flirting all semester ever since Jake's party when Lenny had driven her home. He didn't want to be the only one not jumping off the top rock, and he certainly didn't want her to think less of him.

'I can do this,' he said with feigned bravado. 'It'll be OK, Farrah, really. It's your turn, you go.'

She hesitated but, after an encouraging smile from Lenny, nodded and walked to the edge. She glanced back at him, giving him a heart-melting smile just before she leapt off. He was stunned by the silence of her fall as she disappeared from sight, the beauty of that last moment a ghost lingering in his eyes. He heard a splash and hurried to the edge, looking nervously down below. His classmates were positioned around the perimeter of the swimming hole like a crescent moon, some sitting on the ledge of the cove, some treading water. They clapped and cheered, but for a second, Lenny couldn't breathe. *Where is she?* Then suddenly bubbles rose to the surface followed by Farrah. When she broke through, she wiped her face and smiled up at him, ecstatic. He heaved a sigh of relief. She pulled her hand back across her wet hair and the smile fell instantly from her face.

'My cheer bow!' she yelled, her voice echoing off the rocks. She spun in a circle, looking frantically into the water, then dipped her head down and dove under. A moment later, she came up, panting and empty handed. 'I lost my bow! I should have taken it off before I jumped,' she hollered up at him. Then her expression shifted and smiling with pure joy, she yelled, 'It was so incredible, Lenny! Jump, you can do it!'

That was the final bit of encouragement he needed. He would remember the exhilarated look on her face for the rest of his life, he thought. Lenny inched closer to the edge, his toes gripping the jagged rock as it sloped down. His classmates started counting in unison. *1-2-3!* He leapt off and his heart flew into his throat as gravity quickly took over, pulling him rapidly downward. His body plunged into the water, taking his breath away as the cold water swallowed him whole. He kept falling fast until his foot slammed into something hard, sending pain shooting up his ankle. Reaching down, he grabbed his throbbing foot. He was running out of air, his lungs aching, so he dropped his foot and pushed himself toward the surface, pumping his arms and legs. Before he made it very far, a flash of red cut through the murky water, catching his attention. *Farrah's cheer bow!* He swam forward a few feet and grabbed the mass of silky red before he kicked his way to the surface. *I'll be her hero.*

When he broke through the surface of the water, the warm air hitting his face, he sucked in a deep, comforting breath. His classmates swam around him, clapping and whistling. The exiting seniors standing on the rocky bank above cheered his name, 'Lenny, Lenny, Lenny!'

Farrah swam over to him and as she neared, he reached his fist up straight in the air, kicking his legs beneath the surface to stay above water.

'I found your bow,' he said triumphantly, holding it in the air.

Farrah beamed, looking at his hand in excitement, but then her smile dropped. The color drained from her face, and her high-pitched scream ricocheted off the rocks. Lenny looked at his classmates, confused. Tamra's mouth was hanging open and Justin said, 'Dude,' as he shook his head, his eyes wide in shock. One by one, more screams erupted around him.

Lenny looked at his fist and his stomach contracted into knots. Blonde hair draped over his arm, a dirty red bow holding its loose strands together, a gel-like substance clinging to the ends of the strands near the bow – the remnants of a scalp. He yelled out and threw the mass of hair onto the embankment, swimming away rapidly. Somewhere in the distance, ears ringing, he vaguely registered a girl's voice yelling, 'Someone call the police!'

CHAPTER ONE

Margo tapped her fingers along the steering wheel in time to the music pumping through her Honda Civic's speakers. Her chipped nails and torn cuticles betrayed the anxiety bubbling under the surface of her calm demeanor, but she kept her eyes trained ahead and focused on the winding mountain roads. The twists and turns forced her forward, and had each bend not been seared into her muscle memory after all these years, she would have been in danger of crashing as the early morning fog obscured the path from her view. Once the main highway gave way to the two-lane road snaking through small towns as the elevation steadily increased, the tight turns became more treacherous. Steep drop-offs with no guard rails were common, as were cars going far too fast as they veered over the center line. Just as when she was a teenager learning how to drive, Margo gripped the steering wheel tightly as she slowed to coast through each turn, the road sucking into the mountainside and then pushing back out to the edge.

Crashing would have likely been easier, she mused, as a tight feeling spread across her chest. She had barely returned to Lake Moss since the day she left for college fifteen years ago. Choosing the University of North Carolina Wilmington to remain close to her dad, but far enough away to keep the painful memories at bay, she had packed her bags and left. She came home for Christmas and Thanksgiving during her freshman year, but after that, she'd found excuses for each summer and holiday: internships or relationships; whatever was relevant. She had stayed firmly in Wilmington and asked her father to drive to the coast to visit her instead. As the only child with no extended family to speak of except a smattering of distant relatives in France on her mother's side, he had always obliged. But now, she couldn't stay away. After her marriage and life had imploded in Wilmington six months ago, there was nothing left for her. Her small hometown now drew her in like a magnet, pulling her back into the messy web she'd left behind. With each mile, her old fears and insecurities seeped back in, ready to take root in her uneasy mind.

As she drew closer to town, the deep blue peaks of the mountains ahead broke through the fog. They'd learned in ninth grade science class that it wasn't the color of the trees covering the sharp peaks that gave the ridge its blue hue, but a hydrocarbon the trees released to protect themselves from extreme heat. Once released, it mixed with other airborne molecules, creating the distinct color that gave the Blue Ridge Mountains their name. Margo yearned to veer around Lake Moss and drive deep into the folds of the mountains to hide. But she knew she couldn't. Her eyes drifted up from the road for a long second, taking in their staggering beauty as red and pink streaks of sunrise burst around the peaks and broke up the white haze lingering in the warm summer air. A looming force of blue, rolling hills that appeared to kiss the sky, surrounded by lush trees that hugged the bends in the roads and encased waterfalls and babbling creeks. It would have been peaceful if it hadn't held so many secrets.

The mountains, while beautiful, hovered menacingly; jagged peaks jutting into the sky followed by steep drops into dark valleys in the distance. The protector of the town, but had they really protected anyone? They hadn't protected her mother, or her childhood friend. Perhaps they had protected Margo, since she'd made it out alive. For now, anyway. They protected the town gossip mill, which she was sure would still be alive and well. People who grew up in Lake Moss rarely left, and if they did, they surely returned. The cast of characters wouldn't have changed much, she thought with dread. The mountains had also protected the brewery business that kept the town afloat, of that she was certain. No matter where she traveled in the country, she could always find Moss Creek Brewing on tap.

Margo passed the small sign protruding out of the right side of the road reading, 'WELCOME TO LAKE MOSS. Small Town, Big Hearts,' and clenched the steering wheel tighter. The name of the town where she'd grown up, about thirty-five minutes outside Asheville, had always been a source of amusement amongst the youth there. She was sure she'd heard something in history class about there being a small lake present when the town originated generations ago, but as far back as anyone alive now could remember, it ironically had nothing more than thick, winding creeks and rivers. Nevertheless, it had been home, and it had shaped the course of her life in ways she was still trying to correct.

After several minutes of weaving through the dense thicket of trees, she slowed once more as she came upon a familiar site. A deep ache blossomed in the pit of her stomach. Her finger joints throbbed from their sharp grip, the skin white where it curved around her flakey red polish. She took her foot off the gas and hovered over the brake pedal, letting the car slow naturally as she approached. The music playing on the local radio station in the background fizzled into a low, indecipherable hum as she pulled over and finally stopped the car.

Margo knew if another car came by, there would not be enough space for them to squeeze through without going over the faded yellow line and it made her anxiety spike. But this was important; she needed a moment. This spot had been the beginning of the end. It had changed everything. She opened the car door, grabbing the key from the ignition as she stretched her legs, the warm air whipping her long, deep brown hair around so that it momentarily blinded her. But she could see this spot even with her eyes closed. Even after all this time, it still made an occasional appearance in her dreams.

She snapped the door shut and approached the large tree in front of her. There it was: the small 'In Memory' plaque with a cross attached to the tree's thick trunk. It was dirty, the letters slightly faded, but she could still make out the words. Margo reached a shaky hand forward and grazed her fingers across the grooves of the engraved letters. Her mother's name. The spot where her mother had died. A flash flitted through her mind. The sound of screeching tires, a loud crash as the front of her mother's red car smashed into the tree, folding the hood like an accordion. Her mother, blood dripping down her forehead where it rested on the steering wheel, a faulty air bag never deploying. The settlement from the car company they'd received, which later financed her college degree, would never erase the pain that day had caused.

Margo could see her mom's crumpled car in front of her like it was still there. She hadn't been present at the time of the crash, but the vivid images her imagination had conjured were burned in her mind, as if she had been in the passenger seat. In her frequent childhood night-mares, she sometimes had been. After a long moment, she pulled herself away and climbed back into her car. Margo hated driving past this spot but had hoped time had scabbed that wound. No such luck. A long loud horn startled her as a car whipped around the bend behind her, her blood running cold as she braced for impact. For a split second, she thought she was about to meet the same end as her mom. But at the last second, the small car sped around her, driving over the center line to clear her car and laying on the horn repeatedly in anger, the man inside gesturing at her wildly. Margo heaved a few heavy breaths as her heart raced, the car's taillights disap-pearing around the bend up ahead. After a few minutes to calm herself, she started the car and pulled back out into the road, continuing on her way.

As she drove into the heart of town, Margo felt like she had never left. Town Square, nestled right in the center with the mountains reaching up picturesquely behind the short brick storefronts, looked exactly the same. The strings of bistro lights crisscrossing over the quiet streets still glowed, not yet turned off from the night before. The clock tower that stood tall along the wide circular section in the center of Main Street still ticked away every agonizing second that passed. While she spotted a new organic restaurant and home goods country store, none

12

of the small shops from her childhood had changed. Most even still displayed the missing poster for Jessie Germaine in their windows, the tragedy that had rocked the town fifteen years ago. Margo slowed as she passed the antique shop that had given her such pause as a kid, its dusty, creepy old toys and ancient electronics lining the windows. Squinting to see in, she noticed the exact doll that used to haunt her still sitting upright in the corner of the window. Its dirty, porcelain face watched as she drove by, its beady eyes keeping tabs on her every movement.

Blinking rapidly to clear its disturbing glass eyes from her vision, Margo picked her speed back up and turned down an alley that she always used as a shortcut to Pine Road. Pine would lead her to her final destination: home. Or, what used to be home. The trees lining the narrow road felt like they were closing in on her, shrouding her in suffocating shadows as she inched closer to the place where she grew up. The house where her father still lived. Guilt ebbed at the edges of her mind, but she pushed it down. He had understood why she'd left him alone here.

After several long minutes weaving along the bumpy narrow road covered in small rocks and twigs, Margo pulled into the driveway and put the car in park. She stared up at the home's charming exterior, a confusing storm of emotions swirling just under the surface. She had loved this house at one time, its cozy cottage vibes, every inch of its exterior covered in smooth light-colored stones that reminded her of the river rocks her mother used to collect. The few steps leading up to the porch, a small landing shrouded in the shadow of a large stone archway, used to be covered in potted flowers and seasonal décor when her mom was alive. But once it was just her and her dad, the plants too had died and faded into nothingness. The porch was barren today, save for an empty terracotta planter that had been left behind.

Her dad needed her, she reminded herself. Taking a deep breath, Margo reached to turn the key in the ignition, but her hand froze as the radio jingle for Bob's Hardware cut off with an interruption for an urgent news bulletin.

'The remains of a young woman, believed to be Jessie Germaine, were found yesterday. The discovery was made at a secret swimming hole popular amongst local youth, and if confirmed to be Ms. Germaine, would be the first break in the missing person's case that has haunted the Lake Moss community for the past fifteen years. Jessie Germaine disappeared on May 26th, 2004 . . .'

The blood drained from Margo's face, her heartrate accelerating so rapidly she felt it would explode from her chest. She grabbed the wheel and leaned forward to rest her forehead, closing her eyes as the report buzzed in the background. Dizziness swelled, and her palms were slick with sweat. *Jessie? Found? After all these years?* She couldn't believe it.

Tears formed along her lashes, exploding out in bubbling bursts. Throwing her body back against the seat, the tears flowed and her chest heaved. She tried to muster the strength to pull herself together, not wanting her dad to see her such a mess. He needed her to be strong now. But Jessie's body was not the welcome-home gift she had anticipated. Closing her eyes tight, Margo could almost see Jessie's smiling face as she jumped high in the air on the sideline of the football field, her red cheerleading outfit shining under the Friday night lights. Could almost hear her infectious laugh. Memories from childhood all the way until the last time she saw Jessie flashed through

Margo's mind like a flipbook. Jessie was woven through the fabric of her DNA, and as she imagined her dead friend's body being pulled from the water after all these years, every inch of her was blazing on fire from the pain of it all. Would Lake Moss finally uncover the truth?

Forcing herself to stop the flow of tears and take deep breaths that expanded into every corner of her belly, she tried to zero in on what she'd just heard. She didn't think there were any details, but it'd been hard to focus. *What made them assume it was Jessie? They couldn't have an official identification so soon. Is it simply that she was the only option?* Margo had been gone a long time, but her father would have told her if anyone else had gone missing. As she calmed her racing heart, her shock and distress turned into a deep swell of sad finality. Jessie had been her best friend as a child, and her disappearance had rocked Lake Moss to its very core. With no evidence of foul play at the time, the police had suggested that maybe Jessie, with her big and gregarious personality, had just run away, thinking herself too good for this small town after all, taking the heat off them to find her. But the truth had floated to the surface at last. Jessie was dead, and now the whole town would be on the hunt to find her killer.

Dear Diary,

Well, today didn't turn out as planned. I was excited to meet up with Jessie for another tutoring session, maybe finally get her to open up about her problems with Charlie, but she texted me to cancel. I tried to talk her out of it, so close to finals, but once that girl makes up her mind, that's that. I'm bummed, but maybe I can get her to reschedule sometime in the next few days.

She's been including me more lately, and it really seems like I'm getting my BFF back, thank God! At first, it was just tutoring sessions. But recently, she's been asking to come over to hang out on weekends too AND inviting me to hang with her and Cassidy. Cassidy doesn't seem too thrilled but whatever. It's nice to finally be brought back into Jessie's circle, even just a little. I'm sure it'll get even better with time, and maybe Cassidy will get used to me being around. She became a big part of Jessie's life during my dark years, so I dunno if she's jealous or bitter about me coming back onto the scene or what, but hopefully she'll come around.

Anyway, boring night on the home front now without Jessie coming over. Dad is stuck late at the school again grading the huge group project he insists on giving his class right before finals ever year. It always takes him forever, I don't know why he keeps assigning it. So I have a very

16

exciting date with a movie rental, I think I'm gonna go with What a Girl Wants, and order Chinese food for dinner. If Dad's lucky, I'll save him an eggroll. No promises!

CHAPTER TWO

Margo held the large, curved door to her home open as she helped her dad hobble into the living room on crutches. He had just been released from Mission Hospital in Asheville following his knee surgery – the reason Margo had agreed to come home in the first place. Margo was grateful that there was a bigger hospital with the specialist he needed just a short drive away, as Lake Moss's medical system left a lot to be desired. He would need her help as he recovered, and since he was still teaching geography and coaching basketball at the local high school, summer was the best time for him to finally schedule the operation he could no longer ignore. Back in his 'hot shot days', as he liked to call them, he had been preparing to enter the NBA draft as a college basketball star when a knee injury sidelined him and shifted his path to coaching instead. Margo had often found him grimacing on the recliner over the years, a bag of frozen peas resting on his knee and a bottle of ibuprofen sitting on the end table next to him. But now that he had reached his early sixties and was nearing retirement, he realized he couldn't put the inevitable surgery off any longer. And so, Margo found herself drafted as his caregiver.

'Here Dad,' she said as she helped position him on the worn brown leather couch. 'Let me help you.'

'Thanks, kiddo,' he said, and when she gave a loud sigh, a goofy grin spread across his face, still doped up from the anesthesia that hadn't fully worn off. 'I don't care if you're in your thirties now, you'll always be my kiddo.'

Margo smiled in spite of herself. 'OK Dad, let's get you settled and then I'll grab you some water.'

After helping him elevate his braced knee on a stack of soft throw pillows, another behind his head for support, Margo scurried off to the kitchen and grabbed a glass from the dark walnut cabinet next to the sink. In the background, she heard her dad click on the TV as she moved to the freezer to get ice. Over the hums and clinks of the ice chute, she heard a woman's muffled voice from the room behind her say, 'the body found yesterday has now been confirmed to be that of Jessie Germaine, missing for—'

Margo quickly jerked back her hand, nearly spilling ice all over the floor in her haste to quiet the machine.

'—fifteen years. The heartbreaking discovery was made when a high school student jumped off a rock into a secret Lake Moss swimming hole popular amongst the youth. The student accidentally slammed into an oversized cooler resting along the bottom floor of the swimming hole, breaking the latch and allowing a red cheerleader bow, still wrapped around Jessie Germaine's hair, to float loose into the surrounding water. The remains were positively identified using dental records earlier today. The police have not yet released the cause of death. Back to you, Robert.'

'Just terrible,' said a male newscaster as Margo quickly filled the glass with water and returned to the living room. Her dad gave her a pained look before turning his attention to the TV screen. Margo placed the water on the coffee table before sitting back in the nearby recliner, her eyes glued to the news anchors covering the late afternoon updates. An image of the swimming hole she recognized from her senior year was just fading from the screen. 'The Germaine family has asked for privacy as they grieve, and ask anyone who has information regarding Jessie Germaine to please come forward to Lake Moss Police. We'll update you as new information becomes available.'

Margo's eyes were frozen to the TV, focused so intently that the picture began to look like a million vibrating dots of color rather than the reporter who was now covering the high summer temperatures. After what could have been seconds or minutes, she wasn't sure, her dad grunted in pain from the couch next to her. Shaking her head as she snapped back to reality, she looked over and noticed one of his pillows had fallen.

'Oh, Dad, I'm sorry,' she said hurriedly, handing him the water before readjusting his pillow.

'It's OK. Can you hand me one of my pain pills? I'm about due, and I'd like to rest my eyes for a bit.'

'Of course,' Margo said, grabbing the small white paper prescription bag from her purse and fumbling with shaking hands to open the bottle. Finally getting the lid off, she offered him one of the pills and watched him carefully as he took it. Helping him set the glass back on the table, she readjusted his pillows one more time.

'OK, OK, Margo, I'm fine,' he said as his eyelids grew heavy.

'If you're going to rest, is it alright if I pop out to the market? I'll grab us a few groceries for the week before it gets too late,' she said, glancing at her watch.

'Sure, sure . . .' he said as he closed his eyes.

Watching him for a moment until gentle snoring drifted into the silence, Margo stood, grabbed her purse and keys and headed for the door. She checked the thermostat and made sure the air conditioning was set at a comfortable level; it was unusually warm for this early in the season.

Margo arrived at the small grocery store just outside of downtown in a matter of minutes. She wandered through the aisles, browsing for meal essentials that could be easily thrown together over the upcoming days. Her mind drifted as she grabbed a bag of rice with a red and white label off a shelf. Staring at it, she instead saw Jessie's detached blonde hair with its signature red cheer bow still looped around it, floating freely in the very swimming hole where she and her classmates had swum. She couldn't believe that after remaining a cold case with zero leads for so long, a high school kid jumping into the water had brought Jessie's body up from that cooler. She blinked rapidly, trying to push away the images threatening to overtake her mind of students swimming above Jessie's decaying body all these years.

A loud thwack down the aisle caused Margo to jump and suck in a sharp breath. She looked over to see a child reaching up for a can of ravioli. He'd knocked over several neighboring cans in his quest. She hated that being back in Lake Moss caused her to revert to being on guard all the time, like she had been as a teenager. Her nervousness had snuck in at times in Wilmington,

21

but it escalated to another level in this town. Holding a hand to her chest to calm her thumping heart, Margo walked over and handed the kid the can his fingers were just barely grazing.

'Thank you!' he hollered out before running down the aisle after his mom and turning left at the endcap, disappearing from view.

After returning the fallen cans to their rightful place, Margo quickly finished her shopping and moved to the register. She waited her turn as the women at the register talked amongst themselves.

'I heard the boy actually *grabbed* a fistful of her hair and didn't realize till he was swinging it around above the surface like a lasso.'

Margo inched forward, straining to hear every detail. If there was one thing you could rely on in this town, it was gossip. She reached for a pack of gum on the shelf near checkout, positioning herself for better listening.

'I heard it was that Lenny boy,' the other cashier said. 'He's big for his age, built like a brickhouse which is great for the football team, but you know . . .' She raised her penciled-on eyebrows dramatically, grabbing an onion and keying in the produce code.

'Oh, yes,' the first cashier said, nodding. 'Makes sense then how he went down so far and knocked right into that cooler. I heard they've been pulling junk out of that swimming hole all morning. Imagine, kids swimming around in there all these years not knowing she was stuffed in a cooler down below their feet.'

The customer tutted, 'just awful,' as she grabbed her bags from the second cashier. 'I'm so glad my Katy is too young to have gone swimming there. Those poor kids are probably traumatized.'

'I know, can you imagine?' the cashier replied. 'You have a good day now, Bailey.'

Bailey gave a strained smile and a half-wave as she left the store. Margo looked around for a moment and then stepped forward casually, unloading her items onto the small conveyor belt.

'Did you know her?' the cashier asked Margo as she scanned her items.

'What?' Margo asked, her mind racing.

'Jessie Germaine. Did you know her? I moved to this town about six years back to help my sister out with the kids after her dog of a husband skipped town, so that was before my time. But her missing posters are still hung all around town. Her family must keep replacing them,' she said and pointed one long, pink acrylic nail to the wall. Margo followed her gaze and saw Jessie's bright smiling face in black and white just below the word 'MISSING' in bold red. Now, an age-progressed photo showing what current-day Jessie might look like appeared next to the original photo of the eighteen-year-old version. 'You look around how old she'd be now, right?'

Margo swallowed a lump forming in her throat. 'Oh. Yeah, I knew her when we were kids.'

'What was she like?' the cashier asked eagerly, leaning forward and loudly popping her gum. The other cashier, who was filing her nails, stopped and leaned in as well.

'Oh,' Margo said again, caught off guard, unsure how to answer. She desperately wished they would just finish scanning her groceries and let her go home. 'Well, it was a long time ago.'

'Come on, give us something,' the cashier pushed.

'She was . . . well, bold. She was beautiful and had a personality much too big for this place, which is probably

23

why some people thought she ran away. If she wanted something, she wouldn't let anyone or anything stand in her way.'

The cashiers were engrossed, hungry for more details, but it felt wrong, talking to them about Jessie. Margo had kept her locked away in a dark corner of her mind all these years, not letting herself feel the pain of those memories. She cleared her throat and pushed the remaining items on the belt toward the barcode scanner.

'I'm sorry, I'm in a bit of a hurry.'

'Oh,' the cashier said, disappointment clearly etched on her face, creasing the thick layer of foundation she'd caked on. 'Sure,' she said, flicking her hair over her shoulder and finishing scanning the items in silence, sharing the occasional glance with her co-worker.

On the drive home, Margo decided to take a detour. She remembered a small, old stone bridge that overlooked the now infamous swimming hole and couldn't resist taking a look for herself. The scene drew her forward, as if the car was driving itself and she was just along for the ride. She didn't even remember taking those last two turns.

Margo parked her car off to the side and climbed out, seeing a few people she recognized from high school standing near the bridge. It was roped off, but they were standing as close as they could get, peering over the edge at the action below. She walked up to them, not sure if they would recognize her. She wasn't popular in high school, not like Jessie.

'What's going on?' she asked someone she remembered as Lauren Mills, a mousy girl she'd sat next to in AP English. Lauren had always been first to raise her hand to answer questions.

Lauren looked at her, squinting before a look of recognition lit up her face. 'Oh my, is that you, Margo Sutton? I haven't seen you around here in ages!'

Margo gave a strained smile, 'Yeah, it's been a long time. Just moved back so I could help out my dad.'

'Oh, yes, I heard he was having surgery. How's he doing?'

She tucked her short dark hair behind an ear, looking at Margo expectantly. Margo wasn't sure Lauren had ever said this many words to her in the entirety of the time they were in school together. Even though Lake Moss was a small town, Margo hadn't realized that her father's surgery would be such a hot topic.

Lauren seemed to sense her hesitation. 'Oh, you know how this town is. Everyone was in a tizzy wondering who was going to lead the summer basketball camp while he was out of commission. And of course, it wouldn't be near as fun to watch the games with someone else on the sideline. I hope you don't mind me saying, it's no secret that Shane Sutton has always been easy on the eyes. He was kind of our only option for schoolgirl crushes back in the day; all the other teachers were so much older. It made going to class much more interesting,' she said with a coy smile.

Inwardly, Margo groaned, remembering how all the girls had fawned over her dad, batting their eyelashes as they lingered to ask questions after class just to get a private moment with him. Instead, she forced a small laugh, 'Ah, yeah I can see that. Well, then everyone will be very relieved to hear the surgery went well, thanks for asking. Hopefully he'll be back on his feet in no time. So, what's going on down there?' Margo asked, directing the conversation back to what she really wanted to know.

25

Lauren looked out across the bridge. 'Nothing too earth-shattering. They went back in this morning to search more heavily after finding the cooler that Jessie was in, and they've pulled a few nasty old appliances out of there so far.'

Margo strained to look over the edge and saw a rusted fridge with chains wrapped around it, dripping with water, slowly being pulled up to the top of the bridge by a large truck with a winch. On the other side of the truck was a pop-up tent the investigators were using to examine the appliances as they were pulled out. She wondered if they'd actually found anything of importance. Divers in the water below the dangling fridge continued searching the area. Margo's stomach leapt into her throat as she looked over the edge, the steep drop down to the water below dizzying from this vantage point. She took a step back and steadied herself. As she glanced over at the tent, Margo spotted Chief Healey, older now with a belly paunch and a slight stoop to his shoulders, directing officers to keep the curious onlookers away from the area. His motions stopped when he spotted Margo. Placing his hands on his hips, he narrowed his eyes. Margo nervously raised her hand in greeting, not sure if he remembered her. She slowly lowered her hand after he didn't return the gesture. Turning around, he abruptly continued barking orders. Even now as an adult, Chief Healey's intense stare made her feel like a child with her hand caught in the cookie jar. She turned back to Lauren.

'So, what, someone's been using the swimming hole as a dumping ground?'

'Apparently,' Lauren said, then leaned in closer and lowered her voice. 'I bet it was that trashy family up the road, the Buckleys. I mean, I'm sure you've seen their yard, right? Always piled high with junk like this,' she gestured toward the fridge that was now making its way over the lip of the bridge. 'Their lawn looks like a hoarder opened a scrap yard.' Margo leaned back, trying to escape the smell of tuna salad on Lauren's breath.

Nodding, Margo looked around at the others watching the scene unfolding below. A small shrine of candles, flowers and stuffed animals had started forming along the entrance of the old bridge that she hadn't noticed on her way in. Two people she didn't even recognize were holding each other as they stood near the small stash of tokens for Jessie. Anger mingled with her distress as she watched their irrational grieving. They didn't even know Jessie, not the real Jessie, not like she did. She was just a girl on a poster to them. They weren't her friends, why were they acting like they were at their grandmother's funeral? The way they attached themselves to a tragedy that had nothing to do with them was ghoulish and disgusting.

Margo spotted a reporter setting up an interview just behind her. A slightly overweight woman was standing with her back to Margo, running her hand along her strawberry blonde hair in an unsuccessful attempt to calm the frizz. She couldn't see who it was from behind, but the moment the woman started talking, Margo recognized Shannon Welch's nasally voice from high school.

'It's just so crazy, after all these years . . .' she shook her head, the bubble of tears evident in her voice. 'We were such good friends, everyone loved Jessie. She was that beautiful, enigmatic girl everyone looked up to. I can't believe she's finally been found. I'd always prayed she had just run away and would come back someday,' Shannon paused and sniffled a few times. 'Now we just

27

need to find who did this to her so we can all have some closure . . .'

Margo couldn't believe her ears. Shannon and Jessie were never friends. Shannon sometimes clung to the edge of the cool kid group at lunch or in the halls, trying desperately to infiltrate. She'd frequently witnessed Shannon hanging on Jessie's every word in awe, but she couldn't remember Jessie ever spending time with her or reciprocating the attention. Clearly Shannon hadn't changed, still forcing her way into whatever exciting thing she could latch onto.

Margo remembered waking the day after Jessie went missing, how thick with panic the air had felt. She shook her head at the memory of the jumbled pocket-dial voicemail she'd woken up to on her phone just after her father informed her that Jessie hadn't come home the night before. The blur of Chief Healey in her kitchen, asking if she'd seen or talked to Jessie. The way the town had turned upside down looking for her but found nothing. Margo's life had changed so permanently in that moment. That was something these fake grievers would never understand as they inserted themselves for attention. She and Jessie weren't as close in the end, sure, but in elementary school, they'd been best friends. And in the last year before Jessie disappeared, their connection was rekindling. Margo had hoped they'd be like sisters again. But obviously, that wasn't in the cards; they'd run out of time.

Looking around as she got ready to head back to her car, Margo spotted someone along the edge of the trees, peering out from behind a thick tree trunk. Squinting, she saw it was Bobby Buckley, one of the sons from the family down the road that Lauren had been talking about. Margo didn't know him well, but everyone in the town

28

knew who they were. He was intently watching as the police removed the appliances from the water, looking nervous. He scratched at a red patch on his arm, moving his weight back and forth rapidly. Margo's pulse quickened as he looked in her direction and their eyes locked. After a long moment, he slowly backed away into the shadows. Deciding she couldn't take any more of this morbid scene, she waved to Lauren and hopped in her car, pulling it back onto the dirt road. The sun would be setting in the next hour or so, and she was hoping to get a run in before it got dark to clear her mind. After ten minutes driving along the winding roads, she pulled up in front of her house and rushed in to put the groceries away, check on her dad and change.

Back out in the driveway, Margo stretched in her black Adidas jogging shorts and tank top, grateful the heat of the day was finally tapering off. After loosening up her limbs, she set out up the narrow road. There was a two-mile loop that would take her up the mountain and around a small community of homes nestled in the trees. It would also take her right past Jessie's house. When she'd itched to explore outside as a kid, Margo's mom had given her reference points in their neighborhood marking how far from their house she was allowed go. Her mother had always been a bit uptight, the border of her anxiety holding Margo to a specific radius like a fluctuating noose. It clenched tighter to their house whenever her mom feared potential danger was near, and then loosened as her dad convinced her mom that Lake Moss was a perfectly safe place for Margo to walk around. Jessie's house had always been within the loop of the noose, allowing them to become close as kids.

As Margo ran, she breathed deeply, her lungs welcoming the familiar air despite not having worked out in this altitude in ages. Feeling the tension in her muscles easing with every pump of her arms and legs, Margo slowed to a jog as she approached the Germaine house. She stopped at the big oak tree she and Jessie used as home base for countdowns during lengthy games of hide and seek. She could almost hear her own voice yelling, 'Eight . . . nine . . . ten! Ready or not, here I come!' Margo leaned against the tree, memories of finding Jessie behind a boulder down near the creek or inside a cabinet in her garage rushing to the forefront of her mind's eye. A tear fell onto her hand and she quickly wiped it away before she took a deep breath and resumed running, turning her back on the Germaines' home.

She'd frequently used this route on her jogs growing up. The web of quiet tree-lined streets that linked back down to her house was more peaceful and interesting to her than running into town and around the square like most Lake Moss joggers did. The pressure of a small town was suffocating sometimes. All those eyes watching, waiting to snap up any morsel of drama they could latch onto. Margo preferred the less traveled path with fewer spectators. As she looped around Stone Creek Drive heading back to her home, the sun dipped down behind the ridge of the mountains, shadows from the trees stretching out like creeping fingers up ahead.

A squeak and a blast of wind from flapping wings swept past her and she ducked her head as she slowed. In the summer, bats and their babies became a frequent sighting as the sun slunk down or slowly rose in early morning hours. As a young child, her mother had told Margo a story about a bat getting tangled up in her friend's hair in her youth. The story had scared Margo to the core. But now she wondered if it had been an old wives' tale, an easy way to get young Margo back into the house without argument before dark. Still, the sound of bats caused a familiar shiver up her spine. Margo looked around, trying to find the bat, but it had already sailed into a hiding place somewhere in the trees. Margo picked up the pace, never liking to be out running alone after dark. Within seconds, the mountains drowned out the last rays of the sun as dusk blanketed the street. Short, small bursts of light sporadically bloomed up around her as lightning bugs announced their presence. When she turned down her street, she was winded and slowed to a brisk walk, using the last fifteen or so yards to her house as a cool-down.

Suddenly someone jogged up behind her and whooshed past, causing Margo to jump and nearly scream, stumbling off to the side out of surprise. She came to a complete stop, instinctively reaching inside her shorts pocket for the pepper spray she never went anywhere without; something she'd picked up from her mom. Heaving to regain her breath, she watched as the man jogged down her street. She couldn't see him well with the light receding, but he was tall and wearing a similar outfit to hers with the addition of a baseball cap. Right as he passed her house, he turned his head back and looked at her. Margo squinted, trying to see if she recognized the man. But she couldn't make out his face under the rim of his cap. He turned his back to her and sped up to a full run. Margo slowly released the pepper spray from her grip as he disappeared from sight. Seeing people jogging on these roads had always been rare, and the interaction made the hairs on her neck rise.

* * *

The cool water rolled over Margo's skin, making her feel like she could breathe again through the suffocating heat of summer. She pushed her belly up toward the sky, floating on her back as she took in the tops of lush green trees and clouds swirling into different shapes overhead. She felt at peace, closing her eyes and breathing in the fresh scent of foliage. Moving her arms like she was making a snow angel on the surface of the water, she kicked her legs gently and smiled. Then, Margo felt something hard bump against her foot.

'Ow!' she yelled out as the serenity she'd felt was replaced by a sharp pain.

The sun moved behind a cloud, shrouding her in shadow as she righted herself and reached down below the surface to grab her foot. When she pulled up her hand, it was coated in a thick layer of blood. The intensity of the red seemed to dull the vibrancy of everything around her. Something bright floated a foot away from her, beckoning her forward. She reached for it, and her fingertips brushed against a soft, silky texture. She held up the fabric, squinting to make it out in the darkness now that the sun had gone down. Long, dirty blonde hair wrapped in a large red cheer bow dangled from her hand. She opened her mouth to scream, but no sound came out.

'Hey, what are you doing with that? It's mine, give it back. I need it for the rally,' an eerie, breathy voice rang out from the shoreline behind her. Margo whipped around, and there was Jessie, standing in her cheer warm-up suit. She held a perfectly manicured hand to her head, where blood was pouring down her face in long, dark red rivers. She was pale, her lips blue. She stared at Margo for a long moment, her eyes turning glassy and her body becoming rigid.

'Margo?' she said in a sharp whisper, before reaching her bloody hand in Margo's direction and falling forward into the water, leaving a trail of red as she slowly sunk beneath the surface.

'JESSIE!' Margo screamed out as she shot up in bed, drenched in sweat, her heart racing. Looking around her dark childhood bedroom, she grabbed her phone off the nightstand and saw it was 4:03 a.m. She threw it back down and ran her hands through her hair, trying to calm herself down, but it was useless. Flinging the quilt off her, she jumped out of bed and hastily opened the bedroom door. As quietly as she could, Margo rushed down the short hallway to the bathroom and closed the door behind her, the rational side of her brain cautioning her not to wake her dad battling with the panic washing over her. Leaning over the sink, she turned the faucet on and splashed her face with cold water. She gripped the sides of the white porcelain basin and looked up into the mirror. She stifled a scream. Her own face stared back at her, blood slowly trickling down from her fore-head in the reflection, her face pale. Darting a hand up to the site of the wound, she wiped frantically at the spot. Margo looked down at her hand as she pulled it away, steeling herself to see how much blood lingered on her fingertips. But her hand was clean. Looking back up into the mirror, her injury-free face peered back anxiously, her chest heaving. *Please don't let the night-mares come back*, she pleaded with dread. Blinking a few times to clear the gory image from her mind, she slowly made her way back to bed.

She lay down and pulled the quilt up to her chin, feeling it stick to the cold sweat along her chest. Afraid to close her eyes again, Margo stared at the ceiling until the sun broke through her drawn curtains, unable to rid herself of the stream of red streaking through her mind. Shutting off her alarm a minute before it could sound, she wondered what new discoveries lay ahead.

CHAPTER THREE

Margo parallel-parked her car along Main Street in one of the spots across from the drug store. She crossed through Town Square, which was really a circle, and made her way up to the long brick building. The stretch of stores the building housed along this side of the square was covered in climbing vines. When she'd last seen it years ago, the vines had only covered Tasty's Ice Cream parlor on the end. But now, the creeping vines had reached the pharmacy all the way at the other end as though they were devouring the building whole.

When she reached the pharmacy's red door, she pushed it open causing a little bell above her to ring out. A few heads turned in her direction before going back to their shopping. Forcing a small smile for the pharmacist, she bee-lined down a nearby aisle to grab allergy medication. After two weeks in Lake Moss, being surrounded by trees constantly was doing a number on her allergies after living coastal for so many years. She forgot how much her eyes itched and congestion mounted without medication. Squatting down to scan the lower shelf for her favorite brand, she froze as she heard someone on the other side of the aisle start talking.

'I just can't believe there are no new leads since that poor girl's body was discovered,' said a hushed female voice.

'Well, you didn't hear it from me,' another quiet but excited woman's voice replied, 'but my son knows someone close to the investigation, and they told him that a pregnancy test was found with Jessie's remains.'

'Get. Out!' the first woman said, her excitement evident at this juicy development.

Margo's stomach clenched and she gripped the bottle of pills in front of her. Surely after being waterlogged all these years, a pregnancy test wouldn't show any results. It would add suspicious motives to the men in Jessie's life, but not much else. Still, she couldn't quiet the anxious feeling welling inside her. As someone who had once been close to Jessie, she knew Jessie had her share of secrets. Were they all about to come to light?

'Well, it had to have been Charlie Abbott's baby, right? They were dating at the time she went missing. I know she was eighteen and all, but a teen pregnancy would have really thrown a wrench in the Abbott family's pristine reputation,' the second woman continued.

'You know that family has more money than God would know what to do with; they practically run this town,' said woman number one, a hint of resentment seeping into her words. 'If anyone could have a problem like that taken care of, it would be the Abbotts.'

The women's voices trailed off as they walked away from the aisle and Margo shot up, her mind racing. Of course people would suspect the Abbotts if it was confirmed, or even rumored, that Jessie had been pregnant at the time of her death. The Abbotts owned Moss Creek Brewing and were responsible for most of the town's economy and tourist trade. Because of their success, Lake Moss had morphed from a sparse, uneventful stop on the path to Asheville, into a quaint, picturesque town with tourists coming in to tour the brewery and enjoy the charming small businesses. The Jensens had opened a lovely B&B years back that was always full during summer and especially during fall foliage season, when outsiders flocked to take in the lush, colorful trees as they changed to warm hues. The farmer's market on summer Sundays was also a hot ticket with visitors and locals alike anxious for fresh, home-grown produce, hand crafted goods and home-made pies along with beer tastings. Even Asheville residents made the trek to explore the market's goods. All because the Abbotts had put Lake Moss on the map. They were like town royalty and had every police officer and elected official eating out of the palm of their hand for decades. Their only son, Charles Abbott III – Charlie to everyone at school – was their pride and joy and heir to their fortune. It was reasonable for the town to suspect them; Margo was sure the Abbotts would stop at nothing to protect their family name.

Not paying attention to where she was going as she hustled to the register, she bumped into someone and bounced backwards, her allergy medicine falling to the floor with a loud *clack*. She let out an involuntary squeak as the contact startled her.

'Oh, I'm so sorry,' a smooth, deep voice said as the man she ran into bent down at the same time to pick up her fallen box.

'Don't be, it was my fault,' Margo said as her cheeks

flushed from embarrassment. She finally looked at him as the two stood back up and she couldn't believe who was standing in front of her. 'Wait . . . Austin Hughes?'

A look of sudden recognition flitted across his face and he ran a hand over the short, warm brown stubble blanketing his chin, smiling at her. 'Well as I live and breathe, it's Margo Sutton. What are you doing back here?'

'I could ask you the same thing, I saw on Facebook you'd moved out of state,' she said, smiling up at him.

Margo had always been tall for a girl at five-foot-ten, so growing up it had been hard to get any guys to pay attention to her since most were her height or shorter, unless it was one of the popular athletes who didn't acknowledge her existence. Between her nerdy looks and her sad family history, it hadn't exactly been easy to meet boys. But Austin had been different, tall and stringy and just a little bit awkward. But most important to Margo, he'd been kind. After reaching high school, neither one of them had made their way into any cliques. Sensing each other as kindred spirits as outcasts from the circles of jocks, cheerleaders and brainiacs, they'd found themselves sitting at the same lunch table one day early in freshman year. And then, were lab partners in science class. By some unspoken agreement, they'd also sat next to each other in AP English. They'd quickly become friends, one of Margo's only allies after she and Jessie started running in different circles.

She felt bad, looking at him standing in front of her now, that she'd put their friendship on the back burner when she'd started befriending Jessie again in their senior year. She couldn't believe how much he'd changed since high school, now looking more rugged and handsome than the skinny nerd she remembered. But he still had the same chocolatey brown eyes that turned up at the corners when he smiled, his lips pulling up higher on the right than the left, causing that cute dimple to appear on his cheek. She'd seen the occasional photo of him pop up on her Facebook feed over the years, but he looked even better in person.

'My dad had to have knee surgery, so I moved back to help him out,' Margo continued.

'Ah, I'm sorry to hear that, I hope he's doing alright,' Austin said, placing his hands in the pockets of his dark blue shorts.

'Thanks, he's doing well, all things considered. He'll make a full recovery. Just picking up some meds since my allergies have kicked into high gear now that I'm back. What about you, what brings you back to town?'

'Glad to hear he's on the mend,' Austin said. 'Yeah, I moved to Atlanta for college and then fell in love with the city . . . decided to stay to build my career. I'm just here temporarily for a work assignment. Do you remember the show *Into Thin Air*?'

Margo's heart thumped faster. She remembered seeing him post about changing jobs but hadn't realized it had been to work on *that* show. 'Of course I do. I always watched it with my dad growing up. It was surreal when they came and covered Jessie's disappearance back then. It was pretty hard to watch that episode, to be honest.' She swallowed the lump threatening to form in her throat and looked over her shoulder momentarily as someone walked a bit too close behind her, brushing against the back of her shirt. She'd forgotten Lake Moss's inability to recognize personal space. Margo turned her attention back to Austin. 'I heard they were doing a reboot, but I didn't realize it was already filming. You're working for the show now?'

'Yep,' Austin said, 'I'm on the crew as the lead sound tech. Once our production team heard that Jessie had been found,' he took a solemn pause, giving her a sympathetic smile before continuing, 'they decided it would be great to come back and film a follow-up episode to run in the new season, see if they can drum up any new evidence after all these years. Her episode was one of their most viewed in season nine. When I mentioned I was from here, they jumped at bringing me along. Figured it would help getting through to the townies since I'm not as much of an outsider. But I don't know, it's strange being back, isn't it?'

'Yeah,' Margo said with a big sigh. 'It's like nothing and everything has changed all at once. It's gonna be weird having camera crews running around, getting everyone all worked up again.' She paused, trying to contain the tears that threatened to explode to the surface whenever she talked about Jessie. 'But I'm glad you're involved. At least you knew her,' Margo said softly.

Despite the years that had passed since they last saw each other in person, Austin still seemed safe and trustworthy, like a security blanket from her childhood that she just rediscovered. His presence had always soothed her, the way he talked in a steady cadence and always seemed so at ease. Back in school, he'd tried to protect her from the bullying she'd faced, or at least comfort her after any torment that couldn't be stopped in the moment. While they hadn't talked much in recent years beyond the occasional like or comment on Facebook posts – Margo too caught up in the intensity of her marital problems – it was like no time had passed as she looked at him now. The show coming back to do a follow-up on Jessie's case made anxiety swell in the pit of her stomach, but she felt better that if the story was going to be told, at least it was by someone she knew. And, Margo thought, he was probably right that the town would open up to him more than an outsider, although she wasn't sure how much it would help in the end. When Jessie's episode had aired in 2004, just months after she vanished, the tip line had produced little more than town gossip and a slew of unconfirmed Jessie sightings that went nowhere.

'Yeah, I'm hoping that by being involved I can help show the town and Jessie in the right light, maybe even help uncover some truths since I know the cast of characters a bit. Not that we were close with that crowd by any means,' he said with a light laugh. Margo smiled wryly, and after a long moment Austin said, 'But how are you? You got married, right? I remember seeing some photos a few years back. Is your husband here with you?' He looked around as if expecting a man to jump out from behind the cleaning products aisle.

'Oh,' Margo said, her cheeks flushing, looking down at her feet. 'No, that actually didn't end up working out. It's part of the reason I came back. There wasn't a whole lot left for me back on the coast.'

She couldn't quite meet his eyes as she admitted her marriage failure. Seeing pity etched on people's faces made her feel like a sad, pathetic victim. She'd gone quiet in her online presence since her marriage blew up, unable to face more people knowing the infuriating truth. She already felt terrible enough at the way her husband had treated her, cheated on her, and threw her away like trash. She didn't need other people pointing out how awful it was. And beyond that, Margo felt extra embarrassed because here was this handsome, kind man from her childhood, seeing how much her life had fallen apart, while he lived out his dream job. She came back to Lake Moss at the lowest of lows, and he came back riding in on a train of success.

'I'm so sorry to hear that,' Austin said. His voice was so gentle and understanding, that she looked up and locked eyes with him. Instead of pity, she saw empathy. That was something she'd always liked about him, his ability to listen without judgment. And, who knows, maybe he had been through something similar. If she was any proof, social media was like a highlight reel, rarely showing what was happening behind the scenes. 'Listen,' he said, clearing his throat and making his voice upbeat again. 'I'm going to be in town for a few weeks working on the show.' She appreciated that he was steering her out of dangerous territory, saving her from delving into her messy relationship. 'If you're up for it, maybe we can get together and catch up over a drink?'

'That would be really nice,' Margo said with a smile, tucking her long hair behind her ear. 'Here, what's your number?' she asked, taking her phone out of her bag.

After exchanging numbers and agreeing to meet up in a few days, Austin bid her goodbye and exited the store with his shopping bag. He'd told her he was staying at his parents' house while they were traveling for the summer. Margo paid for her allergy pills and walked out to her car, her mind reeling from the encounter. Not only was one of her only friends from school back in town, but she couldn't believe *Into Thin Air* was back and determined to solve Jessie's case on film. She'd heard so many stories of other disappearances getting solved from tips called into their show's hotline after airing. Even though Jessie's first episode hadn't produced results, would this one . . .?

CHAPTER FOUR

After Margo finished putting the dinner dishes into the dishwasher, she excused herself. She walked down the single-story home's hallway to her bedroom and closed the door. Going to the small wooden desk near the window where she used to do her homework, she pulled out her laptop and moved the book she'd been reading over to the right side of the desk before plugging her laptop in to charge. She opened the job search page she'd been perusing earlier and hit refresh. She wasn't sure where she wanted to live now that she had nothing holding her to Wilmington, but she figured job opportunities would influence her options. She'd quickly crossed Lake Moss off the list. Not only was she reluctant to move back permanently, but there were zero job postings in her field. Instead, she looked at larger cities like Asheville, Charlotte, Charleston and Atlanta. She'd even considered spots in Virginia and Tennessee. A fresh place with new faces seemed like the best idea.

As she scrolled through the openings, images of Jessie and the rumors surrounding her disappearance swirled around Margo's mind. Her thoughts drifted back to when she'd discovered the voicemail, the pocket-dial from Jessie's last known night alive. Margo had forgotten to keep her phone on her that whole evening, so she hadn't even realized there was a voicemail until the following morning. She remembered the sun breaking into her room, the smell of her dad's coffee brewing in the kitchen wafting down the hallway, when a frantic knock came to her bedroom door.

'Come in!' She'd yawned, rubbing her tired eyes, her voice scratchy.

'Margo,' her dad rushed in, panic evident on his face. She shot up to a seated position in bed, gripping her quilt so that it scrunched up in her fingers. The last time her dad had looked this distressed had been when he had to tell her that her mother was dead. 'It's Jessie.'

Margo remembered that morning distinctly, as if she were reliving it in present time, the way her stomach had clenched and a chill, unseasonable for late spring, had blanketed her in goose bumps. 'Something bad's happened, hasn't it?' she'd asked.

'She never came home last night, Margo. Her parents think something may have happened to her. She said she was going to a tutoring session with you, but you told me that she'd cancelled. Did she come over anyway? Did you hear from her? Her parents are worried sick. I just can't imagine if you didn't come home one night . . .'

He trailed off, his face pale with worry, his crystal blue eyes squinting as his eyebrows knitted together. Margo felt like she was going to throw up, but she was frozen, unsure what to do or say. 'No, I didn't tutor her last night, sorry Dad. She cancelled at the last minute, like I told you. I didn't hear from her. They have no idea where she is?'

Margo choked the words out, fear and worry stringing them together like imaginary punctuation marks that made them short and disjointed. It could have been her imagination, but her dad seemed relieved at her answer. That he could rest a little easier in the small comfort of his daughter not being connected to this other parents' nightmare.

'OK, well, Chief Healey is here,' he said, a bit strained. 'He wants to ask you a few questions, but just tell him the truth, OK? Tell him what you told me.'

She was still in a haze as she grabbed her robe to cover her thin pink shorts and tank top and promised she'd be right out. Then she picked up her phone and noticed the missed voicemail from Jessie the night before, shock pulling her back down to her bed. Quickly listening to the message, she forgot to breathe until the message had played in its entirety. Pulling the phone away from her ear with a shaky hand, she realized there was nothing on the message other than muffled, unrecognizable voices and static. Nothing that would give them a clue about what happened to Jessie. She listened one more time with the volume all the way up to be sure. It had clearly been a pocket-dial, inaudible. Jessie was notorious for them, her phone always nestled among lip gloss and pieces of bubblegum. This wasn't the first accidental dial Margo had received from her.

Margo exited the room with her phone tucked into the pocket of her white terry robe. It was surreal, seeing Chief Healey sitting at her kitchen table with a mug of steaming coffee across from her dad. The last time she'd seen him, he'd been sporting a baseball cap, coaching his son's Little League team at the baseball diamond not far from the school. Seeing him there in his official uniform was unsettling.

'Margo,' he said, 'your dad was just telling me that you didn't see Jessie for tutoring last night like she'd told her parents. Is that true?'

Margo would never forget the way his inquisitive green eyes burned into hers. She'd heard people talk in town about how he was like a human lie detector. Was that what he was doing to her? Reading her the way he did every criminal who crossed the police department's doorstep?

She shook her head, saying in a soft voice, 'No, sir, I didn't tutor Jessie last night. She cancelled our session.'

He nodded, running his hand across his bare chin, clean-shaven unlike most of the men in the small town. 'What about by phone? Did Jessie text or call you last night? Or leave you any messages?'

Her heart stopped. Did he already know she had a voicemail from Jessie? Had Jessie's parents given him access to her phone records right away? After listening to the message, Margo knew there was nothing of value on it; it probably wouldn't help but it couldn't hurt to let them listen. Reaching into her pocket, she took out her phone and placed it on the kitchen table gently.

'I just saw a voicemail on my phone when I woke up this morning. It's from Jessie.'

Chief Healey lit up, his hand darting forward to grab the phone. Her father hesitated, as if he was torn between protecting his daughter's private property and helping them find Jessie. 'May I listen to it?' Chief Healey asked, the phone already gripped in his large, calloused hand.

Margo nodded and said, 'OK. But I've listened, and there's nothing there. It sounds like a pocket-dial. Jessie was always doing that, especially to anyone she had keyed into her favorite shortcuts. It just sounds staticky and muffled.'

He looked disheartened but said, 'All the same. I should still take a listen and see if our team can get anything else off it. May I take it with me? You can come by the station in a few hours to pick it back up.'

Margo and her dad shared a look before she said, 'OK.'

'Did Jessie ever mention running away, or anywhere she wanted to visit?'

'No, she never said anything like that to me. And with college just around the corner, why would she take off now?'

'Maybe she was seeing someone? Someone other than Charlie?'

Margo tensed for a second, looking at her dad as she mulled over her answer. He was looking at her seriously, like she held all the answers to Jessie's personal life. She shook her head, pulling her thoughts together through the cloud of nerves and confusion. 'No, but her and Charlie were having problems. She said they fought a lot and she was thinking of breaking up with him.'

'She told you that?'

'Yeah, she said she was going to talk to him. That was a few days ago. I don't know if she did or not. She never mentioned anyone else though.'

Chief Healey looked at her for a moment, making Margo feel anxious. He stared at her with such intensity, it was hard not to squirm under his gaze. Then he rose and said, 'OK well thank you for your help. If you think of anything else that might be helpful, or if Jessie gets in touch with you in any way, please let us know.'

'I will, Chief Healey,' Margo had said, nodding.

Shaking her head to bring herself back to the present and pulling her hair up into a big messy topknot on her head, Margo wondered if updated technology had helped get anything more off the message, or if the police had dismissed it as unhelpful like she had. Just as she forced herself to refocus on the job search page, her phone dinged with an incoming text.

'Hey, Margo! Are you free tomorrow evening for that drink? I have something I'd like to pick your brain about.' It was from Austin. Margo smiled.

'Absolutely!' she texted back within seconds, as a warmth spread through her at the thought. 'How about we meet at Grizzley's around 6?'

'Perfect,' he texted back immediately. 'I'll see you there.'

September 3, 1995

Dear Diary,

My very first entry! I'm so excited to finally have my own diary. A place to write down all my secrets and no one but me can see them. Jessie got this really cute pink Hello Kitty diary with jewels on it when she went to Asheville with her parents but Mom wouldn't let me go with them. She said lots of recent crimes made it too dangerous. Anyway, when Jessie showed me her diary, I wanted one too. After a week of begging, Mom finally took me to a store in town to see if they had one. They didn't have a cool Hello Kitty one like Jessie's, but I found a cute yellow one with a cartoon dog on the cover. Mom wasn't happy that it had a lock on it but there was only one that didn't have a lock, an ugly brown one with no pictures or cartoons on it! No way was I getting that one. I'd be too embarrassed to show it to Jessie. Mom gave in and let me have it, and I'm the only one with the key!

Now for my secrets. I don't have that many but one thing I haven't told Mom and Dad about is that Jessie and I became blood sisters yesterday. Jessie saw it in a movie and said it would bind us together as best friends forever. She took a knife from her kitchen and we snuck down to the creek behind her house. She read something she called a blood oath, about what we promise each other as blood sisters, and she made me repeat it after her. Then she cut her palm with the knife and made me put my hand out. I was scared but I did it anyway. It hurt because she pushed the knife down so hard I cried out and pulled my hand away. But she grabbed my hand back and clasped it in hers, palm to palm. Then we both said 'I swear this oath, my lifelong pact to my blood sister. No one shall break our connection as it is set in blood.' Jessie and I are now connected always and forever.

CHAPTER FIVE

Margo was being followed. A group of townspeople had formed an eerie pack and were slowly walking toward her, loudly whispering behind open hands and falling in step like a horde of gossiping zombies. Their judgmental voices layered on top of each other, a symphony of razor-sharp, hissing words that drowned out everything else.

She tripped and fell, and just as they closed in, Margo sprung up in her bed panting and running her hands through her hair, tangled from tossing and turning in the night. Another nightmare. She'd had similar dreams as a kid, usually about her mom's accident, but she assumed she'd outgrown them for the most part. She'd thought maybe the one she had on her first day back was a one-off from Jessie's remains being discovered. But here they were again, haunting her whenever she closed her eyes. She got up and crossed over to the window, pulling back the ruffled white linen curtains and peering outside.

Margo always loved the view from her house growing up. It was private; the few neighbors she had weren't visible from this vantage point facing their backyard. The house was nestled deep in the trees, but you could still make out the tips of the mountains peeking over the top of the tree line. The sun was starting to rise, casting everything in a warm amber glow as it lightened the night sky. Deciding there was no point in trying to get back to sleep, she grabbed her clothes and crept out to the bathroom to shower and get ready to face the day.

Margo cooked breakfast and as she and her dad ate, he asked, 'You sleeping OK, kiddo? You look tired.'

Margo shook her head. 'Just a few nightmares. Probably just from coming home after all these years. Slipping into old patterns, I guess. But I'm fine.'

Her dad stopped chewing and his eyebrows scrunched together. 'I hope they aren't back. You worked so hard to get over them when you were a kid.'

Margo leaned across the table and clasped her dad's hand. 'I'm fine Dad, really,' she said with a smile, trying to reassure him. While she was concerned about the nightmares reappearing in her life, she didn't want to worry her dad. She could deal with them.

He looked unconvinced but nodded and went back to eating. After breakfast, she spent most of the day helping him with chores around the house. As a teen after her mom died, her dad had helped distract her from the pain by making her his little assistant. They'd hammered nails and she would hand him tools as he fixed leaky pipes under the sink, and any task that he could invent to keep them occupied. The physical labor had helped keep the grief at bay, until night came and it seeped into her dreams in the quiet, still house. Margo had become an introvert after her mom died, sticking close to her dad's side and withdrawing from all her friends and classmates. Besides occasionally hitting baseballs lobbed up by her dad in the backyard to release her pent-up emotions, playing handyman with him was one of the few things that helped give her a sense of peace and purpose.

Her dad still wasn't back to one hundred percent but had become pretty adept with his crutches. It was nostalgic and soothing, pushing the nightmare further away as she followed him around, crossing off tasks on his list. Once the evening rolled in, Margo excused herself from watching TV to get ready to meet Austin. She had nervous butterflies fluttering around her stomach, but she tried to ignore them as she sorted through her closet. She was excited to reconnect, and she couldn't deny how handsome he'd become.

Margo opted for a deep blue sleeveless wrap dress that made her warm brown hair and eyes pop, donning silver hoops from the jewelry box on her vanity. She closed the box quickly, her discarded engagement and wedding rings taunting her from within. She hadn't been able to bring herself to get rid of them, but it felt like they were mocking her. Trying to shake off the anger and sadness at her failed marriage, she leaned forward in the mirror to apply her favorite berry lipstick. Admiring the soft waves she'd styled into her hair and the way her outfit came together, she felt a surge of confidence. She slipped into a pair of light brown open-toed flats, grabbed her leather cross-body bag and headed out to her car.

Margo got to Grizzley's before Austin. Looking around she spotted two open seats at the far end of the small bar. Grizzley's was a step nicer than the only other local pub, with its black leather booths along the walls and carved wooden stools at the bar. Several iron and glass chandeliers were positioned throughout the large room giving it an upscale feel. There was also a beautiful brick-lined patio just beyond the glass double doors along the back wall that backed up into a hillside, surrounded by vibrant foliage. But it was too warm to sit out back; Margo didn't want to be a sweaty mess when she saw Austin. She gave a smile and a wave to Lance, the bartender who she recognized from high school. While they hadn't been friends, he had always been kind and never took part in taunting her like Charlie Abbott had. His warm brown skin glistened in the light from the chandelier above the bar as he came closer to her.

He glanced at her and then squinted, as though he was trying to place her in his memory. She wasn't surprised he hadn't immediately recognized her. It'd been fifteen years since he would have seen her, and she hoped she looked different than the plain, timid girl she used to be. Especially since she'd taken extra care this evening.

As he walked over to close the gap between them, he snapped his fingers and pointed at her. 'Margo Sutton?' he asked, his head cocked to the side. Margo smiled and nodded. 'I'd heard you were back in town,' he said as he set a cocktail napkin down on the bar in front of her. 'How's your dad doing?'

Margo inwardly grimaced at how hard it was to stay under the radar in a town like Lake Moss, even for a former wallflower like herself. She was shocked that Jessie's disappearance had actually gone unsolved for this long since everyone knew everyone's business.

'He's doing well, thanks for asking. Should be back up on his feet in no time.'

'Great! Glad to hear it. My nephew will be relieved, he was hoping to get a few more summer ball camps out of your dad before he retires.'

'I'll be sure to let him know; he'll love to hear that.'

Lance smiled, his thick, dark beard stretching along his beaming face. 'So, what can I getcha tonight? Our happy hour specials are up there on the board,' he said as he pointed back over his shoulder. Margo looked up and took it in.

Moss Creek Pilsner $5

Peak City Chardonnay $4

House Martini $4

Margo desperately wanted to order a dirty martini, but if it was more of a 'low-key beer night' for Austin, she didn't want to come off as aggressive. 'Oh, great. I'm meeting someone, so I think I'll wait till they arrive to order. But thanks,' she said, pulling out her phone to check for any missed messages. Her phone screen was blank.

'Oh, no problem at all. I'll be back with you shortly,' he said as a guest on the other side of the bar flagged him for a refill.

As Margo was putting her phone back into her purse, she looked up and saw Austin strolling in through the door. He smiled as his eyes fell on her, making his way over to where she sat. He was wearing a slim-fit green t-shirt and dark gray shorts. She couldn't help but notice he had nice calves, but she forced her gaze upward and smiled as he got closer and pulled her into a hug. She breathed in his scent, a mix of woodsy and clean linen. It felt comforting and familiar, despite how odd it was to be hugging a man other than her husband. *Ex-husband*, she reminded herself.

'Hey, Margo, thanks for meeting me. Sorry I'm a few minutes late, got caught up on a call.'

'Oh, no problem!' Margo said, hating how enthusiastic her voice sounded. She tried to relax.

Lance made his way back over to them as Austin sat down. 'Well, if the person you were waiting for isn't Austin Hughes,' he said and reached his arm across the bar. Austin smiled as they shook hands. 'How you doin' man?' Margo remembered Austin tutoring Lance in math junior year. Tutoring the popular jocks had saved Austin from getting bullied like the rest of the outcasts. The athletes couldn't afford to fail and get suspended from their respective teams, so Austin had been their savior. She'd forgotten he'd known Lance better than she had.

'I'm good, Lance, thanks. How about you?'

'Oh, can't complain,' Lance said as he placed a napkin down in front of Austin. 'The town is getting all worked up again, but it's good for business. A little slow right now,' he said looking around, 'but it'll pick up later.'

'Glad to hear it,' Austin replied. 'We'll start giving you some business right now. What do you think, Margo? Martinis? Seems like an occasion that calls for more than a beer.'

Margo beamed. *Yes*, she thought, *this is going well already*. 'That sounds perfect. Dirty, please.'

'Same here,' Austin said and handed over his card to start a tab.

'You don't have to do that,' Margo insisted as she shuffled in her purse for her wallet.

'Don't be silly, I don't mind. I'm just glad we can catch up,' he said with another wide smile.

The way Austin looked so genuinely into her eyes, it felt like the most attention she'd had in years. It made her realize that it had been a long time since her ex had looked at her in that way, like she was the only one in the room who mattered. It was nice, although almost disconcerting. What if he didn't like what he saw?

'Thanks,' she said, and she straightened her napkin on the bar in front of her for lack of knowing what else to do with her hands until she had a drink to hold.

'So,' Austin said, turning in his chair to look at her better. 'What have you been up to the last fifteen years? I remember you went to UNC Wilmington. What have you been doing since then?'

Margo laughed. 'I can't believe it's been fifteen years. I ended up staying in Wilmington after school. I got a Criminology degree, but after going through all my courses, I realized I just didn't have the stomach to be a lawyer.' She looked up gratefully as Lance placed her dirty martini on her napkin. She reached for it at the same time Austin reached for his and said, 'Oh, good! Cheers,' and they clinked glasses. She took a long sip, savoring the path it burned as it coursed through her. She needed some liquid confidence.

After Austin took a sip from his and placed it back on the bar, he said, 'Really? How so? You always seemed like you could handle anything. High school wasn't easy, but I was always impressed with the way you pushed through the tough times and still managed to graduate with straight A's.'

Margo flushed. 'I'd planned on going into criminal law since that was what interested me most. But it was too much pressure. If you were good at your job, there was a high probability that at some point in your career you would either be keeping a guilty person out of prison or trying to put an innocent person behind bars. It was just too heavy. I realized I couldn't live with that guilt.'

Austin nodded, taking another sip. Margo mirrored his action. 'That makes sense. So,' he said, looking at her intently, 'what did you do instead?'

'Well, I still really loved learning about criminal justice so when I had a meeting with my academic advisor in my senior year and mentioned how quickly I could type out a paper on deadline, she suggested I look into a nearby court stenographer program. Technically my job title is court reporter, but most people think that means I'm a journalist,' she smiled. 'It was an easy transition since some of my pre-law courses already fulfilled half the requirements, so I took the plunge and went for it.'

'Wow that's really interesting; I've never met anyone who does that. So, you basically sit in the courtroom and type out everything that happens?'

Margo nodded and took another sip. Talking about it made her nostalgic, she missed her job. 'That pretty much sums it up. All the interesting cases and evidence, minus the pressure to prove anything and no one's fate was in my hands. It was the best of both worlds.'

'That's awesome. Are you transferring to a job here or do you plan to go back to where you were?'

Margo grimaced, taking another sip. 'Unfortunately, I don't have anything to go back to. I left my job in October last year, so I've been looking for jobs elsewhere. I'm not sure where I'll land.'

'Oh, I'm sorry . . . why did you leave it? If you don't mind me asking,' he said, taking another sip.

'It's OK,' Margo replied. 'I left for my husband, well, ex-husband. It's pretty clear now that wasn't the best move. He'd been saying for years that he wanted a family and dreamed of his wife being a stay-at-home mom the way his mom raised him. He was in a fairly important position at a financial consulting firm, so he was busy all the time and didn't want his kids raised by a stranger. When things started getting rocky and I felt him pulling away from me, I quit as a sign of good faith that I was ready to commit to our future. Needless to say, it didn't save our marriage.' Margo took a big swig of her drink.

'That's terrible, I'm sorry,' Austin said and reached a comforting hand over to rest on hers where it sat on the bar. It only lasted for a second before he withdrew it to take a sip of his own drink, but Margo's skin felt warm and tingly from the touch. 'Is it nosey of me to ask what happened with your marriage?'

'No, it's fine,' Margo said, although nerves swelled in her belly. This was the first time she'd spoken out loud about what happened. She hadn't even gone into any of the gruesome details with her dad, claiming she wasn't ready. But here she was, willing to air her dirty laundry to the man sitting in front of her. There was something comforting about Austin that drew her in, and she was sure the stiff drink also helped. 'He had been pulling away for a while and I wasn't sure why. He was always cagey about where he was, which of course, created tension and distrust in our relationship. He was upset that I'd quit without telling him, saying he never asked me to do that. Then we started bickering over everything, even the smallest things like who was supposed to do the dishes or who forgot to take the trash out. And then he just started working later and later. Sometimes he wouldn't get home until long after I'd gone to bed. Eventually, I found out he was cheating on me with one of the secretaries at work . . . the ultimate stereotype.'

Austin flinched and said, 'Oof. That's rough.'

Margo's mind flashed back to that pivotal moment. She was supposed to meet an old co-worker for lunch following a hair appointment but had gotten home early after they had to reschedule last minute. She planned to surprise Mark with her early arrival so she didn't text him to let him know. When she walked up the stairs, she heard Mark on the phone with someone. His voice floated down the stairwell, 'I love her and I can't leave her. I just can't do this anymore. We need to end things for both our sakes or we're going to end up hating each other. I really hope we can try to remain friends.'

Margo's breath caught in her throat and she grabbed the handrail to steady herself. He was breaking up with someone; her fears of his infidelity had been true. Margo marched up the last few steps and called out his name. Mark whipped around, his eyes wide like saucers as he slowly placed his phone down on their bed.

'I knew it! You can't deny it after what I just overheard, Mark!'

He was tongue tied and couldn't get any words out, opening and closing his mouth several times. Margo cocked her head and narrowed her eyes, waiting for him to say something. A ding came from her purse. Her phone had been buried in her purse on the back seat on her way home, so she hadn't heard it ring while she was grabbing things from the trunk. When she pulled the phone out of her purse, she saw a voicemail. From Mark. The one he was leaving as she walked in. It was his girlfriend that he loved and couldn't leave, not her.

Shaking her head at the memory, she said to Austin, 'He left me a message breaking up with me and that's when I found out about his affair.'

Austin's face crumpled and he said, 'Wow, what a cowardly move.'

'Right? It was mortifying *and* the final nail in the coffin; you can't come back from your husband asking for a divorce on a voicemail. He filed pretty quickly. I stuck around for a few months, trying to figure out my next moves, but with no job and my dad's surgery on the horizon, it didn't make sense to stay and fight for a life that had disappeared before my eyes. So, here I am.' Margo gave a heavy sigh.

'That's horrible,' Austin said, but thankfully, without pity. Something in his eyes seemed to understand her pain. 'I'm really sorry you had to go through that. Your ex sounds like a dick.'

Margo snorted unattractively into her drink as she took a sip, laughing. 'Yes, he truly is.'

'Well, I know it was a series of unfortunate events that brought you back to Lake Moss, but I'm glad you're here. It's really nice to have a friendly face around,' Austin said.

'Yeah, it's really good to see you,' Margo replied. 'You said you're a sound tech for *Into Thin Air*, right?'

'Yeah, when the crew was here for the original "Jessie Germaine" episode all those years ago, I hung around the set because I was intrigued by the filming process. One of the sound guys, Dave, took me under his wing, showed me all the equipment and put the idea in my head. He said he loved it and thought I would too. He recommended a sound engineering program in Atlanta. Since I'd already gotten into Georgia State, I decided to change my major from Business to Music Technology. Dave and I kept in touch over the years, so when I graduated, I contacted him again for advice on how to break into the industry. He connected me with a few smaller production companies who were looking for PAs. I started at the bottom, basically getting coffee and food for the crew. It was awful, a lame reality show about a group of doomsday preppers.' Austin glanced at her and laughed. 'I've worked on some really bad

62

shows. But I've worked on some great ones too. Did you ever watch *Say It Loud*?'

'Oh, I loved that show!'

'Yeah, it was great working with that team. We were even nominated for a couple of awards for our work.'

'That's amazing, Austin!' she said, bumping his shoulder with her own.

'Thanks. The host of that show always reminded me of Mr. Girabaldi, though, with that creepy goatee,' Austin said, shooting her a look.

Margo laughed and then at the same time, they both furrowed their brows and said, 'When you come to *my* class, you come to learn!'

They laughed, remembering their stern English teacher who reprimanded students with that line any time he caught someone not paying attention.

'You're so right, he did look like Mr. Girabaldi. Well, that's really great that you've found something you love to do,' Margo said.

'Yeah, even during the bad shows, I've loved every minute of my career. And it led me back to Lake Moss and Jessie's disappearance, so I feel like I've come full circle.'

'I'm not surprised they're reprising *Into Thin Air*. It was such a hot ticket back then, I can't believe it ever got cancelled. And the town was thrilled when they chose to spotlight Jessie's case, considering no one trusted the police investigation. I can feel that same energy this time around, that air of hope that her case might finally be solved. When did you get into documentaries?' Margo asked, intrigued.

'I ended up doing a stint with a documentary producer and really fell in love with that style of filming. When I heard *Into Thin Air* was doing a reboot, I really wanted to be a part of it considering the connection I had to the show. The documentary producer I worked with connected me with a buddy of his on the *Into Thin Air* crew when they were getting everything lined up to go back into production in December, and I was able to land the sound tech job. We were already in the middle of filming a few cases when the news of Jessie's body being discovered broke. The producer, Amy, knew I had a connection to Lake Moss and Jessie, so she was excited to have me on board. And now I'm heading up her sound crew. I guess being from Lake Moss had some benefit after all.'

'One person's tragedy is another's good fortune,' Margo said with a sad smile.

'Isn't that the truth,' Austin nodded. 'But I'm grateful to be a part of telling Jessie's story.'

Margo nodded. 'So, what cases have you worked on so far? If you don't mind me asking.'

'Some pretty interesting ones actually. Jessie's case isn't the only one they are revisiting. Remember that Stacy Mennell case they aired in the final season of the show's original run? The one where she was talking on her cell phone with her boyfriend while walking home from her job and someone grabbed her off the street. Her boyfriend heard everything and called the police, but they never found her.'

'Oh yeah, that one haunted me.' Margo shivered. 'So creepy.'

'Yeah, so we did a second episode with all the tips that have come in over the years, I'm hoping it leads to some breaks in the case. We also did an episode on a pretty noteworthy cold case, a college student named Lauren Spierer from 2011 in Indiana. She was partying into the early morning with a bunch of guys at one of their apartments and then left to walk home but was never seen again.'

'I remember seeing that one in the headlines, and I think one of the Kardashians tweeted about it.'

'Yeah, it was a pretty high-profile case at the time. It's crazy that they still have no new leads. But it's been interesting digging through all the cases with the show.'

'I'm sure,' Margo replied. There was a short lull, and Margo started fidgeting.

'Can I ask you something?' Austin said as he flagged Lance to refill drinks.

Bless him, she thought as she pushed her empty glass forward. 'Anything,' she replied.

'I'm sure you remember how secretive the police were during Jessie's initial investigation, and how they refused to participate in the show in 2004.'

'Of course I remember, it made them look so shady. I don't think anyone believes they did any serious investigating when she went missing.'

'Exactly. Well, Amy had a long chat with Healey when we got to town. She told him that the show would have no choice but to paint them in an unfavorable light if they wouldn't cooperate this time. She reminded him of what a bad rap they got, not only in Lake Moss, but across the country people were saying how they'd bungled the case. I wasn't there, but Amy's pretty convincing and unrelenting. She told him that this was their chance to change that narrative, show that they had actually investigated by giving information on the case now. Show everyone that they *are* trying to solve Jessie's case. And, well, Healey actually agreed. His name has been raked over the coals not only for that, but also for that botched drug case when the evidence went missing.'

'Oh yeah, didn't Healey throw that poor new deputy under the bus to save his butt?'

'That's the story, even though he denies it. Anyway, his reputation has never recovered and now he's eager to clear his name and rustle up some good press to outweigh the bad. And Amy said she'd keep him in the loop on anything we find while filming. So, he finally handed over the police report. It's heavily redacted but it's more information than we had before. She noticed that your name came up in the report.' Margo tensed. 'It said you received a pocket-dial message from Jessie the night she disappeared. Amy has submitted a formal request for a copy, but we've been told it'll take some time. So I wondered if you might still have it saved somewhere?'

'Oh,' Margo took a pause. 'No, I'm sorry I don't. It was on my old flip-phone, so I guess when I got a new one, the message went with the old one.' Austin deflated a little. 'Sorry, I thought since I gave it to the police that they'd have it on file.'

'They do, we just thought it'd be quicker to get it from you if you still had it. They're cooperating but not exactly rushing to hand things over. I knew it was a long a shot, I mean, who keeps voicemails for fifteen years, right?' He gave a chuckle.

'Was there anything helpful in the report?'

'I haven't seen it yet. She handed it over to our research team and they are hunting down any leads they find. Since I said I knew you, Amy wanted me to ask. But hey, she got Chief Healey to do an interview!'

'Oh my god, she did?'

'Yep. She sent me over the link to the rough cut so I could clean up some background noise. Hey . . . do you wanna see it? We could head over to my house and watch it. I have my whole sound set-up there.'

'Oh wow! I'd love to. Let's finish up these drinks and get going.'

'Cheers!' Austin said, and they clinked their glasses.

They finished their drinks over small talk about Lake Moss and who they had run into since returning, before Austin closed his tab and they headed out. While Margo and Austin had been friends in school, she'd never been to his house. He'd said the library or her house were quieter than his, where his three siblings were always running around. Looking back, Margo remembered the butterflies she'd had when she'd been alone with him back then. She'd never told him about her crush.

Austin got settled at his equipment station that he used for editing and manipulating audio. Margo sat in silent fascination as Austin worked his magic. He had oversized headphones on, his face screwed up in concentration as he fiddled with various knobs and settings. Margo sipped the glass of wine he'd poured upon their arrival. All of a sudden, the monitor lit up showing Chief Healey sitting at his desk at the police station, a running timer frozen at the bottom of the screen. Austin pulled off his headphones and hit the play button.

The producer's strong, deliberate voice came from off screen. 'Chief Healey, I'd like to thank you for talking to us today. I know you had a hard time of it when Jessie Germaine went missing. Can you tell us why you chose not to release any details of the investigation until now?'

'It was the first big case my department had ever had at the time. I'd only been Chief for a year. Sure, we'd get robberies and car accidents, things like that, but nothing like a missing persons case. I conferred with a few other

67

departments across North Carolina when tips came in, and I was advised to keep things close to my chest. They said the media would blow things out of proportion and start accusing people, but if they didn't have any information to go off, it would be milder. Since they had more experience than me on cases like this, I took it to heart. But as you mentioned, that didn't go well. It created distrust in our department and our investigation. And I assure you, we did investigate,' he said with a pointed stare at the camera.

'What can you tell me about Jessie's disappearance?'

'At the time, there wasn't much evidence at all. She was last seen by her brother, riding her bike away from their house in the early evening. And then, nothing. We interviewed all her friends, classmates, and family. No one had any idea where she went. But then we got some accounts of a trip she said she was eager to take. And we found some information hinting at that plan on her home computer, so it seemed likely she'd just run off. Not many people who we interviewed said they'd put it past her. It wasn't out of the realm of possibility that she'd simply taken off on an adventure somewhere she deemed more exciting,' he said with a shrug.

'OK, let's talk about the discovery of her remains. What can you tell me about her cause of death, the state of the remains, anything you're able to share.'

Healey looked down momentarily and then took a big breath. It was strange seeing emotion from the man who'd only ever appeared stern and commanding. 'She was found in a sealed ice chest at the bottom of a swimming hole popular with local high school seniors. We had a medical examiner and forensic team from Asheville come in to help examine the remains and the cooler. No fingerprints or DNA from anyone other than Jessie were found. With it being in the water for so long, that's not surprising. Her flesh had dissolved into a gel-like substance at the bottom of the cooler, leaving only bones and hair behind.' He paused for a moment, swallowing hard. 'We actually got lucky that she was wearing that bow in a ponytail when she died. When her scalp melted away, the hair was kept together by the bow. Which was what led to the discovery; her hair and bow had floated up out of the cooler when it was jostled open. But from her skull we were able to determine that the cause of death was blunt force trauma to the head. It was caved in on the back side.'

'I see. So other than her body, there was no other evidence to be found in the cooler?'

'Well, that's all we can share at this point.'

Amy paused and then said, 'There have been some rumors around town that a pregnancy test was found inside the cooler with her body. Was Jessie pregnant when she died?'

Healey pursed his lips. 'As I said, I can't comment any further on what was found.'

'OK, well then hypothetically, if Jessie was pregnant, would you be able to tell from the state of her remains?'

'*Hypothetically*, it might be too hard to tell if it was before the fetus had developed a skeleton.'

'So let's assume for a minute that Jessie was pregnant. Does that open up possibilities of who her murderer could be? A lot of people have pointed the finger at Charlie Abbott, her boyfriend at the time.'

Healey visibly tensed. 'I'm not comfortable discussing who is and isn't a suspect in an on-going investigation.'

'But surely Charlie has to be at the top of the list?'

Healey gave her a long look, his nostrils flaring as he inhaled deeply. 'Look, I said I'd give you an interview, but I'm not going to throw innocent people out there to be attacked by the media. We have no evidence that indicates anyone in particular at this stage of our investigation. And that's all I'll say about that.' He crossed his arms across his chest.

Austin clicked the stop button and turned to Margo. 'There's not much more than that. He talks about the history of the brewery a bit, the small family-like vibe of our community, but not much more about the actual investigation.'

'It seems like he's still intent on protecting the Abbotts at any cost.'

'Yeah it does. From what I've heard, they still have the police and Healey under their thumb.'

'The part about her remains . . .' Margo shivered.

'It's horrible to think of her like that,' Austin said sympathetically. 'I'm sure we'll be editing out some of the more gruesome details, but Amy will keep as much as possible.'

'And to think her cheer bow is what led to her remains being discovered,' Margo said, shaking her head.

'I know; something so small led to something so big.'

'So are you guys going to interview the Abbotts?'

'Yeah,' Austin replied, grabbing what looked to be a production calendar off the desk near him. 'We're interviewing a lot of the people connected to Jessie over the next two weeks.'

'Guess I didn't make the cut,' Margo said jokingly. Truthfully, she was relieved no one asked her to be involved. The last thing she wanted was to be interviewed on camera.

Austin gave a small laugh. 'No, I figured you would appreciate if I didn't volunteer you as someone who was missed last time. I also know you well enough that you would have come forward if you knew anything helpful. And that you prefer to be behind the scenes,' he said, smiling at her.

Margo was grateful. 'Thank you,' she said. 'This is bringing back so many old feelings and memories. I've always liked to imagine Jessie out there somewhere living her best life, drinking champagne on a yacht or leading a meeting in some boardroom, to make myself feel better.'

'I think everyone hoped that was the case,' Austin said softly.

Margo took a deep breath and exhaled all the sad feelings. 'OK, so what are the next steps? I'd like to help, if I can. Now that my dad is a little more mobile, I don't have as much to do. Maybe I can help set up interviews or take notes or something? I know you have a whole crew for this, but an extra pair of hands could be useful, and you'd be saving me from terrible boredom,' she asked hopefully, praying she wasn't coming off as too forward.

Austin looked like a lightbulb had clicked on, his eyes bright with the excitement of an idea. 'Actually, maybe there is a way for you to help. You have a lot of know-ledge of this town and the people in Jessie's life. With your legal expertise along with the ability to write out notes quickly from your stenographer career, I bet I could sell you as a real asset to my boss.'

'Wow, really?' Margo asked. She was pleased, but surprised. 'You think she'd go for it?'

'Someone on the team has to conduct pre-interviews this week to make sure we have an understanding of what information we can get from each person before their official interviews, help direct us on what to ask to get the most interesting answers on screen. And we need to ensure they're still willing to talk on camera. I wonder if I could spin to my boss that as locals, we'll have an easier time getting them comfortable enough to open up. It's worth a shot.' Austin shrugged one shoulder.

Margo leaned back in her chair and took a sip of the wine she was nursing. 'I'm in if you are.'

CHAPTER SIX

'I really thought I was going to have to convince her,' Austin said as he handed Margo an iced coffee in her front yard. 'But Amy was eager to hand off the pre-interviews to me and give the OK on bringing you in.'

'Really? That's great. I thought we'd be facing an uphill battle for sure,' Margo replied, taking a sip and relishing the refreshing nutty, slightly sweet flavor.

The summer heat was already creeping in for the day, and iced coffee with oat milk and one pump of vanilla was her favorite. She was thrilled, and quite frankly surprised, to find out their small-town café had started catering to the non-dairy crowd.

'I did too,' Austin said, taking a sip of his own drink. 'She thinks we may have an easier time talking with everyone connected to Jessie. While most of the locals are champing at the bit to see themselves on TV, the ones who actually matter seem to be a little more resistant to outsiders poking around.'

Margo took another long sip of her coffee. 'That makes

sense; you know how this town is. But with the killer still out there, everyone from Jessie's immediate circle is still a suspect. I actually re-watched Jessie's original episode last night, just to refresh my memory on who was interviewed back then, and what they said.'

'I did that too just before I got back to Lake Moss. It's interesting watching it again now that so much time has passed, right?'

'Totally. As a court reporter, over the years I've developed a pretty good sense of when someone is lying or reciting prepared answers. And I have to say, most of Jessie's circle back then seemed heavily rehearsed. There were a lot of repeat words and phrases.'

'I noticed that too.'

'But then you had all these other small clips of our classmates claiming to know her so well and crying like they were best friends or something, but none of them were actually close with her. They were all gushing about how perfect and nice Jessie was. It reminded me how they all used to copy everything she did, what she wore, how she talked, how she styled her hair . . .'

'Yeah, I thought the same thing. It was like jumping back in time for an hour. Remember when she wore her belt with the huge buckle backwards and the next day almost every girl was wearing it that way?' Austin shook his head.

'Oh yeah, that was the worst! It was like, clothing tramp stamps.' She and Austin laughed together at the memory. 'So glad that trend didn't last long. Anyway, as someone who actually knew Jessie, I'm excited to help out and see where the investigation leads.'

'Yeah, it's going to be great,' Austin said, and then his face lit up. 'Before we go, guess what I got!' Margo cocked her head to the side. 'Yesterday we finally got a copy of that pocket-dial message. I was able to clean it up a bit,' he said as they walked toward his Jeep, looking proud at his own skill. Margo froze for a second, her heartrate kicking up a beat. What had he unearthed after all these years? She hopped onto the seat, the air conditioning easing away the sweat that had begun to build on her brow.

'Really?' she replied, trying to keep her voice even. 'What did you hear?' she asked, doing a poor job of masking the anxiousness in her voice.

Instead of answering, he plugged his phone into a dock in the middle console and looked at her with a smile, 'Hear for yourself.'

What am I about to hear? she thought. *Is the recording finally going to reveal its secrets?*

Austin hit play on his phone and watched her face intensely as she listened. The beginning was still muffled and inaudible, which made her wonder why he had exclaimed with such excitement. As the recording went on, Margo could *almost* hear another voice in the background, but it was too distant, too distorted to tell who it was or what they were saying. She couldn't even tell if it was a male or female. Only that Jessie seemed agitated, arguing with someone, the tone and volume of her voice rising as the recording went on.

Then Margo froze as she heard a name break through the haze at the point where Jessie's voice peaked the loudest. '. . . Charlie! I told you . . .' and then back to indecipherable mumbling. But after another beat, '. . . broke up!' came through. The rest of the message was still impossible to discern, but Austin had unlocked a small piece.

Austin stopped the recording 'I know it's not much,'

he said, 'but it's something. 'Did you know Jessie and Charlie had broken up? I had no idea.'

Margo shook her head, trying to clear her mind of the thoughts flying past at record speed. 'She never said anything definitive. I knew they were having problems, but she didn't go into detail. She just seemed really irritated by him. Of course, I didn't blame her, Charlie was such a jerk. It's a bit suspicious though, right? He never said anything about them breaking up. From what you were able to pull from the recording, she could have been talking to Charlie, or talking to someone about Charlie. Either way, it doesn't look great for him. Do you think anything else from the message is salvageable?'

'Probably not,' Austin said. 'Not to toot my own horn or anything, but I'm fairly good at my job and I have the best equipment on the market. I think this is the only story that recording is going to tell.' Margo leaned back into the Jeep cushion, her mind spinning on this new bit of information. 'Anyway, Amy emailed me a list of questions for each person that's specific to them and their relationship with Jessie. I'll forward it to you so you can read it over on the way. But beyond that, we have free reign if we get a hint of any avenues we feel the need to explore further. And she'll want to see your notes of course, in preparation for filming. I really sold her on your stenographer skills,' he laughed.

'Sure. So, who's our first interview?'

Austin grimaced and then said, 'Charlie.'

Margo scowled. 'Oh, great.' She'd never been a fan of Charlie Abbott, and she was not looking forward to seeing him again.

'Yeah, I know, he's not my favorite person either, but maybe he's matured since high school.' Austin shrugged.

76

'Let's hope. I'll never forget how he used to terrorize me back then. Remember how he'd constantly scare me? He found it so hilarious, it was horrible.' Her skin crawled at the memories.

'Oh yeah, he was awful to you.' Austin paused, looking at her intently. 'If you want to skip this interview, I completely understand.'

'No,' Margo replied, shaking her head. 'I want to be there. Even if he's still that same condescending jerk, he can't really do anything to me with you there, right?'

'Yeah, I guess, but I don't want you to be uncomfortable. It never made sense to me why he picked on you so much.'

'When he and Jessie started dating, I was shocked as she used to hate him so much as kids. Every time I saw them, I just stared in disbelief. Maybe I was too obvious about it, because he started lunging at me and yelling 'Boo!' in my face every time he caught me staring. That's how it began. But you know Charlie, once you got on his radar, he never let up. It kept escalating. He'd wait around corners and jump out at me. I'd scream and drop my books and run to the nearest bathroom to hide out of embarrassment. That's when he started calling me "Moaning Margo," like Myrtle, the ghost from Harry Potter that lived in a bathroom crying all the time.' Margo heaved a tense sigh at the memory, feeling the distant sting of the torment even after all these years. 'Jessie told me she asked him to stop once. He said I was obsessed with them and it creeped him out, so he wanted to creep me out in return.'

'What a jerk. You'd think with an ego like his, he'd like people staring at him. He always loved being the center of attention.'

'Well, my stares were in horror, not admiration. Maybe he picked up on that.' Margo shrugged.

'Yeah, maybe. I remember that one time senior year when he broke into your locker and hid inside. And then when you opened it, you screamed so loud, he practically fell out on the ground laughing.'

'That was *awful*. I jumped so hard I hit my back and got a huge bruise down my spine. I don't even know how he jammed his body in there. I mean, we had tall lockers, but still, they were skinny. That locker stunt was the one that finally made Jessie ask him to stop. Even *she* thought he'd gone too far. When Jessie and I started reconnecting, he really didn't like that. His scare tactics started ramping back up again. Remember when he spray-painted "Moaning Margo" with a rudimentary outline of a ghost hovering above a toilet on my locker and claimed he didn't do it? I'm not gonna lie, I'm not looking forward to seeing him again, but I'm not letting him win. Besides, we have the upper hand here.' Margo said, giving Austin a small smile.

'Are you sure?' Austin asked. Margo nodded. 'OK then, you know I have your back. He should be at Moss Creek Brewing. He started helping his parents run the business a few years back. I heard they're getting ready to retire and pass him the reigns completely sometime in the next five years. We've been calling to try to set up a meeting, but he's been avoiding us. Since so many people assumed he could have something to do with Jessie's disappearance, I guess he's reluctant to dive back into the whole thing.'

'Well, it makes sense he and his family would be considered suspects. One could definitely make the assumption that inheriting a money-maker like that brewery could be worth going to any lengths to protect.'

'That one could,' Austin said with a smirk. 'But I'm hoping if we just show up, he'll agree to chat with us.' Margo nodded. 'OK,' he said. 'Let's get going.'

Margo perused the questions on the way over, relieved to see they were pretty straightforward. Nothing too difficult to remember, and Austin could take some creative liberty in how he asked them. Her phone buzzed with an incoming call, but since it was an unknown number, she declined it. The caffeine from her iced coffee swirled with the adrenaline flowing inside her, causing a tornado of nerves and excitement.

Austin parked his car in the oversized lot at the foot of Moss Creek Brewing's property, and he and Margo climbed out. Margo looked up, taking in the impressive landscape. Since she hadn't returned to Lake Moss as an adult beyond her first year of college, she had never done a tasting there. But she remembered going once as a kid with her parents, getting a sampling of Birch Beer in the taproom at the end of their tour, the consolation prize for those under twenty-one while the adults got the good stuff. She had been in awe then at the brewery's sprawling property and charm, and all these years later, she felt the same.

It looked like a cross between an oversized ski lodge and a warehouse, huge windows lining the front of the building's façade, nestled into the base of the mountains with the peaks rising behind it. It was hugged on two sides by lush green trees, stone walking paths and criss-crossed bistro lights disappearing into the thicket for those looking to combine their visit with a light hike. Margo never understood why anyone would want to participate in a physical activity like hiking while drinking beer, and frankly, it seemed like it could get dangerous. But the trails were gentle and ended in the perfect picnic spot with stunning mountain views. Moss Creek, the brewery's namesake, ran in front of the building and passed through some of the trails. She promised herself she would finally try it one of these days. Maybe Austin would go with her.

'Ready?' Austin asked with a smile.

'As ready as I'm going to be,' she replied, gripping her notebook tightly as they walked up the sloping path to the front entrance.

The flowerbeds lining the walkway were in full bloom, giving off an inviting sweet scent that welcomed them to their destination. They crossed over a small footbridge arching over Moss Creek as they approached the large wooden doors. The gentle babbling of the water as it flowed under them was tranquil in the morning quiet, and Margo couldn't believe they were somewhere so beautiful to talk about something so dark. Austin held the door open for her, and she gave him a 'thank you' as she crossed over the threshold and looked around.

The inside of the lobby area was full of large, exposed wood beams and vibrant greenery dripping from the high ceiling. The far wall behind the host podium was covered entirely in lush green moss, a small water feature in its center parting a path as water trickled down into a fountain base at the bottom. There was a stairwell behind the podium that she remembered from the brewery tour in her youth. It led up to an area high above with huge windows that overlooked one of the brewing rooms, a large, tiled room with metal ceiling beams and a mix of oversized circular copper and silver vessels that connected to the ceiling.

A young blonde hostess wearing a fitted black t-shirt with the Moss Creek Brewing logo on the upper right-hand corner, and the gift shop cashier were chatting at the podium as they approached.

'Welcome to Moss Creek Brewing,' the hostess said cheerily. 'If you're here for our ten a.m. tour, you can wait in the gift shop to my left until the whole group arrives.'

'Good morning,' Austin said. 'We're actually hoping to talk with Charlie Abbott. Is he around?'

'Oh sorry, today is his day off. He's probably still at home considering the time.'

'Do you have his address? We know him from high school and just wanted to have a chat,' Austin said, smiling at the hostess, doing his best to win her over so she'd give them the address.

The hostess tensed and looked back and forth between them before shaking her head. 'Sorry, I'm afraid we aren't allowed to give that out.'

Austin clenched his lips together and nodded. 'I understand.' He gave them a polite smile. 'We'll track him down somehow. Thanks anyway. But hey, can you give Charlie my card next time you see him? Let him know I'd like to catch up?' he said pulling his business card from his wallet. Margo got a quick glimpse and saw 'Senior Sound Technician' was his official job title. The hostess took it and set it down on the stand after a short glance, not looking overly concerned about it.

'If you'll excuse me, I have to take this,' she said as she reached over to answer a ringing phone.

Frustrated, they exited and headed back toward Austin's car. Deep down, Margo was relieved their mission had failed. She was nervous about being in close quarters with Charlie, even after all this time.

'Hey, wait up!' the cashier from the gift shop called out as she rushed out the door, a quick look over her shoulder as she caught up to them. Austin and Margo stopped and looked at her, perplexed. 'You're from the *Into Thin Air* crew, right? I put two and two together when I saw you were a sound tech. Not many of those around here and with the television crew in town I just figured . . .' she trailed off, fidgeting with the hem of her polo shirt.

'Yes, we're conducting pre-interviews before the scheduled on-camera spots. We were hoping to catch Charlie.'

The girl nodded. 'I didn't want to say anything in there, you know, just in case . . .' she looked over her shoulder again as if someone was watching her. 'People here are protective of the boss, mostly out of fear for their jobs, but he's such a creep. And if he did do something to that girl, he shouldn't be protected from that. It would be better for all of us if whatever he's hiding came out.'

Austin nodded sympathetically, 'I'm sure he's not the easiest guy to work for.'

'Doesn't matter,' the girl said, looking over her shoulder again. 'His family runs this town, we just have to get by. But look, if you're trying to find him, his new house is just up the road. Take a right out of here and you'll follow a bend in the road that takes you up an incline into the hillside, about five minutes from here.'

'How will we know which house is his?' Austin asked, looking in the direction she mentioned. It looked like nothing but trees.

'Oh,' she laughed, raising her eyebrows. 'You can't miss it. Such an eyesore on a beautiful piece of property. He bought this mountain-side cabin last year, tore it down and put up a modern glass monstrosity in its place. That

82

poor old house had such charm, but, when you have money, you know?'

Margo nodded, 'Thanks for your help.'

'Sure, anyway, gotta go. Good luck!' she replied before hustling back into the brewery.

'Well, let's go see if we can catch him there. I have to admit, I'm intrigued about this modern monstrosity,' Austin laughed as he opened the car door.

Just as Margo was about to respond, the slam of a car door and laughing children filtered through from a parking spot behind her. Turning around, she saw none other than Tucker Harding, his wife Claire and their three children. Tucker, Charlie's best friend, had been part of Jessie's inner circle in high school. Claire came with that group as part of a package deal; Tucker's long-time high school sweetheart. Margo remembered Claire, a shy but pretty girl. She'd been one of Cassidy's friends since elementary school, but she never engaged in making fun of people like the rest of them. She'd kept to the background, clinging to Tucker. Margo always got the impression Claire was out of her depth with that crowd, but Tucker was obviously taken with her. They'd lived next door to one another growing up and their parents were close friends. Tucker had literally married the girl next door.

Claire was still beautiful, with strawberry blonde hair swept back in a delicate low bun and striking green eyes. After three kids, she'd put on some weight, but it suited her. She had always been very slim in high school. Tucker was holding a picnic basket while Claire was bent over, tying one of the children's shoelaces, but both their eyes were trained on Austin and Margo. As Claire straightened up and leaned in toward Tucker, he whispered something in her ear. They both looked over again at Austin and Margo, Tucker's look pointed whereas Claire seemed more inquisitive.

'That's kind of messed-up to just show up unannounced at Charlie's house. I know y'all are here for *Into Thin Air*, but you made an appointment for my pre-interview, shouldn't you give him the same respect?' Tucker asked tensely.

Claire's eyes widened, shooting him an anxious look. 'You didn't tell me they were coming to speak with you,' she said under her breath.

Tucker replied through gritted teeth, 'We'll talk about it later.'

Brushing past the awkward moment, Austin replied, 'We did try setting up an appointment, but he's been dodging us. We're not trying to be disrespectful, we just want to get to the truth.'

Tucker heaved a sigh and mumbled, 'Whatever,' grabbing hold of one of the children's hands and walking away toward the brewery.

Claire stood resolutely, her eyes bouncing between Margo and Austin. 'Why do you need to talk to Tucker again? Nothing has changed since the last time he was interviewed for the show.'

'It's standard procedure. We're talking to everyone who was interviewed last time.'

Claire pursed her lips, looking like she wanted to say more, but instead she turned and followed Tucker with the other two children.

'That was weird,' Austin said.

'Yeah, everyone is *still* protecting Charlie.' Margo smiled wryly. 'But I guess anyone who knew Jessie well is probably a bit on edge.'

84

'Well, let's get going. Don't want to miss our chance to catch Charlie.'

After they climbed in the car and watched the retreating backs of the Harding family disappear in the distance, Austin pulled out of the parking spot and drove off in the direction they'd been given. The path up the hillside darkened as the trees crowded in on the narrow road, blocking out the sunlight except for brief breaks where it burst through like a beacon driving them forward into the next patch of shadows. The cashier was right; it was a house that couldn't be missed. The thicket of trees cleared at the turnoff from the road into Charlie's long driveway, the house immediately visible. It was tucked into the side of the mountain, a large concrete and glass rectangular home jutting out with sharp angles, in stark contrast to the beautiful nature around it. The driveway curved in front of a set of oversized glass doors, so Austin pulled around and stopped a few feet past the door. There were no other vehicles in sight, no obvious clues to anyone being home.

Exiting the car, they looked around as they approached the door, their reflections staring back at them in the perfectly streak-free glass. Austin pressed the doorbell and it echoed loudly inside. After a few moments, Charlie bounded down a spiral staircase on the far side of the first floor and slowed as he approached them. His face went from curious to bothered, but he answered the door anyway.

Throwing it open he said, 'Austin Hughes? What do you want?' Then his eyes landed on Margo. At first it seemed like he didn't recognize her as he looked her up and down, a disturbing smile on his face. But then the smile slowly fell and his brow furrowed. 'Margo?'

Margo nodded and took a step back, not sure how Charlie would respond. But a little part of her smiled that he hadn't immediately recognized her, that she'd changed enough from the nerdy girl who'd rarely paid attention to clothing and hairstyles into someone poised and put together; attractive.

'Hey, Charlie. We're sorry to barge in,' Austin cut in. 'But my producer on *Into Thin Air* hasn't heard back from you and we really need to get a pre-interview in before we start filming. Would you mind giving us a little time, we probably don't need more than like, twenty, thirty minutes max? We'll be as quick as possible,' he said with a smile.

Charlie's gaze turned to Margo again and he gave her a long curious look, as if he was thinking, *Why the hell are you here?* Margo looked down. Maybe he was even irritated that he'd checked her out before he'd recognized her.

Charlie looked annoyed as his eyes traveled back to Austin, and maybe a little nervous. He took a deep breath and rubbed his hand over his tousled hair that was sticking up in different directions, as though he'd just woken up. When he was younger, he had a very rich-boy Justin Bieber-esque look about him with blond hair always perfectly swooshed over, and a seemingly endless supply of new, trendy clothing. Now, he had the same icy blue eyes and good looks of his youth, but his hair was cut short, and his face a little puffier than she remembered. He had a light stubble on his face, like he hadn't shaved yet today, and Margo couldn't help but admit to herself that the man *was* handsome. While still giving off the air of an over-privileged, confident jock, his looks had matured, and he clearly took care of his body, his biceps bulging under his t-shirt.

Finally, he relented and threw the door open wider to allow them in. 'Thanks, I promise we'll make it quick,' Austin said. As Margo walked past him, careful not to get too close, she smelled a hint of licorice and sickeningly sweet florals swirling in the air.

'Well, you're going to tell Jessie's story one way or another, aren't you? May as well give you my side of it,' he said with a scowl. Then his eyes moved to Margo. 'What, are you Austin's little assistant now or something, Margo?'

Unfortunately, he was just as cocky and patronizing as Margo remembered. Part of her hoped he'd feel apologetic toward her, maybe even embarrassed at the way he'd treated her. That didn't seem to be the case. He still found a way to belittle her.

'Margo is a skilled transcriber now, she's worked on a ton of criminal cases,' Austin replied for her, and she was grateful for his support. 'I asked her to help out taking notes while she's in town.' Charlie looked skeptically at Austin. 'Anyway, we appreciate your time all the same,' Austin said, as he walked into the entryway, Margo tight on his heel. 'Wow, this place is . . . something else,' Austin commented as they walked through.

Everything was shiny black marble, glass, and leather. The ultimate, stereotypical rich boy bachelor pad. There was even a zebra print rug in the shape of the animal in the living room under his black leather sofa and chairs. Margo grimaced, hoping it was a replica and not the real thing, but she wouldn't put anything past him.

'Amazing, isn't it?' he said, gesturing around at the home. 'Had it custom built myself.' Charlie puffed out his chest at his accomplishment.

As they moved further into the house, Margo was more and more amazed that someone actually lived there. It simultaneously felt like a sterile museum and a dirty playboy mansion. But her jaw dropped when he led them toward the kitchen. On the backside of the black and steel kitchen were floor to ceiling windows. And the view on the other side took her breath away. A long infinity lap pool looked out over the mountain valley, shades of blue and green peaks reaching up to kiss the sky.

'Can I get you a drink?' Charlie asked, although his voice lacked any sense of genuine hospitality.

Margo stuck close to Austin's side as they halted while Charlie grabbed one of his own family's beers out of the stainless-steel fridge with a digital screen on the front listing the grocery items he was getting low on. His appliances were the ultimate in luxury. *Geez, do they cook the food for him too?* Margo thought, a hint of jealousy creeping in. She glanced at the digital clock on his microwave. 10:30 a.m. was a bit early to start drinking. But from the looks of his crumpled clothing and tired face, maybe it was hair of the dog from the night before.

'No,' Austin said, sharing a look with Margo. 'That's OK. Like I said, this won't take long.'

'Suit yourself,' Charlie said with a shrug as he walked past them. They followed him over to the leather sofa in the living room.

'I know you're not excited to talk to us,' Austin started. 'But you should know, everything I'm going to talk to you about, my producer plans on using in the show either way. So this is your chance to tell your side of the story.'

Charlie leaned back and took a sip from his bottle. He set the bottle down on an end table roughly. 'Alright, let's get on with it then.'

Margo flipped open her notebook and clicked her pen

to the ready position, fully prepared to let Austin take the lead and stick to what she was good at: taking notes. Maybe she could stay out of Charlie's crosshairs by remaining silent.

'So, what can I tell you two that you don't already know? I haven't learned anything else about Jessie in the last fifteen years that I didn't know when the police interviewed me back then.' He leaned back, crossing his arms and giving them an intense stare.

'That's OK,' Austin said, trying to be genial. 'Just a few basic questions to make sure we have all the details we need for filming the episode. And we really appreciate you agreeing to do an on-camera interview as well; it's going to be very impactful for the show.' Charlie straightened up in his seat, and Margo knew that Austin's flattery had worked, priming Charlie to feel important and more willing to answer.

'Fire away,' he said, looking at Austin with intrigue.

'Great. Ready?' Austin asked Margo, who nodded and poised herself to start writing. 'OK, first off, pretty standard, can you tell us about the last time you saw Jessie?'

Charlie looked at Austin for a long moment before answering, as if carefully considering his words. Or perhaps, Margo reasoned, he was just trying to remember details from so long ago. 'It was at the end of year rally earlier in the day before she disappeared. You remember the one, at that outdoor amphitheater near the school where they always held the assemblies in nice weather. Lining us up on those grassy tiered seating platforms, the teachers with megaphones trying to hype us up from the stone stage.'

Austin and Margo nodded, and Austin said, 'Oh yeah, how could we forget?'

'Well,' Charlie continued, 'You know the cheerleaders

always perform, and your dad,' he gave a quick, pointed look at Margo, 'had the basketball team up on stage near the cheer squad to do the senior salute.'

Margo squinted, looking back into her memories. She remembered the annual rally just before finals week and could see Jessie shining in her cheerleading outfit bouncing around the stage. She started scribbling notes, not wanting to fail at her task by getting lost wandering down memory lane.

'Anyway,' Charlie said, 'After the rally, Jessie pulled me aside behind the stage.'

'What did she want?' Austin asked, fishing for details.

Charlie stood up and started pacing the room, picking up his random decorative orbs, tossing them up in the air and catching them before putting them back down. 'What do you think she wanted? To hook up. We made out behind one of the trees until the guidance counselor, Mr. Gilmore, found us and freaked out so we split. After that, I high-tailed it out of there. And because I'm sure you're going to ask,' he said with a smug smile, 'I was with Tucker that night when she went missing. We were hanging out playing pool while my parents were out of town. You can confirm that with him.'

Austin paused for a second before saying, 'Are you sure you and Jessie were making out that day? We heard recently that you'd broken up.'

Charlie's eyes narrowed into slits. 'Where did you hear that?'

'Well,' Austin said, glancing quickly at Margo before turning his attention back to Charlie. 'A message Jessie left someone on the day she went missing was recently recovered, and in the message, it's pretty clear she's saying the two of you had ended things.'

'A message? What message?' Charlie asked sharply, like he didn't believe it existed.

'That's beside the point,' Austin said. 'But if Jessie did break up with you, some people may point to that as motive. Are you sure that really is the last time you saw Jessie? Or maybe that had happened at another rally? It was a long time ago, after all.'

'What the hell are you getting at?' Charlie fired at Austin, towering above him. Margo wondered if it was some sort of power-flex. They were on his turf to ask him questions about his newly discovered dead girlfriend. Well, ex-girlfriend.

'I'm not getting at anything,' Austin replied calmly, trying to diffuse the rising tension. 'Just wondering if maybe you're confusing the dates and that was a different rally you're thinking of? If you had, in fact, broken up like Jessie said in the message, did she break up with you?'

Charlie huffed and shot a glance at Margo, like he assumed she was the one who'd given this information. But he quickly turned to reply to Austin, acting like Margo was not worthy of his time. *He really hasn't changed much*, she thought. Margo prepared herself to make notes on whatever came next.

'Jessie didn't break up with me. I broke up with *her* and she was the one who didn't want anyone to know, OK? She was embarrassed.'

'So, you and Jessie *had* broken up, then? Why? If you don't mind me asking,' Austin said.

'Honestly? When she started hanging out with *you* again, Margo, she complained all the time about how I acted, or how I treated her. Don't act like you didn't get in her ear. Everything was fine between us before you came along and got it into her head that she deserved better than me.' Margo started shaking her head to deny his accusation, even though it was partly true. But he turned his attention fully back to Austin before she could react. 'I couldn't take it anymore, so I broke up with her. There were plenty of girls waiting in line to take her place, so why would I stay with her if she didn't appreciate me?' Even after so many years had passed, Charlie still seemed angry, as if it had just happened.

'What about the last time you saw her at the rally then?' Austin pressed.

Charlie looked annoyed but answered anyway. 'She pulled me aside and told me not to tell anyone we split, OK? She'd heard one of the girls on the cheer squad was flirting with me and wasn't ready for people to know I was available. She thought it would look better if we just acted like we broke up when we went off to college in different cities. She was desperate to maintain her popular reputation, and she knew I was the reason for that. She was a nobody before she dated me,' he said with a cocky grin. Margo despised Charlie and his over-inflated ego more and more with every word he said. After a tense, quiet minute, he continued. 'Look, the one you should really be talking to is Cassidy.'

'Cassidy?' Austin asked. 'Why her?'

'Well, for one,' he paused and pointed an intense look at Margo, '*they* were best friends, which you both know,' Charlie said, as if to say to Margo that Jessie wasn't really her friend. Then he switched his attention back to Austin. 'But beyond that, Cassidy was getting jealous and resentful of Jessie toward the end. You remember all those beauty pageants Cassidy did? She'd done them for years to save money for college. She eventually got Jessie into them too during senior year. Cassidy had always won the local and regional circuit, until Jessie swooped in and started beating her every time.'

Margo nodded along as he talked, remembering Jessie talking about the pageants. She'd loved the attention.

'Anyway,' Charlie continued. 'There was a huge pageant coming up like, a week after Jessie disappeared. Cassidy was desperate to win because it had a huge college scholarship as the prize for first place and her parents couldn't afford to pay for Duke. She needed the money. She asked Jessie not to do that pageant because Jessie's family didn't need the money for college, but Jessie refused to bow out. She loved being in the limelight and couldn't wait to get up there and beat all the other girls, including Cassidy. Cassidy was furious. If anyone in Jessie's circle has reason to hide something about her disappearance, it would probably be her. Oh, and guess what? With Jessie out of the way, Cassidy won that pageant.'

Margo's writing hand froze as she and Austin shared a look. This was the first time anyone had brought up this potential motive for Cassidy, but as Jessie's friend, Margo had known it was a bone of contention between them. Margo had assumed that was one of the reasons Jessie had been spending more time with her than Cassidy near the end.

'Cassidy is on our list to talk to as well, so we'll make sure to follow up on that.'

'Good,' Charlie said, sitting down in a sleek black chair across from them, clearly satisfied that he'd pointed the finger away from himself.

'So, to confirm, you were with Tucker on the night Jessie disappeared? Sorry, just have to get the details locked down for the boss,' he said, giving a convincing empathetic smile that Charlie fell for easily.

'That's right, at my house. And no, there's no security camera footage or anything like that. But he'll confirm it.'

'Great, thanks so much,' Austin said as he and Margo stood to leave, and Charlie mirrored them. 'Just one more quick question and we'll be on our way.'

'Shoot,' Charlie replied.

'Have you heard that Jessie may have been pregnant? Do you know why she had a pregnancy test on her when her body was found?'

There was a tense, awkward pause. Charlie seemed shaken, but Margo couldn't tell how genuine his shock really was. Finally, he said with much less confidence than before, 'I don't know anything about that.'

Austin looked at him steadily. 'Well, thanks again for your time. The team really appreciates it and we'll be in touch with you to schedule your recorded interview so that you can tell your side of things on camera.'

Charlie nodded. 'I'll see you two out.' He led them back to the front door. Charlie reached out to shake Austin's hand, and then looked at Margo. She put her hand out just as Charlie turned on his heel and walked away. Clearly her being there had brought back all the resentment he'd felt toward her in high school. Margo rolled her eyes and dropped her arm back to her side, exiting with Austin and stepping back out into the morning sun.

'Well, that was interesting,' Austin said, looking at her.

'It sure was,' Margo said, holding the notebook tightly in her hands.

CHAPTER SEVEN

The next day, Margo was in her room gathering her notebook and pen into her purse, waiting for Austin to pick her up for their drive into Charlotte. She couldn't find her back-up pen, the one she always carried in case her favorite ran out. Her phone rang while she was on the floor, seeing if it had fallen under the bed. She straightened and grabbed the phone out of her purse just as it abruptly silenced on the second ring. But when she looked at her phone, there was no missed call. Could it have been her dad's phone? She walked out to the living room where her dad was lounging in his recliner watching the news.

'Did you just get a call?'

Her dad glanced at his phone sitting on the end table next to him and picked it up.

'Nope, nothing. Why?'

Margo bit her lip. *Am I hearing things?* She didn't think so, it had sounded so close to her. She shook her head and said, 'Nothing, just thought I heard something.'

She walked out to the backyard and over to her

bedroom window to investigate. The glass on her window was clean and smudge free, allowing a clear view in with her curtains pulled to the side to let the sun light up the room. As she glanced down, she saw the grass and dirt underneath her window showed a slight depression, like the tips of two shoes. She whipped her head around, looking into the trees for any sign of movement, feeling like she was being watched. She didn't see anyone, but the hair rose on the back of her neck. Looking back at the indents, she crouched down and saw a partial striped pattern from shoe soles in the mud. Someone had been looking into her room. Margo swallowed hard and took a deep breath, trying to quell the panic rising inside her.

Austin honked in front of her house, causing her to jump. She placed a hand on her chest when she realized it was him, begging her heart to stop thumping so intensely. She didn't want Austin to see her looking frazzled, afraid he would ask her to step back from helping with the interviews if he was worried about her. With one glance back at the impression in the dirt, she straightened, took a deep breath to calm the fear surging through her, and ran into the house to grab her purse. Waving to her dad with a last deep breath, she ran out to Austin's car.

'Hey!' he said. Then his eyebrows clenched together. 'Everything OK?'

Biting back the truth, Margo tried to convince herself that maybe she was outside near her room at another time and simply hadn't realized she may have left footprints. Maybe she was just getting carried away. She smiled and said, 'Everything's fine. Let's hit the road.'

As the mountains faded into the background in Austin's rear view mirror, Margo couldn't help but think about how crazy it was to be on this adventure with him. If someone had told her a few months ago that she'd be driving around with Austin to interview people about Jessie's death, she would have thought them mentally unstable. Yet here she was. Austin's 'Timeless Classics' playlist on Spotify was flowing through the speakers as she watched the scenery change on their route to interview Cassidy.

'Margo?'

'Sorry, what?' Margo asked, looking over at him in the driver's seat. She hadn't realized how badly she'd zoned out watching the cars zoom past on the highway. Charlotte was about two hours from Lake Moss, a fairly straight shot on 85 minus a few small towns that lie between. He laughed and nodded at where her phone sat in the nook inside the passenger side door.

'I said, are you going to get that? Your phone's ringing.'

'Oh, god, sorry. I don't know where my mind went just now,' she said, picking the phone up and looking at the screen. Her body tensed as she quickly hit the decline button and threw it down in her lap.

'What's wrong?' Austin asked, stealing quick glances at her before darting his eyes back to the road. 'Who was it?'

'My ex, Mark. He won't stop harassing me, constantly calling. After *he* was the one who broke *my* heart. Our lawyers are handling the divorce so there's no reason he should need to talk to me. The nerve of this guy,' Margo trailed off, looking back out the window as a tractor trailer sped by.

'What could he want now? He was the one who ended things, wasn't he?'

'Right, like he was the one who cheated and then left me to be with his secretary. Filed the divorce papers

97

immediately and essentially took custody of all our shared friends. What else could he possibly take from me now? I left my job, I left town. He won. But he just keeps calling.' Margo leaned back and crossed her arms sharply, finally looking back over at Austin. His lips were pursed, his eyes turned down slightly at the corners.

'I'm sorry he's giving you a hard time; I wish there was something I could do to help. Have you answered any of the calls to see what he wants?'

'He just keeps leaving messages saying he wants us to talk. I think he's trying to assuage his guilt at blowing up my life and I'm not about to give him that satisfaction. Even when we were together, it was always about him and his career and what was best for him. I don't think he ever truly cared about how his words and actions affected me. I would have done anything to make him happy, but he was just . . . impossible.'

'Relationships are hard,' Austin said back, giving her a sad smile.

'Tell me about it,' Margo heaved a loud sigh. 'I get the feeling you kind of understand where I'm coming from. You haven't been married, have you?' she asked, her eyes narrowed.

'No, but I came pretty close with my last girlfriend. I really thought that she was the one, but there was always underlying tension in our relationship. She complained about my job constantly coming first, and her second. Looking back, I know she was right. But I'd started making more time for her so I thought things were getting better. I even bought a ring,' he barked a short laugh. 'I must have jinxed it. About a week before I was planning to pop the question, Julia was offered a job in Chicago and it was a huge promotion. How could I tell her no?'

He glanced at Margo and she nodded. 'But I couldn't leave Atlanta. I'd finally paved my way into steady work with a few production companies after doing grunt work for years. I knew if I went with her to Chicago, I'd have to start all over again. I just didn't think I could do it and honestly, I loved Atlanta and had no desire to move. I was a little wishy-washy with her when she asked if I'd come with her. I was hoping to put it off until I knew myself if I was willing to go. But then we started fighting all the time; she kept hinting that I was going to choose my job over her yet again. It had created a rift we couldn't come back from. When she left for Chicago, that was it. The ring is still buried in my sock drawer back home. I haven't wanted to even look at it to get rid of it.'

'I'm sorry, I understand how you feel. You put so much energy into someone and then poof, it's gone. And you feel like you just wasted years of your life on the wrong person.'

Austin sighed. 'Yeah, that pretty much sums it up. But in hindsight, I can see that I put her on the backburner too much, took her for granted, thinking she'd stick around. My job still means a lot to me, but I can see there needs to be more balance. I thought we'd at least stay friends, but too much was either said or left unsaid. I haven't talked to her since she left, other than seeing her pop up occasionally on Facebook. So at least for me, it's been a clean break. I've been able to focus on work and move forward. It sucks that Mark won't just leave you be after all he's done.'

'Yeah, very true.' Margo grimaced. But she was grateful that her relationship failure wasn't a point to be embarrassed about with Austin. He didn't see her as failing; he understood. It felt good to have him on her side now that she'd lost most of her friends in the divorce. Only one of her and Mark's shared friends continued to check in, but even that felt forced. 'I'm so ready to be done with him,' she continued. 'Hopefully he gets the hint soon.'

'Hopefully,' Austin agreed, and then looking at the smile stretching across Margo's face he also smiled. 'What?'

'This song is my *jam*!' Margo said, turning the volume up and letting Hall and Oates' *You Make My Dreams* pump through the speakers.

Pushing aside all sad, depressing memories and awkwardness of years gone by, they started singing at the top of their lungs, dancing in their seats and releasing the pent-up feelings bubbling below the surface. It was cathartic and hilarious, as neither of them had very good singing voices. It was the freest Margo had felt in a long time. They continued to laugh and sing along with the playlist for the rest of the drive with intermittent small talk about the artists and concerts they'd been to. When *Rapper's Delight* came on, high school memories came exploding to the surface.

'Oh my god, remember when Mrs. Romero made us create a Spanish rap song and we had to perform it for our final project?' Austin asked

'Ugh, don't remind me! I almost threw up before my rendition of *La Esquela Perdida*.'

Austin burst out laughing and Margo followed suit. 'Hey, it was far better than my *No Mas Tarea*!'

'Yeah, I'm sure she didn't appreciate you calling for no more homework, especially when the entire class joined in on the chorus, screaming out "No Mas Tarea!" every time.' Margo and Austin laughed. 'But you did receive quite the round of applause.'

Margo couldn't believe how easy it was to be around

him, and she almost forgot about the task that lay ahead: interviewing Cassidy. As they neared the exits that led into uptown Charlotte, they saw the skyline pop into view, full of interesting architecture, including a building that looked like it had a purse handle on top and another with layered tiers that resembled a crown. It wasn't called Queen City for nothing. Margo hadn't come into Charlotte much growing up, but the few times she had with her parents, she always thought it was strange how the downtown area was referred to as 'uptown'. But that was exactly their current destination, as Cassidy now worked in finance at the Bank of America building.

Austin parked in a nearby parking garage, grabbing a ticket from the machine. When they approached the banking corporate center and looked up, Margo was in awe of how beautiful the 'crown' building looked up-close, the metal and windows shimmering in the sunlight. Austin texted Cassidy as she'd requested to let her know they'd arrived, and she sent back a quick, 'Be right there!' After a few moments, Margo saw a familiar face break out into the sun, looking around.

Cassidy hadn't changed a bit. She was still stunning, if not more so, and Margo immediately felt self-conscious. The shame of not being accepted by the popular kids had stuck to her, like a scar that was always there no matter how much she tried to cover it up. Besides looking a bit older and more mature, most of Cassidy's features remained so identical, it was uncanny. Her long, chocolate brown hair bounced in waves that cascaded over her shoulders. A mauve lipstick accentuated her plump, pouty lips, a warm bronzer highlighting her defined cheekbones. She had perfectly manicured eyebrows, and an expert-level winged eyeliner framed a set of thick eyelashes. Cassidy could bat her eyes and the boys would no doubt come running like they had in high school. It was not a surprise to anyone that she was a regular first-prize winner on the pageant circuit. She was confident and gorgeous.

If Margo was honest with herself, she had always been envious of Cassidy. Not only was Cassidy one of the 'it' girls, but she had also replaced Margo by Jessie's side for a few dark years after Margo's mom had died. At Eloise's funeral, people had looked at Margo and her father with pained expressions. Maybe it was just too much sadness to look at that close-up; the kind of sorrow that makes people uncomfortable. It had been easy to pull away and hide. And when Margo had come out of her protective cocoon of isolation, Jessie, like Cassidy, had blossomed into one of the prettiest girls at school, quickly earning them both a spot in the popular crowd. All Margo had gained in that time was an awful string of recurring nightmares and another two inches in height. By the time her cloud had lifted enough to realize she missed her friends and her life, she'd been left behind as they all formed new high school cliques. When Jessie had started spending time with Margo again in their senior year, much to Margo's joy and relief, Cassidy wasn't thrilled with Margo tagging along, taking some of Jessie's attention.

It was strange, seeing Cassidy approaching her and Austin now. Margo hadn't seen her since graduation, and in Jessie's ominous absence, they hadn't had any reason to interact that day. Then Margo had gone off to UNC Wilmington, and Cassidy had gone to Duke University, another point of jealousy that Margo had tried not to hold on to. Cassidy was not only beautiful, but she'd always been smart and ambitious too. Margo felt the old familiar intimidation creeping in as they closed the gap.

102

She hated the way she still yearned for Cassidy's approval all these years later, but she forced a smile on her face anyway. All of a sudden, she was unsure of how to talk to the force of a woman in front of her.

'Well look who we have here,' Cassidy said when she reached them, pushing sunglasses down from the perch on top of her head to cover her eyes as she squinted into the afternoon sun.

'Hey, Cassidy,' Austin said and extended his arm to shake her hand. 'Thanks so much for meeting with us today.' She shook his hand before turning to Margo.

'Sure, thanks for coming to me. There's just no way I could get back to Lake Moss right now, I've been slammed at work. Long time, no see, Margo.'

She extended a hand which Margo shook, unable to read how genuine Cassidy was being now that her eyes were shielded. Margo wished she'd brought shades of her own.

'Fifteen years,' Margo said as she dropped her hand back to her side. Did Cassidy feel as awkward about this reunion as she did? She couldn't tell, but knew she needed to keep things friendly so she didn't mess things up for Austin. 'It's good to see you.'

'It's good to see y'all as well. I hope you don't mind walking a few blocks, it would be easier for us to go chat in the park. I told my boss I was taking a lunch break, and I don't really want anyone at work hearing me talk about this.'

'Sure, no problem at all,' Austin said. 'Lead the way!'

Cassidy smiled and brushed past them, walking fast for someone in six-inch heels and a pencil skirt. But then again, Margo thought, she'd had a lot of practice in her pageant days. Margo was useless in a pair of heels, and she'd never really needed them anyway. Mark hadn't liked when she'd donned them as he wasn't much taller than her.

Austin and Margo took a few quick steps and caught up, walking in time with her as they crossed the street filled with businesswomen and men as they went about for their lunches and appointments. After a few minutes, they reached Romare Bearden Park, a small greenspace in the center of uptown, lined by a waterfall wall lit up with rainbow lighting, and stunning architectural views peeking out from above. With the nice weather, there were several small groups picnicking, their dogs running around chasing each other. Just like Moss Creek Brewery, this felt in stark contrast to the topic they were about to discuss.

'Will this do?' Cassidy asked as she led them to an empty black metal bench near the water feature.

'Works for us,' Austin said, and Margo nodded. The three of them sat down, Austin in the middle.

'Listen,' Cassidy said, leaning in and lowering her voice, pushing her sunglasses back up on her head. 'Jessie was my best friend, and her body just being found like that . . .' she shivered, searching for the right words. 'It's not that I don't want to help. And maybe the show will dig up something new. But I'm not sure I'm comfortable talking on camera about any of this. I've worked my ass off for this job, and I don't want to do anything to jeopardize it.'

'I can have a talk with my producer,' Austin said reassuringly, 'make sure we are really specific about what's on and off limits?'

'Can this just be off the record for now? I'll give you guys some backstory; I know you knew her too,' she looked across Austin at Margo, her voice a bit challenging, her eyebrows arched up as if it was a question.

Maybe, Margo thought, Cassidy was still holding on to the old habit of competing to be Jessie's best friend. Much of the time Margo had spent with Jessie, it was just the two of them. But Jessie had invited her along a couple of times with her and Cassidy for shopping or ice cream. There was one weekend where Jessie had invited herself and Cassidy over to Margo's for a sleepover, but when Margo opened the door, it was just Jessie standing there with her overnight bag. Margo had asked why Cassidy hadn't joined them, but Jessie had just replied, 'Oh, you know Cassidy. Girl is always being dramatic about something!'

A kid screamed in excitement a foot away from them and Margo was brought abruptly back to the park. As quickly as the strange tone had trickled in, Cassidy's voice switched back to normal business. 'So, I'll answer some questions to get you set up. But I just can't commit to being on the show right now.'

'I understand,' Austin said, dragging Cassidy's lingering gaze on Margo back to him.

Margo couldn't quite read Cassidy's expression. It seemed cheery enough given the grim circumstances that brought them all together, but there was something Margo couldn't fully place about the look in Cassidy's eyes. She knew Cassidy excelled at putting on a performance after years of cheerleading and pageantry. Was she performing for them now? *Why would talking to us jeopardize her job if she has nothing to hide?*

'Thank you,' Cassidy said sweetly, laying a hand gently on Austin's knee.

Margo tensed, heat flushing to her cheeks. Cassidy had never given Austin the time of day growing up. Had he gotten attractive enough to be worth her time? Margo knew she had no claim on Austin, they'd just reconnected after all, but her old attraction to him had come rushing back and her skin crawled at the way Cassidy was leaning toward him now.

Cassidy slowly retracted her hand, Austin giving her a polite smile, and then she said, 'Well, let's get started then. I don't have too much time before I need to get back.'

Austin cleared his throat, 'Sure thing, are you ready, Margo?'

'Ready when you are,' Margo said, her notebook opened, pen poised.

'Great,' Austin continued. 'I'm going to dive right in since we're short on time. Did you know Jessie and Charlie had broken up before she went missing?'

Cassidy paused for a moment and then said, 'Yeah, I knew.'

'I just can't believe she didn't tell me they broke up right when it happened. I knew they were fighting a lot near the end and that she was considering it, but I thought she would have called me once she pulled the trigger,' Margo blurted out before she could stop herself. She shot a quick, remorseful glance at Austin, but he was watching Cassidy.

Cassidy's eyes darted to Margo. 'Jessie told *me* everything, but she didn't want anyone else to know, so close to graduation and all.'

'But I was her friend, she'd been confiding in me about their issues, she could have told me anything. I would have kept her secret.'

A shadow of ugliness took over Cassidy's face. 'You were her *tutor*,' she snapped.

Margo flinched. Again, she internally chastised herself for speaking at all. It wasn't her place. This was Austin's job, not hers. She vowed to keep quiet for the rest of the interview and looked back down to her notes.

106

'Did you know there was a possibility that Jessie was pregnant when she disappeared?' Austin interrupted, having no doubt sensed the tension that sprouted up.

Cassidy didn't answer right away. Her face relaxed and she looked at Austin thoughtfully, like she wasn't quite sure how much to say. 'I knew there was another guy in the picture, but she was super secretive about it. She wouldn't even tell *me* and *I* was her best friend. I mean, I guess it's possible.' She shrugged, tossing her long hair over her shoulder on one side. Margo didn't miss the not-so-subtle dig in her direction.

'Another guy?' Austin said, turning to share a quick confused glance with Margo. This was the first time they'd heard anything about Jessie seeing someone else. 'No one else has mentioned another guy. Did she tell you anything about him?'

'Not much,' Cassidy said. 'Just that he was a step-up from Charlie. I think maybe he was older or something, because she wouldn't tell me who it was, and I never saw her flirt with anyone in particular at school. Maybe he was a student at the community college or worked in town or something.'

'Do you think Charlie knew she was seeing someone else?' Austin asked.

Cassidy looked off at the dogs chasing each other not far from where they sat, thinking. 'Couldn't say for sure, you know how he is. But if he did know, he probably would have been pissed.'

'We spoke to Charlie recently. He said we should talk to you because of the pageant competition after Jessie disappeared. That you won that big scholarship money to pay for Duke. He said Jessie had been taking the wins out from under you ever since you introduced her to the circuit. But with Jessie gone, you won the pageant and the money,' Austin said.

Cassidy grimaced and looked down as she picked at the nail polish on her thumb. '*That bastard*,' she whispered angrily under her breath. And then louder, 'Of course *he* would say something like that. Jessie was my best friend.' She ran a hand anxiously through her hair, tousling it. Her constant references to being Jessie's best friend were clearly for Margo. 'Was it annoying that she kept winning after it had been my thing all those years? Yeah. But not enough to *kill* her. We had fun doing them together, getting all dolled up and practicing our talents. I know I needed that scholarship more than her, but I could have found the money another way, gotten a loan or something. He was probably just trying to divert attention away from himself.'

'Why would he need to do that? Didn't he break up with her?'

Her eyes widened slightly before she shook her head. 'Did he tell you that?' Cassidy barked a short laugh. 'What am I saying? *Of course* he did. Jessie broke up with *him*, not the other way around. He was livid.'

'Are you sure?' Austin asked.

'Absolutely,' Cassidy said with confidence, nodding. 'She told me she was planning to cut ties now that she had this other more interesting guy going on and had me pick her up at Charlie's house after she did it. She said she was glad to be free of him.'

'So what kept you from telling anyone about the other guy all these years? Didn't you want to help find her?' Austin asked.

'I was a stupid, selfish kid. I had my own things going on. And she'd entrusted me with this secret that I felt I had a duty to protect. Deep down, I'd convinced myself she just ran off with this guy and was living her best life somewhere. I didn't want to blow up her secret if she wanted to be left alone. I figured the truth would come out without me. But now, with her body being found . . . well clearly, I assumed wrong. It's time that all the cards get laid on the table, isn't it?'

'OK, so, can you confirm when the last time was that you saw Jessie before she went missing?'

'Oh, yeah, easy,' Cassidy said. 'It was at the end of school rally earlier that day. We cheered together and then I asked if she wanted to come over later that night to watch the *American Idol* finale. My pageant talent was singing so I was obsessed, and it was our thing to watch it together. She said she couldn't come over because she was grounded for backing her car into a tree, but when I offered to come watch it at her place, she said she'd already promised her brother, Brandon, that she'd help him with something while she was homebound. I asked her what they were doing, but she said it wasn't important. At the time, I wondered if she was actually meeting up with the guy she was seeing, but that's all she told me, and we didn't talk again after that.'

'Was there anyone else that Jessie spent time with outside of your circle? We know she spent most of her time with Margo, you, Charlie, Tucker and Claire, right?' Margo noticed how Cassidy's mouth turned down slightly on one side when he'd mentioned Margo's name. 'But other than the mystery man, can you think of anyone else who might be worth talking to who may have been missed the first time around? You knew her so well, after all,' Austin asked, playing into her sense of importance to Jessie. Smart tactic, Margo mused.

Cassidy was silent for a second before leaning in and

lowering her voice like she was about to tell them a dirty secret. You could take the girl out of Lake Moss, but the proclivity to gossip was bred deep. 'I don't want to get anyone in trouble or anything, but there is one other person I don't think anyone ever talked to. No one really knew about him except for me.'

'Who was it?' Austin asked, eagerly.

'Wylie Hooper,' she said, looking smug as she leaned back. 'You remember him, right? That kinda chubby hipster dude with the long hair who worked at the Abbott's brewery? Always wearing flannel, had that long beard?'

Margo squinted, pulling a hazy image to the forefront of her mind. 'Vaguely, I never interacted with him, though. Austin, did you know him?'

Austin shook his head. 'Same. Everyone knew who everyone was in town, but I never had anything to do with him. What was his link with Jessie? She seems a bit out of his league, no? You don't think *he* was the other guy, do you?'

'Oh, god no! Nothing like that.' Cassidy laughed. 'But he made Jessie the hero of our group.'

'How so?' Austin asked, curiosity etched across his face. Margo couldn't believe she had no idea where this was going.

'Well, Charlie used to sneak beer from the brewery for our parties in the cove. He got really cocky about it and took too much one time and got caught. His parents flipped. They took away his keys and instructed the staff not to let Charlie into the storeroom. So, the group was out of luck for a bit. But then, Jessie went with Charlie to the brewery after hours one night because he'd left his favorite jacket there. Jessie was wandering around, and apparently caught Wylie doing something dodgy.'

'Do you know what he was doing?' Austin asked, Margo was furiously scribbling notes.

'Not sure. Rifling through papers in the manager's office or something, Jessie didn't specify. But it was big enough that she was able to trade her silence for free beer whenever we wanted. She had us covered the rest of the school year after that.'

What had Jessie stumbled upon, Margo wondered. It had to have been something pretty major if she was successfully blackmailing an adult. It certainly sounded like a plausible motive if the police got wind of it. They'd have to look into it further.

'The Germaines are holding a funeral service for Jessie. Will you be coming back to Lake Moss for that?' Austin asked.

Cassidy sighed. 'I want to, I really do. I'm just so busy at work. But I'm gonna try to come the day of the service at least, I should be able to take one day off.' Cassidy's phone pinged loudly and she looked down at the screen. 'Shit, I gotta go,' she said, jumping up and pulling her sunglasses back down. 'I'm sorry, my boss is looking for me.'

Austin and Margo stood. 'Thanks so much for talking to us. This was really illuminating.'

'I'm glad,' Cassidy said. She shook both their hands and they said their goodbyes. As she turned to walk away, Austin quickly shouted out after her.

'If you change your mind, you have my number. Call or text me anytime, we would love to get you on camera, even if it's just to talk about the Jessie you knew.'

'I'll think about it,' she said, waving over her shoulder as she disappeared into the crowd.

'Wow,' Austin said as he turned to face Margo once Cassidy was gone from view.

'Yeah, I can't believe that she didn't tell anyone any of that until fifteen years after the fact. It's almost like she didn't want the case solved until now. Maybe that's why she doesn't want to be on camera? Surely your producer would ask why she didn't come forward before and she's worried she'll come off like she has something to hide?' Margo shrugged.

'Yeah, she was always self-absorbed though, wasn't she? At least we have some new information to use in our questioning. Amy is going to be stoked.'

'For sure,' Margo said, giving a smile. 'And hey, sorry I butted in there. It came out before I could stop myself. I'll do my best to keep quiet from now on.'

'No, it's OK,' he replied. 'And it seems to have provoked her a bit, which wasn't a bad thing. It led to some good information'

'OK good, I was worried I was going to mess up the interview. Anyway, want to grab a quick bite before we head back?'

'Absolutely, I've heard there's an awesome custom sandwich shop across the street. Wanna grab one and eat it out here since it's so nice out?'

'Sounds great,' Margo said.

After eating, Margo and Austin made the drive back to Lake Moss, bouncing theories about the case off one another and going over their plans for upcoming interviews in light of the new information. While they hadn't spoken to the whole cast of characters in person yet, the dirty laundry getting aired after all these years was giving them a lot to think about. Charlie of course felt suspicious, but the addition of Wylie to the mix was interesting.

112

Austin called Amy on the drive to let him know they had to add Wylie Hooper to their list, and she was ecstatic with the development. After rounding a tight bend, Austin turned onto the street that led to Margo's house and slowed the car. Margo looked down at her phone as they approached, pursing her lips at a string of unanswered texts that had come through from her ex.

Margo collapsed into the chair at her desk tucked away in her childhood bedroom, her mind reeling from all the memories these interviews were stirring up combined with the stress of the looming final stages of divorce. It was the end of an era. It would be a relief for the i's to be dotted and the t's to be crossed and have a clean break. She flipped open her laptop screen, deciding to distract herself by browsing social media to see if anything new or interesting had popped up since she left Wilmington. She hadn't spoken to many of her old friends there, knowing that they were likely still seeing Mark around town, but she couldn't help wondering what they were all up to. Navigating to her Facebook page, she perked up when she noticed she had a few notifications waiting for her. The first was alerting to the post for the Weekly Wins on her Carolina Courts group page where others in her industry shared the highs and lows of the cases they worked on, job openings, and more. After that was a notification that Delia, one of her friends from her last job, had posted a link on her wall about one of their favorite restaurants closing. 'Ugh, bummer!' Margo typed out in the comments, pushing down the disappointment that their first communication since she left Wilmington was so impersonal, rather than a text or call. Margo had sent a text to Delia a week ago that had gone unanswered.

Navigating back to the list of notifications, Margo froze with her finger above the trackpad, a tremor in her hand giving away the ice shooting through her veins.

'Gessie Jermaine has sent you a friend request.'

Was this a sick, cruel joke? Someone flipping around the first letters in Jessie's name to torment her upon her friend's body being discovered? Margo couldn't fathom who would do such a thing. She knew she wasn't necessarily popular in this town, but was she *that* unpopular? Her cursor hovered over the blue confirm button, then she moved it over to delete, sure nothing good would come of accepting a request that was clearly a troll trying to mess with her. Or perhaps it was Charlie resuming his scare tactics with her after their interview. She wouldn't put it past him. Staring at the small profile picture next to the notification, she leaned closer to the screen and squinted. She recognized that photo. Clicking on 'Gessie Jermaine', she bounced over to their profile page to get a better look at the enlarged image. Memories circled around just out of reach like a dog chasing its tail, and she grappled with where she recognized the picture from. Then, with a wave of nausea, it clicked. The small sliver of an arm barely showing along the edge of the photo's frame is what gave it away, because on its wrist, was a small braided bracelet she would recognize anywhere.

In the photo, Jessie was giving a coy smirk sitting at a wooden table, her hair pulled up in the signature red cheer bow that she adorned so frequently in high school. The sight of the red fabric made Margo's stomach churn, the image of it floating away from Jessie's decaying body fresh in her mind. There was a notebook open in front of Jessie, and next to her, cropped almost fully out of the photo, was Margo herself. It had been taken during one of their tutoring sessions in the school library by someone on the Yearbook committee. It hadn't made the cut for print, but Margo had asked them for a copy of it one day when she walked by the computer lab and saw them working. She had posted it to her Myspace page, so proud to have been reconnecting with her beautiful friend, hoping some of Jessie's popularity would rub off on her and make her less of an outcast. Someone had found and saved the photo, purposefully removing Margo to use on their fake page. It was hard to wrap her head around the fact that someone would do something so mean-spirited during such a tumultuous time.

She scrolled down the page, but due to privacy settings, there wasn't much else to infer from the profile. The only other visuals she could see were a scanned newspaper clipping showing the cheerleading squad at the final football game their senior year, Jessie front and center, and then a photo of the taped-off crime scene at the swimming hole where Jessie's remains had been discovered. A cold, clammy wave enveloped Margo as she stared at the images. The page felt sinister and every fiber of her being was shouting at her to click delete on the request. But before she knew what she was doing, her curiosity overcame her. What if there was more information visible once she confirmed the request? Would it become clear who was behind it? Would it point to Jessie's killer?

She clicked the blue confirm button and was hit with a punch to the gut as she realized no further information had been loaded to the page yet. Ready to reverse course and block the account, she was taken aback by a notification popping up on Facebook Messenger. Opening its panel, she saw the new message at the top was from the very account she was about to block. With a shaking hand, she opened the dialogue box, bracing herself. There in the gray chat bubble, the words danced tauntingly in front of her eyes.

'Nobody likes a snoop. Stop meddling and leave Lake Moss before it's too late.'

Before Margo could even process what she'd just read, a lump in her throat forming thicker with every word, a photo popped up in the dialogue box. She gasped, pushing her chair back in surprise as if she'd been burned. The photo had been taken that very morning. In it, Margo was climbing into Austin's car outside her house as he smiled over at her. The photo had clearly been taken from behind the tree line near Margo's home.

Three bubbles appeared and Margo braced herself for whatever this person was going to say next. Finally, the words appeared on the screen. 'It would be a shame if you met the same fate as your so-called "BFF".'

Anxiety swelled in her chest, thick and heavy like someone was pressing down, trying to crush her. Her heart thumped wildly in rebellion against the pressure, her lungs constricting with each choppy breath. As the reality of someone watching her from the shadows took root in her mind, the image of the footprints outside her window zooming back to the forefront, blackness crept into her vision. She pushed back further from the desk, leaned forward and put her head between her legs as she took sharp rattling breaths. It had been a while since she'd experienced a panic attack, and she mentally kicked herself for not getting her Xanax prescription refilled before returning to Lake Moss. She should have known she couldn't cope on her own here, but she hadn't realized Jessie's body would turn up and cause everything in her to implode.

116

After a few long minutes that felt like hours, Margo straightened up and closed her eyes, breathing deeply and feeling the anxiety taper off as her belly expanded. *It's just a message.* She reminded herself. It was creepy, but it was just a stupid Facebook message, someone trying to scare her. Probably Charlie, like he did in high school. She could picture him sitting there behind his laptop getting a kick out of imagining her fear as he typed out the words. The thought of the smug look on his face angered her. She wasn't a timid kid anymore. Taking control, she X'd out of the message without responding and quickly blocked the account. She wouldn't give them the satisfaction of knowing they got to her, and she certainly wasn't going anywhere. Not yet, anyway.

CHAPTER EIGHT

When Margo walked out of her bedroom, trying to shake off the lingering bad vibes from the mysterious message, her dad was standing just inside the living room. He was leaning on his crutches, his brow furrowed in worry.

After staring at her for a second he said, 'I need to talk to you about something. Can you come into the kitchen? I made coffee and thought we could have a chat.'

Margo hesitated before saying, 'Sure. Is everything OK?'

He paused for a moment before saying, 'Everything's fine, Margo. We just need to talk.'

She followed him into the kitchen, nerves mounting with each step. He seemed concerned, what could be so serious? She was already on edge from the Facebook message, and now this. They poured their coffees and walked over to sit at the dining table across from one another. The tension in Margo's body was almost painful, her muscles screaming at her to release their strained state. What bomb was her dad about to drop on her? After the explosion of her marriage and Jessie's remains being found, she wasn't sure she could take another hit.

Her dad sat with his hands around his mug. He started to talk, but then shut his mouth. There were tears in his eyes as he looked up at her. 'Dad, what is it? You're scaring me.'

He exhaled and leaned onto the table. 'I just spoke with Mark.'

Margo's hackles immediately went up. *Mark called my father?!* It crossed such a line, she couldn't believe he'd stooped so low. How would she feel if she called his mom and told her what a lying, cheating son she had? Her face grew hot, her hands gripping the mug tightly. 'Why did Mark call you?'

'Margo, he told me what you've been doing. Leaving voicemails and calling him constantly.'

'I haven't called Mark at all in the past week or two, he's been the one calling and texting me! I don't know what he's talking about. And even if I did call him one or two times right after I got to Lake Moss, what, I'm not allowed to call the man I was married to for eight years?' She was getting angrier with each passing second.

'Margo, you've called him almost fifty times since you split up. He told me how you went onto Diana's Facebook page and posted a nasty comment before she could block you. You've left thirty-two angry voicemails and texted him at least a hundred times. Yes, he counted.'

Margo's mouth dropped open and she puffed out a loud breath, feeling trapped. 'I can't believe he called you. Like I said, I stopped trying to contact him weeks ago. Those calls were over a period of months, Dad! And that was mostly when their engagement news was still fresh. That woman stole my husband and then bragged about it publicly. She humiliated me,' she said, gritting her teeth.

'Diana posted a photo of her and Mark announcing

119

their engagement, yes. And I understand how much that must have stung. But she wasn't bragging about ruining your marriage, you two aren't friends on Facebook so she didn't think you'd see it. She didn't even tag Mark in the post.'

'It crushed me! Dad, he cheated on me with his secretary and then they announced their engagement just three months later! How do you expect me to react to him getting engaged so soon after we split? And not even having the guts to tell me about it first before I saw it on Facebook?'

'Margo, I'm not defending his actions, but he said for months before his affair even started, you accused him of cheating. He said you even showed up at his work and berated him in front of his co-workers because there were two women helping out who weren't on his team. Margo, you almost got him fired.'

Margo exhaled and slammed her body back into the chair. 'So, you're saying it's my fault he cheated? Dad, I quit my job to focus on getting pregnant because that's what *he* wanted. But after I quit, he pulled away even further. Even if he wasn't cheating at first, he eventually did prove me right. How can you take his side over mine?'

'I didn't say I was on his side, Margo,' her dad said calmly, trying to diffuse her anger. 'I'm livid with him for cheating on you and I told him so. But I don't hear you denying any of this.' Margo remained quiet, but glared at her father, feeling betrayed. 'He admitted he did want to start a family and pressured you even though you weren't ready, which was wrong. But he said he never asked you to quit your job and once you were at home all the time, you got more and more convinced he was lying and cheating.'

'He didn't ask but I knew it's what he wanted. He told me constantly about his mom being a stay-at-home mom and how amazing his childhood was because of that. Of course he wanted me to stay at home.'

'I understand why you made that decision. But what about all the messages and phone calls? You guys split up six months ago. He played a couple of messages for me and Margo, I've never heard you sound that upset before.'

'Again Dad, that was weeks, some of them months ago even, before I came to Lake Moss. Everything was still fresh before I left Wilmington. I don't understand why he's bringing it up now. The engagement announcement was like a slap in the face. How was I supposed to sound? Happy?' He looked down at his coffee and shook his head. 'Why aren't you on my side?' Margo slammed her fist down on the table, sloshing her coffee over the side of the cup.

'Margo, please hear me out. I *am* on your side. I'm always on your side.' He reached over and clasped Margo's trembling hand. 'But you can't fall into that trap every time you see something about their relationship online. Mark even said he saw your car outside Diana's house a couple of times before you left town. I know you're saying you've eased up now that the shock has worn off and I believe you. Mark's just worried you'll start up again, and you haven't been answering his texts or calls to talk to you about it directly. I'm worried about you. That's the *only* reason I'm bringing this up, not to defend Mark. This paranoid behavior . . . it reminds me of your mom.'

Margo shrank back, a sharp pain in her chest as he vocalized the fear that had always simmered under the surface. 'Mom was paranoid about things that weren't real, imaginary threats. This is real, it happened,' she said defensively in a low voice, willing it to not be true.

'We never talked much about your mom's mental health, but I know it affected you. Yes, she worried a lot, but her paranoia was always based on something real. We just didn't tell you every detail because you were so young. I didn't want to scare you, or have you think less of her. She loved you.'

'What are you talking about . . . based on something real? I know I was young, but I could tell when her fears seemed . . . excessive. She once thought my friends were planning to kill me and wouldn't let me do anything outside of school for a week!' Margo replied incredulously, the repressed memory sky-rocketing out of her. She'd loved her mom so much, and desperately wanted her to be *normal*, but the truth was, moments like that had occurred more than Margo's memory would let her admit at times.

'And that was because she'd watched a *Dateline* episode about three girls killing another girl because a boy one of the girls liked wanted to date her instead. She internalized it, letting it invade her own life.' Her dad dropped his head before looking back up at her. 'Let me start from the beginning. It's about time you knew the whole story.'

Margo watched her father take a sip of his coffee, stalling. 'I'm not sure I want to hear this, Dad,' Margo said with trepidation, her anger dissipating with the shift of the conversation.

The image of her mother was already tenuous, threatening to disintegrate and leave her with a mere ghost of an unstable woman. She wanted to remember her mother as fondly as she could, not look back through a lens of despair and pity.

'I think it's important you do,' he replied, looking pointedly at her. After a pause, he said, 'As you know, we met when I was the starting point guard on the basketball team during our senior year of college. We fell in love quickly and intensely. We dreamt of me going to the NBA, the glamorous life we would lead with her on my arm, traveling the country for games.' He paused, running a hand through his salt and pepper hair, looking sad and tired, but also, nostalgic. 'Then I blew out my knee and the doctors said I probably wouldn't play again, not professionally anyway, crushing my dreams not only for myself, but for what we had envisioned for our future. So, we started making new plans. Then, one day there was a story on the news about a woman getting raped on campus. They hadn't caught him and your mom became convinced that she was next. She wouldn't leave her apartment and missed two weeks of classes. Finally, I offered to walk her to and from every class. I even showed up late to a few of my own so I could do it.'

'That was sweet of you,' Margo said quietly.

'Yeah well, after she got back to classes, another story came out about some break-ins in the area. And your mom got fearful again about someone breaking into her apartment. She had me install new locks on the doors and windows, but even that wasn't enough. She wanted me to sleep over every night. If I couldn't for some reason, she'd call me constantly telling me she thought someone was outside watching her. I essentially moved in with her after that. She'd wake up every few hours thinking she heard something. Eventually I convinced her to talk to a counselor at the school.'

'Did the counselor diagnose her?'

'Not an official diagnosis. Since it was free through the college, her counselor was a grad student seeing patients for his required clinical hours. He said that she displayed symptoms of paranoid personality disorder, but he was reluctant to make it an official diagnosis because she didn't quite hit all the marks. He described her as similar to an empath, someone who feels everyone else's emotions and internalizes them. It made sense because anytime we'd go to a party or were in a crowd, she'd come home emotionally exhausted. For your mom, emotions were airborne. She caught them like other people caught colds. The counselor had his advisor prescribe her medication, and he forbade her watching the news or reading the newspaper whenever possible. Over the final few months of school, she got better and we got re-swept up in feelings of excitement for our future. She'd grown up in a small mountain town in France until she was ten, when her parents died in a car accident and she moved to the states to live with her Aunt Bea. She had always wanted to raise her kids in a similar environment.'

'Were you already engaged?'

'Not yet, but we'd discussed getting married. We looked at a map and narrowed it down to a few places Eloise liked that had open positions in our fields, and we started sending out our resumés. I was offered the position at Lake Moss High and Eloise was thrilled. We moved here, got married, and everything was great for a while.'

'So what happened?'

'Your mom got pregnant and stopped taking her medication. She was afraid of potential side effects. I kept a close eye on her and she seemed fine. But by the end of her second trimester, she started getting worried because you weren't moving around much. From all the books she'd read, she knew by that time you should have started kicking. The doctor wasn't concerned, he said babies are all different and everything looked good. But Eloise wasn't convinced. We went to a specialist in Asheville and that doctor said the same thing.'

'Let me guess, Mom still wasn't convinced?'

He shook his head. 'Nope. She became depressed and was certain she was carrying a stillborn. She stopped getting out of bed and I had to coax her to eat. I talked to a doctor on my own and he said all I could do was make sure she was still eating and staying hydrated. But since she was already experiencing depression, he warned me of the risks for post-partum depression, gave me some pamphlets to prepare myself. But I was only twenty-four, I didn't know what to do.'

'But surely when I was born healthy, Mom was fine?'

'It actually happened before that. All of a sudden in her seventh month, you started kicking. The paranoia and depression just melted away. Your mom became herself again, eagerly planning for your arrival.'

'Did she get post-partum depression?'

'No, my fears were unfounded. For the first few months, it was amazing. She was thrilled to be a new mom and we loved you so much. We felt so blessed.' He paused, seeming to work out how to tell the rest. 'But then a woman on a TV show she loved lost her baby to crib death, and Eloise was certain that was going to happen to you too. She'd wake you up during the night to make sure you were still breathing. Sometimes I'd wake up in the morning and she'd be sleeping on the floor next to your crib.'

'So that's how it all started up again, then,' Margo said sadly.

Her dad nodded. 'After that, any time she saw a news report about a kid going missing or a home invasion or whatever the current crime headline was, she'd become paranoid about it and our whole lives would be turned upside down. But this time, she was resistant to going back on her medication. She thought she was just being cautious, keeping her family safe.'

'God, Dad, how did you take it?'

'I loved her.' He shrugged. 'And I loved you. I knew she was sick, that it wasn't her fault. I just held on to the hope that one day she'd go back on her medication. I did everything I could to shield you from the brunt of her paranoia, but I know I wasn't always successful.'

Margo felt such sadness over what her parents had endured. With this new information, many things that her mother said and did suddenly made sense. Margo remembered watching her mother closely every day, craving desperately to see her face light up with joy. Eloise's expressions had ranged from confusion to sadness to fear, most of the time all within one day. But when she did switch over to a loving smile, enduring the rest of her moods had been worth it. They were electrifying. Those were the moments Margo tried to hold on to, to drown out the darkness lurking in the corners of her memories. But she also remembered her mom breathing a sigh of relief when her dad came home from work every day, as if she'd been holding her breath since he'd walked out the door that morning.

'I knew she was having a hard time, but it didn't seem out of control. She just seemed over-protective, sometimes overreacting because she was worried about my safety.'

'Well, once she was done breast-feeding, I did convince her to take her meds again and start seeing a therapist.

But for some reason, the meds weren't working as well as they previously had. We tried several different medications and only one had any noticeable impact. It toned everything down but didn't make it go away completely. That was the best I could do at the time.'

'Was she still on them when she died?'

Her dad shook his head sadly. 'She went off them because she'd started experiencing fatigue and nausea, having a hard time sleeping. She read up about side effects and got scared. She stopped taking them about a month before her car accident. I tried to talk her out of it, tried convincing her to try out a new medication instead, but she refused to take the "poison pills". She started getting paranoid again, convinced someone was going to hurt you.'

'Yeah, I remember in that last month, she wouldn't even let me ride my bike to the creek.' Her dad nodded. After a long pause, Margo steeled herself to ask the question that had haunted her every day for the past twenty years. 'Dad, did Mom kill herself?'

He swallowed a couple of times, and tears gathered in his eyes again. 'I don't know for sure, honey. I really don't. But there's a part of me that thinks she might have.'

A river of tears finally exploded over Margo's lashes as she nodded, leaving streaks down her flushed cheeks. 'Me too,' she whispered.

Her dad reached across the table and gathered Margo's hands into his own. 'So, you see why I'm worried about you, don't you? I've always kept a close eye on your behavior, worried that you might have inherited some of what haunted her. And while you were a little obsessed with getting good grades, you always seemed OK. You never did anything that concerned me. Until now.'

Margo furrowed her brow, looking at her dad. After hearing the extent of her mom's mental health struggles, her tears dried up at her father comparing their actions. Her face hardened as she wiped her face with the back of her hand. 'Are you really saying you think what I've done is on the same level of Mom's behavior? Isn't it understandable, considering Mark cheated? And can't you see I'm doing much better now than I was right when the split happened?'

'I don't know. Margo. I get that there were issues in your marriage, but this is how it always started with your mom. Nothing too concerning and maybe even explainable. How could I tell her not to worry about a break-in when it had just happened to someone else in the same neighborhood? But then it would spiral out of control and consume her entire life. I just don't want you to go down that path.'

Margo shook her head and leaned back in the chair. Yes, she had gone a little far after she found out about the engagement, but still she felt justified. Anyone would have felt the same, perhaps done the same, or even worse. Her dad comparing that to how her mother behaved hurt her on another level.

She puffed out her cheeks and exhaled. 'I don't know what to say, Dad. I really don't think my behavior is anywhere near how Mom acted. I think most people would feel the way I do and would understand. You've never been cheated on so I don't expect you to get it. But . . . I hear you, I know I can't act like that again, and I haven't contacted either of them in a while. I'm moving on I swear, you don't have anything to worry about.'

He looked at her for a long second before conceding defeat. 'Look I'm not trying to scare you and you're right,

I don't know what that feels like. But it would make me feel a lot better if you went and saw Jazz, at least for a few sessions. She's still practicing. And you did say you'd had another nightmare. She helped you so much with them when you were younger. So look at it as heading those off before they get worse. It can't hurt.'

Her dad was looking at her in a way that made her feel like a teenager again, like he needed to fix everything. As much as Margo felt he was overreacting about Mark, he was right that the nightmares were back. Even more than she'd admitted to him.

Margo relaxed her shoulders and nodded. 'OK, I'll make an appointment if that makes you feel better.'

'I appreciate that.'

Margo nodded and they both rose from the table. As she tried to shake off her feelings from the conversation, a layer of anger hung just beneath the surface and refused to dissipate. Walking over to place her cup in the dishwasher, Margo pulled out her phone to send Mark a text admonishing him for worrying her dad for nothing. Why did he think it was appropriate to contact him after all this time, when she'd clearly calmed down and moved on? Her dad was just recovering from surgery and now was worried about her too which he did not need. But instead of sending the message, she scrolled through her call and text history with Mark and realized she really *had* spiraled after their engagement post. Scrolling down all the texts she'd sent, all the calls she'd made, it was overwhelming. While her anger felt justified, there was no point in starting back up again. It was time to leave it in the past for good, so she locked her phone and put it back in her pocket. Not really sure what else to do, she started making dinner. Her dad's talk had left her feeling anxious and caged in as she boiled pasta and chopped lettuce for a salad.

When she was done prepping, she grabbed her phone and texted Austin, 'Wanna grab a drink at Stout? Hopefully you're not sick of me after spending all morning together, but I need to get out of here.'

A minute later her phoned dinged. 'Still stuck in a meeting. Should be done soon, meet you in a bit? ☺'

She replied quickly and then plated the food for her dad, setting him up in front of the TV. She grabbed her purse, applied lip gloss and a hint of blush, and ran her fingers through her hair in the hall mirror. Wanting to be comfortable, she anxiously threw on a pair of her favorite jeans, a tank top and Converse sneakers. She waved goodbye to her dad, telling him she wouldn't be home late. Things felt a little tense between them – it would be good to get some space.

CHAPTER NINE

On the drive to meet Austin, Margo rolled down the windows and let the warm evening air wash over her, trying to let her bad mood escape out into the night. Looking to distract her whirling mind, she turned on the radio and fiddled with the tuning buttons. They didn't get many good stations up here, but she found a classics station playing *Every Breath You Take* by The Police and turned it up, singing along loudly as she eased the car around the dark bends in the road. Her tension floated out on the words, making her feel calmer with every passing verse.

By the time she pulled into the parking lot at Stout, her body felt more relaxed. She entered through the large double doors and looked around, a pool table in one corner and a vintage jukebox in another. It reminded her of the hole-in-the-wall bar near her college where she and her dad would shoot pool when he came to visit. He always went for stripes. She shook her head, trying to get her dad out of her mind and focus on meeting Austin. The bar was lively but not packed. Considering it was a weeknight, she wasn't surprised. Margo took it all in, barn wood walls with lit beer signs hanging throughout, high vaulted ceilings and a square wood wrap-around bar in the middle of the room.

She hopped onto a bar stool near the entrance to be visible to Austin when he arrived, and asked the bartender, 'Hey, which Abbies do you have on tap right now?' She had to admit, the Abbotts knew how to make a great beer. He handed her a laminated menu.

'Alex, can I get another?' a man a few seats away asked, holding his finger up.

A minute later Alex came back to where she sat. She glanced up from the menu. 'I'll have the Moss Falls Pale Ale.'

'Coming right up!'

While he poured her beer, her phone dinged inside her purse. Pulling it out, Margo hesitated. She was afraid to see what was waiting for her, the threatening Facebook message she'd received floating to the forefront of her mind. Trying to shrug off the ominous feelings swirling inside her, she took a deep breath and opened her messages.

'Heading your way!' Austin had texted.

'Great, see you soon!' Margo replied, relief surging through her that it was just him.

Dirty Little Secret by The All-American Rejects blared from the jukebox as her eyes wandered over the other patrons. She noticed several guys she vaguely remembered from high school shooting pool but didn't recognize anyone else. While she sipped her beer, the aromatic earthiness pairing well with hints of lemon and cloves, Margo tapped her foot on the bar stool along with the music, anxious for Austin to arrive. She was never the type to go to a restaurant or bar alone and it made her feel uncomfortable and exposed. Suddenly, someone was next to her, their breath hot on her cheek. She was over-powered by the smell of whiskey thick and suffocating, mixed with a potent cologne. Margo became instantly nauseous from the blend of licorice and floral notes, transporting her back to the whiff she had gotten on Charlie's doorstep.

'Well, well, well, Margo Sutton all by her lonesome. What are *you* doing here?'

She turned and found herself face to face with Charlie. His eyes were glazed over, clearly drunk. *Really* drunk, by the sway of his body. Most of the stories she'd heard about Charlie in high school centered around him being drunk. Perhaps he had a drinking problem. If so, managing a brewery probably wasn't the best idea.

'Hi Charlie. Just having a drink,' she said, pointing to her beer.

'Well would you look at that, miss goody-two-shoes drinks! That's rich!' he slurred. 'Must work up quite a thirst poking your nose in where it doesn't belong.' He smiled, showing all his teeth, a steely edge to his words. Margo leaned back to put some space between them. 'You've never belonged here. I'm not surprised you're trying to insert yourself into the one big thing to happen to this town.'

'You're drunk,' Margo said sternly, trying to ignore the sting from his words. 'Maybe you should sit down and have a glass of water.'

Charlie smacked his hand down on the bar top, the loud *thwak* making her jump. 'The thing is Snitch Bitch, I don't answer to you. You always were a nobody, trying to creep into our group, trying to latch on to Jessie. You were obsessed with us. What a joke, like we'd ever want a nothing like you hanging out with us.' He laughed loudly and then reached over and grabbed Margo's beer, taking a long drink before slamming it back down on the bar. Beer sloshed over the sides and Margo quickly grabbed the stein and moved it out of his reach, sopping up the mess with a napkin.

'I never wanted to hang out with *you*, Charlie,' Margo said, pointing her eyes at him. 'But I *was* friends with Jessie, whether you liked it or not.'

'You weren't friends. You were her tutor! And somehow you managed to convince her I was a bad guy. It was your fault we broke up!' he yelled, leaning in. Some of his spit landed on her cheek. Slowly, Margo wiped it away, anxiety swelling inside her, making the beer in her belly turn sour.

'What do you want, Charlie?'

He narrowed his eyes so intensely, it seemed they might be sucked into his face and disappear. 'What do I want? Hmm let's see.' He snapped his fingers. 'I want you to stop running around like Austin's little sidekick asking questions about me and Jessie. It's none of your damn business!' He jabbed a finger into her chest roughly. 'And you know what else? Here you are taking notes while I'm interrogated about where I was that night, but what about you, Margo? Where were you that night? You were obsessed with Jessie and apparently still are with the way you're *desperately* trying to cling to her through this show.'

Margo bit back a retort on the tip of her tongue about it not being her fault the show was interested in him. She knew it would fall on deaf ears. In his liquor-soaked mind, she was guilty by association, because to Charlie it was still Margo's fault he'd lost Jessie all those years ago.

Alex wandered over. 'Settle down Charlie. I don't want any trouble tonight.'

134

Charlie looked at him with his eyebrows raised. 'You don't want trouble? Well then kick this bitch out because that's all she is,' he slurred.

Charlie stepped an inch closer and Margo stood up from the stool to back away. Their exchange had taken an aggressive turn, and she was beginning to fear what he would do next. She'd heard rumors in high school about Charlie's temper, and whatever he'd had to drink was starting to reveal his true colors. But looking at his smug, entitled face, she felt her resolve strengthening. She thought back to every time Charlie taunted her or jumped out of the shadows to scare her. She'd bowed down to him all through high school, but she wasn't a kid anymore and she wasn't about to let this pompous asshole push her around. Pushing down her fear, she inched closer. Charlie was tall, about six foot three, but with Margo's own height of five-foot-ten, she wasn't much shorter.

'What is it you're afraid of, Charlie? Are you worried I might find out some ugly truth about you? Maybe that you had something to do with what happened to Jessie?'

'Screw you, Margo!' Charlie said before pushing her, harder than she expected.

If she'd been more petite like Jessie, she would have fallen, maybe even been hurt. Instead, she stumbled back and caught herself on the bar as Charlie advanced toward her again. His friends rushed over and were about to pull him away when, out of nowhere, Austin jumped in between them.

'What are you gonna do, Charlie? Hit a woman? That's not a good look in the middle of your ex-girlfriend's murder investigation, is it?' Austin said.

'Fuck off Austin! Mind your own business.'

'This *is* my business,' Austin said calmly, but with an edge to his words.

'I said, stay out of it,' Charlie snarled through clenched teeth.

Austin was only an inch or so shorter than Charlie, but was easily thirty pounds less. Margo was impressed that he didn't take a single step back. Charlie's face was bright red and screwed up with rage. He was breathing heavily, his fists clenched so tightly that his knuckles were white, anger bleeding from every pore. One of Charlie's friends finally tried pulling him away, but he resisted, yanking his arm from his friend's grasp.

Alex interrupted the commotion. 'Charlie, it's time you and your friends leave.' He looked at Charlie's friends. 'Get him out of here.'

Charlie glared at him. 'My family owns this town! Those are my beers you've got on tap,' he said, pointing to the numerous beer taps labeled Moss Creek. 'You don't get to tell me to leave, *Alex*!' He spat out his name like an insult.

Alex stared at him with one eyebrow raised and slowly crossed his arms across his chest. Alex was a big guy and his biceps bulged as he stared Charlie down. Finally, Charlie realized he was out-muscled and relented when his friend grabbed his arm again, pulling him toward the door. Before it closed, he yelled out, 'You better watch your back, Margo!'

Margo's bravado evaporated as her adrenaline subsided, and she let Austin lead her back to the bar stool. She rubbed her arm where she'd caught herself on the bar. *That's going to leave a mark.*

'Are you OK?' Austin asked.

'Yeah, I'm fine, just a little shaken up,' she said with a weak and unconvincing smile. Austin's face was flushed and he looked ready to punch someone. She'd never seen him angry before. She placed a hand on his where it rested on the bar and he softened. 'Thanks for stepping in at the end there, who knows how far he would have gone.'

'I'm sorry I didn't get here sooner. Why don't I order us a round?' Margo nodded and Austin put his fingers up to Alex, asking for two of what Margo had been drinking.

'You got it!' Alex replied, 'And hey, thinks for stepping in, man. Beers are on me. Charlie gets so belligerent, but that's the first time I've seen him go after a woman,' he said, looking over to Margo and shaking his head.

'Wow, I feel so special,' she said with a wry smile.

As Alex poured the beers, Austin asked, 'So what brought all that on, anyway?'

'Mainly alcohol, I assume. But he seemed really pissed off that I was with you for the interview. I think he still blames me for Jessie breaking up with him.'

'He's always been a hothead, but I've never seen him take it that far before. I really am sorry my meeting held me up. I should have been here to stop him sooner.'

Margo smiled, 'No apology necessary, your intervention saved the day. With that temper, I have no idea what he's capable of. I'm not gonna act like I didn't tell Jessie she deserved better than him, but it seemed like she already knew that.'

'Guess it's easier for him to blame you than to admit he was the reason they were having problems, especially now that he's under a microscope with the investigation ramping back up.'

Margo nodded. 'Yeah probably. I just don't understand how he's basically remained the same person since high school, no growth whatsoever.'

'Yeah, me either. I mean, he has been coddled by his rich family this entire time. If someone is constantly getting you out of scrapes without repercussions, it's pretty difficult to grow into a better person.' Austin paused and leaned in, 'You know, I heard he barely graduated college. His dad had to make a call to an old friend so he could retake a final he'd bombed. It sure pays to have rich, influential friends,' Austin finished with a shrug.

Margo smirked, the rumor making her feel a little better. 'Why am I not surprised by that?'

Alex came back and set their beers down. Austin and Margo chatted as they sipped. Despite their efforts at small talk, the mood had already been ruined. Austin seemed disappointed that the night had taken a dark turn, and Margo couldn't blame him.

'Hey, why don't we finish these beers and get out of here. I want to show you something.'

Margo looked at him inquisitively. Austin had an excited smile on his face, a twinkle of a secret in his eyes. 'I'm not sure I'm going to be much fun tonight.'

Austin bumped his shoulder against hers. 'Come on, I think you're going to like this. Give me a chance to turn things around.'

Margo found it hard to resist his hopeful expression. And was she wrong, or was he flirting with her? While her schoolgirl crush had started seeping back in, she hadn't been sure if he was feeling it too. 'OK, sure,' she replied after a short pause, smiling in return.

They downed the dregs of their beers and as they walked outside, Austin said, 'You can ride with me, we aren't going far and I can drop you off at your car after.'

Margo climbed in the passenger side of his Jeep. 'Where are you taking me, Austin Hughes?' she asked.

'It's a surprise,' he replied coyly.

Austin drove around the backside of the bar, where the slope of the mountain began to curve up. He turned onto a narrow dirt road that Margo didn't even notice at first. The car rumbled over the uneven surface for several minutes, pebbles and twigs kicking up against the doors and windows as the car pulled them up the mountain. Finally, Austin stopped and turned to her.

'The rest of the way is on foot, but it's not far.'

She resisted asking him again where they were going and instead, exited the car. Austin leaned across the passenger seat and pulled a small flashlight and flask out of the glove box before climbing out as well, piquing her interest. Margo followed him down an overgrown path through the trees, sidestepping roots poking up through the dirt. After only a minute, Austin stopped and pointed the flashlight up into the trees. At first, Margo didn't see anything except moss-covered trunks and limbs. She was about to ask Austin what she was supposed to be looking at, dark in the woods, when she saw it. Rungs of a ladder leading up to what she originally thought was a thick tree. Instead, the form of a small rickety structure up in the trees started to take shape the longer she stared – a wooden tree-house of sorts perched on four wooden stilts. The wood had the same green tinge that the trees were covered in, camouflaging within its surroundings.

'Whoa! What is this?' Margo asked.

'It's a really old weather observation tower. Remember that topographic map assignment your dad gave in sophomore year?'

Margo nodded, thinking back to the midterm assignment where, after a few weeks of him teaching the class how to read a topographic map, he handed them one of

Lake Moss. He then loaded them into the basketball team's van and blindfolded them as he drove them up into the mountain. Their location had been marked with a red X and they had to find their way back to the main road using only the map.

'Well, I think your group took the southern route, but mine took the eastern route. It took longer so of course we didn't win, but I saw this as we were traipsing through. No one else saw it because I stayed on the edge of the group and it was a bit further into the forest than where we had walked. I didn't say anything, but kept thinking about it,' he said, peering up to the towering wood box. 'After class I talked to your dad about it, and we looked it up together. Apparently, it's from before Lake Moss formed as an official town. They'd built this as a way to monitor when storms were coming in. Come on up!' Austin said excitedly as he tucked the flashlight in his back pocket and started climbing up the rungs on the ladder.

Margo followed him up a bit hesitantly, not trusting the old wood to hold their weight. Thankfully she made it to the top after a minute of careful climbing and found him dusting off the surface of the platform surrounded by walls on three sides and a roof. One side was completely open.

Margo whistled. 'Look at that view!'

They could see far into the distance at this height, and it was breathtaking. The moon illuminated the tops of the mountain range, the cloudless sky dotted with more stars than she'd ever seen before. Margo almost felt like she could reach up and touch one. Fireflies blinked sporadically over the expanse. They sat down with their legs dangling over the open edge. Margo kept her eyes pointed upward, afraid she would lose her nerve if she looked down.

'Wow, I feel like King and Queen of Lake Moss up here presiding over our small kingdom.'

Austin pulled the small flask out of his front pocket and took a swig before turning toward her. 'Care for a drink, milady?' he said in a terrible impersonation of a British accent, leaning forward in an exaggerated bow.

Margo laughed. 'Why thank you, milord.' She took the flask from his outstretched hand and took a drink of what turned out to be either bourbon or whiskey, the alcohol burning the back of her throat. 'Why didn't you ever tell me about this place?'

Austin shrugged. 'I don't know. It was kind of my secret place where I'd come anytime I needed space. I got overwhelmed pretty easily back then. Actually, I almost took you here the day Charlie locked you in the girl's bathroom. You seemed like you needed space too. But then you left right after school and I couldn't find you.'

Austin glanced at her warily, obviously not wanting to bring back the bad mood Charlie had caused earlier. 'Yeah, that was a *great* day,' she said, sighing heavily before taking another swig. 'His hatred of me really ratcheted up a notch after that because my dad got wind of it somehow and reported it to the principal. Charlie always blamed me for getting detention and that my dad benched him in the next basketball game. He started calling me "Snitch Bitch" after that. I'm not sure if that's better or worse than "Moaning Margo",' she said with a wry smile, looking at Austin. But he didn't return her smile.

He looked away and then said, 'I never told you this, but I was the one who told your dad.'

Margo's eyes popped open wide. 'What? Really?'

Austin looked guilty as he turned his gaze back to her. 'I thought I was helping. I was so sick of Charlie teasing you all the time and getting away with it. He just went too far that day. I didn't consider that he'd blame you since so many people witnessed it. But I should have known. I ended up making things worse for you and I didn't want to admit that back then, I felt terrible.'

Margo looked at him for a moment. 'It's OK. You were trying to help, and he probably would have continued to torment me anyway. He did get more aggressive after that, but it was also around the same time Jessie and I were reconnecting. I'm pretty sure that's what really turned his amusement in teasing me into actual hate. Him getting punished was just the cherry on top.' Reluctant to let herself dwell on Charlie yet again, Margo shook her head and then smiled. 'Do you remember that tiny, pitch black closet in the photography room when we took Yearbook freshman year? The one where we loaded our film into the canisters to be developed?'

Austin laughed. 'Oh yeah, it was like a five-by-five-foot coffin.'

'There was one day when you asked to skip the line and come in with me because you needed to get done quickly to go write a paper?' Austin nodded. 'That was when I knew we'd be friends.'

Austin smiled and cocked his head. 'Why that day?'

'That room wasn't designed for two people, so we kept bumping into one another, knocking things over and saying sorry each time because it was so dark, trying to load our film in this tiny space. Then all of sudden you stopped moving and laughed. I asked what was so funny and you said something like, "Doesn't it seem like Mr.

Roper could be outside the door thinking we're getting it on in here?".'

'Oh my god, I can't believe I said that.' He smacked his forehead with his palm. 'It just came out and I was mortified because, why would anyone our age know who Mr. Roper is? My mom loved *Three's Company*, so I'd watch reruns with her while I was doing my homework. You were so nice to laugh along and not call me a dork.'

'That laugh was genuine because I *did* know that show. Must have been a thing with our moms because my mom had a big crush on Jack Tripper. She even had a t-shirt with his face on it.'

'That makes me feel better.' He paused and smiled at her. 'I'm pretty sure my mom had a crush on him, too, but she'd never admit that in front of my dad.'

'Oh, my mom made her crush *very* apparent with my dad.' Austin and Margo laughed together. 'What you said that day in the film room was so perfect. And I immediately thought, "Oh yeah, we're gonna be friends",' Margo said, thinking back fondly about the show from the 70s and 80s that had seemed so silly in the 2000s. But she'd loved the characters, especially the nosy landlord, Mr. Roper, who would only let Jack live in the same apartment with Chrissy and Janet because Jack pretended to be gay. It was one of her favorite memories of her mother, the two of them snuggled on the couch, laughing over jokes that so often went right over Margo's head.

'Why didn't you say anything?' Austin asked.

'I don't know,' she replied, shrugging one shoulder. 'You know I was kinda shy back then.'

She passed the flask back to Austin and he took another sip, looking at her. 'Yeah, it was one of the things I liked about you. Everyone in high school was so loud and hungry for attention. You were never like that. I knew I wanted to be friends with you since the first day of Mrs. DeMarco's Algebra class, freshman year. She called on me to answer a question, but I wasn't paying attention, I was drawing in my notebook. And you turned around, saw my panic and mouthed the answer to me. I was so grateful. I didn't have many friends; my best friend moved away the summer before. And honestly, I never really fit in with anyone after that. Outside of tutoring, I didn't know what to say to any of them. Except you.'

Margo felt her face flush as they took a long look at one another. Suddenly feeling the shyness of her youth creep back in, she looked away. 'Do you come back to Lake Moss often?' she asked.

'A couple times a year. Usually at Christmas and Thanksgiving, sometimes my mom's birthday if I can get away. You?'

'This is my first time back in about fourteen years.'

'Really? Why?'

Margo shrugged and looked over the dark landscape. 'The minute I left this place I felt like a different person. It was like the weight of expectation and judgment had been lifted and I could be whoever I wanted to be. And the dark memories from my mom's death and Jessie's disappearance weren't suffocating me anymore. The first day of college, I made friends and spoke up in one of my classes. In both instances I kept expecting someone to mock me or call me names, or even worse, totally ignore me. But they didn't, they were actually interested in what I had to say. And then the few times I came back here, I felt like I reverted right back to the old Margo again. I hated it. The anxiety and sadness I felt the minute I crossed over the town line. So, I made my dad come visit me instead.'

144

'I know what you mean. Even though I came home over the years, it's not like I hung out with anyone from school when I got here. I stayed with my family and was always itching to leave after a few days. I could be leading a team in Atlanta one day, and then come home and feel like a nerdy nobody the next. The funny thing is, I don't feel that way this time. I'm having fun grabbing drinks and doing interviews with you, even though the circumstances are grim,' he said with a smile.

Margo's body warmed. She'd said too many goodbyes in her life, it was nice to welcome someone back in. 'So am I. Jessie's body being found is horrible, but I'm glad we've reconnected. And now that you mention it, I'm not feeling like old Margo this time either. Does this mean we've grown? Are we *adults*?' she said with an exaggerated horrified expression.

Austin clutched his heart. 'Oh god, I hope not!' he exclaimed, laughing.

They reminisced for a while longer about teachers they loved and hated, about school projects they'd worked on together and the countless times they did homework at her house, snacking on chips and cookies while their classmates went to football games and parties. Finally, they called it a night since Austin had an early morning with his team. They climbed down from their view in the clouds and Austin steadied her when she came down off the ladder, his hands lingering on her hips for a long second. The drinks she'd had were sneaking up on her, making her feel unsteady.

'Actually, do you mind just driving me home? I'm not sure I should drive.'

'Of course! I guess partying with the crew all the time has upped my tolerance.' They both gave a light laugh. 'But what about your car?'

145

'I can grab it tomorrow on my run. I'll just adjust my route to include passing by Stout.'

Austin nodded and they climbed in the car and headed back to her place. After parking his car in the driveway, she turned and smiled. 'Thanks for tonight. I really needed it. And thank you for showing me your secret spot.'

'No problem. I had fun.'

'So did I,' she replied, and they looked at each other in silence. She wondered if he might kiss her. But the minute she had that thought, she wondered if it was too soon after the separation. She *felt* ready to move on, but was she really? The conversation with her dad was still fresh in the back of her mind. Maybe talking with Jazz about everything first wasn't such a bad idea.

Margo broke the look and said goodnight, climbing out of the car. She watched from just outside her front door with a wave as Austin drove away. As she turned to put her keys in the lock, somewhere behind her she heard glass breaking and a scuffle, followed by dogs barking. She whipped around, holding her keys and pepper spray out like a weapon, wondering if she would actually start spraying if someone was there. But there was no one, just the inky black darkness dotted by porch lights. The dogs continued to bark. She had an eerie feeling like she was being watched, the hair on the back of her neck standing up and a chill washing over her. As she looked around, she kept expecting Charlie to jump out of the shadows. Overcome by fear, she ran into her house, frantically closing and locking the door behind her. She rushed to the window in the front room and peeked through the curtains. She scanned the area, feeling like she was missing something in her periphery.

'What are you doing?'

Margo jumped and spun around. Her hand flew to her

chest. 'Oh my god, Dad! You scared me! Why are you sitting here in the dark? Were you waiting up for me?'

'Kind of. Must have dozed off.'

'Dad, I'm not a kid anymore, I can take care of myself,' she said, even though she didn't feel as confident about that as she had that morning.

'I know, I just wanted to make sure you were OK. After what happened today, I feel awful.'

Margo walked over to the couch and sat next to her dad. 'I'm alright, Dad. Just a little shaken up by everything.'

'Are you still upset with me?' he asked, looking shameful.

Margo sighed. 'Maybe a little.' She gave him a weak smile. 'I love you Dad, nothing will ever change that.' Finally, he gave her a small smile in return. Looking back over her shoulder briefly at the front door she said, 'Dad, do you still have the security system active? I noticed you haven't set it since I've gotten home and I told you when I had you replace mom's old system a few years back that you should at least be using it at night.'

'Oh, that thing,' he said with a dismissive wave of the hand. 'I've been fine all these years. I don't think anyone's going to break in and mess with me. I stopped paying for the police monitoring a year or two ago because it was constantly going off and that piercing sound was so loud, and then the phone would be ringing off the hook to check on me, it drove me crazy.'

'Constantly going off for no reason? Or you kept forgetting about it and setting it off?' Margo asked with a small smirk.

He gave a short laugh and ran his hand across the stubble on his chin, 'Maybe a bit of both, who can really say.'

'It would make me feel a lot better if we could set it at night, at least while I'm home. With everything going on with Jessie's body being discovered and the town getting all worked up . . .'

He took a long look at her and then nodded. 'OK, Margo, whatever you want,' he said, and she was sure right now, he would agree to anything to win back her favor. 'I'll help you log into the app on your phone in the morning so you can turn it on and off from wherever. It's a pain running to that keypad every time it goes off. But you can turn it on for tonight if you want, you just have to type in 9035 on the panel near the garage door to turn it off when you're ready to disable it.'

'Thanks, Dad,' she said, sighing with relief that the alarm would help keep watch over her. 'I'll turn it on after I get ready for bed. Speaking of which, do you want me to help you to bed? It's getting late.'

'No, I can manage,' he replied, getting up from the couch and leaning on his crutches. Before he walked down the hall, he turned back to her. 'Sleep well. I'll see you in the morning.'

'Night.'

Margo ran her hands down her cheeks and exhaled. She was exhausted. She went to the bathroom and washed her face. As she was brushing her teeth, she heard what sounded like a trashcan being kicked over right outside the long thin bathroom window. She pulled the curtain aside mid-brush, the mint from her toothpaste making her gag as she inhaled sharply and looked around outside. The Avendales' security light was on and their trashcan that was out on the curb for pick-up tomorrow was knocked over. She knew the most likely explanation was a bear or some other animal, but part of her couldn't help but wonder, could it be Charlie waiting for her to let her guard down? In his drunken state, knocking things

148

over was probably inevitable. Margo shivered. She finished getting ready for bed, double-checked all the locks and windows were secure and turned on the security system from the keypad before closing her bedroom door behind her. After she turned out the light, she peeked out her curtains one last time. The night was dark again and the dogs had quieted. Hopefully whoever or whatever had been lurking outside was long gone. But again, she felt uneasy, like she was being watched as she closed the curtain, blocking out the moonlight and saving her from any prying eyes.

September 12, 1999

Dear Diary,

I am so mad at Mom! She has been so hard to deal with this week. On Thursday Dad dropped me off at school because Mom was having one of her bad days. But then she showed up with a sack lunch like she thought I forgot mine, but I didn't. She was screaming my name and reaching her arms out to me. Her hair was sticking up all weird and her clothes were totally wrinkled. Everyone laughed at me. Jessie grabbed my arm and marched me into the school. I felt bad for leaving Mom like that, but she was so embarrassing. And then everyone started calling my mom a bag lady and other things. I tried to tell them she just gets sad sometimes, but they wouldn't listen! Jessie got so mad that she told them to shut up or they'd regret it. She even called Brad a dummy and Charlie a jerk. It was so brave because those guys pick on everyone and we always try to stay out of their way. We heard Brad is moving away at the end of the year so maybe that's why she wasn't scared of him, but I couldn't believe she said that to Charlie. It made me feel so much better that Jessie stood up for me.

THEN, today Mom completely freaked out again! She dropped me and Jessie off to see Blast From the Past, but Jessie talked me into seeing Jawbreaker instead. It's R-rated so we had to sneak in. It's about some girls who accidentally kill their friend and cover it up. It was so good!

But Mr. Henderson caught us when we walked out and told Mom. After we dropped Jessie off, Mom screamed at me the whole way home because I lied. She's acting like I killed someone! I called Jessie later and her mom didn't even care. She didn't get grounded or anything. Why can't Mom be cool like Jessie's mom??

CHAPTER TEN

Margo drove past Town Square, turning at the familiar road that led to her old therapist, Dr. Jasmine Johnson's house. She took patients at her home in a shed turned office in her backyard. The last time she'd seen Jazz was the day before Margo left for college. Her dad had made an appointment for her to address any worries she might have about leaving home for the first time, even though she hadn't seen her therapist for a few years by that point.

After her mother died, nightmares plagued Margo. They all involved her mother crashing her car in various horrible ways. Sometimes it was a deer in the road, causing her mother to swerve on the wet pavement. Sometimes the slick surface had simply caused her mom to lose control. But other times, her mother drove the car directly into the tree of her own volition. Those were the worst ones. They were the ones that Margo feared were the truth, that her mother had chosen to leave her, had chosen death over raising her daughter. She didn't leave a note and there were no witnesses, so they could never be sure. Margo would wake up screaming and

152

crying. The nightmares came so frequently that her father had put a small mattress in her room and slept next to her the first year as comfort, holding her close when she woke up shrieking in the dark.

It had rained the day her mother's car crashed into that tree not far from their home. That road, if you took it far enough, led right out of town. Margo often wondered if her mom had decided to leave them, but then chose to leave life altogether instead. She'd fought with her mom about the movie she and Jessie had snuck into the night before the crash, a memory that still haunted her. That's when Margo had started to wonder if her mother was too strict, too protective, too . . . everything. She was used to her mom's rules and perpetual check-ins, her eyes darting around constantly whenever they were in public. It had been so ingrained into her childhood that it seemed normal. When Margo woke up the next morning, her mom's car was already gone and her dad didn't know where she was. Until the police had shown up on their doorstep and everything had fallen apart . . .

Running away from those memories was something Margo had become fairly adept at all these years. She shook her head and exited the car, walking around the side rock path toward Jazz's office. Everything looked pretty much the same, tomato and herb garden on her left, green grass bordered by bright yellow black-eyed Susans on the right. The shed had been repainted a soothing pale blue, but the wood shingles at the top were still there. Jazz greeted her warmly, her black hair now mostly gray. More wrinkles gathered around her face as she smiled, but her golden-brown skin was still as radiant as ever. The old gray couch inside the office had been replaced by a tan leather loveseat. After Margo sat down and Jazz pulled out her notebook, Margo began fidgeting.

'It's been a long time, Margo; it's good to see you. How have you been?'

'I was doing pretty good until these last few months. They've been harder than most.' Margo summarized what had happened in her life since she'd last seen Jazz, the words flowing easily as if they'd never stopped having appointments. College, her stenographer career, her marriage falling apart, and then reconnecting with Austin to help with the interviews. There was so much to catch her up on that it took up half their allotted hour, and she felt like she'd only skimmed the surface. With a deep breath, she continued, 'The reason I made an appointment is because I'm barely sleeping. The nightmares are back with a vengeance. Not of my mom though, these started after I came home, after Jessie's remains were discovered in the swimming hole.'

'I see,' Jazz said, in her usual giving-nothing-away voice. 'What do these dreams consist of?'

'Usually some variation of either being chased, or of me trying to find someone and I can't find them no matter where I look. Sometimes both. And there's always a frantic energy about them, like if I don't find them, they'll die. Usually, it's Jessie I'm trying to get to, but I can never save her. The first one happened the night I came back, right after her body was discovered. I was floating in the swimming hole. And then Jessie appeared on the bank of the water, blood dripping down her face . . .' Margo shivered as she recounted the dream.

'It's understandable that your feelings would manifest in a dream like that, considering the shock of the discovery and the fact that you came back to your hometown after

154

such a long time away. A hometown that you still associate with deep trauma and loss. Memories of your friendship with Jessie coupled with the news coming to the surface when your mind is at rest.'

'Yeah, I thought at first that it was just a blip from the shock, but the dreams haven't stopped. Ever since I got back to town, I've been feeling like there's someone watching me or lurking in the shadows, and then last night I had an altercation with Charlie Abbott at the pub. He was drunk and we got into an argument. It escalated and he pushed me and told me to "watch my back". I feel like I need to keep looking over my shoulder. I hear noises outside my house and think the worst.' Margo sighed, fidgeting with her hands in her lap, trying to keep tears at bay. 'I also got a weird message on Facebook, maybe just Charlie messing with me or something, but it was really creepy. I just . . . I don't know,' Margo said, shaking her head. 'Sometimes I feel like I'm losing my mind. I mean, we live in the mountains. There are critters all over the place knocking over trash cans and scuttling through the woods. I try to tell myself that when I hear or see something, but it's not working. I just feel like someone is out to get me.'

'Well, that would explain what's manifesting in your dreams. Why did you argue with Charlie?'

'He was upset that I've been poking my nose in the investigation with Austin, asking questions about Jessie. Honestly, I don't know why he got so upset with *me*, though. Austin was the one asking the questions. I guess he blames me for him and Jessie's relationship falling apart,' Margo shrugged. 'He always teased me at school though, so honestly, I wouldn't be shocked if he's holding on to a ridiculous teen grudge. He got in trouble a couple of times, benched from games and detention. Doesn't seem like he's gotten over any of it. He always had a quick temper. And he was drunk, I'm sure that didn't help.'

'I want to go back to your use of the phrase "out to get you". It's interesting. What would that be in your eyes? How could someone "get" you? Is it a physical threat you're feeling? Or is it emotional?'

Margo paused and thought about it. 'I guess both. After what Charlie said, yeah I'm worried he'll get drunk again and come after me. But it's more than that. I just feel like there's someone watching me, waiting for me to make a mistake and pounce. That sounds dumb doesn't it?'

Jazz smiled. 'No, it's not dumb. What kind of mistake are you worried about making?'

'I don't even know! That's the problem; it's some weird abstract feeling. I feel afraid a lot of the time, and even though I know it's ridiculous, I can't stop feeling this way.'

Jazz made a few notes and then looked back up. 'Margo, I think what might be at play here is the guilt coming back from your mother's death. It was a "mistake" way back then when you snuck into that movie, a "mistake" that you argued with your mom rather than fessing up and apologizing. And then she died, and you thought it was your fault. You used that word, "mistake," often when you were a child and you spent the rest of your school years trying to be perfect. Perfect grades, perfect daughter. You beat yourself up for years and when we left off, you'd seemed to have eased up, allowed yourself to forgive your younger self. But perhaps it's still there in the background, lingering. And with the confirmation that Jessie isn't just missing but also dead, it makes sense that you'd connect the two in your dreams. Let me ask a question. How has your work life been?

Are you hard on yourself when you make a mistake professionally?'

Margo looked down at her hands and searched her memory. 'Honestly Jazz? I can't remember making a mistake at work.' Margo sighed loudly, feeling like she hadn't eased up on herself like Jazz had assumed.

Jazz widened her eyes slightly. 'Never? It's quite normal to slip up once in a while.'

Margo shook her head. 'I usually triple check everything I do so that doesn't happen.'

Jazz nodded, staring at her intensely. 'What about your home life?'

Margo barked a short laugh. 'I've made many mistakes there. Including believing my husband when he said he wasn't cheating,' she replied bitterly.

'I'm talking about more practical matters. Like, forgetting to pick something up from the store, or missing an appointment.'

Margo took a deep breath. 'I suppose I have. I missed an important doctor's appointment once . . . and one time, I was really busy going over urgent work documents and forgot a big dinner for Mark's company. I'd turned my ringer off so I could get the work done and when I looked at it later, I saw a bunch of missed calls. I showed up twenty minutes late. He was furious; it was one of our biggest fights.'

'Alright. How did those instances make you feel? Did you beat yourself up over your errors?'

'The doctor's appointment, yes. I felt awful because I incurred a hundred-dollar cancellation fee that we couldn't afford at the time; it was before he got his huge promotion.'

'How did Mark react?'

'I didn't tell him,' she replied sheepishly. 'I wrote a check from my personal account.'

After a pause, Jazz asked, 'What about the dinner?'

'I didn't have to beat myself up because Mark made me feel terrible enough on his own. He was so angry that he wouldn't talk to me for days. He'd been hoping to take a new role that had opened up and a few of his colleagues were also vying for the position. He was the only one invited to the dinner because he was part of a couple and his boss's wife wanted an even number at the table. Mark thought it was his chance to get in with the higher-ups. But then I showed up late and frankly, not looking my best as I had to rush to get ready. I was a sweaty, disheveled mess when I arrived. Mark was so embarrassed.'

'I understand that Mark was upset with you. But how did *you* feel about it?'

'I hated myself. How could I have messed up something so important to the man I loved?'

'But couldn't it just be that you are human, and you made a mistake? You didn't do it on purpose, right?'

Margo clenched her lips together. 'Maybe I did, though.'

Jazz's eyebrows came together. 'How so?'

'I don't know. Maybe I did it unconsciously. Mark has always been a flirtatious guy and every time I went to a work function with him, he'd introduce me to all these women who were so put together and beautiful. I felt plain next to them. They seemed so taken with him and they barely even looked at me. The new position would have made him their supervisor. I'm not gonna lie, it scared me.'

'So, you think you were late to the dinner so he wouldn't get the promotion? Because you were worried that he'd cheat on you with one of these women?'

158

'I don't know! Maybe I'm just *that* screwed up, Jazz.' She hadn't examined her motives this closely about anything in years. Reliving those moments with Jazz made her rethink her harsh reaction to her dad's concerns; perhaps he really did have a reason to worry.

'Is that what Mark told you? That he thought you'd done it on purpose because you are screwed up?'

Margo looked down shamefully. 'Something like that.'

'And you believed it?'

'Honestly, it made sense. He'd picked up on my jealousy with these women before and I couldn't say one hundred percent that I didn't do it for those reasons. I don't think I did, but when he said it that way, it seemed possible. He eventually did get the promotion, but that moment shifted things in our relationship. From then on, everything felt like my fault, like by trying so hard to make things up to him, I was actually just pushing him away.'

'I'm going to let you in on something,' Jazz said, leaning forward to rest her forearms on her knees, clasping her hands as her rings lightly *pinged* against each other. 'Not everything we do has some mysterious inner motive. Sometimes we just react, we make mistakes, and sometimes mistakes have consequences.'

'I guess. But since I'm so careful to avoid mistakes in every other area of my life, it's hard for me to believe that I accidentally messed up so badly.'

'We all do our share of overthinking, of reading more into our actions than we actually intended, especially if someone else is reflecting those thoughts back to us. But that doesn't make you screwed up. It makes you human.' She paused, leaning back thoughtfully. 'I have a homework assignment for you. Well, two actually.'

159

Margo smiled and rolled her eyes. She remembered Jazz's assignments, like when she'd had Margo pick up her childhood diary again to record her thoughts about her Mom every night before bed, and when she told Margo that she had to start a conversation at school with someone, anyone, to break out of her seclusion.

'Before our next appointment, I want you to do a visualization exercise. Lie down in a quiet room and reimagine that night when you were late for the dinner. But change the narrative. Imagine that it was a simple mistake, an oversight that millions of people make every day. If it helps, change the characters. See it as an episode of your favorite show, or movie. See the same scenario but with other people in the main roles. Then when we talk again, I want you to tell me if you still feel like it might have been intentional.'

'OK, I'll do my best,' Margo said.

'And secondly, do you still have your diary?' Margo nodded. 'Start making entries every night before bed. Get everything out like you used to. I think it'll really help.'

'I can do that.'

'Great.' Jazz glanced at the clock. 'Wow, that's the hour already. But if anything comes up for you, give me a call. We have another appointment scheduled for next week, but we can move that up if needed. Next time we can talk more about what happened in your marriage. Some of that may be spilling over into the nightmares too. I just want to caution you not to be too hard on yourself. And I'd also like you to start writing down your dreams when you wake up. The nightmares are what really concern me. Remember all the work we've done in the past and try to use the tools I gave you back then as well. Do you remember the rubber band trick?'

160

Margo held up her wrist to show the black hair tie resting snugly against her skin.

'Good. If you need pulling back to the present because the anxiety is overwhelming you, just snap it gently a few times to ground yourself.'

'Thanks Jazz. I appreciate you seeing me again after so many years.'

'It's good to see you. And to see you doing well, all things considered. You're being very articulate about your feelings, given everything that has happened with your marriage and career. It used to be so much harder for you to open up.'

Jazz walked Margo to the door and waved goodbye. As Margo backed out of her driveway, she realized the tension in her body had lessened, she wasn't gripping the wheel as tightly and she felt more optimistic than she had when she'd arrived. It was like a weight had been lifted, the weight of thinking she was losing control of her mind. *Like my mom.* She shook her head to clear out that thought and drove back toward her house, looking forward to seeing Austin the next day for their interview with Wylie.

As she rounded a bend in the road, she spotted a car behind her. She watched the car as it took all the same turns she did. Fear poured back into her veins, chilling her as it spread like venom that obliterated all the calmness Jazz had just instilled. Her breath became rapid as she kept her eyes on the rearview mirror, certain the car was following her. She turned down the road that led to her house, and the car also turned. She felt like she was going to throw up. Should she call someone? Austin maybe? But then, the car turned off on the last side road before reaching her home and disappeared from view, swallowed up by the trees lining either side. After pulling the car into the driveway and turning it off, she rested her head on the steering wheel and exhaled, her heart pounding. All the work she'd just done with Jazz, vanished in seconds. If she was being honest, she still believed that car might have been following her.

CHAPTER ELEVEN

Margo woke early the next day disoriented, the remnants of a dream fleeing from her mind as she strained to hold on to them. She tried to write it down in her journal as Jazz instructed, but it was mainly anxiety left in its wake. Feeling groggy, Margo made her bed, taking the time to do it properly. It had always irritated Mark when she insisted on making their bed so precisely every morning. He didn't see the point since they didn't use half the decorative pillows she'd stack neatly on top. But her mother had ingrained this in her, the two of them pulling the sheets tight while singing a song her mom had made up about tucking corners and fluffing pillows. Continuing the tradition kept that connection to her mother alive. After swiping her palm over the top of the patchwork quilt her mother had made her to smooth it out, she shuffled out of her room and quickly disarmed the security system before grabbing the newspaper from the front step for her dad. Walking back into the kitchen, she started the coffee and popped a bagel in the toaster. With a big yawn, she pulled her hair up into a loose bun on top of her head and ran her fingers over the small circular mark the elastic band had left on her wrist, thinking how so many things leave traces behind even after they are long gone. A reminder that they had once existed, refusing to be forgotten. Jessie and her mom were no exceptions.

She sighed as she looked at the yellow numbers on the microwave reading 7:47, her dad wasn't awake yet. After she ate, Margo rinsed her dishes and stuck them in the dishwasher. Then she made an omelet for her dad. She plated his food and placed it on the kitchen table just as he tottered into the kitchen. He looked at her with a smile which quickly fell when Margo gave a tight smile in return. She was caught in her complex web of emotions; she was still shaken up by her interaction with Charlie, the car following her home, and the lingering nerves that crept in with the darkness, invading her dreams. And on top of all that, she now had to cope with someone sending her that disturbing Facebook message. Every time her phone went off, a chill coursed through her bones as she wondered if they'd strike again. She didn't feel safe awake or asleep.

'What do you have going on today? You didn't make any for yourself?' he asked as he looked down at the food.

Margo took a sip of her coffee then shook her head. 'No. Austin is picking me up to go interview Wylie Hooper in Asheville and we're planning to have brunch there. I had a bagel earlier that should carry me over.' She glanced at the clock. 'Speaking of, I need to hop in the shower. We'll be back before dinner, but there's some leftover lasagna in the fridge that you can warm up for lunch.'

Her dad nodded and Margo rushed down the hall to get ready, trying to push Charlie's threats to the back

164

of her mind and focus on the day ahead. After showering, putting on makeup and throwing on her favorite red sundress, she still had a good fifteen minutes before Austin was set to pick her up. Looking in the floor length mirror, a memory of her mother popped into her head, wearing a similar red dress to the one Margo was wearing now. Margo was nine and they'd gone to a local creek for a picnic one day, just the two of them. They'd had so much fun splashing in the water and eating cucumber sandwiches cut into small squares, feeling like proper ladies. That is, until some guys arrived across the creek and began jumping in the water, splashing and screaming loudly. Her mom became convinced their spot had become too dangerous and forced Margo to quickly help her pack up the basket and leave. Margo hadn't understood what the danger was, but her mom had been so sure.

She smiled despite the abrupt ending that day had come to, clutching the memory of how beautiful her mother was. Sometimes she was afraid as the years passed that she would forget, that the visuals would start to fade. But she held on to them tightly, wanting to keep her mom alive in her mind for as long as possible. While Margo did get her mom's chocolate brown hair and eyes, the rest of her face resembled her dad. She'd always hated her button nose, much preferring her mother's long aquiline features and cursing that she'd inherited traits that favored her dad's side. Not that he was unattractive, quite the opposite as everyone she grew up with had constantly made very clear, but she wished she could see more of her mom when she looked in the mirror.

Margo jumped up and went out to the backyard, sitting down next to the small rock waterfall and tiny pond she and her father had made together as a memorial to Eloise Sutton. Her mom had loved collecting river rocks. She'd spend hours by the banks of the main river they went to frequently, looking for the perfect rocks – they had to have something special to them, but Margo never knew why she chose some over others. When she and her dad were going through her mother's belongings months after she'd died, Margo cried when she came upon the box of rocks, telling her dad she couldn't bear to throw them out. So, they'd decided to build this tribute in her memory.

Margo reached under the side of the largest rock surrounding the pond, where there was a secret crevice she'd discovered one day, formed by the way the shape of the rocks nestled into the earth. She pulled out the metal box, rusted along the edges and covered in Hello Kitty stickers. She couldn't believe it was still there, dirty but intact. The metal lid squeaked open revealing Margo's favorite mementos from her childhood, her own little time capsule. An old locket her mother used to wear with a photo of her and her dad on one side, Margo as a baby on the other. Margo's first-place ribbon from the local fifth-grade spelling bee; she'd made it to regionals and lost on the word 'duplicitous'. A small snow globe from Niagara Falls when they'd visited for her dad's birthday one year. The program from her mother's memorial service at the church. There were notes from Jessie as well, secrets passed back and forth to one another, the bubbled letters BFF at the bottoms near her signature, back when they were still best friends forever.

Underneath all this were photos and movie ticket stubs. She smiled, rubbing dirt off the fading ink. They didn't get too many good movies at the small theater downtown, so every time there was a movie they actually wanted to see, it was a treat. Looking at the fading stub on top labeled *Blast From the Past*, a 3:30 showing; she frowned and quickly shoved the stubs back into the box.

Margo rifled through the photos next, the first one of her and her parents at the county fair, all holding caramel apples next to a funhouse mirror, laughing at deformed versions of themselves. A tear slipped down Margo's cheek. She'd been twelve years old the day of this photo, just a few weeks shy of her mother's death. Margo put the photo down and tried to stop the tears from flowing, tilting her head back and sniffing deeply. Unable to stop it, the memory of her mom's funeral crashed in on her. The entire town had come to the cemetery after the church memorial to watch as Eloise was lowered into the ground. Margo stuck next to her dad, gripping his hand with her own so he wouldn't leave her too. The Germaine family had stood next to them on the grassy hill next to the casket, Jessie pulling Margo's other hand into her own when Margo's sobs had risen above the reverend's words.

Margo heard a twig snap in the trees that surrounded her backyard and she leapt up, frantically scanning the area. She caught a flutter of movement somewhere to her left and stared pointedly in that direction. Margo snapped the hair band on her wrist a few times. *Probably a squirrel or rabbit*, she thought hopefully, trying to quell her lingering fear that someone was watching her. After no one revealed themselves, she shook her head and went back to the box. It was broad daylight; she would be fine in her own backyard. Nevertheless, she was on high alert now and her tears dried up.

The next photo was from Halloween when she and Jessie went as characters from *Sailor Moon*, an anime girl squad cartoon show that Jessie had been obsessed with. Margo had only liked it because Jessie did. Another photo was from Jessie's tenth birthday, Jessie holding up a large piggy bank she'd gotten as a gift, the goofy pig's smile matching the ones on their own faces. Next was a photo of Jessie at the top of a cheer pyramid. She was so tiny, she always ended up at the top. Margo touched Jessie's smiling face on the glossy paper, wondering how it had all gone so wrong. She looked over the mementos sprawled out on the grass in front of her. The keepsakes were all from before her mom died. After that momentous shift in her universe, not much had seemed worth keeping.

Margo's phone dinged in the pocket of her dress, startling her out of her sad memories. She slowly pulled it out and saw an alert from Instagram. She hadn't looked at it in a while, avoiding it because she didn't want to see photos of Mark and Diana. But she'd finally blocked him the other day and dipped her toe back into browsing the posts, adding the occasional meme that made her laugh to her story. Luckily none of their shared friends had posted anything with them included so she hadn't had to look at their happy faces. Margo hoped that was out of concern for her, but since she hadn't really heard from any of them since she left, she wasn't so sure. After navigating to her Instagram messages, she saw a message from a college classmate laughing at a post she'd shared the other day. Then, noticing a new message request in the top corner, she clicked it with a mix of curiosity and trepidation. A weight plummeted into the pit of her stomach when she saw a new messaging waiting from the handle Gessie_Jermaine. Before opening the message, she navigated to their profile. Like her own, the account was set to private so she couldn't see the person's posts, if there even were any. But the profile photo was the same one used in the Facebook message she received from the same name.

She hesitantly clicked back to the message. In it was a photo of Mark and Diana at their engagement party, staring at each other with big smiles, champagne glasses in their hands. A group of friends, some of her own, were gathered around with glasses hoisted in the air. Just one line accompanied the photo, a quote she vaguely remembered from somewhere. 'While you are too busy minding other people's business, who is busy minding yours?' – Edmond Mbiaka. Margo felt sick. The sting of seeing Mark and Diana celebrating was quickly replaced by fear that this person had discovered something so personal about her. She hadn't posted anything about the divorce online, but they'd still found this ammunition against her. Margo accepted the message and replied, 'Who is this? Why are you doing this to me?'

In response, another photo came through of her walking out of Stout, the night she'd had the confrontation with Charlie. It was cropped in on her face with a bit of the bar's neon sign peeking out from behind her head. Her eyes had been scratched out. The message 'Keep digging and you'll see,' appeared.

Margo's lungs deflated quickly and painfully like she'd been hit by an oncoming train. She asked again who it was, but no reply came. She stared at the message for a long moment before cold fear took control and she hit the block button. Who could it be? Would Charlie go through this much effort just to scare her off?

Margo heard the crunch of tires in front of her house. She rushed to shove everything back in the metal box and returned it to its hiding place. Standing and taking a deep breath, she tried to shake off the dark cloud engulfing her. Her hands continued to tremble, so she shoved them in the pockets of her dress. With one last look around, she walked around the side yard and spotted Austin walking up the front steps.

'Hey!' she called out, trying to keep steady, hoping he didn't hear the quiver in her voice.

When Austin saw her, he smiled, forcing that adorable dimple in his right cheek to pop to the surface. 'Hey,' he called back. 'Wow, you look great.'

Margo looked down at her dress, pulling her hands out to smooth the fabric nervously. 'Thanks,' she said before looking back up. 'Just need to grab my bag and tell my dad we're leaving.'

'OK, no rush, I'll be in the car.'

Margo went in and grabbed her things, hollering out a goodbye to her dad who was now settled on the couch watching a soccer match. She tried to push down thoughts of the messages, not wanting to worry Austin right before an important meeting. Asheville was only a thirty-minute drive from Lake Moss and their conversation naturally turned to Jessie's murder.

'The thing that has always baffled me about the police investigation is, they were pretty quick to jump to the "she most likely ran away" party line.' Austin said, his eyes trained on the road ahead. 'But when we looked at the report, there were just a bunch of unsubstantiated tips called into the tip line. Most were anonymous so they couldn't follow up. The only mention of an actual person was Shannon Welch saying Jessie told her she was going on some trip.'

170

'I can't believe that,' Margo said, shaking her head. 'Shannon was such a gossip and was constantly creating fake rumors so people would pay attention to her. She's hardly reliable and she wasn't even friends with Jessie. I saw her showing off for the local news crew after Jessie's body was discovered too . . . it's absurd. I haven't heard any mention of plans to leave town from any of Jessie's inner circle like Cassidy or Charlie. And she never said anything to me, either.'

'The only solid thing in the report is a note about her search history on her computer, a B&B she had looked up. But there wasn't even an actual reservation, like the police led everyone to believe.'

Margo raised her eyebrows. 'It's the sloppiest investigation I've ever seen. And with my job, I've seen a few. It's no wonder Healey's anxious to redeem himself.'

'Yeah, he seemed pretty intent on wrapping her case up as a runaway and getting the heat off the department. But that clearly backfired.'

'I honestly thought he was in way over his head with this case. Her parents always remained adamant that Jessie never would have run away and left all her personal belongings behind. She'd never tried to run away before, there was no reason to.'

'So, who seems like the most likely suspect at this point?' Austin asked.

'Well, obviously Charlie is my first pick. I've seen his anger first-hand, so it doesn't seem out of the realm of possibility that his temper got away from him one night and he covered it up. But I also got a weird vibe from Tucker and Claire that day at the brewery. I don't know what their motive would be if they're involved, but why would they be concerned about what might come out in the interviews?'

171

'I agree, Tucker seemed annoyed and it's strange he hadn't told Claire about his interview. And Claire seemed like she didn't want us to talk to Tucker again, didn't she?'

'I got that too.'

'And then there's Cassidy. I'm not sure the pageants are enough of a motive, but it could have been an accident. And she had gotten into Duke, so I don't think she would have let anything mess that up. If it was her, I could see her trying to cover her tracks so it didn't ruin her pristine future. She doesn't seem like a violent person, but I could be wrong, it's not like we know her *that* well.'

'Yeah, I'm not sure what to make of Cassidy. She's got this great career now that she clearly loves, and I get that. But she seemed so reluctant to come back to Lake Moss and I wonder if that really was all about her job or if there's more going on there. I mean, her best friend's body was just discovered after fifteen years. Why doesn't she want to be interviewed this time? I would have thought she'd be anxious to help catch Jessie's killer. But she did also seem excited to tell us about Wylie. Maybe that was to point the finger away from herself?'

'I was wondering the same thing . . . Oh wait, I think this is it,' Austin said, squinting out the windshield and pointing to a small red brick building nestled in between a yoga studio and an Italian café.

Margo looked at the sign reading 'Hooper's Brews' and whistled. 'It's cute! I could go for a beer before brunch.'

She smiled at Austin and his gaze lingered on her for a second before he turned and unbuckled himself. As Margo got out of the car, her phone rang. She pulled it out of her bag and saw 'Unknown Number' yet again on the screen. She was tempted to answer it and confront the mysterious caller. But she didn't have time for that right now, so she declined the call. Maybe this time they'd leave a voicemail and she could end the mystery once and for all. But another part of her worried what that message would be. Charlie threatening her? Her social media stalker coming at her through the phone now? Mark trying a different tack? Nothing but disturbing heavy breathing? Before her mind ran too far away from her, she snapped the hair band two times, shook off the foreboding feeling and threw her phone back in her purse.

When they walked into the brewery, the scent of hops, rosemary and something sharp lingered in the air. The brewery had concrete floors and tall ceilings with exposed pipes giving it an industrial feel. Trendy abstract close-up photos showing the fermentation process were scattered across the brick walls. The subliminal message was effective; Margo could almost taste the beer. The place had a diverse crowd, a mix of hipsters with beards and man buns abounded throughout, pretty girls decked out in summer dresses, and two handsome young guys holding hands where they sat at the end of the bar, laughing with the group sitting beside them. Margo appreciated the friendly, relaxed vibe.

Neither Austin nor Margo had known Wylie well since he'd been older than them when they were in school. Nevertheless, the rugged, handsome redhead behind the bar was not what she was expecting. She remembered him as slightly pudgy with a long red beard and scraggly, unkempt hair. Now he was fit, clean shaven and a wealth of rugged appeal. He was flirting with a blonde woman at the far end of the bar, pouring her taste after taste, when he spotted them and walked over to take their order.

Austin put out his hand and said, 'Hey Wylie, not sure if you remember me and Margo from Lake Moss? I'm Austin, my producer let you know we were coming?'

Wylie's eyes lit up in recognition. He looked at the clock. 'Sorry, time flies when you're having fun, I lost track of the hour. Can I get you anything? I don't want to brag, but my beers *are* the best,' he said with a proud smile.

The man exuded charm and allure naturally, Margo had to give him that. Asheville sure had changed him for the better. Margo felt herself staring, unable to look away. His gaze landed on her and he winked, causing her cheeks to grow hot. She was mortified and hoped Austin hadn't noticed her blushing.

'I'd love a beer, what do you recommend?' she asked as she bent forward over the bar to get a closer look at the 'on-tap' board hanging behind it.

Austin shot her a look and she realized her question had come across as flirtatious. She quickly straightened back up and looked away.

Wylie leaned on the bar and said, 'Oh you have to try Hoop's Sour Ginger IPA. It's my personal favorite,' he said, grinning.

Austin leaned in toward Wylie and said, 'We'll take two then.'

Wylie glanced at Austin like he'd forgotten he was there. 'Coming right up! Then we can talk in the back.'

Wylie wandered away to pour their beers. Austin looked at Margo with a knowing grin. She waved a hand in front of her face. 'It's hot in here, he should turn on the air conditioning.'

Austin shook his head and laughed. 'The air conditioning is on, Margo.'

She quickly pulled her hand down and blushed again, embarrassed at her body's involuntary reaction to Wylie. Especially in front of Austin, who she was realizing she had a crush on again after all these years.

'Oh, I guess you're right,' she said dismissively, trying to think of something to change the subject.

Wylie came back with their beers, saving her from herself, and led them to a large room in the back that they used for special events. They sat down at a long rustic wood table with live edges, the sunlight pouring in from the bank of floor to ceiling windows giving the room a warm glow, before taking sips of their beers. The flavors hit Margo's tongue with such intensity it felt like her entire body was shocked awake.

'Wow,' Austin said with a long whistle. 'That's amazing.'

Wylie smiled widely. 'It's good, right?'

'Oh yeah, so different than any other beer I've had. No wonder you've got such a good crowd out there. Well done, Wylie,' Margo replied, going in for a second sip.

He sat back, satisfied that he'd impressed them. 'I do my best. So, what did you want to talk about? Your producer, Amy, was it? Was pretty vague on the phone,' he said, now fully addressing Austin. 'I didn't really even know Jessie.'

Margo and Austin shared a look. Austin took the reins while Margo pulled out her notebook and pen. 'We interviewed Cassidy Quinn the other day and she said you actually did know Jessie.'

Wylie's skin paled a few shades. 'What do you mean?' he replied slowly.

'Look Wylie, I'm gonna be straight with you. She said something about Jessie blackmailing you to sneak her and her friends beer. Is that true?'

Wylie deflated and leaned back in his chair roughly. After a moment he said, 'Well, I don't work for the Abbotts anymore so I guess they can't fire me.' He sighed heavily and dropped his hands into his lap. He seemed hesitant to speak and his eyes darted around like he was looking for an escape. Finally his gaze came back to them. 'I'd been saving up money for years to open this place,' he said, spreading his arms out and looking around his brewery with a soft expression. 'It'd always been my dream. I'd worked for the Abbotts learning the craft since I was sixteen, doing grunt work at first and then working my way up as I got older. I knew this was what I wanted to do with my life and working for them was my way in.'

Margo looked around the room too and had to concede, he'd built a lovely place, and from the taste of it, amazing brews. 'You've done a great job with this place, Wylie.'

'Thanks.' He gave a half-smile before continuing. 'I had enough money saved to open a small spot, but I needed more than that. Brewing beer is like a science, there's so much that goes into it – if you want to make great, complex beer, that is. The Abbotts had that down pat. All I needed were some basic recipes to start experimenting from. Well, and I wanted their unique yeast strain. It had developed amazingly over the years. And not for nothing, I had a big part in that. I just couldn't resist. It takes years to develop that type of house character in a strain, and I knew I'd build off what they'd done once I got to Asheville, so it wasn't going to be a copy; no one would be any the wiser. I had my own ideas. What's the harm in getting some help to get started, right? It's not like I'm competing with Moss Creek. They're national and in a league of their own compared to what I'm doing here.'

'And Jessie caught you?' Austin asked.

Wylie frowned. 'Yeah. It was after hours. I didn't think anyone was still there. I was closing up the place and decided to go into Mr. Abbott's office and see if I could find anything useful. All of a sudden, Jessie was standing there in the doorway watching me rifle through his filing cabinets, asking what I was doing. I tried to lie, but she knew I had no business in his office. So, I came clean and asked her to keep quiet. What did it matter to her?' Wylie shrugged. 'She agreed not to turn me in, but said she wanted something in return. Wanted to be the hero for her friends, you know? I was stuck in a hard place. I said I would do it and she promised not to tell Mr. Abbott.'

'That's it? You just gave her beer and she never said anything?' Austin asked.

'I mean, come on, you knew Jessie. At first it was a six pack here and there, but then it became more frequent and higher quantities; it got risky. I started to worry that Mr. Abbott would notice so I started buying beer with my own money so I wouldn't get caught, but I couldn't afford to keep that up and still save for my own brewery. Every time I saw that girl, she looked at me with this snide, knowing look. She just loved holding it over me.' Wylie shook his head, looking off to the side like he was reliving it right then and there.

'Did she ever tell Mr. Abbott?' Austin asked slowly.

'Nah. Honestly, I think she just liked taunting me with it. Keeping me in fear of her so she could get what she wanted. She seemed to get off on it. You both knew her, she could be really intense when she had her mind set on something.'

Austin and Margo shared another look, not disagreeing

177

with him. 'When was the last time you saw her?' Austin asked.

Wylie squinted, thinking. 'Geez, we're talking fifteen years ago. I guess the last time I can remember was about two weeks before she went missing. Yeah, that was it. I kept expecting her to come back for more beer because it was a weekly thing by that point, every Friday night after Mr. Abbott left for the day she'd show up at the back door. But then she skipped a week and I thought maybe she was letting me off the hook.' Wylie shrugged again.

'Do you remember where you were the night Jessie went missing?' Wylie's face pinched in, like he assumed Austin was accusing him. 'Sorry, I'm asking everyone that question.'

Wylie's face relaxed a little, but his eyes remained narrowed. 'I was at HopCon the entire week she went missing. I went every year after I turned twenty-one. It was the only thing I splurged on while I was saving up money. I didn't even know about her disappearance until I came back that weekend. And of course, everyone was talking about it.'

Margo kept taking notes while Austin thanked Wylie and told him they'd be in touch to set up a day for an on-camera interview if he was willing. The tension of the earlier question seemed to dissipate as they talked.

Wylie looked excited at the prospect, but he leaned in and lowered his voice. 'Look, I'm happy to answer questions about Jessie in a general sense since she hung around the brewery all the time. But I'm not going to admit on camera that I was supplying underage kids with alcohol or that I was stealing from the Abbotts. Either of those could tank my business and get me in some deep legal trouble. If I'm asked about that, I'll deny it. So, if we could skirt around that somehow, then I'm in.'

'I understand,' Austin said, clearly disappointed. Wylie's confession would add some real color to the mystery of Jessie's story. 'I'm not sure my producer will want an interview without that, but I'll ask her and see what she says.'

Wylie deflated, probably hoping to sneak in some free advertising for his brewery on national television. 'Maybe I could offer further insight into the brewery, and Jessie and Charlie's relationship since they were there so much? Those two were so hot and cold, either madly in love or fighting like they were in it for the heavyweight championship . . . I'd really love to do an interview if we can make it happen.'

'I'll see what I can do,' Austin replied.

Austin should show the producer Wylie's photo, Margo thought. That would probably tip the scales in his favor and make her find a way to include him. If he did do an interview, Margo was sure hundreds of women who watched the episode would be glued to their televisions, swooning over Wylie Hooper and planning their next trip to Asheville. They finished the last of their beers and Wylie gave them both a nice growler – a large amber jug to-go – of the sour beer they'd just had.

Austin shook his hand and as they walked to the doors, he whispered, 'If I tell my producer he admitted that about Jessie, she'll want to use it.' Austin looked around the room. 'And he's right, his reputation would be gone if people found out he stole the yeast strain and served underage kids. I'd hate to ruin his business. And who knows what kind of legal troubles it could bring.'

179

His expression was strained as he contemplated what to do.

'Yeah, that's tough. I know you love your job, but it would be hard to live with tanking Wylie's reputation and career, especially if it ends up that he didn't murder Jessie. And after that interview, I don't know about you, but I really don't think he had anything to do with it.'

Austin shook his head. 'I don't either, but who knows for sure, right? I never would have thought something like Jessie's murder would have happened in Lake Moss period and here we are.'

'Could you just tell your producer that he denied it when we asked?'

'Yeah, I could. I just don't know if that's the right thing to do in the middle of a murder investigation. My producer already knows Jessie had something on Wylie.' He heaved a deep sigh. 'For now, I'll tell her about his alibi and say he wouldn't talk about his deal with Jessie. Maybe our researchers can confirm his alibi and take him out of the running as a suspect and it'll be a moot point.'

As they approached the door to exit the brewery, Margo glanced back. Wylie was back to flirting with the blonde woman from behind the bar. She threw her head back, laughing at something he'd said. The woman was petite, and Margo had to admit, looked a little like Jessie, the age progression photo from the missing poster floating to the forefront of her mind. Wylie caught her looking at him and his smile became slightly strained. Austin opened the door for Margo, and she tore her gaze away, following him down the block to their planned brunch spot. Margo's mouth was already watering at the thought of the crab mac n' cheese and fresh oysters

Austin had gushed about. But in the back of her mind, she kept thinking about Jessie and Wylie's secret transactions. Was it really all about the beer? Or did Wylie have a type? And if there was more going on between them than he'd admitted, maybe he'd been jealous of her relationship with Charlie. Was that enough of a motive?

February 16, 2004

Dear Diary,

Jessie and I had another tutoring session today. I feel like we are totally turning a corner and becoming besties again. After we finished a practice test, she leaned in and started complaining about Cassidy! To me, can you believe it? Her and Cassidy are supposed to be sooooo close, but apparently Cassidy is getting on her nerves lately. She was all, 'Cassidy is being such a sore loser! Like it's my fault that the judges think I'm prettier than her. And now she's sooo whiney because she misses the attention and the prizes! Girl needs to get over it!

It was the first time Jessie has confided in me about her friendship with Cassidy. I thought Cassidy had totally replaced me, but it seems like I'm finding my way back in after all! I mean it was so dumb of Cassidy to ever suggest Jessie do the pageants with her anyway. Jessie IS way prettier and is a magnet for attention. Cassidy never stood a chance. And then Jessie talked about the dress Cassidy wore to school today. She said it looked like someone threw up on her. Which is weird because when I met Jessie after school for our session, she was talking to Cassidy and saying how cute the dress was. I guess Jessie was just being kind and didn't want to hurt her feelings. It's so nice not being the one talked about, for once.

182

CHAPTER TWELVE

Margo woke up, shooting straight up in her bed. She was clammy, her heart pounding. *Another nightmare.* She wished so desperately they would stop. Writing in her diary wasn't helping this time, not like when she was a kid. She picked up her cell phone off the nightstand with a shaking hand and scrolled through her notifications, quickly spotting a text from Austin.

'Wanna meet up before we interview Tucker today?'

Grateful for a distraction, she quickly tapped out a reply. 'Absolutely. I'll grab us some coffees and meet you in Town Square in an hour?'

'Perfect,' he replied, putting a smile on Margo's face, pushing the bad dream further back into her subconscious. She was intrigued to see what Tucker had to say after their weird moment outside Moss Creek Brewing.

Throwing on a pair of linen high-waisted shorts that tied in a bow around her waist and tucking in a light-weight t-shirt, she quickly ran a brush through her hair and applied light makeup. She turned off the security system and hurried into the kitchen, knowing she needed to make sure her dad was settled before she left for such a large chunk of the day.

She started cracking eggs for a veggie omelet when she heard him hobble into the kitchen behind her. 'Hey, I'm almost done making your breakfast if you want to take a seat. Then I'll need to run out to meet Austin,' she said without turning around.

'You don't have to do that, Margo, I can make something for myself.'

'It's OK, I don't mind,' she said, turning around to grab him a plate.

'You look tired, sweetie, are you sleeping alright?' he asked, studying her expression. 'Is it the nightmares again?'

'Um, yeah, but it's nothing,' Margo said, not meeting his gaze.

'Margo, you remember how bad the nightmares got after your mom passed, and how much that fear invaded your waking hours too. It's not good for you, kiddo. I'm sure all this stuff with Jessie's body being found is dragging up a lot of emotions. I don't want to see them terrorize you again.'

Margo still couldn't bring herself to look at him. 'I know, Dad. I'm trying to manage it, really. I've already spoken to Jazz about them, and we have another meeting on the books. It might just take some time to get them under control.'

'Maybe you should step away from helping Austin. He can do it without you; it's his job after all, not yours.'

'No,' Margo snapped quickly. Then softened. 'No, I want to keep working with him on it. The interviews won't go on forever, I'm sure the dreams will subside eventually.' Hoping to stem the tide of this conversation,

184

she turned and placed his plate on the table. 'Do you need anything else before I head out?'

'No, no, go meet your friend,' he said with an annoyingly knowing smirk.

She ignored it and grabbed her bag before heading out to her car. Margo picked up two coffees and freshly baked croissants from Peak Java near Town Square. It was only a block from where she and Austin planned to meet, making it an easy pit stop. Holding his coffee and the pastry bag in one hand, she took a sip of her coffee with the other. Margo had them add an extra shot of espresso to her latte, and she could almost feel the electric jolt from the caffeine buzzing through her.

Exiting the café, the summer air engulfed her and she regretted not getting her latte iced. She made her way over to a bench and settled herself to wait for Austin, flipping through her notebook. She wanted to be fresh on every detail from their previous interviews before going into the one today with Tucker. He was the final piece of Jessie's popular clique, and also happened to be Charlie's alibi.

As Margo sat there reading, she heard a group of women's voices break out in loud chatter in the quiet street behind her. Turning to look over her shoulder, she saw three women from the local businesses coming together in one of the alleys, lighting up cigarettes for a smoke break. One had on an apron from the hair salon, one a grocer uniform, and the other Margo didn't recognize. The women were oblivious to Margo's presence, gossiping loudly about their guests that morning.

'Ya know,' the one from the salon said in a high-pitched, nasally voice. 'Did I ever tell y'all that I saw Charlie Abbott the night Jessie disappeared?'

'Oooh, no! Spill!' one of the other women said excitedly, like she'd just won the lottery.

Margo scooted closer in their direction on the bench, craning her neck to hear every detail.

'So, I was out here, minding my own business, takin' a smoke break, ya know, even though I wasn't supposed to after already taking two earlier in the day but whatever.' The other women laughed. 'When I saw a car pull up out there on the far side of the alley near the back lot,' she continued, hooking her finger over her shoulder. 'At first, I didn't think anything of it. But then I heard some shoutin' and looked over. They were under that streetlight so they were lit up, and wouldn't you know, it was Charlie Abbott and Jessie Germaine arguing in the front seats. It must have been one of Charlie's parents' cars, because it wasn't that truck we always saw him driving around.'

'Wow,' the grocery woman said. 'You saw them arguing? You're sure it was that day?' They were rapt with attention.

'I sure did. And it was definitely the right day. I remember being a little shaken up the next morning when I saw on the news that she'd gone missing, but truth be told, I didn't think too much of the argument. Jessie had gotten out of the car after a minute and slammed the door, storming off. Charlie got out of the car too and ran after her, grabbing her arm and whipping her around. But she shook him off pretty quick and walked off. He yelled something like, "Fine, be that way! I don't need you," and climbed back in the car. He sped off in the opposite direction.' She shrugged one shoulder.

'Wow,' grocer woman said again, the third woman smacking her gum loudly as she stared in amazement. 'And you didn't tell anyone?'

'They seemed to have made a pretty clean break, so I just assumed whatever happened to her had to have been later after that. Plus, my boss would have had my ass if I'd gotten caught taking that extra smoke break. I couldn't afford to lose my job. He'd already written me up twice. And can you just *imagine* if I'd run my mouth and sent the police after the most powerful family in town? Innocent or guilty, they would have run me right outta Lake Moss.'

'So true,' the third women said, shaking her head. 'But that's just plain creepy now that her body has been found.'

'I know, right?' salon woman said, excitement in her voice at finally sharing this nugget of information. Margo could only imagine how hard it was to keep to herself.

'It wouldn't have done much good anyway,' grocer woman said sympathetically. 'I mean, you remember the police were pushing the story that Jessie probably just ran away and would show up one day when she was ready to come back. And remember how badly the police botched that drug bust a few months before she disappeared? Useless, just useless they were. It's no wonder no one in this town tells them nothin.'

'That's true,' the salon woman said, clearly placated. 'I couldn't believe when all that evidence just disappeared.' The other women shook their heads, making a *tsk tsk* sound. 'And of course, Jessie's case seemed like a hot mess from the get-go, especially with the Abbott family being a little too close to the missing girl for their own comfort. I'm sure they were hand-in-hand with the police tryin' to protect Charlie. Who knows what was real and what wasn't? Well, anyway, just been on my mind lately with all these new rumors swirling about.'

'Anything particularly juicy?' the grocery woman asked, hungry for more.

'Well, I heard some ladies in the salon yesterday talking about how Charlie is saying the last time he saw Jessie was at the rally right after school that day. Suspicious, isn't it? To lie about something like that?'

Margo could tell the woman was getting great joy out of the other two hanging on her every word. Was what she said true? Or was she just fishing for attention. It was hard to tell, but nevertheless, an interesting addition to consider.

The third mystery woman spoke up now, leaning in and lowering her voice, but Margo was grateful she could still make out the words. 'I don't know, if it was me? I'd put my money on that Tucker boy.'

'Tucker? Why's that? Isn't he a respectable family man now?' the grocer asked.

'You remember that senior prank, don't you? My little sister was in their class so she came home bursting at the seams to talk about it.'

'I don't think I remember any prank,' the salon woman said. 'What was it? I was a bit out of the loop on what the school kids were up to, I was a few years out at that point.'

'Jessie had apparently goaded Tucker into pulling off the senior prank to steal Mr. Abernathy's bowling pin. Remember? Every class did it.'

'Oh, that's right. It's been so long since high school, my memory isn't so great anymore,' the salon lady replied, tapping her finger against her head.

'So, Tucker tried it, but he got busted and suspended from school. He was freaking out, livid with Jessie, because he'd gotten into some fancy college with a morality clause in his acceptance, and he was terrified they were going to rescind his offer. Sounds like pretty good motive to me.'

188

'Didn't his dad get involved though and had it removed from his record?' the grocer asked.

'Not sure, but if his dad did have to step in, I'm sure he wasn't too thrilled with Tucker,' the third woman said. 'He's an intimidating man, big and brooding. I would not have wanted to be in his crosshairs.' The other two made appreciative noises of agreement. Margo's head was spinning. Thinking back, she did remember Tucker getting in trouble for that prank senior year. She hadn't realized that Jessie had played a role in it.

'Hey, Margo,' Austin said with a smile as he climbed out of his car where he'd parallel parked across from her. She was so engrossed in the gossip she hadn't even noticed him arrive.

'Oh, hey!' she said back, standing and greeting him with a hug. 'Here's your coffee, and there's a croissant in the bag with your name on it.'

'Great, thanks!' he said gratefully. Margo noticed Town Square felt quiet again and turned around to see the ladies returning to their respective shopfronts. That was all she was going to get from them today, but it had been full of intel that she needed to share with Austin immediately.

'Wait till you hear this, though,' she said, and quickly recounted everything she'd overheard. His eyes were wide with intrigue.

'Well things sure haven't changed around here, have they?' he laughed.

'Not at all,' she said, returning his smile.

'You know, I do remember that prank thing being a big deal when Tucker got caught. But it totally slipped my mind until now.'

'Same here,' Margo replied. 'And I didn't realize that Jessie had any connection to it.'

'Which store did the first woman go into? My producer may want to interview her about seeing Charlie and Jessie fighting that night.'

Margo shielded her eyes with her hand from the bright sun. 'The salon, right over there,' she said, pointing her finger at the small white shop with photos of women in different hairstyles lining the front window.

'OK, thanks. You know what?' Austin said, looking at his watch. 'We have time before we need to meet Tucker. What do you say we pop over to the school and see if they'll give us any information on his alleged suspension or what happened with that prank.'

'Let's do it,' Margo said. 'If you want to leave your car, I can drive this time.'

'After you,' he said, with a gentlemanly sweep of his arm. She smiled, and they made their way to her car to head to Lake Moss High for the first time in fifteen years.

CHAPTER THIRTEEN

As Austin and Margo walked up the familiar brick steps of their old high school, vivid memories flashed behind Margo's eyes. The throngs of students pushing into the school, joking around while Margo stood on the outskirts, watching. Charlie and his bully football teammates throwing poor pimply Frankie Taylor into the trashcan that still stood on the other side of the steps. Margo waving to Jessie as she passed by with Cassidy on their first day of high school, the two girls laughing and whispering instead of returning her wave. The shame she'd felt at being forgotten by Jessie, unable to bounce back from the two years Margo had spent withdrawn and grieving.

Jessie had been so stunning it was hard not to stare when Margo passed her in the halls. She'd morphed into a striking beauty with pixie, elfish features, her upturned eyes and cupid's bow lips no longer too large for her face. Her eyes were so big it had seemed like she was peering right into your soul, seeing every last secret. Charlie used to make fun of her in elementary school, calling her Dobby, the house elf from the Harry Potter books, which was a bit kinder than the Moaning Myrtle reference he'd donned on Margo. But all of a sudden, the two were the most beautiful couple in school. In some ways, Margo had felt betrayed, like Jessie had switched to the dark side. Jessie had hated Charlie when they were younger. It seemed Jessie had changed in more ways than just appearance while Margo had been hiding from the world.

Austin opened the heavy front door and the familiar halls greeted them, now painted a dusky beige rather than the stark white she remembered. They walked up to the admin desk, recognizing Mrs. Baker, who was still the school administrator after all these years. Luckily, the school was still open due to summer school, but the halls were quiet, the smattering of students likely in class at that moment.

'Austin Hughes and Margo Sutton! What a sight for sore eyes. What are you two doing here?'

'Hi, Mrs. Baker,' they said in unison, feeling like students again. Margo hoped that time they'd spent volunteering as student aides in the front office had paid off and would make Mrs. Baker open up to them now.

'Do you have a second to chat? I'm working on the *Into Thin Air* production crew and we had a few quick questions.'

'Well, look at you, Austin! I'm impressed, you've really made something of yourself!' Margo noticed Austin blush and she stifled a smile. Like herself, Austin seemed to have a hard time taking compliments. 'Sure, I'd love to be interviewed!' In this small town, Margo knew most people were itching to be a part of the new episode, except for the key players it seemed. 'Come on back to my office.' They followed her to the small office off the reception area and sat down across from her desk. 'So, what can I do for you two today?'

'We had some questions about Tucker Harding.'

'Tucker? Not sure how helpful I'll be but go ahead and shoot.'

'Were you aware of his suspension for stealing Mr. Abernathy's bowling pin trophy?'

The annual prank that each class before them had accomplished was a source of competition amongst each senior class. Mr. Abernathy was a strict teacher and a harsh grader. He was also a champion bowler. He'd won a regional tournament some years before and always had that engraved trophy on the shelf behind his desk in the classroom. He'd frequently use bowling analogies that exasperated his students. The prank was their way of getting back at him, telling him not to take himself so seriously. And each class came up with new and inventive ways of returning the trophy before the end of the year, like leaving it on the roof of his house or in the back seat of his car. Margo could never figure out why he still kept it at the school, knowing that the goal of every incoming senior class was to steal it. But maybe he secretly hoped he'd catch one in the act and feel the satisfaction of enacting justice. It seemed with Tucker that he'd gotten his wish.

'Of course!' She put her hand up to one side of her mouth like she was telling them a secret, lowering her voice as she looked around. 'Between us, I always thought Mr. Abernathy took that silly little prank too seriously. He always got it back so why make a big stink about it?' She shrugged. 'But he had Principal Lawson's ear so when they finally caught a student in the act, he was excited to have someone to make an example of.'

193

'But we heard the suspension was removed from Tucker's permanent record. Is that true?'

Mrs. Baker shook her head in disapproval. 'Oh yes. Tucker's dad, Clint, was friends with Principal Lawson. They'd gone to college together at that all boys private school, Hampden-Sydney, the one Tucker himself got into. The ethics code was strongly enforced, and Clint was afraid if the college found out about the suspension for stealing, they'd rescind his acceptance. He came by after classes ended when we were preparing for commencement ceremonies and was only in Principal Lawson's office for twenty minutes before Lawson told me to remove the suspension. Boy's club, I swear,' she said, shaking her head again. 'But seeing as how I thought the suspension was a little harsh in the first place over a harmless prank, I didn't argue. Clint was a bit intense, and I heard that he'd donated a significant amount of money for the new scoreboard we needed which I'm sure helped grease the wheels.'

Austin shot Margo a quick glance. She was furiously jotting down notes in shorthand but caught his look. 'So, it was just wiped clean? Like it never happened?' Austin asked.

'You betcha! Lucky for Tucker his dad had the right friends and the money to help his cause.'

Austin rose from his chair and Margo followed suit, tucking her notepad and pen into her purse. 'Thanks for your time, Mrs. Baker,' Austin said.

Her face fell. 'That's it? No other questions? Do you want me to do an on-camera interview? I'd be happy to, you know.'

'That won't be necessary at this stage, we're just gathering some background information. But we really appreciate you being so candid with us, and my producer will reach out if she thinks she can use you on camera.'

Mrs. Baker seemed disappointed but nodded and walked them to the door.

'It was nice seeing you again,' Margo called out as they walked down the steps.

'You too, dear. How's your dad holding up?' she asked.

'He's recovering well, and eager to be back. Thanks for asking,' Margo replied.

Mrs. Baker smiled, 'Glad to hear it.'

They jumped back into the car and set out toward Tucker's place, not far from the school. Tucker and Claire's home was modest, a small white house with green trim, a tiny front yard littered with bikes and toys, nestled at the end of a small cul-de-sac, surrounded by forest on one side and similar small homes on the other.

Margo knocked on the door, with weathered paint and crayon drawings all over. She heard kids laughing and yelling from inside the house, Tucker's loud voice booming at them to keep it down. He opened the door a few seconds later. Tucker had always been a good-looking guy, though while Charlie had been strikingly handsome, Tucker had been the epitome of the word *cute*. But now, he'd filled out, clearly lifting weights regularly. His wavy brown hair was cut close and he wore a tight-fitting t-shirt that emphasized his muscles. But Tucker still had that less harsh nice-boy look about his face. He'd never been overtly mean like Charlie, but he'd never stood up to him either, always laughing as Charlie made jokes about his classmates.

'Hey Austin. Margo,' he said, tilting his head slightly toward her. 'Come in. Sorry it's kind of a madhouse around here today. Claire took the day off from work and is having a girls' day with some friends in Hendersonville for her birthday. So, I've got the kids all by myself.'

'You have three kids, right?' Margo asked, thinking back to when she saw them at the brewery.

Tucker smiled, clearly a proud father. 'Yep, three little ones. Eleven, five and three years old,' he said, picking up a small plastic tricycle from their path and placing it to the side. He was acting much more polite than Margo anticipated, almost as if they hadn't even had the awkward moment in the parking lot, but maybe he was trying to play nice for the sake of his portrayal on the show.

'What a handful,' Austin replied with an impressed smile.

'Yeah, but I love them. Even if they are little monsters,' he said with a grin. The noise level in the other room rose another notch. Tucker looked toward the bedroom nervously. 'Sorry, can you give me a second?'

'Sure,' Austin replied. 'We're in no rush.'

Margo and Austin sat down on a dingy beige loveseat just inside the living room while Tucker walked into the bedroom where the kids were playing and shut the door, muffling the noise within. Their house, while definitely small for a family of five, was cozy. The carpet needed a good deep cleaning and their eat-in kitchen off the living room could use major updating, but it felt like a home filled with love. Photos of their kids hung all over the walls and covered most surfaces in the living room. Everyone looked happy in the photos. In one on the fireplace mantel, the entire family was on the slopes of a snowy hill, decked out in ski gear.

Tucker came back into the room. 'Sorry about that. I put on Peter Rabbit so hopefully that'll occupy them until we're done.'

'No problem.'

'So, how can I help you?' Tucker asked as he sat down across from them on the matching beige couch.

'We're doing all the pre-interviews for the new episode of *Into Thin Air*. My producer said she already set up a date to do your on-camera interview?'

Tucker nodded, 'Yeah, it's in a few days. I'm assuming it'll be similar to what we did the first time around?'

'For the most part yes, but some new information has come to light. We just wanted to ask you a couple of questions about the time surrounding Jessie's disappearance.' Tucker looked uncomfortable for a moment, then nodded. 'Just to reconfirm, where were you the night Jessie went missing?'

Without skipping a beat, he replied, 'I was with Charlie. We were watching a movie at his parents' place. We had a few beers and played some pool. I was home by midnight, my parents can verify that.'

Austin nodded and Margo jotted down notes. But she remembered he'd used those exact words in the episode fifteen years ago. It was a little too precise.

'Did Jessie ever mention a trip she was planning?'

Tucker shook his head. 'Jessie and I ran in the same circle but I wasn't her confidante by any means. She never said anything about that around me. If there was a trip, she'd have been more likely to tell Cassidy about it.'

Austin nodded and then took a deep breath. 'OK thanks. We also wanted to ask you about the prank that got you suspended right before graduation.'

Tucker's eyes narrowed. 'What's that got to do with anything? It was a stupid childhood prank. And it happened a month before she went missing.'

'We heard it was Jessie who pressured you into it,' Austin pressed.

Tucker paused, assessing Austin's intentions. 'Yeah, she did.' He looked down and shook his head. 'You knew Jessie, she'd push and push until she got what she wanted. She and Charlie had attempted to steal the trophy the week before, but the janitor caught them sneaking into the school after hours. That really pissed them off. They kept going on about not wanting to be the only class that couldn't do it. Then one night, we were all drinking at the swimming hole. Jessie had brought two twelve packs and between the five of us, we finished them all. I was pretty drunk.'

'Which five of you?' Margo asked glancing up from her notepad. There was a core group, but they sometimes had periphery friends around them, and she wanted to make sure her notes were accurate for Austin.

'The two couples, Charlie and Jessie, and myself and Claire. And then Cassidy. Sorry I still don't see what this has to do with anything.'

'Can you just tell us how it went down?' Austin asked.

Tucker exhaled loudly, clearly getting annoyed. 'Jessie kept taunting me, saying I was a pussy because I wouldn't even try. She was a girl and even she tried to steal the trophy, going on about how she had more balls than I did. Finally, I got mad and said I'd do it, just to shut her up.' His face was red, the memory resuscitating his anger even after fifteen years. Then, realizing how bad that sounded in light of Jessie's death, he cleared his throat and continued. 'I broke into the school through the door at the back of the locker rooms that never latched properly. I managed to grab the trophy and make it out successfully.'

198

'You didn't get caught that night?'

Tucker shook his head. 'Nope. I thought I'd gotten off scot-free. Jessie and Charlie were ecstatic and we went to Charlie's house afterwards to celebrate and decide how we wanted to return it. But the next day I was called to the office. Apparently, Mr. Abernathy had gotten fed up with the prank and installed a camera to catch the culprits. So, there was no way to deny it. I was suspended and my dad was furious. He was already mad at me because a week before, my mom's muscle relaxers went missing and he assumed I took them. I didn't, pills were never my thing. But when I got suspended, it tipped him over the edge and he wouldn't let me go on a senior trip I was planning with my friends. It didn't matter that he couldn't prove I took the pills, because there was solid proof that I had stolen the trophy. So I had to sit at home while Charlie, Lance and the others went on a guys' weekend.'

'Were you angry at Jessie?'

Tucker shot daggers at Austin, obviously knowing what he was hinting at, and said, 'Of course I was. Wouldn't you be? I never would have done it if she hadn't goaded me into it. But my dad said I was in control of my own actions and I only had myself to blame. As an adult, now I can see he was right. At the time, I was angry. But not angry enough to kill her. It was a dumb prank, and after my suspension was done, I got over it.'

'Weren't you worried that it would affect your acceptance to Hampden-Sydney? I've heard they have a pretty strict ethics code,' Austin asked.

Tucker was getting more and more agitated as they inched closer to what they really wanted to ask. Wringing his hands in his lap, his eyes darted to the side sporadically.

Tucker was a smart guy. Margo was sure he knew where Austin was headed. *But he's definitely hiding something*, Margo thought.

'My dad was. I didn't think they'd care that much over one suspension with an otherwise clean record. We all make mistakes. But my dad looked it up and read the code to me which made me a little nervous. I'd worked like hell for the grades to get into his alma mater. But my dad went and talked to Principal Lawson since they were old friends and got him to take it off my record to be on the safe side. So why would I kill Jessie over that? I was in the clear.'

Margo and Austin shared a look. Austin cleared his throat, obviously nervous about confronting Tucker with his next statement. 'We just came from the school. Mrs. Baker was there the day your dad came to talk to the principal. She said that didn't happen until after classes ended, which would have been after Jessie went missing.'

It was like a bomb had been dropped. They sat in a tense silence as Tucker's face reddened and he clenched his fists. One of the kids in the other room started crying loudly. Tucker looked quickly in that direction before turning back to Austin.

'Look, I didn't kill her. And if you're looking to point the finger at anyone it should be Charlie. You know he got rough with her sometimes.'

Margo had a flashback to the bar when Charlie had shoved her. She'd heard rumors about him getting rough with Jessie, but she'd assumed they were just that. Rumors. She couldn't imagine Jessie letting anyone push her around. But then Margo remembered the time Jessie came to school with bruises on her arm.

'What do you mean by rough?' Austin asked, pressing for more details.

Tucker splayed out his hands. 'Nothing major, he didn't hit her or anything like that. But he pushed her a couple of times when they were arguing. I had to pull him away from her once or twice. And then there was that one time at Luke's party.'

'I remember hearing about that,' Austin said, and Margo nodded, more details from the past sliding into place.

'Yeah, they got into a big fight because she was flirting with a guy from another school. I'm pretty sure she did it just to rile him; she loved the drama of it all. But the fight escalated faster than normal because Charlie was wasted. He punched the guy and then grabbed her to pull her away. Somehow, he twisted her wrist in the process. She screamed and we dragged Charlie away from her. He said he hadn't meant to hurt her, but who knows, honestly.'

Margo looked at Tucker inquisitively, wondering why he was suddenly so willing to throw his friend under the bus. 'Aren't you and Charlie still friends?'

'Not like we were in high school, but I guess you could say we're friends in a loose sense. He's still in party mode, just wants to get drunk and rage all the time. I have a family now, it's not all about getting smashed for me anymore. He used to constantly try to get me to go drinking with him when I moved back after college, but I guess he got tired of hearing about my family obligations. We don't really hang out anymore except the occasional barbeque or pick-up football game.'

Austin looked at Tucker for a moment, sizing him up. 'Here's the thing, Tucker,' Austin said slowly. 'Weren't you with Charlie the night she went missing? You were each other's alibis. So how could Charlie have done it if he was with you?'

201

Tucker's face grew red again, his left pectoral jumping up and down as his agitation grew. *Or is it guilt?* He looked like a caged animal, his eyes darting around like he was trying to come up with a story, a way to escape, seeing how he'd slipped up.

'I don't have anything else to say. I've got to get back to my kids. You can see yourselves out,' he said dismissively.

He rose from the couch and went to open the bedroom door where he'd closed the kids in at their start of their conversation. Margo looked at Austin and they both widened their eyes quickly at the turn the conversation had taken. It was clear Tucker wasn't being completely honest with them. They rose and left the house, the screams from the kids fading as they hopped in the car. They were both silent as Margo drove away. But she was sure they were thinking the same thing. *What is Tucker Harding hiding?*

CHAPTER FOURTEEN

The next morning, Austin and Margo sat across from each other at a small window table at Blue Mountain Café, the diner just outside of downtown. It had the best breakfast food around, and Margo was glad to see that hadn't changed in all the years since she'd come here as a kid. It had been her favorite place to eat with her parents, and later just her dad, because it was built to resemble a tall tree-house. The tables and chairs were all chiseled out of trees, with live edges creating a rustic feel. The café had three differently named levels, all accessible by a steep circular staircase, offering stunning views of the Blue Ridge Mountains. Margo had requested her favorite level, The Ridge, at the top where you could see miles and miles of forest and fluffy clouded skies; it always felt breathlessly high up there. She and Austin took their time savoring the last bites, talking over their plans.

'It's nice that the Germaines decided to hold a funeral service for Jessie, now that her remains have been released from evidence,' Austin said, taking a sip of his coffee and gesturing to the waitress walking by holding a coffee pot for a refill.

The thought of Jessie's remains made the bite of bacon Margo was chewing turn to dust, sticking thick in her throat as she tried to swallow. She pursed her lips and nodded as the smiling server asked if she too wanted her coffee topped off. Margo nudged the cup in her direction, grateful for the hot swig helping dislodge the trapped bacon bits as she took a sip.

Clearing her throat as Austin looked at her, she said, 'Yeah, I mean, I know from experience that closure isn't *really* a thing after the death of a family member, but I hope that it helps them, everyone really, to say goodbye.'

'Jessie's brother, Brandon, came back in town for the service. Apparently, he hasn't been back since Jessie disappeared.'

'Oh, wow, really?' Margo asked, losing her appetite despite the several bites remaining on her plate.

She leaned back into the chair, looking out the window as rain flecks speckled the glass, obscuring her view of the mountains. Behind the veil of water, she could just make out the swaying greenery. Reaching up to her face and wiping an eye, she realized a few tears had fallen. Hastily sweeping them away, she kept her eyes glued to the window, embarrassed to let Austin see her distress. He was silent, giving her the moment. Margo watched as the rain picked up its pace, like Lake Moss itself was crying for Jessie.

Margo sniffled, and began running her fingers repeatedly through her long hair where it draped over her shoulder. As soon as she noticed her hands were shaking, she dropped them to her lap under the table and clasped them. Margo hated funerals. Ever since attending her mother's as a young teen, she avoided them religiously. But she would need to go to Jessie's. Not only would she be expected to attend, she was close to Jessie after all, but it was the right thing to do to support Jessie's family.

'Are you OK?' Austin asked, looking at her with concern.

'Sorry, I'm fine, it's just . . .' she took a long sip of water, setting it back down and sniffling again as she returned her hands to her lap to still them. 'I'm just so heartbroken for Jessie's family. For what they must be going through right now. I spent a lot of time around them as a kid, and they're such great people. I haven't even seen them since I've been back or given them my condolences. I keep telling myself at least they can bury her now, but . . .'

She trailed off as a few more tears blazed a hot path down her cheeks. How could she ever look them in the eyes at the service? They had to have heard she was back and noticed her absence. She pulled up one of her hands and fidgeted with her silverware on the table, aligning it precisely next to the plate. Austin reached over and set his own hand gently over hers, halting her movement. She looked up and gave him a sad smile, the weight of his hand comforting.

'I'm sorry,' Austin said, giving her hand a light squeeze. 'I know this must be hard. You knew Jessie a lot better than I did, and I forget that sometimes. I just get so wrapped up in the job . . . I hope I haven't been insensitive.'

'No reason to apologize,' Margo said, pulling her hand back as he lifted his own. 'You've been great. I know this is a huge opportunity for you.'

He gave her a grateful smile. 'Well, Amy thinks I should go try to talk to Brandon and her parents. They've been hard to get on the phone, trying to maintain privacy from press and nosey neighbors, but she's hoping if I just show up that they'll give me a chance. I understand if you don't want to come, but . . .' he trailed off.

'No,' Margo said, sitting up straight and trying to quiet the anxiety and sadness battling to consume her. 'I should be there. They may be more willing to talk to you if they see me.' She forced a smile, trying to put on a brave *I swear I'm OK* expression for Austin's benefit, but it felt more like a grimace.

Nevertheless, Austin seemed grateful. Margo had to face them eventually, and better to do it in a smaller setting first than amongst the crowd at the funeral service.

'Thanks, Margo. I think we should try to confirm Cassidy's story with Brandon. Remember she said that Jessie claimed to have plans with him that night? That's why she couldn't watch *American Idol*? Maybe he can tell us what they were doing and where, see if it leads to anything new.'

Margo nodded, taking a final sip of coffee as the waitress placed their bill face down on the table. Austin was quick to scoop it up, pulling his wallet out of his pocket.

'You don't have to do that, Austin,' Margo protested, trying to reach for her bag on the seat next to her. 'You're going to have to let me pay at some point.'

'It's a business breakfast, right? I'll expense all . . .' he looked down at the receipt and laughed heartily as he said, 'twelve dollars of it. Man, I miss prices like this.'

Margo laughed and let go of her purse. 'OK, fine. But the next meal is on me.'

Margo and Austin opened the restaurant's door and crouched over, bolting for Austin's Jeep a few spaces away from the entrance. By the time they got inside and snapped the doors shut, they were soaked. Neither of them had realized a pop-up summer storm was on the radar today. They laughed as they took in each other's appearances.

'Well, this certainly looks professional for an interview, doesn't it?' Austin said as he shook his head like a dog after a bath, sending water flying everywhere.

Margo held up her hands to shield herself, but she was already so wet from head to toe that it really didn't matter. It felt good to laugh, pushing down some of the anguish she'd been consumed by just moments ago. Her black cotton t-shirt dress clung to her body, her hair plastered along the side of her face and collarbone.

'You know, I think salvaging this is probably impossible. My house is pretty close to the Germaines', why don't we make a pit stop to get dried off and change. I'm sure my dad has something you could borrow, you're both freakishly tall.'

Austin laughed again and turned the key to start the engine. 'Thank god, otherwise you'd tower over me!' he said.

After their pit stop, they left Margo's house, this time armed with umbrellas and towels to lay down on the car seats. The Germaines' house was nestled slightly further up in the thicket of trees at the top of a narrow, windy road. It was part of the reason they'd been so close as children. Margo's mom had been friends with Jessie's mom, sharing babysitters and taking turns watching the girls in a pinch. Jessie and Margo had formed an instant bond from all the time spent together at a young age.

As Austin navigated the bends in the road, Margo smiled sadly as pieces of memory flashed through her mind at lightning speed of all the times in her youth she'd traveled this very road. Her mom in the driver's seat, matching long brown hair whipping around with the window down. Playing in Jessie's yard, running around carefree as their moms drank a glass of red wine on the front porch. Lying on Jessie's bed next to her as they did their homework, Mrs. Germaine bringing them a plate of freshly baked brownies as a treat. Finding tadpoles in the creek behind Jessie's house. There had been so many good memories, before Margo's world had fallen apart. She pushed them all down, refusing to cry again.

The windshield wipers and falling rain momentarily obscured Margo's view of the house as they approached, but when Austin brought the car to a stop, she knew they'd arrived. She caught glimpses of the house through the swipes of the wipers. Growing up, Margo had always loved the Germaines' house. It was like someone had mashed together a traditional southern home with something from a small German village. The bottom half was all red brick, but the top half was painted off-white and had bold dark brown vertical boards spaced evenly across the façade. The area above the entryway was a steeply pitched triangle roof, with a dark brown tip and the same brown framing the second-floor windows. The large wooden door was rounded on top and adorned with oversized black metal brackets and sconces normally alive with fire on either side. Even though everything had changed, here, it was exactly the same.

Popping open their umbrellas, they hurried up to the front door and Austin pressed the doorbell. Margo was comforted to see that her favorite decorative aspect as a kid was still there too. An oversized brass lion door-knocker fixed in the center of the door. After a few seconds of standing in the warm, damp air, the door creaked open to reveal Brandon. He looked from Austin to Margo, and once his eyes landed on a familiar face, he opened the door more fully.

'Margo?' he asked as he leaned against the door frame. 'Been a long time.'

'Too long,' Margo said apologetically. 'I should have come sooner.'

The full head of hair Brandon had in his youth was replaced by a short buzzcut and a receding hairline. A stubble goatee framed his lips, which were pursed like he couldn't quite decide what to make of Margo. After a moment, his eyes trailed over to Austin.

Austin cleared his throat and stuck out the hand that wasn't holding his umbrella. 'Austin Hughes,' he said. 'I went to school with Jessie as well.'

Brandon sized him up for a long moment before Margo decided to move things along. Her ankles and legs were getting wet again as the breeze carried rain under the umbrella. Despite the warm summer temperature, she was getting a chill from the combination of the water and the anxiousness swelling inside her.

'Brandon, would it be alright if we came in?' she asked kindly. 'I'm afraid we've already had to do one wardrobe change today from the weather. You know how these storms get.'

'Oh,' Brandon said, after a brief hesitation. 'Sure, come in.'

He pulled the door the rest of the way open and stepped to the side, gesturing them in. They gave him gracious smiles as they stepped inside, closing and shaking out their umbrellas the best they could before Brandon snapped the door shut behind them.

'Sorry,' he said. 'You wouldn't believe the amount of press and nosey folks we've had snooping around since Jessie was found.' His voice cracked a little on the last words, and Margo's heart ached as it pounded harder in her chest.

'I can only image,' Margo said. 'We're sorry to barge in unannounced. We heard you were back in town, and I realized I hadn't yet been by to pay my respects to you and your parents. Are they home?'

Brandon ran a hand over his head, rubbing it in a circle before putting his hand back down and into his pants pocket. 'No, they, uh, were having a hard time with everyone snooping around. They decided to stay at a hotel in Asheville for a few nights while I finished up the funeral arrangements. It was just too hard on them, but they'll be back for the service.'

Margo nodded, looking around as she tried to ignore the nausea and anguish clashing inside her, twisting her stomach in knots. In contrast to the despair of its inhabitants, the house was still bright and cheery, although the drawn curtains and overcast skies cast it in dark shadows. The walls, a light green-gray hue, were accented by white trim and ceilings and light hardwood floors.

The furniture was a mix of traditional wood and cozy fabrics, a bright white kitchen visible on the far side of the first floor past the dining room and formal living room, just like Margo remembered. She could almost see young Jessie sitting at the breakfast bar, snacking on popcorn and begging her mom to take them into Asheville for an adventure. Margo smiled sadly as the visual faded, and she turned her attention back to Brandon who was watching her expectantly.

'I'm sorry, I'm sure this has been horrible for all of you. We won't take up too much of your time. But we were wondering if we could ask you a few questions about Jessie.'

'Why would you need to do that? You knew her,' Brandon asked, looking skeptical as he walked into the living room and sat in one of the armchairs near the fireplace. Margo and Austin followed him into the room, perching themselves carefully along the edge of a love seat, trying not to get anything wet from the rain.

'I'm working on the show *Into Thin Air*, and we're in town hoping to tell Jessie's story and uncover the truth of what happened to her,' Austin said, choosing his words very carefully. Brandon's cheeks flushed red and he turned on Margo.

'Is that really why you came here? To interrogate me? I thought you were here because you actually cared about Jessie and the fact that you *used* to be like a part of this family. Wow, people really do change,' he said sharply as he stood up to end the meeting.

'No!' Margo said hastily, also jumping to her feet. 'I *am* here because of Jessie. I am. But Austin is trying to make sure Jessie is portrayed properly, so it's not a bunch of strangers who didn't even know her storming around acting like they did. I'm helping him because I care about Jessie's narrative too. And I didn't want a stranger intruding, asking these questions. Please, just give us a chance,' Margo pleaded.

Brandon considered her carefully for a long, tense moment, before finally sitting back down in his chair. With a sigh of relief, Margo sat back down next to Austin. The guilt at encroaching on his grief was building, but she hoped they could ask their few questions and then leave him in peace.

'Thank you,' Austin said. 'We'll try to be as quick and respectful as possible.'

Brandon grunted and nodded, crossing one leg over the other and leaning back. 'OK, well let's get it over with then. I'd rather you get the story right. Nothing

211

about how this town has handled Jessie's disappearance has been respectful.'

'How so?' Austin asked. Margo listened carefully, deciding it would put off Brandon to take out her notepad. She would jot everything down the second they left the house.

'Besides everyone's lack of personal boundaries?' Brandon scoffed. 'Our family is in mourning. Jessie is dead, discarded like fish food. Our world has collapsed *again*, yet all anyone cares about is getting a look behind the curtain and contributing gossip to feel like their sad lives are important.'

Austin nodded, his eyes sympathetic and kind. 'I'm sure that's been horrible. But our goal is to get justice for Jessie. Not to make things worse for you, I hope you can see that in time.' Brandon huffed and crossed his arms, but didn't say anything, so Austin took that as his cue to continue. 'Can you tell us a little about your relationship with Jessie? Just to give some color to her life growing up?'

'Exactly the kind of relationship you would expect when your dad remarries and has a new baby with wife number two. Jessie was their pride and joy. It didn't leave a whole lot of room for me, but I got by.'

'It sounds like maybe you didn't have the best relationship, then?' Austin asked. Margo was squirming internally. She knew that Jessie and Brandon had always been at odds, but he was still a grieving brother. The line of questioning was making her deeply uncomfortable, but she knew it had to be asked.

'Look, at the end of the day, she was family. Siblings don't always get along, especially at that age. I won't deny I was jealous of her and the royal treatment she

212

got from our parents. She always got what she wanted, whereas I had to work hard to get things for myself. When she turned sixteen, they bought her a brand new car with a big stupid red bow on it,' he paused to take a sip from the glass already sitting on his end table. Margo hadn't noticed it before, it looked like whiskey. She wished he would offer her one as she tried desperately to push away the mental image of Jessie's red cheer bow floating to the surface of the swimming hole. 'But *I* had to work two jobs to pay for half of my car myself when I turned sixteen. She got everything handed to her, but she still acted like the world owed her something. It drove me crazy.'

'I'm sure that was hard,' Austin said. 'Your younger half-sister getting all the attention, everything coming so easily to her. I'm sure it led to some fights between you two; I know my siblings and I would get into it pretty good growing up. It must have been a confusing and difficult time for you when she disappeared.'

Brandon eyed him up curiously, took another sip, and set the glass back down hard on the end table. 'I'll be the first one to admit that Jessie was spoiled rotten and always got her way. She was difficult to love at times, but I *did* love her, OK? We drove each other crazy, like all siblings do, but I would never have laid a hand on her. You hear me?' Austin nodded, about to say something when Brandon continued. 'It makes me sick now, the way her name is being dragged through the mud with all these rumors swirling about her being pregnant. It's a disgrace. After Jessie went missing, I couldn't stay in this town anymore. My parents' grief filled up every room. I know it was probably wrong to leave, but it was too much for me to handle. And the way the police messed up everything from

213

the start, acting like she ran away to try to cover up the fact that they couldn't solve it? Maybe even to protect the Abbotts who had the biggest motive? What a joke, I couldn't sit around and watch their mockery of an "investigation",' he said with air quotes. 'But I came back for the service, I owed them that much and to pay my respects to Jessie. This town though,' he heaved a heavy sigh, 'makes me want to get right back in the car and get the hell out of dodge.'

'I understand how you feel,' Margo said.

'Yeah,' Brandon said. 'I know you had a hard time here too growing up. I forgot you know how it feels to lose someone in this town.'

Margo grimaced, trying not to let thoughts of her mother distract her from the conversation at hand.

'So,' Austin said, steering the conversation back on topic. 'Cassidy told us that the night Jessie disappeared, she'd told her she couldn't hang out because she was grounded and had plans to help you with something. Do you remember what that would have been?'

'I have no idea why she told Cassidy that,' Brandon said, looking perplexed. 'I definitely didn't have any plans with her that night. I was out with a buddy of mine when my parents called panicking because they couldn't find her. I drove around town looking for her until early into the morning.'

Changing tactics, Austin asked. 'Well, did you see her go anywhere that night after the school rally?'

'I saw her creep out of the house and ride off on her old pink bike before I left to meet my friend. I told the police that. She'd backed her car into a tree a few days before, so it was in the shop. That's why she was grounded. My parents rarely disciplined her, but my dad was furious at her recklessness,' he said, squinting as he

214

thought back fifteen years. 'That's part of why I drove around looking for her after my parents called. We were worried she may have crashed her bike or something when she wasn't at any of her usual haunts. But, obviously, I didn't find anything.'

'You mentioned the police potentially protecting the Abbott's with their incorrect narrative about Jessie running away. Do you have any reason to believe Charlie or his parents were involved?'

'Besides the obvious?' Brandon scoffed. 'Charlie was and still is a pompous ass. I never liked him or the way he treated Jessie, like she was his property. It wouldn't surprise me if he was capable of murder, and we all know his parents have the money and connections to make anything disappear.'

'Did Jessie talk about a trip she wanted to take, like the police suggested they'd found evidence of? I never heard her talk about anything like that and was a little shocked when it came up back then,' Margo asked.

Brandon shook his head vehemently. 'There was no trip. At least not one she told me or my parents about. I mean she had places she wanted to go, like everyone, but nothing specific. We always felt the police glommed on to some rumor so they didn't have to do their jobs. Or wouldn't do it because of the Abbotts.'

Margo and Austin nodded in agreement.

'Would you be willing to talk on camera for the episode? It would be really great to involve her family in some way.' Austin asked delicately.

'I don't think I'm up to that, man, it's just . . . I just need to get through this funeral. When my parents are back, you can ask them. They're avoiding calls but I'll try to give them a heads-up to screen for your number.'

215

'Thank you, and we understand. If you change your mind, please feel free to text or call me or Margo any time,' Austin said, slipping a business card out of his wallet and setting it down on the coffee table in front of the couch.

Deciding not to bother Brandon any longer, they gave heartfelt condolences for his loss and thanked him extensively for his time as he ushered them out the door, openly relieved the questioning was over. When they got into Austin's car and started the engine, the local radio station was broadcasting a breaking news update. Austin cranked up the volume.

'The appliances pulled out of the local swimming hole where Jessie Germaine's remains were discovered, have been linked to a local family, the Buckleys, who live just a few minutes from the site in question.'

Without waiting for the announcement to finish, Austin immediately started dialing his producer. They quickly discussed whether or not a pre-interview with the Buckleys was needed, but decided it was better to catch them off-guard so they couldn't make their stories match. They hadn't been interviewed the first time the episode was filmed, so this had potential for some big on-air reveals. Amy said she would work on getting an on-camera interview set up quickly and would be back in touch with the schedule. Austin looked at Margo as he put the car in reverse and pulled out of the driveway.

'Well, this just keeps getting more and more interesting, doesn't it? Austin said.

Margo nodded, jotting down all her notes from the talk with Brandon as Austin drove her home. When he dropped her off, she watched as his car disappeared from view, thinking about how Brandon said that he and Jessie had no plans the night she disappeared. As she turned to walk up the path to her front door, she saw something out of the corner of her eye dart from the side of her house into the trees. She rushed over and crouched behind some bushes, squinting at the tree-line for movement. Branches swayed as though something had just disturbed them, but there was no one in sight. Margo snapped the hair band a couple of times against her wrist as her mind ran away from her. It *could* have been a coyote or a deer. When nothing else emerged from the foliage, she went back to her front door and went inside. The minute she entered the house, something felt off. The presence of another person vibrated through the air, causing a prickling sensation along the back of her neck. She'd dropped her dad off at a friend's that morning to catch up before meeting Austin for breakfast, so she knew it wasn't him. She still had another half-hour before she had to pick him up. She looked around the house and spotted the back sliding door was open, the screen door closed, letting fresh air in. She didn't remember her dad leaving it open earlier and quickly pulled it shut and latched the lock.

She went to her bedroom and somewhere in the distance, she heard a loud engine rev, followed by a vehicle peeling away loudly. Margo moved to the window but before she pulled it open, she smelled a sickeningly sweet scent and her heart leapt into her throat. Licorice and floral notes. Looking around, she noticed her pen cup from her desk had been knocked over, the pens scattered along the carpet. With jittery fingers she quickly set the alarm system from her phone. As her legs gave out, she sat down on the bed and heaved a deep breath. Charlie had been in her room.

February 27, 2004

Dear Diary,

Today was a weird day. It started out great!
Jessie came up to me at school before second period
and set up a tutoring session for later. Luckily
Charlie wasn't around to mess with me. But when
she got to my house after school, she asked where
my dad was and when I said he was still at school,
she was bummed that he couldn't help us. She
asked if we could go study at her house instead
since her mom had made our favorite brownies. I
haven't been to her house since we were kids, so
I was excited to be invited over again. We were
having a great time reminiscing and gorging on
her mom's awesome snacks.

But then Brandon came home and he and Jessie
got in a huge fight. He wanted to watch a movie
on the big TV in the living room but Jessie had
an episode of Friends on and wouldn't give up the
remote. Brandon got so mad and called her a spoiled
brat. She called him a loser and that really set
him off, I'd never seen him so angry. He tried to
take the remote from her but she put it behind
her back and they were like, rolling on the ground
fighting for it! They used to fight when we were
kids, but now Brandon is a big guy and I was so
worried, I didn't know what to do so I just stood
there. But finally he gave up and screamed how
she always got her way and someday she was gonna
pay for being such a selfish bitch. Jessie just
called him a jealous jerk while he stomped to his

bedroom to watch his movie. He slammed the door so hard the whole house shook.

After he left, Jessie told me how he's not going to college and is just filing papers at some office a few towns over. She called him some pretty nasty names and said he's so jealous of her that he's always starting a fight over something. As kids it was pretty obvious that Jessie was her parent's favorite, even though they always told Brandon they loved him just the same. Jessie said she couldn't wait to go to college and be far away from him. I'm going to miss her. It's been so nice becoming her confidante now that she and Cassidy are fighting about the pageants, so even if we are far away, I'm sure we'll text and call all the time.

CHAPTER FIFTEEN

'. . . In a statement released by the police yesterday, the appliances were connected to the Buckleys, a family who live less than a mile from the swimming hole. Which sparks the question, could the cooler also belong to them, and if so, what is their connection to Jessie Germaine? We'll update you when new information becomes available. Steve, back to you,' said the local news reporter as she stood in front of the Buckleys' property.

Margo and her dad sat on the sofa, watching the report with interest. Margo had been hoping for more of an update. But so far, no additional details had emerged. When the news moved on to another story, her dad turned the volume down.

'The Buckleys? Really? I find that hard to believe. They usually keep to themselves.'

'I remember their one son, Bobby, a bit from growing up and have seen him around town. But I didn't know him very well. He was kind of an outcast, but he seemed harmless. They do live right down the road from where she was found though,' Margo replied with a shrug.

'Their older boy, Tommy, played on the team one year. He was pretty good. But then his dad, Roy, made him quit so he could get a job and help out the family when he turned sixteen. I tried talking to Roy, but he wouldn't budge. Said basketball wasn't going to do him any good in the real world. Even though I disagreed with him, Roy was respectful, if a little dismissive. I've never heard of any violence in that family, none of their kids got into fights or anything like that at school. It just seems hard to believe.'

'Yeah, I agree. But they have to investigate every lead and it doesn't seem like they have very many.'

Margo's phone rang and when she saw Austin's number, she smiled and answered. 'Hey!'

They hadn't planned anything for that day because Austin said he was going to be busy with the production team. They were scheduled to begin filming interviews soon.

'Hey Margo. So, Amy talked to Mr. Buckley and convinced him and his son Bobby to do an on-camera interview. They'd like to clear their name publicly of any scrutiny. Since it wasn't planned, we had to squeeze it in today. I was wondering if you'd like to come and watch? Maybe take some notes. You might see something we don't.'

'Oh wow! Yes, I'd love to come. What time should I be there?'

'I can pick you up in twenty. It's happening quickly as the statement by the police has caused a stir.'

Margo glanced at her watch. She'd already showered but would need to change and throw on some makeup. 'OK, that works. Thanks for including me, Austin.'

'Of course, I'll see you soon.'

Margo turned to her dad. 'Are you OK making yourself lunch? Austin's coming to pick me up and I'm not sure how long I'll be gone.'

'I'll be fine. Have fun kiddo!' he said with a knowing smile. He must assume they were going on a date but she didn't have time to correct him. She knew he wanted her to step back from helping Austin, but she wasn't going to do that.

After quickly throwing on a flowy midi-skirt and a white button-up with the sleeves rolled up to her elbows, she applied makeup and then decided she needed a little more color. She rarely wore bold lipstick, but she wanted to look put together for the production crew, so she grabbed a bright red from her makeup bag. As she rubbed her lips together, loving the way the color popped, she thought, *Who am I kidding? This is all for Austin.* She smiled at herself in the mirror. Austin honked and she grabbed her handbag, checked that her notebook and favorite pen were still there and rushed out the door.

The minute she saw Austin in the front seat, she couldn't keep the smile off her face. She hopped in the car and buckled herself in.

'Hi,' she said breathlessly.

'Hey there, you look good,' he said, that dimple flirting with her.

She smiled in return, trying to keep her cheeks from flushing and keep her cool. They were heading to an interview regarding a murder investigation, not dinner and a movie. She did her best to push her confusing but exciting feelings for Austin aside and focus on the task at hand.

As they got closer to the Buckley property, the tension in Margo's body ratcheted up, replacing the butterflies

222

that had been there at the start of the trip. After a few minutes, the road became encased in long shadows as they drove a familiar stretch where the trees grew together above the road, moss dangling down from the entangled branches, reaching for the car like long skinny fingers ready to pluck them up out of their path.

Behind the canopy . . .

From the main road, they turned right onto an old mountain road, the tree branches so overgrown at the entrance that an outsider probably wouldn't even know it was there. Margo hadn't taken this path since her youth, but she would never forget it. The road led deep into the woods where there were no public parks or businesses, just dense forest, creeks and rivers, and the now infamous swimming hole. Austin turned right at the next bend. This road was clearly more worn from use as it led to the Buckleys' property. As the town of Lake Moss grew and progressed, people began building houses closer to the town, rather than far out in the forest, away from society and modern amenities. But the Buckleys had remained in their secluded home for generations, never showing signs of wanting otherwise.

The car inclined up the slope at the edge of their property. Margo had never been down their road before, but she'd had an idea of what to expect and she was not mistaken. The Buckleys had been called 'the trash family' behind their backs at school, and now Margo could see why. There were piles of rusty appliances, toys, planks of plywood and panes of scrap metal scattered around their yard. An old Chevy sedan missing its wheels sat off to the side on cinder blocks. The hood was propped open and tools littered the edges. Margo wasn't even sure how many kids the Buckleys had. There were two in high school with her, one a grade above and one two grades below. Bobby Buckley had been several classes ahead of her but was the one she'd seen around town the most.

After they parked alongside the other crew members' vehicles, Austin walked with her to the area where the show's equipment was set up. There were two men standing on the porch, one sitting in a chair.

'Those are the stand-ins, the second team. They stay in the spot we're going to shoot so we can light the scene and check audio. When we're ready, we'll bring in the first team, which in this case is the Buckleys.'

'Shouldn't you be over there checking the sound?' Margo asked.

'Nah, my crew is setting everything up. Once they're done, I'll go over, double-check everything and test, but doesn't look like they're ready just yet.'

'Oh interesting.'

Austin explained the process to her and all the terminology, including the different call times on the call sheet he shared with her.

'They should be calling the first team in shortly. Once we start filming, we'll do several takes and when Amy is happy with what we've got and we're ready for the last shot, she'll do a martini call out.'

'Martini? Are we having happy hour on set?' Margo asked with a laugh.

Austin smiled, 'Not literally, it's just a slang term to say we're done, time for martinis!' He laughed. 'But then the crew still needs to wrap out so it's a little misleading.' He talked her through all the other crew members around set. There were the grips laying down the dolly track for the camera to move smoothly, and the gaffers who were finishing setting up lights on C stands with sandbags to hold them steady as well as placing silk screens over the lights. Austin led her over to a brunette woman wearing jeans and t-shirt that read 'Do it on film!'

'This is my producer, Amy. This is Margo, who's been helping me with the notes.'

Amy's face lit up. 'Oh, so nice to meet you. You're notes have been great, thank you so much.'

'Not a problem, just glad I could help,' she replied with a smile.

Austin's first assistant came over and said they were ready for sound check. Amy waved and walked away to talk to one of the crew members. Austin led Margo over to an area he called 'Playback Village' where there were monitors set up to show the scene they were shooting. He said when they began rolling, she could watch from there but until then, as long as she didn't get into the shot, she could go wherever she liked. Margo watched as he walked over to the crew and pointed her out. She waved awkwardly as several of them looked her way.

Production vans littered the driveway and people with walkie talkies hanging from their waistbands swarmed the area. The huge high-tech camera was being loaded onto the dolly track. Margo felt out of place and not sure what to do with herself. She spotted Chief Healey and a deputy standing off to the side, watching it all unfold. Were they still there from questioning the Buckleys themselves? Or perhaps they'd simply heard through the grapevine that the crew was interviewing and wanted to be present. Either way, Healey didn't look pleased, his face pinched in and his arms crossed tightly over his chest. He glanced at Margo for a second, then looked away, more interested in what the crew was doing.

Margo perched on a large boulder sticking out of the

ground near Playback Village, out of the way but still in view of the monitors. She watched Austin give orders to young production assistants and test the equipment. Seeing him so in charge and skilled at his job was making her like him even more. He became someone else; a confident, sexy man. This other layer of his personality was a definite turn-on. She hadn't been sure she could ever feel like this again after her husband, but the feelings bubbling up felt beyond her control.

After another half-hour of set up, Amy called out 'First team!'

They had set up an old chair for Roy Buckley on the sagging porch, all the hoarding glory in full view of the camera in the background. Margo glanced at the monitor and it was a compelling shot that said so much about this family. After a few minutes, a production assistant led Roy Buckley out of the front door. He was limping with a cane, followed by Bobby Buckley. Bobby made eye contact with Margo, and she wondered if he remembered seeing her while the appliances were being pulled out of the swimming hole. Maybe she should have told Austin about that, but it'd slipped her mind until now. After Roy sat down, Bobby stayed standing by his side, his hand on his father's shoulder.

'That's great, just like that,' Amy said. Austin held the boom mic out over their heads, just out of the frame. 'OK everyone, quiet on the set! We're about to start. Caleb, the slate?'

Amy motioned to a young man with the clapperboard marked with *Into Thin Air* on the top, *Buckley Family* on the bottom, and a 1 in the 'Take' box. He held it out in front of the Buckley men and said, 'Take One!' before he clapped the arm down.

226

'Thank you for taking the time to speak with us today Mr. Buckley. We know it's been tough since the police made their announcement that the appliances found in the swimming hole alongside Jessie Germaine's remains belonged to your family. Can you tell us how those appliances came to be there?' the producer asked.

'Well, they *shouldn't* have been there,' Roy said with an annoyed glance up at his son. Bobby looked away. 'We got a notice from the city that a complaint had been filed about our property havin' too much trash on it. Bunch of nosey nellies if you ask me. We're the only ones who live out here so who cares what our place looks like? I had a mind to tell 'em to go to hell. But the notice said we could be fined if the "trash" wasn't reduced. Well, let me tell you, I've found some treasures in this *trash*,' he said, sarcastic emphasis on the last word. 'Hell, I even fixed up my old truck usin' parts other people threw away.' He harrumphed and looked off to the side.

'I'm sorry to hear that Mr. Buckley.'

'Call me Roy. Yeah, well, we don't have money for frivolous things like fines. So I helped my boy here load a few of the appliances up in the truck and sent him on his way to the dump with a dolly. And, well . . .' he looked pointedly at Bobby. Clearly Roy was not happy that Bobby had brought all this attention onto his reclusive family. Bobby looked sheepish, his face reddening at the underlying anger from his dad.

'Bobby, can you tell us why you discarded the appliances in the swimming hole instead of taking them to the dump?'

'I had plans to go tubin' that day with my friends. But when we got the notice, my dad told me I had to do this first. My friends didn't wanna wait for me and if I'd gone

227

all the way to the dump forty minutes away, by the time I got back they woulda left without me. I asked my dad if I could do it the next day, but he said we'd have to pay if we didn't take care of it as soon as possible.'

'We'd never gotten a notice before, so I didn't know how strict they were going to be about that fine. It said "immediate removal" or something like that. I didn't want to take any chances,' Roy interrupted, his rough, gravelly voice justifying his actions.

'Yeah, so I decided to take the back roads and just dump everything in the forest and then go back the next day to take them to the dump. But then I saw the old bridge that towers over the swimming hole. I knew the seniors used it to party, but no one else went there. So I figured that was easier and I wouldn't have to go back to move anything. I pulled the truck bed up to the edge and used the dolly to drop them over. It wasn't much, a broken fridge, some scrap metal, a coupla microwaves and an old metal school desk. Then I left and picked up my friends,' he shook his head. 'The desk had my older brother's name scratched into it. That's how they knew the stuff belonged to us. I know it was wrong, but I was just a kid who wanted to hang out with his friends.' He shrugged, looking embarrassed at his younger self's stupidity. 'It was the only time I ever did it.'

'Bobby, when was this?'

'I was eighteen at the time,' he scrunched up his face, trying to do the math. 'That would make it the summer of 2001, I guess.'

'So, about three years *before* Jessie went missing.'

'Yeah, I guess so.'

'Bobby did you see Jessie around the time of her disappearance?'

228

Bobby shook his head. 'Nah, I didn't even know her. I hear those kids out there sometimes late at night. But they leave us alone, so we leave them alone.'

'I know it's a been a long time, but do either of you remember what you were doing the night she went missing?'

'I do actually,' Roy replied. 'It was my Bobby's birthday that night. Bobby and I were target shootin' most of the day in the woods behind our property. Then we had a birthday dinner. We had cake and watched TV.'

'Since you were in the woods near the swimming hole, did you see anything? Did you see Jessie or anyone else?'

Roy glanced up at Bobby. 'I don't think so, do you son?'

Bobby shook his head. 'I don't remember seein' anyone while we were shootin'. But remember that car we saw on the road later?'

Amy perked up, leaning forward in her chair. 'What time was that?'

'We got home just before sunset. My wife was making a special dinner for his birthday and she wanted it to be a surprise. She handed me a coupla beers and we sat on the porch until it was ready, probably about an hour later,' Roy replied.

Bobby nodded in agreement. 'We saw this car. We'd see cars zoomin' around out there from time to time, probably seniors goin' to and from their parties, but this one stood out because it was actin' real strange. It was gettin' dark out so the headlights caught our attention. We saw the car drive past, then a minute later it came back. Then the car stopped, pulled forward a little, then stopped again and sat there for a few minutes. We thought maybe they were lost and might need directions, but then it made a U-turn and drove away.'

229

Margo hitched a breath at the revelation. This was the first time anyone said they saw anything out of the ordinary that night. This could be huge. She looked over at Healey and his mouth was hanging slightly open, his arms now dropped to the sides. He whispered something to the deputy who pulled out his small notebook and wrote something. The next question from the producer pulled Margo's eyes back to the set.

'Did you see what type of car it was, or the color?'

Margo tensed, leaning forward in anticipation of his response, but Roy shook his head. 'Nah, it was too dark. A lighter color is about all I could say, wouldn't you Bobby?' he said, looking up at his son.

'Yeah, maybe gray or off white? I can't be sure. But it was a car not a truck or SUV.'

Margo exhaled the breath she hadn't realized she was holding, and she could sense the blanket of disappointment that came down upon the crew at the lack of details.

Amy called out, 'Print that!' From Austin's quick rundown of the filming process, Margo knew that meant Amy was happy with the scene and they could lock it in. The clapperboard came in again and the interview moved on to the background of the Buckley family and their desire to remain living in the woods. Margo started to zone out and her eyes wandered around the property again. Austin had warned her that filming could get boring with all the stops and starts. She heard a faint squeaking and searched for the noise. A young girl with loose blonde braids was trying to ride a rusty, faded pink Huffy bike around a small patch of concrete behind their shed. The bike was too large for her, more suited to a ten- or eleven-year-old. The girl appeared to be around only five or six. The bike still had a few metallic tassels hanging off the handlebars, making Margo smile. She'd had a similar bike growing up but hers had been light blue. She rose and wandered over to the girl. When she walked up, the girl smiled at her and lost her balance, nearly toppling over. Margo rushed to help her steady the bike back up.

Margo crouched down. 'Hi, what's your name?'

'I'm Molly. That's my dad over there,' she replied, pointing to Bobby.

'Hi, Molly. I'm Margo. How old are you?'

She held up her fingers. 'I'm five and half. But I don't know how to make a half with my fingers.' Margo chuckled. 'Can you help me? I'm just learning how to ride and my mom's too busy.'

'Sure!'

Margo held on to the back of the bike while little Molly pulled her feet up onto the pedals. Margo moved the bike forward while Molly pumped her skinny legs shakily. The chain was so rusted, Margo was surprised it still moved with the pedals. Just as she was about to let go, Margo glanced down at the bike and spotted a sticker on the back of the seat, faded and peeling at the edges. The glitter still sparkled in a few spots. She let the bike go and Molly squealed with delight. As Margo watched Molly ride around in circles, she searched her memory for that sticker, certain she'd seen it before. Suddenly she remembered, a chill shooting down her spine. When Jessie and Margo had still been best friends in elementary school, they'd covered their matching bikes in stickers. Margo had been jealous of the name sticker on Jessie's bike. Her mom had found one for her birthday that read 'Jessie' instead of 'Jessica'; Jessie had hated her full name.

Margo ran over to Molly who'd just put her foot down and almost dropped the bike because she couldn't reach the ground properly from the seat. Margo caught the bike before it fell and Molly jumped off and started hopping over a chalk hopscotch sketched onto the concrete nearby, quickly losing interest in the bike. Margo leaned down and inspected the sticker. Like the bike itself, it was covered in dirt, having no doubt sat in one of these piles outside for who knows how long. Margo rubbed the pad of her thumb on her shirt, then licked it and wiped off the dirt. With the layer of dirt gone, she could faintly see an 'essi' on its surface, the rest had faded away. She looked the bike over and most of the other stickers she remembered were gone, but there were still remnants of a *Sailor Moon* sticker on the handlebars. This had to be Jessie's bike, the one her brother said he saw her riding when she rode off that fateful night. The J and E must have worn off over time.

She walked the bike back to the production area and caught Austin's attention, widening her eyes so he knew it was important. He motioned for his assistant to take over and then walked over to Margo.

'What's up?'

'I was just over there with Molly and she was riding this old bike. Austin, I think this is Jessie's bike, the one she rode off on that night that no one ever found. Look at this sticker,' she said, pointing to the blue-glittered sticker. 'Jessie got that sticker for her birthday. Her mom had to look everywhere to find one that said Jessie instead of Jessica. I was jealous because I could never find a Margo sticker, so my mom called all over North Carolina until she found a store that carried it and got me one for my own birthday a couple of months later. It's faded, but I'm sure this is her bike.'

Austin inspected the stickers for a moment. 'Considering how old and rusty the bike is, it could be it. I'll tell the assistant producer and see what they say. Thanks,' he said, smiling at her before he ran back.

There was a flurry of activity, whispers and looks in Margo's direction. Then they cut and Amy was informed of the discovery. She walked over to Margo and asked the details of the bike. Margo reiterated what she'd told Austin but included the info about the *Sailor Moon* sticker as well. Amy thanked her and walked back to the set with the bike. Both Bobby and Roy were looking at Margo and the bike, their foreheads scrunched in confusion. A glance at Healey showed he too was looking at her with intensity. She wondered if she should have taken it to him instead, but the moment was gone.

The clapperboard slapped down again, making Margo jump, and Amy leaned in. 'What can you tell me about this bike?'

Roy grunted and looked up at his son. Bobby shrugged and said, 'I don't know. I'm pretty sure that's been in one of these piles for a long time. We find things all the time and if we think it'll be useful, we just bring it back. People are always dumpin' things in the woods. Can I look at it?'

'Sure,' Amy said, pushing the bike toward Bobby.

He looked it over, squinting at the details. 'Oh yeah, I found this in the woods with Darren, my younger brother. It was sittin' against a tree but looked like it'd been there for a while. It was covered in dirt. We assumed one of the high school kids left it when they were partying or something. I remember because Darren wanted to give it to our younger sister, Martha. We couldn't afford a new bike and all we had were ten speeds. She was too small for them. She was so happy when we brought it home.' Bobby straightened. 'Why are you askin' about this bike? That was years ago.'

The producer paused and then said, 'Because the sticker on the back seat reads "e-s-s-i". The first and last letters have faded but we think that it may be the bike Jessie rode away on the night she disappeared.'

Margo stole a glance at Healey and saw him whispering again to his deputy, pointing in the direction of the bike.

Roy's face grew red and he struggled to rise from his seat. 'We're done here. I've given you your interview, now get the hell off my property.'

As soon as Amy yelled 'Cut!' Healey and the deputy walked over and briefly talked to her before grabbing the bike and wheeling it toward the police cruiser.

Amy called out, 'Is the gate good?'

After a few minutes of conferring with the crew, including Austin, the assistant hollered out, 'The gate is good!' Austin came over and explained there were no problems with the equipment or memory card so they could proceed with the wrap out.

Margo pumped her arms, winded from the jog she'd decided to take after she got back from the Buckleys'. The weather was less hot and humid today, so she'd taken advantage of the cooler breezes blowing through the mountains. She avoided jogging past the Germaines' house, not wanting to run into Brandon again. She felt badly about questioning him in their interview when he was clearly grieving. She'd see him and his parents tomorrow at the funeral anyway. Instead, she chose an alternate route that was longer because it took her into the forest closer to town. The path through the woods was beautiful with streaks of bright sun breaking through the trees. Growing up, she'd taken this path only a handful of times, eager to break up the monotony of her workouts.

But today's run told her how out of shape she was, the longer route making her feel older than her thirty-two years. She decided to be easy on herself and slowed to a standstill, leaning over and resting her hands on her knees while she caught her breath.

After a minute, she started a brisk walk through the trees. Cardinals and Carolina Chickadees were having a lively conversation creating a symphony of chirps. As Margo rounded a bend where the path took her back to the main road, she saw something further in the woods to her right. Margo walked closer and crept up to a tree, squinting and wondering if it was a coyote or, worse, a bear. The figure moved and Margo gasped. There in the forest up the hill, were Cassidy and Tucker. They were too far away for her to hear what they were saying over the bird concert, but they seemed to be arguing. Cassidy gestured wildly while Tucker stood with his arms folded tightly across his chest. Tucker shook his head, said something angrily back and turned to walk away. But Cassidy grabbed his arm and turned him back around. Her voice rose and Margo heard a few words. 'She . . . can't . . . down . . . hide . . .'

Margo took a step forward in the hopes of hearing them better and she stepped on a fallen tree limb, snapping it loudly and sending rocks and leaves sliding down the slope. She ducked quickly behind the tree. When she peeked around the edge, Cassidy and Tucker were looking in her direction. Her heart was pounding. Tucker shook his head and put his hands up as if to say he'd had enough, backing away from Cassidy. She turned hastily around and stormed off in the opposite direction. Margo waited a few minutes before coming out from behind the tree. They were both gone. When she turned around to head back to the main road, she froze. Just yards away from where she was standing was a bobcat, its head hunched down, a raised ridge along its back as it eyed her warily, its ears lying flat. Frantically she perused her memory on what to do. In all her time growing up in these mountains, she'd only spotted bobcats from afar. Her heart pumped faster, her chest heaving up and down as she stared the animal down, its yellow eyes watching her every move. She remembered that she shouldn't run away but should back away slowly. No sudden movements.

Quietly, she moved her foot back and took a step, then another, until her back hit a tree. The bobcat's nostrils flared as it growled a low hum. Margo's fear overcame her, and she closed her eyes as she pulled herself behind the tree. She heard leaves and twigs snap as the bobcat moved, but it seemed to be moving farther away, rather than toward her. She stole a glance around the tree and saw it dash off into the forest. Exhaling, she tried to calm her breath before starting out again. As Margo resumed her jog back on the main road, she thought about the exchange between Tucker and Cassidy. While she wished she could have heard more of what they said, what was intriguing was that Cassidy was here in Lake Moss when she'd told them she would have a hard time taking even one day off to attend Jessie's funeral. Yet here she was, the day before, in the woods arguing with Tucker. What could they have to argue about? And why would they be doing it in the woods, why not just meet up somewhere in town? They were hiding something, but how dark was their secret and how far would they go to protect it?

As she slowed her pace to cool down, the zipped pocket of her shorts that held her phone vibrated. She quickly pulled it out. Unknown number again. This was the fourth time in two days she'd received a call from an unknown number. Margo was always careful not to give out her number or sign up for anything that required she share it unnecessarily. She was tempted to answer it but denied the call and slipped it back into her pocket with a shaky hand. Deep down, Margo feared whoever was on the other end of the line. She wondered again if her social stalker had escalated and gotten ahold of her phone number.

She walked the rest of the way to her house, her mind obsessing over worst case scenarios. Margo sat down on the lawn to stretch out her muscles, but the tension from the unknown had seeped in and they remained taut. Her phone buzzed again and she froze. She was afraid to look at her screen, nervous that it might be another threatening message. Taking a deep breath to steel her resolve, Margo pulled out her phone and saw a voicemail notification. Was the unknown number and her social stalker one and the same? Had they finally left a voicemail? Or was her mind running away with her and this was someone else entirely?

The message was only three seconds long. She clicked on it and pulled it to her ear, wondering if the answer was about to be revealed. She heard some muffled sounds and just before the message ended, there was a whisper of something. She turned the volume all the way up and listened again. At the end, she heard what sounded like someone muttering under their breath – '*Crazy bitch*' – before the phone clicked off. Margo's blood ran cold. She listened to it a few more times, trying to place the voice, but it was barely audible. She couldn't even tell if it was a man or a woman. It was like an afterthought, as if they'd considered leaving a message but decided against it at the last minute and hung up in anger. She was no closer to the answers she so desperately needed. Margo quickly looked up from her phone and scanned the landscape around her. Was someone watching her right now? A dog barked from a few houses down, making her jump. She stood and walked into the street, looking in the direction of the dog still barking. When the house came into view, the dense trees next to it were moving, as though someone or something had just dashed into the woods.

CHAPTER SIXTEEN

Margo repeatedly smoothed the wrinkles out of the black tailored dress she used to wear to court as she shifted her weight back and forth in line next to Austin, biting the inside of her lip. He looked handsome in his slim black slacks and crisp white button-down. His black jacket was draped neatly over one arm, and he gave her a quick smile as he folded up the cuffs of his shirt until they sat snuggly midway up his forearms.

There had been an early morning shower that day that had turned into partly sunny skies for the funeral service. The lingering humidity in the air had made them damp and sticky as they stood around Jessie's gravesite, laying flowers and saying their goodbyes. While the Reverend spoke of such deep loss, reliving bright moments in Jessie's life, Margo caught Charlie slyly texting on his phone, not paying attention. A moment later, she saw Tucker pull his phone out of his pocket and look at a message. He shot an angry look at Charlie, shaking his head slightly, before shoving his phone back in his pocket and turning his attention again to the service. Charlie had continued to stare at Tucker's back long after Tucker had looked away. Margo wished she knew what was said. She, Austin, and her father had stood near the back of the crowd, Margo having a hard time witnessing the devastation on Mr. and Mrs. Germaines' faces as they cried through the service. She'd felt sick every time she looked at the casket, imagining what was left of Jessie lying inside.

At the end, she had taken a deep breath and forced herself to approach Jessie's parents to offer condolences, and it had been almost unbearable. Jessie's mom cried as she hugged Margo, thanking her for being such a good friend to their daughter, and how grateful they'd been when she'd tried to help Jessie get her grades up in the end. Even though she was thanking Margo, her words were soaked in sorrow. Margo felt pale and clammy despite the warm air, brushing off their thanks and mumbling, 'I'm so sorry for your loss,' so many times that the words soon seemed to have no meaning at all. Afterwards, she and Austin dropped her father back at home under protest. He wanted to comfort and support Margo, but he was hot and tired from working his way around the uneven ground of the cemetery on his crutches. Margo convinced him that he'd properly paid his respects; that the Germaines would understand given his condition and he could go home to rest; she would be OK since she had Austin by her side.

Now, she and Austin were back at the Germaines' house for the funeral reception, surrounded by everyone in Lake Moss that Margo had so artfully avoided all these years. It was suffocating, and despite the spacious rooms, Margo felt like anywhere she turned she would surely run right into someone. Austin nudged her shoulder and she gave him a grateful smile; glad she at least had him. She'd told him about the altercation between Cassidy and Tucker in the woods, and he had agreed that it was suspicious. While they were here to pay their respects, they were also on high alert. So many suspects under one roof made it a crucial time to observe.

Brandon had avoided them at the service and now at the reception, clearly still not pleased with their questioning his relationship with Jessie. Margo couldn't blame him. The line moved and Margo and Austin stepped forward, accepting the plates they were handed as they neared the table holding a wide spread of catered food, donated by Gillian's Grill, a restaurant downtown that boasted all organic food. The smell of sweet southern barbeque filled up Margo's senses as she got closer, but she couldn't decide if she would keep any food down with the heartbreak surrounding her on all sides.

A young man holding a tray covered in bottles of Moss Creek Brewing beers walked by and she quickly flagged his attention. He paused long enough for her and Austin to each grab a bottle before moving on to the next crowd of people. She wondered if the Abbotts had donated their products to the reception, too. Taking a sip, she felt her anxiety calm ever so slightly as the crisp amber liquid weaved its way through her senses.

She'd known it would be hard coming back to this town, but she hadn't realized she was going to be thrown into the den of haunting moments from her youth so head-on. Memories were crashing over her in waves everywhere she looked. There was no escape from the suppressed emotions fighting to explode just under the surface. Part of her wanted to pay her respects quickly and get the hell out of there, but she had to continue on this journey. She had to get through to the other side.

Once it was their turn at the food table, Margo and Austin helped themselves to barbeque ribs and chicken, buttery mashed potatoes, grilled asparagus and warm rolls. Finding a quiet window ledge to eat along, Margo forced herself to take a bite. It was so delicious, she momentarily forgot she was too distressed to be hungry and ate half her plate before Austin nudged her.

Placing her fork down she asked, 'What is it?'

'Look,' he said, gesturing out the window into the backyard where he'd been looking intently as he ate.

Most of the mourners were inside enjoying the air conditioning, but there was a small group on the far side of the yard, looking tense and agitated. Charlie and Tucker were standing nose to nose, Tucker's back to the house. Charlie's face was contorted in anger and he appeared to be yelling. Off to the side, Cassidy was gripping her beer bottle tightly against her chest, looking on the verge of tears. Next to her was Tucker's wife, Claire. Her blonde hair was swept up in a bun, her green eyes a mix of sadness and confusion.

'Let's go see what's happening,' Margo said as loud, muffled voices started to filter in from the outside. Austin nodded and followed her lead. They dropped their plates into the garbage can just beside the back door. Once they stepped outside, they could hear the argument at hand.

'I don't know what you were thinking!' Charlie yelled, inching even closer to Tucker. 'I thought we were on the same page.'

'Just back off, man! You've been trying to control this entire thing since day one. You need to chill.'

'Chill?' Charlie spat. 'You know damn well why I've been trying to control this. And don't act like it wasn't saving your ass too,' he said, shoving Tucker, causing him to stumble back a few steps.

'Stop it! Both of you!' Cassidy yelled, taking a step forward. Claire looked lost and worried, like she'd wandered into a place she didn't belong. She gave Cassidy a strange look that Margo couldn't quite place.

Margo and Austin kept their distance, not needing to get very close to make out every word. 'What do you think they're fighting about?' Austin asked quietly, looking like he just stumbled upon a smoking gun.

'Not sure. Maybe Tucker told Charlie he'd made a slip in his interview with us.' Margo shrugged, watching intensely.

'Back off, man,' Tucker growled again, stepping forward and pushing Charlie back. Charlie took a half-step back before lunging forward and cracking Tucker across the jaw with a right hook. Tucker stumbled, holding his face and looking like he was about to counter-attack. They were both seething.

'Please, stop!' Cassidy cried out, stepping in between them and looking imploringly at Tucker. 'Just walk away, Tuck, He's not worth it. We're at Jessie's funeral for Christ's sake!'

'Tucker?' Claire finally said quietly, her face etched with concern.

Tucker looked back and forth between the two women before finally dropping his tense arms down to his side. 'You're right, he's not worth it. Come on, Claire. Let's get out of here. We'll pay our respects on the way to the door.'

Claire reached out and he grabbed her hand with one last long look at Cassidy, then Charlie, whose chest was still heaving, before turning and walking toward Margo and Austin to go back inside. Tucker froze momentarily when he saw them, and Margo noticed Charlie and Cassidy were also staring in their direction.

'What are you looking at?' Tucker asked, pushing past them into the home.

'Just getting some fresh air,' Austin said back. 'Come on, let's head back inside,' he said under his breath. The look on Charlie's face was unsettling, his eyes boring into Margo, like she was the cause of every bad thing in his life. Cassidy just seemed incredibly sad as she watched Tucker and Claire's backs retreating through the door. Margo dragged her eyes away and followed Austin into the house. She could feel Charlie's stare lingering on her as she retreated, causing her anxiety to swell.

'That was interesting,' Margo whispered as they blended into the crowd, trying to shake off Charlie's threatening vibe. A few seconds later, she saw Cassidy and Charlie walk inside, but Margo wasn't up for a confrontation. Charlie still looked like he was poised for a fight, and Margo was convinced he'd been in her bedroom. That, combined with the fact that she still wasn't sure if he was the one stalking her on social media, made her want to put as much distance between them as possible. There was no need to poke the bear.

'Are you ready to get out of here soon?' Margo asked, itching to go home and take a long shower to wash off the feelings of the day.

'Yeah, are you OK alone for a sec? I just want to run to the bathroom really quick.'

'Oh,' Margo said, looking around to see where Charlie had gone but she'd lost sight of him. 'Yeah, sure, I'm fine.'

'I'll be back fast, I promise,' he said, squeezing her arm before cutting a path through the gathered mourners.

After he left, Margo noticed through the newly formed gap in in the crowd that Cassidy was rushing toward the front door, trying to shield her face as she cried. A few heads turned her way, looking sympathetic at her pain, before returning to their conversations. Curious, Margo followed Cassidy outside and looked around frantically. But Cassidy hadn't gone far, standing off to one side near the driveway and lighting a cigarette with a shaking hand as tears flowed down her rosy cheeks.

'Come on,' she mumbled with the cigarette held between her lips, her red lipstick rubbing off on the white paper as she clicked the lighter repeatedly.

'Are you OK?' Margo asked, walking toward her.

Cassidy jumped, startled by the intrusion.

'Oh, Margo,' she sniffled, taking the cigarette out of her lips. 'I didn't see you there. I swear, I don't normally smoke, it's just . . .'

'It's fine. I think everyone gets a pass today,' Margo said, giving her an empathetic smile. 'Can I?'

'Um, sure, thanks, I'm useless right now,' Cassidy said, pulling the cigarette back to her mouth with trembling fingers and handing Margo the lighter. Margo held up a hand to block the breeze and quickly lit the cigarette for her.

'Thanks,' Cassidy said, seeming to settle as she exhaled deeply, blowing the smoke straight up into the air. 'I'm sorry, do you want one?'

'Oh, no, that's OK.'

Cassidy nodded, looking up at the tops of the trees as she worked with obvious effort to stop the tears from falling.

'Are you alright?' Margo asked again. 'I saw you rushing through the crowd looking upset, so I just wanted to—' Margo asked hesitantly.

'Why do you care?' Cassidy snapped, wiping her nose with the hand that wasn't holding the cigarette. 'It's not

245

like we were ever friends. We were in the same orbit because of Jessie, but that wasn't exactly my choice.'

Margo's stomach churned, twisting in knots. Maybe it was a mistake following Cassidy out here. After a long moment, Margo turned to go back inside. 'Sorry,' she muttered under her breath.

'Wait,' Cassidy said with a huge sigh, turning to look at Margo directly and placing a hand on her arm to stop her from leaving. 'Sorry, I'm a mess. I know you saw what happened out back earlier, you know, the whole crew back together. Well, minus Jessie.' She looked down at her black patent leather heels, twisting the pointed toe of one back and forth on the pavement.

Margo knew there was no point denying it, and Cassidy was vulnerable; this could be her chance to find out what was going on. 'Yeah, I did. What was that all about?'

'The fight? Oh, you know the guys, they can be so hot-headed,' Cassidy said evasively.

Deciding to take a swing, Margo said, 'I never knew Tucker as well as you did.' Cassidy snorted, taking another drag of her cigarette. Margo noticed her hand was still shaking as she brought it up to her mouth. Margo pushed forward, 'Do you think he could be considered a suspect? I've never seen him angry like that, is he capable of . . . murder?' It was hard to say the last word, but she choked it out.

'What? Tucker? Absolutely not,' Cassidy said vehemently, coming to his defense with zero hesitation, shaking her head vigorously.

'Not even with the suspension? People have been talking about how upset he was with Jessie for pushing him into that senior prank. I know Charlie is his alibi, but after that fight, I don't know, I just had to ask,' Margo said quietly, watching Cassidy closely.

Cassidy's face darkened, pinching inward. 'How dare you storm back into town on your high horse, interrogating us like you're a freaking detective? Tucker would never have hurt Jessie,' Cassidy spat at her.

'I'm sorry, I didn't mean—' Margo started, trying to de-escalate the situation. This was not going how she'd envisioned.

But suddenly, Cassidy's face relaxed and she sighed heavily again. She silenced Margo by putting her hand up. 'No, I'm sorry. It's not you. It never was. It was Jessie. And now that I'm back in this town, it's so easy to slip into old behaviors with . . . everyone. I almost didn't make the drive out here this morning; the thought of seeing everyone again filled me with dread.' Margo caught the lie and considered calling her out on it, but Cassidy was being so open with her, she worried that pointing out she'd seen her the day before would put her on the defense again. Cassidy paused and swallowed a few times, seemingly working up to say something important. 'When Jessie started hanging out with you during senior year, she'd needle me about it, like she was trying to make me jealous. I couldn't understand why she wanted to hang out with you all of a sudden, after years of making fun of you.'

Margo flinched, feeling the old sting of rejection. She'd always assumed Jessie just put up with Charlie's taunts and maybe stuck up for her at times. But apparently, she'd joined in.

Cassidy saw the look on Margo's face and her shoulders relaxed slightly. 'Sorry, I didn't say that to hurt you,' she said, looking down at the ground. 'I just . . .' Cassidy's eyes darted back up. 'You know she wasn't the nicest person, right? That she could be really cruel?' Margo nodded, remembering a few times when she'd seen Jessie make fun of some of their classmates behind their backs. She hadn't thought much of it, trying to win back Jessie's favor and never being on the receiving end of her harsh words, she rationalized to herself that it was just Charlie and popularity getting in her head. That it wasn't the real her. It was hard, now, hearing she'd said hurtful things about Margo too behind closed doors. 'Well anyway, anytime she brought you up, she was always slyly pitting us against one another. And it worked. I resented you, felt like you were trying to take her away from me. I fell right into her trap.'

'I hate that she did that,' Margo replied, shaking her head, a little shocked by this admission from a woman who'd only shown disdain for her up till now.

'My ego wouldn't let me fully admit until recently that she'd manipulated me into hating you. When you showed up with Austin, all those feelings came back and I started thinking about Jessie and how she manipulated everyone, including me. I wasn't very nice to you, back then or when you came to Charlotte. I'm trying to be better, but obviously I've got more work to do.'

Margo placed a hand on Cassidy's arm. 'I understand. This whole time Austin and I have been doing these interviews, it's been hard not to retreat back into the old timid Margo too. This town sure doesn't bring out the best in people.'

Cassidy nodded, looking at her thoughtfully. 'I just don't understand why you would think between the two guys, that it could possibly be Tucker? Everyone knows Charlie and Jessie fought constantly, and no one has any idea where he actually was that night,' Cassidy shook her head with her eyebrows raised and looked back at the trees.

'Wait, what?' Margo asked, and Cassidy snapped her eyes back to Margo, looking like a deer caught in headlights. Margo, realizing that Cassidy had let something slip accidentally, pushed on. 'So, Tucker and Charlie weren't together the night Jessie disappeared?'

Cassidy bit at her lip, throwing her cigarette stub down and crushing it with the toe of her shoe. Running a hand anxiously through her hair, she looked around to make sure no one else was within earshot. She clenched her lips together, trying to stifle the tears that were threatening to fall. She gulped a couple of times, but the tears slipped down her cheeks anyway.

'Look, Tucker couldn't have done it, OK? Please just leave him alone.'

'How can you be so sure?' Margo asked gently.

And then, like she was lifting a weight that had chained her down for a long time, she blurted out, 'Because he was with me!' throwing her arms up in the air before dropping them to her sides.

'What?' Margo asked. 'Why was he with you?'

'Come on Margo, you're smarter than that,' Cassidy said. She looked anxious, but also a little relieved. The truth dawned on Margo, and it must have shown on her face. 'There it is,' Cassidy said, with an anguished smirk. 'Tucker and I were hooking up senior year.'

'Wasn't he with Claire then?' Margo asked.

'Yes, and Claire was my friend. I was terrified of her finding out. Tucker was the only guy she'd ever been with. I knew it was wrong, that it would destroy her. I was a shitty friend, you don't have to tell me that,' she said, looking in the distance. 'But I was so drawn to him, so deeply and madly in love with him. We just . . . couldn't help ourselves. We didn't mean for it to happen.'

'Why didn't he just break up with Claire and be with you, then? If you loved each other?' Margo asked, genuinely surprised. She'd never had any inkling of this affair.

'I mean, come on, you've seen Claire. Perfect, sweet, pretty little girl next door. We didn't want to hurt her, but also, his parents desperately wanted him to be with her. They *adored* her. She was the picture-perfect housewife, and their parents had been friends for ages. I don't think they understood my ambition. They wanted their son to settle down in Lake Moss near them and have the quintessential American life, picket fence, little kids running around. Well, they got their wish,' Cassidy grimaced.

'So, you guys ended things? Eventually?' Margo asked, understanding how claustrophobic the pressure of that type of life could feel.

Cassidy started crying again, unable to make direct eye contact with Margo. 'All three of us were going off to different colleges. It was the perfect excuse to finally get what we wanted. He could use the distance as a reason to end things with her delicately, and then after college graduation, we could finally be together in the open since enough time would have passed to seem less suspicious.' She choked out a sad laugh. 'He came and visited me at Duke once or twice a year, and it was like we had never been apart. I really thought he was going to be my happily-ever-after.'

'So, what happened?' Margo asked, completely engrossed.

Cassidy looked down at her feet again. 'He went home for a long weekend a few weeks before graduation. He'd done a good job of letting Claire down gently and I was

250

supposed to go with him so we could finally be seen around town together, setting up to announce our relationship in the upcoming months. But I got stuck on campus, working on a huge final group project that I couldn't get out of, so I had to cancel. He was so upset, he thought maybe I wasn't taking our relationship seriously and we got in a huge fight. One night that weekend, he had a few too many drinks and ran into none other than little-miss-girl-next-door herself.' Cassidy paused, wiping tears from her face. 'Anyway, they hooked up and Claire got pregnant with their first little rugrat. And that was that. He did the honorable thing and married her when he found out. Our epic journey to make our way back to each other came to a screeching halt.'

'Oh, Cassidy, I'm so sorry. That must have been devastating.'

'Yeah,' Cassidy sniffled, looking up. 'Well, anyway. It's why I don't come back here very often. It's too hard, seeing them with their kids. I can see in his eyes when he looks at me that he still feels what I feel, but it's too late for us. I have to just stay away.'

Margo and Cassidy had never been close, but in this moment, she felt a deep kindred sadness for her. Margo's own relationship had blown up in her face too, but in such a different way. Still, heartbreak recognized heartbreak.

'Did Jessie know?'

Cassidy looked up at Margo, a long intense stare, before saying, 'Yeah she did. I could never hide anything from that girl. She made snide comments a few times, nudging me toward Tucker right in front of Claire. You know how she was. Tucker was paranoid that she'd let the cat out of the bag. Especially after they got in that big argument over the prank. He said some pretty mean

251

things to her and was worried she'd tell Claire about us as payback. But she didn't. Anyway,' Cassidy said with a deep sigh, 'I just didn't want any of this to come out, it would devastate Claire, and her children don't deserve that. But you see why Tucker couldn't have killed Jessie, now, don't you? He was *with* me, that whole night.'

Margo nodded, ready to mentally cross Tucker off the list in her head of those from Jessie's circle with both means and motive. But at the same time, if they were truly in love, people might question how far Cassidy would go to protect him. And what had they been arguing about in the woods the day before? It could look to the outside world like they were a team, in on it together somehow. Although, the whole debate was a moot point if no one ever found out about the affair. But Jessie *had* taunted Cassidy and Tucker with their secret. Had she pushed Tucker too far after the prank? And if so, was that motive? It seemed like a stretch that one of them would kill Jessie just to keep her quiet, but Margo reasoned anything could technically be possible. She'd seen headlines of people killing for much less, over a parking space, being unfriended on Facebook, hell, she even remembered a headline about a man killing his mother because she refused to buy him Avril Lavigne concert tickets. And she remembered from one of her criminal trials the way a lawyer had laid out a compelling defense based on how teenagers' pre-frontal cortex, which controlled decision making and impulse control, was the last part of the brain to mature, still developing well into the early twenties. What was more interesting, Margo reconciled, was that Charlie's alibi had just been blown wide open. *What is he hiding?*

'There you are,' Austin said as he came out the front door looking around. 'Are you ready to go?'

'Sure,' Margo said, giving Cassidy one last look. 'Take care, Cassidy.'

Cassidy gave her a nod, and they parted ways to their respective cars. Margo watched as Cassidy drove away.

'What was that all about?' Austin asked finally, like he couldn't hold it in a second longer.

'You'll never believe what she just told me.'

March 4, 2004

Dear Diary,

OMG. So today, Jessie's annoyance with Cassidy seems to have hit a new level. I guess Cassidy was like, begging her NOT to do some big pageant that's coming up. She's still been whining about losing, apparently her parents are mad about all the money being wasted on voice lessons and outfits and everything.

Anyway, I was walking through the school parking lot today and I saw Jessie and Cassidy arguing behind a tree. Jessie was like, 'You're the one who convinced me to sign up for these stupid things! I can't help it if I'm better than you.' And Cassidy was all like, 'You don't even need the prize money! And pretty soon my parents aren't going to let me do them anymore!' Then Jessie was like, 'That's not my fault! People expect to see me up there now. I'm not just gonna quit.'

And THEN. This is what was so crazy, Cassidy like, totally got in Jessie's face and said 'I mean it Jessie. Drop out. It's not some stupid game, it's my future! If you don't stop . . .' And then Jessie smiled and took a step closer and they were like, nose to nose. And she said, 'You'll do what?' Jessie was always so fearless.

Cassidy just huffed and stormed off. Jessie walked off in the other direction. I was gonna run after her and see if she wanted to talk, but then Charlie came out of the school and she plastered on a smile and bounced over to him. No thanks! I know he's rich and cute and all, but he is the WORST. I don't understand what she sees in him. I know it gives her status, but she could do so much better.

CHAPTER SEVENTEEN

On the way to Tucker's house the next day to confront him with their new information, Austin pulled into the small gas station nearby to fill up. Margo decided to pop inside to grab a few bottles of water while he was at the pump, walking down the aisles to the cooler in the back. Her phone dinged inside her pocket and she was almost scared to look, but her curiosity took over and she pulled it out. It was an email from her lawyer giving a status update on the progress of the divorce. It seemed to be going well; he said that he thought the last round of asset negotiation was going to be final. She tapped the back button, relieved the divorce would soon be done for good, and scanned her other emails quickly. Her breath caught in her throat when she saw one from GessieJermaine@gmail.com. Her social stalker had found her email address. She looked up and saw Austin pumping gas through the storefront window. Should she tell him? She looked back at the email and clicked into it.

'Don't stand too close to the fire, you might get burned,' the message read. A gif file was attached so Margo nervously clicked and a window opened up to play the animation. It showed a photo taken across from the Germaines' house, from the day of Jessie's service. In the photo, Margo was lighting Cassidy's cigarette for her, outside by the garage. Then suddenly, blood started dripping down from the top of the frame, covering the photo in red. Margo felt like she'd been stabbed in the chest, an acute pain making it hard to breathe. Her hands shook as she watched the gif again and again, unable to tear her eyes away. Finally, she exited out of her mail app in frustration. *Who is doing this? Is it Charlie? And if so, how far will he take it?* A chill ran through her at the thought. She couldn't imagine anyone else in Lake Moss having this much animosity toward her. If their purpose was to get her to stop looking into Jessie's case, the person with the most fingers pointing at them was Charlie. Glancing back up, she contemplated running outside to show Austin, but was startled by a man in a police uniform pulling out a bottle of cold brew coffee from the refrigerated case beside her.

'Oh, Margo, hey,' Brent, who she'd gone to high school with, said as he laid eyes on her.

'Hey, Brent,' Margo said back, giving him a polite smile, trying to block out the anxiety inducing message lurking in her phone. 'How are you doing?'

'I'm alright,' he said, 'it's been busy with the investigation kicking back into such high gear. Had to grab a little extra jolt.' He shook the bottle back and forth.

'How's the investigation going?' Margo asked, trying not to sound as eager as she really was for details.

'Ah, well, you know I can't talk about that. Chief's got everything on lockdown. But he's cooperating with the show investigation this time, so it'll be public at some point.'

Margo sighed. 'I understand you're in a tough position. It's just been a frustrating couple of weeks for me. First Jessie's body is found, and now I think Charlie Abbott has been trying to scare me like he used to. He seems pissed that I'm poking around in the case, and I worry what he's capable of. I know his family is powerful, but is he even being considered as an official suspect?'

Brent straightened up, tensing. 'I'm sorry, Margo. I've been given really strict orders not to talk about or go near Charlie or the Abbott family. I'm afraid I can't give you anything else. Healey would have my badge.'

So, her suspicion about Chief Healey protecting the Abbotts rather than prioritizing solving the case was right. Just then, the door opened and Austin stepped in.

'Hey, Margo, you get lost or someth . . .' He stopped in his tracks when he saw who Margo was talking to. 'Oh, hey Brent, how's it going?'

Brent gave Margo a sympathetic smile and sidestepped around her. He gave Austin a quick handshake and placed his drink down at the register. 'Hey Austin, it's going alright. Gotta get back on patrol though. I'll catch you guys later.'

After paying, Brent quickly exited out into the sun. Austin gave Margo a quizzical look as she paid for two bottles of water, but she stayed quiet till they got back to his car. She was on the verge of showing him the stalker messages but chickened out. She was afraid he would either cut her out of helping with the show in the name of her safety, or that he would jeopardize his job by confronting Charlie to see if it was him. Whoever was messing with her, she didn't want to put Austin in their sights too. On the way to Tucker's, Margo filled him in on the conversation with Brent. After arriving, they sat in Austin's parked car a couple of houses down from Tucker's. They wanted to be sure he was home before knocking on the door. After waiting fifteen minutes, Tucker came out to the front yard and turned off the sprinklers, before walking back inside. Austin looked at Margo with an anxious smile.

'Let's go.'

They exited the car and walked up to the door, skirting the wet lawn. Tucker answered, looking surprised to see them.

'Oh, hey . . . what's up?' he asked, scrunching his forehead, his mouth set in a hard line.

'We just had a few follow-up questions if you don't mind.'

'My on-air interview is tomorrow. Can't it wait? I'm really busy.' He glanced nervously behind him.

'It shouldn't take long. We just wanted to ask you about your relationship with Cassidy Quinn,' Austin said quickly, as if he was afraid the door would be slammed in front of them.

Tucker's face went white then slowly flushed bright red.

'Honey, can you make sure the trashcans are out by the curb for pick-up tomorrow?' Claire called out from inside the house.

He glanced back again, his eyes darting frantically. 'Yeah, I'll do that now!' He stepped outside and quickly shut the door behind them, ushering them to the part of the driveway that was not in view from inside the living room. 'Look, I don't know what you're talking about. But this is my family, my home. You can't just come here insinuating that I'm cheating on my wife!'

Out of the corner of her eye, Margo saw Claire in one of the bedroom windows folding a shirt and craning her neck to look at them suspiciously. When she caught Margo looking at her, she quickly moved away.

Austin cocked an eyebrow. 'We never said you were cheating on your wife. Are you?'

'No!' Tucker leaned in and glanced quickly at the front door, then back at Austin. 'I love Claire. We're happy. I don't know where you got this idea from.'

After a pause, Austin said, 'We got it from Cassidy. She told us that you two had been hooking up since high school behind Claire's back. Frankly, she said you guys were in love and had plans to reconnect after college. But then Claire got pregnant and you couldn't leave her. Is that true?'

Tucker's nostrils flared and his face turned a shade darker. 'Yes, alright, it's true!' He shook his head and looked to the side. Then he whipped his head back toward them. 'But that doesn't mean I don't love Claire and my kids. They are my whole world. This can't get out. It's been over with Cassidy for years. I won't admit this on camera if you decide to use it. In fact, I'll cancel the interview right now!' Tucker hissed out.

Austin shook his head. 'I'm not planning on telling my producer about the affair. I'm not interested in ruining your marriage. That's your business, not mine.' Tucker seemed to relax slightly. He exhaled and released his clenched fists.

The next-door neighbor's dog started barking on the other side of the fence a few feet from the garage. Margo glanced over and thought she saw the tree next to the gate leading to the neighbor's backyard move. Probably a squirrel, Margo thought, as she focused her attention back on the conversation.

'Then why are you asking about it?'

'The problem is, you were Charlie's alibi that night and he was yours. But Cassidy said you were actually with her. Do you see our predicament?' Austin replied, arching his eyebrows inquisitively.

Tucker shook his head again, and whispered, 'Dammit Cassidy,' under his breath. 'OK yeah, I was with Cassidy that night. But obviously I couldn't admit that when asked for my whereabouts. Charlie came to me and said he had no alibi and asked if I would say I was with him. Since I needed one too, I agreed.'

'Is that what you were fighting about at the funeral reception?' Margo asked.

'That was part of it. I don't want to talk about that,' Tucker said, brushing her off angrily.

'Did Charlie tell you where he was that night? Why he needed an alibi?' Austin asked, trying another angle.

'He said his parents were out of town for a wedding and his dad had asked him to pick up something urgent in Charlotte from one of their suppliers. He said it took him most of the night driving to and from and it was late when he got back. But since no one was with him to confirm what time he returned home, he knew it wasn't a good alibi even though it was the truth. He knew the focus would be on him since he and Jessie were dating.'

'Did Charlie know you and Cassidy were together?' Austin asked.

'No, he never knew. Charlie isn't the most discreet person. He drinks a lot, which I hear you've witnessed first-hand,' he said with a quick look at Margo who tensed. 'I didn't trust him to keep it quiet; he's a mouthy and unpredictable drunk. Cassidy's parents had a basement with its own entrance. We only spent time together there, and sometimes in the woods if the weather was nice. Never seen out in public unless we were in a group. Neither of us wanted to hurt Claire. As messed up as the whole thing was, I did love her too. But it just happened one night, and then Cassidy and I couldn't stay away from one another. I was with her in that basement the night Jessie went missing. I told Charlie I was home alone in my room.'

Austin nodded. 'Cassidy said Jessie knew about your relationship. Weren't you worried she'd tell Charlie or Claire?'

'Of course I was. Cassidy insisted Jessie wouldn't say anything. But Jessie would always make backhanded comments and push me toward Cassidy when Claire was standing right beside us, making it very clear she had the power to blow everything wide open if she wanted. I told Cassidy that she couldn't be trusted. Thankfully, she never actually said anything.'

'Did you ever talk to Jessie about it?'

'A couple of times. But she always acted like she didn't know what I was talking about. She had some elaborate explanation for each time she'd made comments around Claire. It was pointless. I finally backed off and let Cassidy handle it.'

Austin shot a quick look at Margo before saying, 'Someone saw you and Cassidy arguing in the woods the day before the funeral. We were under the impression that she could barely take a day off for the service, much less two. What was so important that she couldn't wait to talk to you?'

Tucker stared at Austin, his nostrils flaring slightly. Margo could feel Austin tense next to her. 'It's personal, none of your business.'

Austin looked reluctant to say more so Margo pushed

forward. 'Was it about your relationship? Or the fake alibi? Maybe Cassidy wanted to come clean?'

Tucker looked around and said, 'Something like that. Look, I gotta get back inside, just leave it be.'

Just then, Claire popped her head out the front door, leaning forward and looking at them confused. 'Tuck? What's going on? Is everything OK?'

Tucker jolted at her voice and plastered a small smile on his face. 'Everything is fine, honey. We're just working out a few details for my interview tomorrow. Almost done.'

Claire glanced back and forth between them until her eyes landed on Margo. She gave her a long, questioning look and seemed reluctant to leave. 'Are you sure?' she asked, her eyes darting back to Tucker.

'Yeah, it's fine Claire, really. I'll be back inside in a minute.' Even Margo could hear the anxiety floating just under his words.

After another long look at Margo and Austin, she slowly closed the door. Tucker let out a loud breath. 'Is that all?'

After a pause while Austin seemingly weighed his options, he said, 'OK, thanks for talking with us. But hey, I have to warn you, you'll need to come up with another alibi. A false alibi for Charlie, a main suspect in the case, is too big not to investigate on camera. And I will have to tell my producer that Charlie's alibi was fabricated. I'll just tell her you did it as a favor to him. Sorry man, but if you back out of the interview now, it may look even more suspicious and get people talking.'

Tucker clenched his lips together and took a deep breath. Then he nodded. 'Fine. I'll tell Claire that I was trying to help out my best friend. That I was in my room that night, like I told Charlie. And if asked on camera, that's what I'll say.'

Austin nodded and they turned to leave. Tucker watched as they walked down the driveway back to Austin's car. Before they stepped off the sidewalk, Tucker called out, 'Hey! If a word of this gets out . . .' he tilted his head forward and looked pointedly at them.

His message was clear, if anyone found out about the affair, they'd be the ones he'd come after.

Driving away from town and up into the gorgeous mountains near Moss Creek Brewing, Margo rolled down the window and inhaled deeply. She'd always loved the smell of the trees in her hometown, fresh and earthy. When they pulled up in front of the Abbotts' grand home not far from the brewery, it struck Margo what a difference a mile or two made. Going from Tucker's small suburban house to the Abbotts' mansion was a shock; a study in the differences between the haves and the have nots. The house, while styled as a chalet nestled into the side of the hillside, was massive and had huge stone columns holding up the portico. The circular driveway could easily fit ten cars. There was even a grand balcony over the portico. Margo could just imagine Virginia Abbott standing up there, greeting her arriving guests with a glass of champagne in her hand. A pond with a waterfall trickled off to the side in the front yard. Margo had never been to the Abbotts' property and was impressed. The house was stunning.

Austin pressed the doorbell and a loud ding echoed inside the cavernous home. A woman wearing a gray and white maid's uniform answered the door and led them to a library with tall, vaulted ceilings off the entryway. She told them to have a seat, waving her arm to matching cream leather-tufted loveseats facing one another across a small oval coffee table, and said she'd let Mr. and Mrs. Abbott know they'd arrived. Austin and Margo took a seat and were silent as they took in their elaborate surroundings. The wall next to them carried paintings with nameplate plaques underneath from a few well-known American artists like George Inness and John George Brown, painters Margo remembered from her elective American Art History college class. She wondered if they were originals or well-done copies. With the Abbotts' wealth, she imagined they could afford originals. The floors were white marble with thick gray veining and had oriental rugs placed strategically throughout.

Margo was in awe of the room. One wall was covered from floor to ceiling with a bookshelf full of beautiful leatherbound books, a rolling wooden ladder angled against the far end. The bordering wall had a massive arched stone fireplace with a chaise lounge and an over-sized leather armchair placed in front, along with a small table laid out with a vintage chess board. As it was summer, the fireplace wasn't lit, but Margo imagined lounging on the chaise, reading a book in front of a roaring fire with snow falling outside in the winter. Along the mantel over the fireplace was a row of Fabergé eggs encased in glass boxes. Margo almost whistled at the sight, but caught herself; the oversized room would surely magnify the sound to all. Next to the fireplace was an antique carved wood writing desk with a vintage type-writer and a stained-glass Tiffany lamp. *Did anyone actually use that desk?* Margo wondered. More likely, it was placed there for show.

Virginia Abbott breezed into the room a few minutes later wearing a long flowy white summer dress and gold strappy Chanel heels. Her hair and makeup were perfectly done. Margo wondered if she'd gotten dressed up for them or if she always looked so put-together in her own home. Margo felt self-conscious about her yellow sundress and cheap brown sandals. She smoothed the dress out while rising to greet Mrs. Abbott, wishing she'd worn lipstick and spent a little more time on her hair that morning. Though everyone knew of the Abbotts, Margo had never met Charlie's parents. They ran in different circles.

'Hello, I'm Virginia Abbott, but you can call me Ginny.'

She held out a hand toward them, her fingers curled forward like the weight of her rings were pulling them down. The massive engagement ring on her other hand glistened when the sunlight hit it, almost blinding Margo. She got a whiff of Ginny's expensive, overpowering perfume and held her breath until she pulled away. Margo had never been fond of perfume and thought most women applied too much. Ginny was no exception.

'I'm Austin and this is Margo,' he said, motioning toward her.

Ginny was beautiful, even now that she was older, although Margo couldn't guess her age. Her blonde high-lighted hair was still lush and shiny, no doubt cut and colored regularly. Not one wrinkle blemished her face, which didn't move much when she smiled, her cheeks refusing to join in. Copious amounts of Botox must be helping with that just under her skin, Margo thought.

'Welcome, can I get you anything to drink?'

Just then, the maid came into the room carrying a tray with a crystal water decanter and glasses. 'Water is fine,' Austin replied, and Margo nodded in agreement.

Ginny looked at the maid, 'Silvia, water please.' The three of them sat down, Ginny perching herself delicately on the edge of the loveseat and Margo and Austin sat back down across from her while Silvia poured them all water. 'My husband should be down in a minute. He's just finishing up a call.'

They sat in uncomfortable silence for a moment. 'Your home is lovely,' Margo said to ease the silence.

Ginny's lips upturned slightly. 'Oh, thank you. We're redoing the kitchen right now so it's just a mess, but we love this place. Plus, we're not far from the brewery so Charles can easily pop over to assist Charlie if there's a problem.'

They smiled at her but said nothing. Margo wasn't sure if Charlie visited his parents much, but she hoped he wasn't there. She had no interest in seeing him. She feared retaliation if he found her in his home questioning his parents. If he *was* her online stalker, the last threatening message still fresh in her mind, she didn't want him to escalate further. Charles's voice filtered into the room, getting louder by the second. His call seemed to be wrapping up.

'Yes, but I won't pay more than a thousand Harry, so do what you have to.'

He entered the room as he clicked off his cell phone and dropped it in his blazer pocket. He too was dressed for the interview, gray slacks and matching blazer, a crisp white button-up and polished brown leather shoes. His hair was fully gray; no attempt had been made to hide it. But it suited him, made him appear regal with his crystal-clear blue eyes. The same eyes Charlie had.

'Sorry about that,' he said as he leaned toward them and firmly shook both their hands. He sat down next to Ginny and took a sip of water. 'So, what can we do for you today?'

Margo noticed how he didn't look at Ginny or sit too close to her. No gestures of affection or even an acknowledgement that she was present. *Not a very loving relationship*, Margo thought.

'We just have a few questions for the *Into Thin Air* episode on Jessie. We don't suspect we'll need you to do an on-camera interview, but some background info would be great.' Ginny and Charles nodded. 'We recently interviewed Wylie Hooper, who used to work at your brewery.'

Charles's expression softened and he smiled proudly. 'Wylie was a great employee. He came to me when he was a teenager and said he wanted to open his own microbrewery one day. He wanted to learn how to brew. I admired his gumption, so, I gave him a job and he worked for us until he had enough money saved to open his own in Asheville. From what we hear, he's doing quite well.'

'You weren't worried about the competition?' Austin asked.

Charles laughed and shook his head. 'Oh no, he never wanted to open a large place like Moss Creek. He was more interested in seasonal craft brews, a smaller place. I thought it was great and encouraged him.'

After a pause, Austin asked, 'Did you know that he was giving beer from the brewery to Jessie for her and her friends?'

Charles's face dropped and he looked off to the side. He shook his head again and looked back at them. 'No, I didn't know that. Why would Wylie give Jessie beer? I don't think he even knew her other than being Charlie's girlfriend.'

Austin paused a beat, clearly deciding how best to word his response. 'He didn't really have an answer when we asked that question, but it seemed like maybe she had something on him and was pressuring him in some way.

I'm not sure of the specifics,' Austin said, shooting a quick look at Margo. After agreeing to keep Wylie's indiscretions off-screen to save him from potential legal and professional scrutiny, neither of them wanted throw Wylie under the bus by telling the Abbotts about him stealing their trade secrets.

Charles looked unconvinced but said, 'It's disappointing, but what can I do about it now?'

'Apparently Jessie approached him after you cut Charlie off when you caught him sneaking beer, and she was relentless. It was their way back in after you took away Charlie's keys.'

Ginny looked at Charles. 'I told you that you shouldn't have trusted Wylie. How many times did I tell you that boy had ulterior motives when he offered to work all those late hours? But you wouldn't listen,' she hissed out, shaking her head.

Charles looked at Ginny. 'Ginny, please,' he admonished her. She took a deep breath and exhaled through her nose, annoyed. Then he looked back at them. 'It's really unfortunate that Wylie didn't just turn them down or come clean to us about what was happening. I thought he had better sense than that. But you can't believe that Wylie had anything to do with Jessie's death over some beer.'

'No, I'm not saying that. We're just piecing everything together,' Austin replied.

'Well, I for one wouldn't put it past him,' Ginny replied, flicking her shiny hair over her shoulder.

Charles looked like he wanted to say something back to her but didn't because they were in front of company. Instead, he shook his head and asked, 'Is there anything else we can do for you?'

'Um, yes,' Austin said uneasily. Margo noticed him shift

in his seat. There was so much tension flying between the Abbotts, it was making Margo uncomfortable too. She kept flipping her pen over in her hand in between scribbling down notes. 'You two were at a wedding out of town the night Jessie went missing, correct?'

'Yes, Lila and Colin Richmond's daughter had been married the weekend before in Raleigh. We stayed a few extra days to visit with friends,' Ginny replied.

'Have you ever used a supplier in Charlotte?'

'Charlotte?' Charles said, his face scrunched up. He glanced at Ginny who looked equally confused. 'No, we've used the same suppliers for years and none are in Charlotte.'

'Do you know where Charlie was that night?' Austin followed up.

'I assumed he was at home like he was supposed to be. He told us Tucker came over and they played pool. Tucker confirmed that,' Charles said stiffly. Margo and Austin shared a look. 'Why don't you just come out with it. You obviously have something you want to ask,' Charles continued, his voice becoming harder, his eyes narrowing.

Austin was understandably intimidated by Charles. He cleared his throat and clasped his hands in his lap before finally saying, 'No, there's nothing specific. We are just confirming alibis from all angles.'

'What you're trying to do is poke holes in Charlie's alibi and we're not going to help you do that,' Charles said angrily. Ginny's mouth dropped open slightly and she looked sharply at her husband. Charles straightened and inhaled loudly, his nostrils flaring as he exhaled. He stared at them for a long second before grabbing Ginny's hand and standing, pulling her up along with him.

270

'We're done here. If you have any more questions you can speak to our lawyer.'

He reached into his pocket and pulled out his wallet. He slipped a card out and handed it to Austin. Margo and Austin followed suit, rising as Austin reached out and took the card. The interview was obviously over.

'Silvia will show you out,' Ginny said stiffly as she followed her husband out of the room. Suddenly, the two of them were a unified front. Austin looked at Margo and widened his eyes. She whistled softly at the change the mood in the room had taken. She assumed Austin was thinking the same thing as her. There were secrets in the Abbott family, and they would spare no expense to protect their own. Unless Charlie decided to be honest with them or more evidence magically came to light, they might never know where he actually was that night.

CHAPTER EIGHTEEN

The next afternoon, Margo walked up to the oversized door at Moss Creek Brewing. The note on the door read 'CLOSED TODAY FOR PRIVATE EVENT.' After Tucker's revelation about the false alibi, Amy decided to catch Charlie on camera with the lie and had instructed Austin not to let the Abbotts know specifics for fear they would tip him off. After entering the brewery, Margo smiled at Austin as he ran over and gave her a quick hug, but it didn't quite meet her eyes.

Austin, unnervingly observant as always, said, 'What's wrong?'

'Maybe I shouldn't be here. Or I can wait in the car,' she said, her nerves at seeing Charlie spiking again.

'Margo, I know he's got you spooked. But I'm with you and so is the whole crew. I wouldn't let anything happen to you. Amy is going to ask all the questions, you'll just be watching from the sidelines.'

'I know, it's just . . .'

'I think having you present will throw him off his game more than if he's just trying to pull one over on the crew. You clearly agitate him, and that can really give us a leg up.'

'So, you're basically serving me up as the sacrificial lamb,' she said, this time giving a genuine smile.

'Pretty much,' he laughed. 'But I have your back. I promise.'

'OK, let's get this over with then,' she said, exhaling loudly and the two of them walked further into the brewery.

Most of the crew was littered around the large room off the entrance setting up equipment near the astounding windows overlooking the mountains. The room took her breath away yet again and she knew it would look beautiful on camera with the blue jutting peaks in the background.

'Amy thought it was a good idea to do the interview here. Since the brewery is the main economy of Lake Moss, she thought it would add color to the episode. I guess the Abbotts are confident after all, that Charlie's alibi is solid. Charlie jumped at the opportunity for the free advertisement,' Austin said with a smirk.

Margo raised her eyebrows. 'I'm sure.'

'We're about to get started, everything is already set up. There's craft services over there,' he said, pointing to a long table off to the side covered in snacks and sandwiches, coffee carafes and a bucket of sodas. 'Help yourself.'

'Thanks.'

'Charlie insisted on a specific chair, so the prop master had to swap it out. But we should be starting soon.'

Margo glanced around, nervously. 'Of course he did. Where is Charlie now?'

Austin looked as though he was trying not to laugh. 'You won't believe this, but he hired a hair and makeup artist for his interview. We offered one to him, but he insisted on hiring his own.'

Margo's mouth dropped open. 'You're kidding me!'

Austin couldn't hold it in any longer and he burst out laughing. 'I wish I was but no, he's over there in the back room getting his makeup done.' He hooked his thumb over his shoulder. 'No one else we've interviewed even asked for hair and makeup.'

Margo joined in and shook her head. 'Why doesn't that surprise me.'

Just as Austin was about to reply, Amy called out, 'First team!'

Seconds later, Charlie came walking into the room with his rich boy swagger. His hair was gelled over from a thin side part, a thick layer of foundation making his face look waxy.

'Where are we doing this?' he asked Austin, barely glancing at Margo.

Amy rushed up and led him to the chair they'd set up near the windows. As Amy called out orders to her team and Austin got his equipment ready, Margo sat down in a chair directly in view of Charlie so she could see every reaction he had. A few minutes later, the clapperboard slapped down, and Amy began talking about the brewery and growing up in Lake Moss. She followed it up with questions about Jessie, their relationship and subsequent break up, and then asked for his whereabouts the night she went missing. Charlie gave all the stock answers he gave fifteen years ago. Finally, Margo knew the gotcha moment was near, and a mix of nerves and excitement swelled in her stomach.

'It's come to our attention that you weren't actually with Tucker on the night Jessie disappeared. He's admitted that he was doing you a favor by lying to give you an alibi. You weren't playing pool with him.'

Charlie cleared his throat and straightened up. He looked like he was trying to maintain his cool, confident demeanor while searching deep for an explanation.

'Oh, that,' he gave a small, unconvincing laugh. 'Looking back, it's so stupid. I was running an errand for my parents and since I didn't get home alone till late—'

'Actually, Charlie, we don't think you *were* running that errand for your parents, either. They confirmed that they don't use any suppliers in Charlotte, which is where you told Tucker you went. Why would you need Tucker to cover for you? Where were you really, Charlie?'

Charlie's expression was suddenly unreadable. He was stiff, his eyes alight like dancing flames, his jaw clenched tight and rigid.

'Did she put you up to this?' he finally asked, gesturing at Margo. She flinched, taken aback. Margo shook her head in silence, slouching back into the chair as if she were trying to disappear. 'You've been gunning for me and my friends since you got back into town,' he spat, leaning forward in his chair.

The producer's assistant was about to run over but Amy held her hand up, as though to say she wanted to see how this played out. Margo stayed quiet, not moving a muscle, afraid to draw even more attention to herself.

'Tucker admitted pretty quickly that your alibi was a lie,' Amy said, dragging Charlie's attention back to her.

'And what, you think you can believe everything he says? Because my friends are all such honest, trustworthy, upstanding citizens?' he scoffed.

'We're just trying to get your side of the story,' Amy

said calmly. 'Why don't you just tell us what you were up to that night?'

Charlie considered her for a minute before leaning back with force. 'Fine. But it's not going to matter, because no one can confirm it anyway, hence the need for Tucker, that prick.'

Margo tensed, anxious for his reply.

Charlie puffed out a breath and looked around the set, like he was stalling for time. 'I was passed out. Alone. At home.'

Margo deflated; the answer was so anti-climactic. 'Passed out?' Amy asked.

'Yeah, passed out,' Charlie continued. 'I'd taken some muscle relaxers and cracked a beer. My parents were out of town and my shoulder was bothering me from a game of pick-up basketball I'd played earlier that week. I just wanted to chill. But they were some potent pills, I wasn't prepared for how quickly they'd knock me on my ass. So, I don't really remember that night past drinking a beer. Next thing I knew, I was waking up on the sofa the next morning. I can tell by the look on your face that you understand why I felt the need to have a better alibi than that. I asked Tucker and he was willing to give me a reliable alibi. Until now I guess,' Charlie said, scowling.

Nodding thoughtfully, Amy said, 'I can see that,' in a tone that implied she understood completely why he'd lied. 'But why would you need to lie to Tucker about taking pills and falling asleep? He was your best friend, surely he'd understand.'

Again, Charlie looked panicked. He clenched his lips together and shook his head. 'I didn't tell Tucker about the pills because I'd taken them from his parents' medicine cabinet, and he got in trouble for it. I didn't think his parents would even notice since it was an older prescription but after he caught the blame for it, I couldn't fess up. He would have been so mad after the way his dad went in on him for it.'

Amy nodded and paused. 'OK let's move on.' Margo could sense she was a bit disappointed in his answer but was pressing on with determination. 'Is it true that Jessie was actually the one who broke up with you?'

Charlie's eyes narrowed and even through the thick layers of makeup, Margo could see his face flushing with anger. This wasn't going the way he thought it would and it gave Margo a sliver of pleasure to see him squirm. 'It was mutual, OK?' he replied defensively. Then he relaxed his clenched fists, probably realizing he was coming off as aggressive on camera. 'It just wasn't working anymore.'

'Why's that?'

Charlie glanced quickly at Margo then back at Amy. 'She was always complaining and saying she deserved better than me whenever we argued. And toward the end, we were arguing almost every day. She got a little too big for her britches after becoming so popular, because of *me*: *I* made her popular,' he said, pointing a finger at his own chest, 'but suddenly she was too good for me. I got sick of it.'

'Can you tell us anything about the rumor that you and Jessie were spotted having an argument earlier in the evening near Town Square, *after* the rally where you initially said was the last time you saw her?' Amy continued, and Margo was impressed with her calm and poised tenacity.

'Fine, you caught me, OK. I confess!' he put his palms out in front of them with a harsh laugh. 'I wanted to talk

277

to her about our relationship, to try to get back together, work out our problems. That girl drove me crazy. But she wanted nothing to do with me. Told me I needed to get over it because there was someone else.'

'Did she say who?' Amy asked eagerly.

'No,' Charlie scoffed. 'I assumed it was a friend of mine or something, otherwise I figured she'd throw whoever it was in my face. But we fought and she stormed off and I went home to unwind. Then I took the pills. That's the big nefarious ending to my story. How'd I do, was that satisfying enough for you?'

Remaining calm despite Charlie's agitated demeanor, Amy concluded with, 'We really appreciate you telling your story, Charlie. I know it's not easy to dredge all this up again. But we are grateful that you spoke with us today.'

Charlie was not mollified by her words. He jumped up from his seat and stomped away from the spotlights and mic booms, while Amy called out to check the gate. He disappeared into a doorway behind the hostess podium.

After the gate was confirmed good, Austin walked over to Margo with one eyebrow cocked. 'Is it just me? Or does no one in this group have an actual rock-solid alibi that can be confirmed?'

'It's not just you,' Margo replied.

'If you can wait a few, maybe we can go grab lunch after we wrap out?'

'Sure, sounds good. I could go for some barbeque from Gillian's. The food at the reception was incredible.'

'Ooh good call. Shouldn't take long,' he said as he walked away with a smile.

While Margo waited for Austin and his team to break down the equipment and pack up, she sat down at a table and scrolled through Instagram. An alert notifying her of a new message popped up and Margo's breath hitched in her throat. Her finger hovered over the little arrow before she clicked. After a long moment, Margo finally tapped into her messages and released a huge sigh of relief. It was from an old co-worker sending her a funny meme of a dog typing furiously in a courtroom. The note under the image read 'We miss you! Your replacement can't type nearly as fast as you haha!' A warmth swelled in her heart that someone from her old life had finally checked in. She replied with a heart emoji and, 'Miss you too! Call me next week so we can catch up.' before clicking back on her screen. But her smile fell as she noticed another message request, this one from someone outside her followers. Pulse racing, Margo clicked in. Her fears were founded. The requestor was using the GessieJermaine handle but had added a 456 at the end. A new account from the two she'd previously blocked. With dread, she opened the message, a morbid curiosity pushing her forward.

There was a thumbnail image of a video revealing trees and the side of a house. She hit the play button. After some rustling, the camera moved around the side of the house and blurred slightly as the person zoomed in. When the camera focused, Margo's hand flew to her mouth. The video was of her and Austin from the day before, interviewing Tucker in front of his garage. But it was too distant to hear what they were saying, seemingly shot from a house or two away. The video only lasted ten seconds but ended on Tucker, his face red and his eyebrows clenched together. The message under the video read, 'Did you think I was lying? One way or another you'll stop asking questions, I'll make sure of it. When you go to sleep under your patchwork quilt tonight, make sure you lock your window. I am closer than you think.'

Margo glanced over at Austin who was zipping up his bag and shaking hands with his crew. She came to a decision. It was time to tell him. The person seemed determined, the gap between when each message was sent getting shorter and the threats more sinister. She had no idea how far they would end up taking it, and she needed someone in her corner.

As Austin walked up to her, his smile slowly dropped as he saw her face. 'I have to show you something,' she said quickly before she lost her nerve. And then, she caught Austin up on the other messages before showing him the most recent video. 'I didn't mention it until now because I didn't want to worry you. I just thought it was Charlie playing another prank on me. But now it seems to be escalating, they keep finding ways to get to me, and I'm not so sure it is Charlie after all.'

Austin played the video a few more times before looking back at Margo. 'Who would be so upset at us asking questions *other* than Jessie's murderer?'

Margo clenched her lips together and took a deep breath. 'I'm freaking out, Austin. With everything going on, I'm worried whoever is doing this could actually end up hurting me. Or you!'

Austin nodded, looking concerned. 'Well, we were confronting Tucker about his alibi with Charlie when this video was taken. Which he ended up confessing was a lie. Maybe this *is* Charlie and he was worried Tucker would do just that. He was pretty pissed in that interview just now. And look, this message was sent a few minutes after he stormed off, so it's not totally impossible for him to have done it after the interview ended.'

'So, you think it's Charlie?'

'Do I think Charlie is capable of something like this?' he held up Margo's phone. 'Yeah, I do. But I don't think he's the only one with something to hide. The timing of it is suspicious, though. Is it OK if I send this video to myself? I'm going to see if some of my guys can get anything off it to tell us who it is.'

'Yeah sure,' Margo said, distracted.

Austin placed a hand on her arm. 'I know this is scary but we'll get to the bottom of it. I promise. I'm not going to let anything happen to you. Now, how about some ribs and mashed potatoes to take your mind off it,' he said with a smile.

Austin was hard to resist so she smiled and nodded as they walked to the exit. Before she walked through the door Austin was holding for her, she glanced back. Charlie strode purposefully back into the room, barking orders at a brewery worker. When his eyes landed on Margo, they hardened and an evil smile lit up his face.

CHAPTER NINETEEN

As Margo finished loading the dishwasher after breakfast a day later, her phone rang. She picked it up and smiled when she saw Austin's number on the screen. Putting it on speaker she said, 'Hey! What's up?'

'Hey! So get this, our show researchers have been taking your notes and fact checking them. Remember how Wylie said he was at that beer convention when Jessie went missing? Well one of the researchers found that he did purchase tickets to the convention, so we thought that was that. But then yesterday when she was searching old Myspace pages of Lake Moss High students for any photos of Jessie from that day, she found one taken after the end of year rally. In the background, after we cleaned the photo up a bit, you can see Wylie and Jessie talking. Well, arguing actually.'

Margo leaned her palms on the counter. 'Wow, what?! So, Wylie *was* in town the day she went missing. *And* he argued with Jessie. He totally lied to us.'

'Exactly! My producer called Wylie last night to see if he'd be willing to talk on camera but didn't tell him what we'd found, and he jumped at the chance. We're squeezing it in today, like, in a half-hour. Do you want to come watch? We took a small crew with us to Asheville to film to contrast his smaller place with Moss Creek Brewing. I didn't want to call you too early and wake you up. But if you hop in the car now you should be able to make it.'

'Sure!' she said a bit too enthusiastically, wincing at the tone of her voice.

'Great, see you soon!' he said before hanging up.

Margo glanced into the living room. Her dad was snoring on the recliner with a basketball game on the television. Luckily, she'd showered the night before, so she ran into her room and threw on a cream linen dress. After applying quick makeup, paying extra attention to her lashes with a few extra coats, she swiped a bold red gloss on her lips. She topped the outfit off with a thick pair of gold hoops. As she looked at herself in the mirror, she wished she had time to do something more to her hair. But it would take about a half-hour to get there and she didn't want to miss the interview. Her dad hadn't woken yet, so she grabbed her bag and quickly wrote him a note.

Out on the winding mountain road, she cranked the air conditioning and drove faster than she normally would, anxious to get there. When she arrived, she pushed through the doors and spotted Wylie standing behind the counter, lights surrounding him in front of his impressive list of beers, talking to one of the crew. Austin popped his head up nearby after he'd adjusted the angle of his boom mic. He spotted her and ran over.

He whistled when he got close, 'Wow, look at you! You dressed up for Wylie, didn't you?' he said with narrowed eyes and a mischievous smile.

283

Normally Margo would have blushed and maybe denied it. But this was Austin, and since they'd spent so much time together lately, she felt more comfortable. Instead, she smiled and bumped his shoulder with her own. 'Jealous?'

Austin chuckled and said, 'Maybe.' He smiled widely at her.

Now Margo was certain she was blushing. 'So did I make it in time?'

'Kind of. Amy already did the first part of the interview, just the background stuff. We took a quick break so we could all grab breakfast since there's so many great food spots nearby. Amy wasn't able to get catering set up on such short notice, so we do walk-away meals when that happens. But we're just about to dig back in with the juicy stuff.' Austin arched his eyebrows for emphasis. 'You can sit wherever you want since we are shooting in front of the bar.

'Austin! We're ready,' Amy hollered out. She gave a quick wave to Margo when she spotted her.

As Austin ran back to his station, Margo positioned herself to the side at a tall table. When Wylie spotted her, he waved and winked. Two females and one male from the crew turned around to see who he was waving to. She recognized a familiar hint of jealousy in their eyes, Wylie clearly having the same effect on them as he did on Margo. She felt her face flush with their eyes on her. The slate had 'Wylie Hooper – Hooper's Brews' penned in white on the front. The arm clapped down with a loud slap.

'Wylie, can you tell us where you were the night Jessie disappeared?' Amy said off-screen.

'I was at HopCon in Kentucky. It's a yearly convention

for brewers. There are panels and product exhibitions, that kind of thing. I go every year.'

After a long pause, Amy said, 'We actually looked into that, and while you did buy tickets, we found a photo from the day Jessie went missing, with you – and Jessie – in the background.' She slowly passed an enlarged photo across the bar top to him. 'It appears as though you were in Lake Moss, arguing.'

Wylie looked panicked, his eyes wide and his skin paling even further. He picked up the photo and squinted at it for a full minute before placing it back down on the bar.

Amy waited for him to say something, but Wylie remained silent. 'Can you tell us where you really were the day she disappeared? And why you lied about it?'

Wylie gulped a few times and his eyes darted around the room, landing on each person before he quickly looked away. Then he exhaled and leaned his elbows on to the bar. 'I didn't have anything to do with her disappearance. I swear. I had planned on going to the convention, like I said. But I was seeing someone at the time. Someone who's married. I . . . she called me the night before I was set to leave. Her husband had to go out of town unexpectedly for work. We didn't get much time together so when the opportunity for a few days together presented itself, rather than just a few hours here and there, I took it. I gave the tickets to a friend and he went in my place. I'm not proud of it.' He shook his head and ran his hand over his hair. 'I was with her most of the time.'

Amy nodded and pushed the photo toward him again. 'So what are we seeing here then?'

'It's not what you think,' Wylie said quickly, panic in his voice. 'Jessie asked me to give her a ride later that night.' He glanced at Austin, surely wondering if he'd told Amy about the beer blackmail. 'She was always at the brewery with Charlie, so we knew each other. Her car was in the shop and she had something important she had to do. I don't know what, she didn't tell me, but she was adamant that it was important, that she had to be there. I knew I'd be with S—' He stopped himself before he said her name. 'I knew I'd be with this woman. I gave up the convention to spend time with her, no way was I going to leave her to give Jessie a ride. She was mad that I refused, she wasn't used to not getting what she wanted and . . .' he glanced at Austin and then Margo, 'and I guess that's what's going on in the photo.'

'So this,' Amy tapped her finger on the photo, 'is the last time you saw Jessie? The *real* last time?'

'Yeah,' he said sheepishly. 'I lied because I don't want to blow up my former girlfriend's life. She's still married and has kids now.'

Amy moved on, asking questions about Jessie and her friends, and his interactions with them. It wrapped up quickly and Margo went to stand by Austin while he dismantled his equipment. After a quick glance at Margo and Austin, Wylie immediately disappeared into the back room.

'Do you believe him?' Austin asked as he released the lever lock on a tripod.

'I honestly don't know what to think. When we interviewed him before, I completely believed him. But he lied before, so there's no way to trust him now. Can you think of anyone who might fit the bill for his mysterious affair in Lake Moss who's married and name starts with an S? Maybe who would have been hanging around the brewery since that's where he spent most of his time?'

Austin finished breaking down his equipment and stacked it all to the side. 'There's a few I can remember seeing around a lot. Stacey Cooper, Stephanie Malitakas and Shanika Williams. But I can't really see any of them with Wylie. At least the Wylie from back then.' He shrugged.

'Yeah same. The only other one I can think of is Sherri Lambert, but she would have been in her forties at that time. Seems unlikely. But I mean, who knows how many S-named women are in that town that we didn't have any interaction with as kids. It could be a needle in a haystack.'

'Well Amy is working in conjunction with the police now that they are cooperating. So I'm sure they'll interview him with this new information and get a name to confirm it off-camera. And our researchers will do some digging too. I don't know, though, do you think we should tell Amy about the beer he was giving to Jessie and the blackmailing? I almost told her this morning but I'm still nervous about ruining his career on the off chance he's innocent. But now that he's back in the suspect pool, I'm worried there's more to his history with Jessie.'

'Yeah, that's tough. But his story about Jessie blackmailing him does match up with what Cassidy told us, so at least that part of it seems truthful. He admitted to those illegal activities to us rather than lie about them which seems a bit odd if he did murder her, unless it was some weird attempt to distract us and gain our trust. I'm really not sure what's best to do at this point. Do you think if you told Amy that she could be discreet about it?'

'Maybe, but now that I think about it, I'd have to admit that I kept it from her too.' He glanced over at Amy who was talking to a crew member near the bar. 'I just started working for her and she's been trusting me with a lot of responsibility. If she knew we omitted this from our notes . . .'

Margo nodded. 'Yeah, I didn't think about that. We don't want to blow up both your careers in one go. I guess . . . let's just keep it to ourselves. For now, anyway. If the police can't confirm his alibi, we could revisit it then and find a way to loop her in?'

Austin's eyes were full of worry. He paused, thinking for a moment, before nodding. 'OK, that sounds like a good plan. If his new alibi holds up, then there's no point in telling Amy. Thanks for coming all the way out here.'

'Thanks for inviting me,' Margo said, smiling. 'I guess I'll head back. You have more interviews today?'

'Yeah, and we'll be here a bit longer packing up before we head to talk with Lenny, the boy who slammed into the cooler and brought her cheer bow to the surface. He's pretty shaken up, but we finally got him to agree to go on camera which should add some nice color to the episode.'

'Oh, that's great. Well keep me posted if anything big comes up.'

'Will do!' he said, smiling.

Their eyes lingered on one another for a moment before Margo reluctantly turned toward the door with a wave.

CHAPTER TWENTY

Margo stood in her childhood bedroom the next day, writing on her old whiteboard hung on the wall next to her closet, where she used to keep track of her homework assignments. The pink floral magnets that used to hold up photos of her childhood were now tacking up photos of all the possible suspects in Jessie's murder, lines connecting the photos to their alibis and motives that she and Austin had come up with so far. Jazz had sent her an apologetic text the day before, canceling their appointment last minute and asking if they could reschedule for later in the week. Margo was disappointed, but somewhat relieved to put off their next session. Talking about personal heavy stuff in the middle of interviewing suspects in Jessie's case was a bit overwhelming. But needing somewhere to focus her energy, Margo had put the suspect board together and was quite proud of her handiwork.

The cast of characters represented on the board was interesting, not one of them could definitively be cleared, but they didn't have any solid evidence to point at any of them either. Their best bet for a believable suspect was still Charlie, but everyone seemed to be tangled in a web of secrets and lies. Unable to stop staring at it, Margo sent Austin a text to see if he could come over later and discuss. He replied that he'd be busy with on-camera interviews and post editing for another day or two but should have a break once they'd wrapped shooting. The doorbell rang so she popped her phone into her pocket and headed down the hallway. *Who could that be?*

She heard her dad at the front door talking to someone. As she got closer, a red light followed by a blue one illuminated their entryway, bathing the living room in a sea of colored lights. *The police?* Margo's pulse rate quickened, a shiver running through her as she rushed to the door.

'What's going on?' she said when she saw two officers starting to lead her dad out of the house. She looked past them at the police car in the driveway, its lights bouncing off the house.

'Margo, it's OK. Everything's going to be fine,' her dad said. Despite his calm demeanor, panic was rolling in and preparing to swallow her whole. She looked at the two officers and saw Brent was one of them.

She directed her attention toward him. 'Brent? What's going on, why are you taking my dad? Can't you see he's still recovering from surgery?'

The older officer that Margo didn't recognize took over guiding her dad toward the police cruiser, Brent taking hold of Margo's arm gently. 'Margo, try to stay calm, OK?'

'Are you arresting him?' she asked, her chest tightening, dizziness creeping in, making it harder to breathe. Margo had already lost one parent, she couldn't handle the idea of something terrible happening to her father too.

Brent looked over his shoulder and watched his partner snap the back passenger side door of the cruiser shut behind Shane before turning back around to face her. Margo had a hard time tearing her gaze away from her dad looking sadly out the window, but she needed answers. She looked desperately at Brent.

'Shane's not under arrest. He's just being taken in for questioning.'

Her stomach turned to lead. 'What questioning? What could he possibly know?'

'I can't really discuss it with you, I'm sorry. But I'm sure we'll have him back to you soon.'

Margo paled, looking back at her dad staring at her from behind the thick glass of the car window. Her body suddenly felt numb and heavy, the axis around her tilting as darkness seeped into the corners of her vision. Her dad's worried eyes and Brent's voice calling out her name were the last thing she registered as she fainted.

Slowly opening her eyes, Margo blinked rapidly as the old popcorn ceiling above her wavered. Her mother had nagged her dad constantly about removing the textured eyesore, but he'd never gotten around to it. Then Margo saw Brent's face hovering above her, blurry and mouthing her name. His voice was a low hum, muffled under the fog she was trying to come out of. Suddenly, reality came rushing back. Her dad. The red and blue flashing lights. She slowly pulled herself up into a seated position from the floor, holding a hand to her clammy forehead and rubbing the tender area above her eyes.

'Are you OK? How are you feeling?' Brent asked, his voice coming into sharper focus.

'A little groggy. What happened?' The world moved around her in waves before coming into focus again.

'You fainted,' Brent replied, his voice heavy with concern as he handed her a glass of orange juice. 'You should drink this. Have you eaten anything today?'

She shook her head, realizing she'd forgotten to eat breakfast. She grabbed the glass and gulped it down. When she was done, she handed the glass back and looked around the room. 'Where's my dad? Did you take him to the station?'

Brent sighed. 'No, he's still out in the car, we wanted to make sure you were OK. Are you feeling better? I really need to get back. Can you try walking to the sofa?'

He offered her his arm and she pulled herself up. The juice seemed to be helping some because she felt steadier on her feet, even though anxiety was still pumping through her. 'Yeah I'm alright.' She looked up at Brent with tears in her eyes. 'You can't tell me anything? Does this have to do with Jessie?'

Brent pursed his lips before saying, 'I'm really sorry but I can't give you any details.'

Margo glanced out at the car with her dad in the back seat. She nodded and said, 'Please be careful with him.'

'We will I promise. Are you OK if I leave now? Do you want me to call anyone for you?'

'I'm fine. And thank you for making sure I was OK.'

'No problem. You should go make yourself something to eat.' He tipped his hat toward her before walking out the door.

The sharp click of the latch made her flinch, the vision of her dad being hauled off by the police burned in her mind. She went to the kitchen and made herself a sandwich, trying not to obsess about what they were asking him at that very moment. Taking it back to the living room, she spotted the large, framed photo on the mantle of her and her dad at her college graduation. He'd been so proud of her that day, telling anyone who would listen that his daughter had graduated with honors.

Margo spent the next two hours pacing the living room and surfing through channels on TV, trying unsuccessfully to distract herself from her worry. *What could be taking so long?* She was anxious to talk to her dad.

A car door slamming startled her and she jumped up, running to the window and throwing back the curtain so aggressively that the curtain rod came tumbling down in front of her. Her dad was hobbling up the path on his crutches, the police car that dropped him off pulling away from the curb. She saw the curtain at Mrs. Avendale's house flutter shut. Surely, that woman was excitedly waiting for any activity from her front row seat. Margo feared it was only a matter of time until she stoked the fires of gossip around town. Kicking away the fallen curtain rod, Margo flung open the door and threw herself at him, wrapping her arms tight around his torso.

'Woah!' he said, almost losing his balance before squeezing her back with one arm, his crutches clenched tight under his armpits. 'It's OK, Margo, I'm home. Everything's fine,' he said soothingly into the top of her hair.

Margo pulled away teary-eyed, and they made their way further inside to sit down on the couch. 'So, tell me what happened. Why did they want to talk to you?'

'It was really nothing. I'm sorry it worried you so much, but they just wanted to get the perspective of a teacher on Jessie. I had Jessie in several classes over the years, and I knew her well since she came to all the basketball games.' Her dad shrugged and looked away. Normally Margo was really good at reading her dad, but now she was getting nothing from him. Was he just tired? Or was that thinly veiled worry behind his eyes. 'They just asked about Jessie around the time before she disappeared, how she seemed, her relationship with Charlie, had I noticed any problems with her, that kind of stuff. Other than her flunking a few tests that she was worried about, there wasn't much I could tell them.'

'You were gone for hours,' Margo needled. 'All that time just to ask how her mood was?'

'Well, it was more than just that, but that's the gist. Everything is fine. There's no need to worry, kiddo.' He placed a hand on her knee and squeezed as he gave a lopsided smile.

Margo wasn't sure what to think, but her dad seemed determined to brush it off as no big deal. Realizing she wasn't going to get much more out of him, she rose from the couch and got him a snack as he turned on the television. After setting his food down on the coffee table, she told him she was going to her room to read. She needed to distract herself from the panic that had crept in since the police came and still hadn't quite dissipated with her dad's surface-level answers. Since Austin wasn't free and she needed a break from staring at her murder-board, she decided to pick back up the book that she'd started reading during her dad's initial recovery right after his surgery. It was a light-hearted romantic comedy which seemed like a good palate-cleanser from the darkness. Moving across the room to pick it up, she froze. The book wasn't where she'd left it. Instead, it was on the opposite end of the desk. She knew she couldn't have left it there, because that was where she always used her laptop since it was closest to the power outlet. Her laptop was pushed to the left to make space for the book.

Her heart started to race, and her eyes darted around the room nervously. Had her dad come in to tidy up one day and not told her? Had she simply moved it while half-asleep and couldn't recall? She picked the book up and restored the laptop to its proper place. As she turned to plop down on her bed and read, she stopped dead in her tracks. On top of her bed, made with tightly tucked corners, was a depression in the surface of the quilt, the ghost of a body left behind. The impression on her pillow looked almost as if a head had rested on it, the memory of its weight captured in the plushness of the down feathers. Thinking back to the day she was sure Charlie had been in her room, she dug her fingernails into her palm, sweat trailing down her back even with the air conditioning on. She inhaled deeply but smelled nothing, no hint of his distinctive fragrance. Was her mind playing tricks on her? Seeing an outline where there may just be ripples in the quilt? She tried to convince herself that her anxiety about her dad coupled with her fainting episode earlier was simply overflowing into the present. She tried to reason that maybe she hadn't pulled the quilt tight like she usually did. Or maybe she'd rested at some point and forgot. But as she backtracked through her day, she didn't remember going near the bed since she'd made it that morning, she'd been focused on the suspect board. Taking her phone out, she quickly turned the alarm system on via the app.

CHAPTER TWENTY-ONE

The next day as Margo walked out to her car on her way to the grocery store, she received a text from Austin.

'Shooting wrapped! I should be done here later tonight. Wanna grab a drink?'

'Sure! But maybe you can come to my place? I finished the suspect board and I thought we could look over it together. I can make dinner and my dad has a nice aged whiskey we can try 😊' Margo replied, smiling as she pulled out her car keys.

She saw the three dots indicating he was replying, and her nerves mounted. Was she coming on too strong, inviting him over for dinner? They hadn't been reunited for *that* long, what if he didn't feel the same as her and was just being friendly, wanting to grab a drink to discuss the filming? Her pulse raced as she waited for his message to materialize. The bubbles disappeared for a moment and her heart stopped.

But then, his text came through. 'Whiskey? Are you trying to get me drunk? 😉 7 pm?'

Margo was flooded with relief. 'What if I am? 😉 See you at 7!'

Margo couldn't keep the smile off her face. She hoped now that they were done with the interviews, something might happen between them. Ever since she'd started hanging out with him, her resentment and anger toward Mark and Diana had dissipated, pushed out to make space for these new feelings. Feelings that were simultaneously confusing and scary and wonderful. While Mark's betrayal and the end of her marriage still stung, she was thinking about it less and less. When she and Mark had called it quits, she didn't think she would ever feel butterflies for someone again. But here she was, despite being plunged into a dark trauma from her past, her feelings for Austin developing with each passing day. He had saved her from herself through all of this, helping her to rise from the ashes of everything she was trying to leave behind.

Still smiling to herself, as Margo clicked the small button on her keys to unlock her car and reached for the door handle, she heard someone behind her. She whipped around with her pepper spray outstretched in her hand.

'Oh my!' Mrs. Avendale said, clutching her heart. 'I didn't mean to scare you, dear.'

Margo exhaled and stifled a scowl. She wasn't in the mood to stymie Mrs. Avendale's curious mind. 'Hi, Mrs. Avendale. How are you?'

'I'm doing well, thank you for asking. It's nice to see you back, Margo, after all this time.'

'Yes, it's nice being home with my dad.' She sighed inwardly, silently urging her to get it over with and ask.

'I saw the police out front yesterday. I hope nothing's wrong. Is your father OK?'

Sly move to feign concern, Margo thought. 'My dad is fine, thanks for asking. Nothing to be concerned about,' she replied with a forced smile.

Mrs. Avendale's face relaxed in disappointment over the lack of a juicy story. But she said, 'Thank god! I was so worried. Well, alright, I'll let you go on your way. Say hello to your father for me and please do let me know if you need anything while he recovers,' she said as she headed back across the street.

Margo put her hand up and waved. 'Will do, Mrs. Avendale.'

The smile dropped from Margo's face the moment she turned back around. She thought about the rest of her day ahead as she reached for the car door handle, realizing just how excited she was to pick out groceries for her newly confirmed dinner date. She looked down and her hand stopped on the handle. Her front left tire was flat. She'd heard noises outside and dogs barking again late last night but had refused to go outside to investigate fully, forcing herself not to let paranoia win. It had been a challenge, but after a quick peek out her window showed nothing, she'd made herself go back to sleep. Now she wished she had looked into it further. Margo crouched down and inspected the rubber, finding a small, clean gash on one side, the size of a small knife. She straightened quickly and looked around. Her skin prickled with a strange, tingling sensation. Was someone watching her right now? A wave of suffocating nausea rushed over her as anxiety took a choke-hold. Even though she was trying her best not to read into things ever since the discussion with her dad, this felt real. There was a physical piece of evidence sitting in front of her. *But it had been real to Mom too.* Was the danger real, or all in her head? Was her mind inventing a perceived threat, filling in blanks of its own accord?

She forced herself to calm down, expanding her belly with a few deep breaths. She lived in the mountains, there was frequently debris littered along the roads that could cause a flat. Her dad had taught her ages ago what to do in a situation like this. She went around the back of the car and spent the next half-hour replacing the tire with her spare temporary one. Popping the flat into the trunk, she drove down to Jimmy's Auto Shop less than a mile away. Jimmy pulled out the damaged tire and placed it on his worktable, inspecting the slash closely.

'So, what do you think?' Margo asked.

Jimmy straightened and took off his glasses, wiping off the dirty lenses with a small microfiber cloth spotted with dark oil. 'Well, there's no way to be sure since whatever punctured the tire isn't still lodged in there. You probably just drove over something in the road. I get at least one of these a week. You wanna buy a new tire? I got the same make and model as your others.'

Margo nodded and followed him over to the tire wall where he grabbed the correct one and then put Margo's car on the lift, raising it up so he could get to work changing it.

'You're sure someone didn't slash my tire on purpose?' she asked, a bit hesitantly but figured it was worth a shot.

Jimmy looked at her wide-eyed. 'Why would someone slash your tire? Ex-boyfriend?' he said with a smirk.

Margo smiled uncomfortably. 'Ex-husband actually, but he doesn't live around here. The puncture is so clean, it just made me wonder if it was deliberate. I heard some noise outside my house last night, figured it wouldn't hurt to ask your expert opinion,' she replied, trying hard to sound nonchalant.

He pulled the spare tire off and flashed her a proud smile. Jimmy had taken over the shop when his father of the same name had retired some twenty years ago. 'Well like I said, I can't be sure. I suppose it's possible. But it seems more likely that you drove over a sharp-edged rock or something in the road. It's easy to get a flat up here, you know that.'

Margo nodded, not entirely convinced. She waited while he put the new tire on and checked the pressure in the others. She handed him her credit card and while he completed the transaction, she ran her finger over the slash in her tire still sitting on his table. It wasn't long, maybe two inches, and had no ragged edges. Jimmy came back and handed her the credit card and a receipt. As she drove away, she couldn't get the image out of her head of Charlie squatting next to her tire late at night, encased in shadows, angrily pushing a knife in as his manic smile glinted in the moonlight.

Shaking off the ominous feeling, she drove to the market. Margo picked up two thick cuts of Chilean sea bass and fresh vegetables. She decided she would also make her famous lemon garlic rice that Mark had loved so much. Margo hoped Austin would like her cooking, maybe even enough to win him over and see her as more than an old friend or investigative sidekick. By the time she left the store, her mind had totally replaced thoughts of the tire with her dinner date, planning what to wear. While Margo loaded her paper grocery bags into the trunk, her pocket vibrated. She slammed the trunk shut and pulled out her cell phone. Unknown number again. She almost answered it this time, but as she was in a hurry to head home and get ready, she declined the call and slipped it back into her pocket. After the short message they'd left a few days ago, she was reluctant to confront her harasser.

Just as she rounded the back of her car to climb in the driver's seat, she spotted a man walking briskly toward her from the far side of the parking lot. He was tall, average weight and wearing a black hoodie over his head, making it hard to see his face. *Why would someone wear a hoodie like that in this heat?* Margo continued to watch the man as he closed the gap, afraid to take her eyes off him with the menacing vibe he was giving. Suddenly his head shot up, bringing his face into partial view. Charlie! The keys and their accompanying pepper spray jingled in Margo's shaking hands, blood pounding loudly in her ears. She took a step back and her backside bumped into the side of her car, causing her to drop her keys. She scrambled to pick them up; he was only a few yards from her now.

She quickly pulled her phone back out, poised to dial 9-1-1. Before she hit the call button she looked up, afraid to lose sight of him for too long. His head was tilted down again, but he was only inches away. She was about to yell at Charlie to stay back, that she was calling the police. She pulled her phone up just as he looked up again, right in front of her, and she almost screamed. But the face looking back at her wasn't Charlie's. He had the same piercing blue eyes but was much younger and scruffier than Charlie. A teenager really. He gave her a confused look as he passed. Her phone was clutched to her chest and she was sure her face was a ghostly shade. She'd been so sure it was Charlie; it had looked just like him. *Maybe I shouldn't have brushed Dad's concerns off so quickly. Did I inherit some of mom's behaviors after all? Is this the next stage . . . seeing things that aren't really there?*

After her breathing returned to normal, Margo headed home. She turned off the air conditioning and rolled down her windows, hoping to blast away the terror lingering in her periphery. The air was warm, but she enjoyed the fresh scent of trees as it rolled in on the summer breeze. She turned the volume up on the stereo and sang loudly along with Tom Petty's *American Girl* in an attempt to regain her good mood. Several minutes later, the tension in her body lessened. She convinced herself that her mind was just seeing what it expected to see with the hoodie guy and the whole slashed tire theory, making her see Charlie everywhere. Jimmy was right about how easy it was to get a flat on these roads; that had to have been what happened. After learning about her mom's condition, the idea that her sensibility was slowly deteriorating scared her more than if Charlie *was* stalking her. She was clinging to that fear now almost like a defense mechanism for her paranoid thoughts, refusing to let her mind get stuck in that state of fear. If she could explain everything away, then she wasn't like her mom after all.

Margo hung a right off the main road, taking her regular scenic backroad that led to her home through a series of small side streets. For years, she'd used this route to bypass the section where her mother had died, unable to look at it without having a breakdown. Now, it was a habit, and she enjoyed the feeling of being lost in the trees. She was on a long stretch of the road when she advanced on a blue truck going well under the speed limit. Frowning as she crept closer, Margo craned her head out the window trying to see the road ahead. Far up ahead was a hairpin turn, but she had time before she came upon it. The road was clear, not another car in sight, so she crossed the center line to pull around the truck and sped up. She was just about to pass it when she spotted Charlie sitting in the front seat, his lips turning up at the edges in a cruel smile. She blinked.

This was no hallucination. It *was* Charlie in the truck. She slammed on the gas, hoping to pass him quickly. Charlie sped up as well, keeping her trapped on the opposite side of the dotted line, unable to cut back in. The turn was rapidly approaching. She glanced back at him and he laughed at the look of terror on her face. Suddenly a horn sounded, loud and long, and she whipped her head back to the road in front of her. She was about to crash head on into a white sedan that had just rounded the curve in the road ahead.

'Shit!' Margo screamed, quickly pulling her foot off the gas and swerving back behind Charlie, just barely avoiding the collision.

With her hands shaking uncontrollably and her heart racing, she steered the car over to the side of the road and stopped on the grassy shoulder. Charlie honked three times and sped off. Margo stared at his truck as it got smaller and disappeared after the turn, sucking in air rapidly, on the verge of hyperventilating. His evil laugh was playing on repeat in her mind, and she was more convinced than ever that Charlie had in fact slashed her tire like she'd imagined. Was he following her? The road they were on was not as heavily traveled since it simply veered around the main road and linked up a few miles down. There was nothing along this road other than beautiful lookout turn-offs and a popular make-out spot for high schoolers. And it was nowhere near the brewery. It seemed too much of a coincidence.

But after the chat with her dad, she was reluctant to tell anyone what she really thought. Charlie had been ahead of her, not behind. She was sure her dad would tell her it was just an eerie coincidence. Although, if Charlie *had* been watching her over the past week, he'd know this was the road she always took home. When her hands stopped shaking again, she started her car and pulled back onto the road. She drove home, one eye trained nervously on her rearview mirror. But oddly, the encounter made her feel better about her dubious mind. She wasn't imagining everything after all.

Margo chopped onions and garlic in preparation for Austin's visit, glancing at the clock. There was still an hour before he was set to arrive. She'd taken a long shower, trying to wash away the sense of unease from her encounter with Charlie. She spent extra time on her makeup and hair to nail that balance of looking nice without looking like she was trying *too* hard. Her stick-straight hair was hard to curl, but she'd managed to add some long waves and was pleased with the results. Her dad limped into the kitchen, his crutches clicking loudly on the hardwood floors.

'Cooking dinner already?'

Margo turned and smiled. 'Just getting things ready.' She sat down at the small kitchen table, wiping her hands on a kitchen towel, and her dad followed suit. 'I wanted to ask if you could eat dinner in your room tonight, if you don't mind. Austin is coming over,' she said, blushing and looking down at the table.

'Austin, huh? You guys have been spending a lot of time together lately.'

'It could be nothing . . . but he's a nice guy. After Mark, I didn't expect to feel anything for anyone, especially so soon. But you were right about it being time to move on, it's been six months. And it's not like I *just* met him. He was always nice to me, and well, lately, it's felt like it could be more.'

'You don't have to justify yourself to me,' he said with a wry smile. 'I'm happy you're finding a way to move forward.'

'Dad, I've thought about what you said. I've been avoiding the subject since our talk, but I know that I went overboard with Mark. Now that I'm not as consumed by his betrayal, I can see my behavior wasn't acceptable. I have my rescheduled appointment with Jazz coming up in a couple of days. She loves talking to me about coping skills and obviously I need to do some work in that area,' Margo said with a light laugh. 'But I'm feeling hopeful for the first time in a long time.'

'I'm really happy to hear that, Margo. Austin was always a nice kid. I think you two would be great together.'

Margo smiled. 'So, what do you think? Can you make yourself scarce tonight?'

'Actually, I wanted to talk to you about something.' He shifted his weight and Margo's curiosity piqued. 'I didn't want to say anything with everything you just went through with Mark, and things have been hectic around here lately. I didn't want to make it harder or more confusing for you. But . . . I started seeing someone about three months ago.'

Margo's eyes popped open wide. 'You have? Who is she?'

It was her father's turn to blush as he fiddled with the saltshaker. 'Her name is Francine. She moved to Lake Moss a year ago when Mr. Duncan finally retired in the Math department. She took over his position. But it took me months to work up the courage to ask her out. The last date I went on was with your mom. I was pretty rusty, to say the least,' he said looking back up at her, smiling with one side of his mouth.

'Dad that's great! Really. I'm sorry you didn't feel like you could tell me. It's been a long time since we lost Mom, and I want you to be happy. I've always hated the idea of you being here alone. I came back to help you recuperate, but here you are dealing with my stuff instead.'

'That's what I'm here for.' He reached across and squeezed Margo's hand. 'Frannie was on vacation with a group of friends, but they got back last week. I've been putting off seeing her; I wanted to make sure you were OK first. But I think it's time. She's picking me up in about thirty minutes and I'll stay at her house tonight,' he said, looking sheepish. 'Don't want your dad cramping your style on your date.'

'Wow, way to go, Dad,' Margo said with a chuckle. 'And technically mine's not a date.' Then she noticed he'd put on a nice shirt and his hair was combed neatly. 'You look really nice. And thanks for telling me, I'm sorry we didn't talk about it sooner.'

He nodded and rose from his chair. 'I'm going to go pack an overnight bag. But maybe we can have breakfast tomorrow so you can meet Frannie? I think you'll really like her.'

'I'm sure I will. And yes, breakfast sounds good. Just text me when you're on your way and I'll whip something up.'

'Thanks kiddo,' he said and left the room.

Margo watched as he walked down the hall and disappeared into his room. It had taken her dad over twenty years to move on from her mom. Maybe it was the tragedy of it all, or maybe he just loved her that much. Maybe he really was trying to put Margo's feelings above his own. Whatever the reason, she was glad he'd met Frannie. It was time for them both to be happy. Looking back now, Margo realized she and Mark were just too different for it to have ever worked. He wanted a white picket fence in the suburbs and a Martha Stewart wife baking in the kitchen and raising the kids, dinner waiting when he got home. Deep down, Margo knew that was never what she wanted. While she did like to cook, what she really wanted was a career and a partner who was her equal. Maybe kids one day if it worked out, but it wasn't her number one priority the way he needed it to be.

Margo glanced at the clock and turned on the oven to preheat. The kitchen filled with delicious aromas as she sautéed broccoli, cauliflower and sliced zucchini in garlic and olive oil. Popping a lid on the pan and turning down the heat, Margo ran to her bedroom to get dressed. She pulled out a long gauzy floral sundress with halter straps that highlighted her long neck. She added dangly gold earrings and while looking through her old jewelry box, she came across a gold bracelet with her name etched onto the front. Her mother had given it to her on her last birthday before she died. On the underside, she'd had, 'To my heart, my love, my daughter. Love, Mom' engraved. Margo had forgotten all about this bracelet. After her mom died, it had been too painful to look at, so she'd buried it under all her costume jewelry in the box, layering more pieces on top as she got older. Margo took the bracelet out and slipped it over her hand. It was designed to be loose-fitting, but it was snug on her adult wrist. Margo almost liked it better this way.

After one last glance in the mirror, fluffing her hair and deciding she liked how it was falling, she made her way back to the kitchen. A car honked outside and Margo ran to the front door, pushing the curtain aside to peek out the window. A gray SUV was idling in front of their house. Her dad came up behind her carrying a duffle bag, struggling to manage the door and his crutches. She quickly reached over and opened it for him.

'You look beautiful, honey.' He kissed her on the cheek and said, 'Have a good time tonight, Margo.'

'You too, Dad.'

As he limped down the walkway, she caught sight of Frannie in the front seat. She had long light brown hair and seemed tall and lithe, not unlike her mother. Frannie waved to her and Margo waved back before closing the door. Realizing she only had a few minutes before Austin was supposed to arrive, Margo took out the fish that had been marinating in foil and slipped it into the oven. She got the rice cooking, and feeling her stomach somersaulting with nerves, she decided a glass of wine was sorely needed. Now that the focus would be on her and Austin rather than Jessie's case, Margo hoped she could be herself, totally and completely, without doubt creeping in.

She sipped her wine in the kitchen and checked the simmering rice that still had fifteen minutes left. A knock on the door startled her. She smoothed out her dress and ran her fingers through her hair one last time before pulling it open. Her breath caught in her throat when she saw Austin standing there. He was wearing fitted jeans and a freshly ironed blue button-up, the sleeves cuffed precisely mid-forearm, his hair styled off to the side. Her heart did a flip.

'Wow,' was all Austin said.

Margo showed him in, and he handed her a bunch of flowers she hadn't noticed him holding.

'Thank you. That's so sweet.' She felt an ache in her chest as her heart pounded.

308

'It smells amazing in here.'

'Hope you like sea bass. It's one of my specialties,' she said as she added the flowers to a vase and placed them on the table in the dining room.

'I love sea bass.'

Margo glanced at him and noticed he seemed a little nervous too. For some reason that made her feel calmer. 'The food has a little under fifteen minutes until it's ready. I thought we could take a look at the suspect board I put together in my room while we wait?'

'Sounds good!'

She walked him back to her childhood bedroom, and Margo flushed as she realized what a *line* that was. And then, that thought spiraled into anxiety about the fact that she was about to be alone. With a man. In her bedroom. Taking a deep breath, she opened the door and gestured for him to follow her. Thankfully, Austin walked right up to the board and started admiring her handiwork. They stood in front of her whiteboard, discussing the different alibis and potential motives. Margo was hyper-aware of how close they were, her skin tingling every time their arms happened to touch.

Austin compared a few bits of evidence to other cases they'd already filmed and Margo shook her head. 'God, your job must be so hard when you work on shows like this. All the cases I saw on the original seasons of *Into Thin Air* seemed so unsolvable. Even in cases like this,' Margo waved her hand at the wall of photos, 'where the body has been found and all the evidence that comes with that, it still hasn't gotten anyone closer to the truth. To spend so much time and effort on something, and in the end, not have it resolved must be so frustrating. And then it's just on to the next devastating story.'

309

'That's why shows like this are so important,' Austin replied. '*Into Thin Air* solved almost twenty cases in its ten-year run. Tips that came in led to arrests and answers. I'm not sure if you remember the Sheila Braverman case with the young woman who disappeared from her dorm in Portland? They caught the killer because of a tip called in to the show, and they ended up finding more bodies buried in the guy's backyard. There's always someone out there who knows something.'

Margo shifted her weight, nodding along with what he was saying. 'Oh yeah, I remember that case being a huge success for the show, it was all over the news. It had gone unsolved for almost twenty years or something, right?'

Austin nodded, 'Yep. I'm hoping by working on these cases, that I'll play some small role in giving the victims' families answers, too. Maybe even the Germaines.'

Margo looked back at the board, 'So, with it all laid out like this, what do you think?' Margo asked.

Austin gave a low whistle as he looked at their lack of solid intel, 'Even though Wylie lied, my gut is telling me it's not him. I think Cassidy seems the most suspicious to me. Or Cassidy and Tucker together. After that interview and what she told you at the funeral, and then you overhearing the two of them fighting secretly in the woods? I don't know, I just feel like she's hiding something more than just the affair, like they both are. It seems silly for her to have killed Jessie over a pageant. But Jessie also knew about the affair with Tucker so that could have played into it, too.' Austin shrugged. 'There's just something off there.'

'I see what you mean. I got a weird vibe from her as well, but at the same time, it seemed like sadness to me.

310

Regret over Tucker, this love that they both had but were never able to let blossom. I think it's hard for her to see him with his family.'

'Then who do you think did it?'

'Maybe I'm biased, but my money's still on Charlie. For all his faults, I think he really did love Jessie in his own way, however messed up that way was. Maybe he just couldn't take Jessie tossing him aside for another guy and he snapped,' Margo shrugged. 'Plus, he's constantly lying about where he was that night, I'm not sure I buy his "I took some pills and passed out" story. And we've witnessed his temper first-hand. After that altercation in the bar, and my flat tire this morning . . .'

'What are you talking about?'

'Oh, right. I forgot I haven't told you about that yet.' Margo recounted what happened with her tire and then her run-in with Charlie on the road, the anxiety she felt at the time creeping back in as she recounted what happened.

'Why didn't you call me right away? That was really dangerous. I know his family is a big deal, but he's gone too far. Maybe I should have a talk with him and tell him to back off.'

'No, please don't,' Margo pleaded. 'I didn't want to worry you or get you roped into whatever he's doing. I thought maybe I'd just run over something on the road. But then what he did in his truck was terrifying. I didn't know what to think, but I don't want to make a big deal out of it. Maybe Charlie is just messing with me like in the old days. He doesn't seem to have matured much. I don't want his family setting their sights on you.'

'I know, but what if he's your social media stalker too? I'm still going to tell him to leave you alone. I'm the one really poking around asking questions, not you. He shouldn't be taking out whatever he's going through on you.'

'Do you think that's a good idea? You might just antagonize him more. And I'd hate for it to jeopardize your job since that's what you came here to do.'

'We're not in high school anymore. I'm not bowing down to him like everyone did back then. He needs to own up to his behavior and grow the hell up. Besides, we already got his interview on camera. He can't do anything to my job.'

Austin was getting worked up, and Margo had to admit, his instinct to protect her made her feel good. She was so used to taking care of Mark, it was nice to have someone want to take care of her instead. Margo glanced back at the board, sizing up the suspects.

'Is there a version of this where they are all involved? Not Wylie necessarily, but the others? Maybe an accident happened at the cove or Charlie's temper got the better of him, and they all witnessed it? Maybe that's why it can't be pinned on any one person.'

'And his friends scrambled to help him cover it up?' Austin looked back at the board and pondered the idea, scratching the scruff on his chin. 'That's not a bad theory actually. The three of them all seem to be hiding something. What if that something is an elaborate cover-up they all took part in?' He turned his gaze back to Margo. 'And maybe that's what he and Tucker were fighting about at the reception, him controlling the situation. Might even have been what Cassidy and Tucker were arguing about in the woods. He was pretty vague and evasive about that. And Cassidy seems like she'd go to any lengths to protect Tucker.'

Margo smiled; that was exactly the idea that had popped into her mind. 'Yeah, it seems very possible. There's just something about how that group interacts that is suspicious and with their current jobs and families, they'd all lose so much if it came out that they'd either killed Jessie or helped cover it up. I mean you saw how worried Cassidy was about her job. It's definitely worth considering. And maybe my online stalker is able to keep tabs on me so easily because there's more than one of them?' Margo was proud of herself for proposing such an impressive theory.

'Have you had any more messages since the last one you showed me?' Austin asked, looking concerned again.

'No, thankfully, but I keep expecting one to pop up every time I open the apps on my phone. I just feel like I haven't heard the last of them yet.'

'Maybe it'll calm down now that we're done filming. But you have to let me know if you get any more, OK?'

'I will, promise,' Margo vowed.

The timer went off in the kitchen and the two of them headed back to serve up the food. While they ate, they took a much-appreciated break from discussing Jessie's murder and Margo's stalker and instead talked about their own lives before their returns to Lake Moss.

'Do you like living in Atlanta?' Margo asked.

'I do. The energy of the city is great and there's so much TV and film production going on there that I'm rarely without work. After growing up here, I craved the excitement of city life with lots of people and a high-energy atmosphere. What about you? What are your plans after your dad is healed up? I'm assuming you're not going back to Wilmington.'

'I'm not really sure what's next. The lease was up on

our apartment when I left. So, I don't have a home to go back to even if I decided that's what I wanted, although, I don't think it is. My employers have already replaced me, so there's nothing left for me there. I do want to get working again though. Originally when I came home, I thought I'd stay here for a few months and decide which direction I wanted to go. But I miss the ins and outs of trials, the lawyers weaving their way through evidence. Especially since we've been interviewing suspects, I'm getting antsy to get back to work. And I'm like you, I prefer living in a more bustling place than this. It's just so quiet. Wilmington isn't a big city, but especially during peak tourist season, there are people everywhere on the beach and in town. I'm having a hard time sleeping lately with the complete silence out here. All I hear are my own thoughts and that's never good,' Margo said, laughing.

'Oh my god, same!' Austin agreed, laughing. After a pause he looked at her. 'Have you started looking? Maybe you should try out Atlanta. They have courts there too, you know,' he said with a sly smile, that damn dimple flirting with her yet again. It got her every time.

'Maybe,' she said, smiling back. 'I've only been there once for a wedding. But I liked it. I have started looking for jobs again, just seeing what's out there. I've been trying to keep my options open, but I've set alerts in a few cities. Raleigh, Charlotte, Savannah, Nashville, and yes, even Atlanta.' She laughed as he beamed. 'So, we'll see what happens and what becomes available job-wise. I even thought of applying somewhere totally far away, like Los Angeles, but I'm not sure I could actually move that far from my dad. As much as I don't want to stay in Lake Moss, I'd like to be close enough to him to see him as he gets older. But beyond that, there's not really anything tying me to one specific place right now, so I guess I could move anywhere.'

'Well, if you decide to seriously consider Atlanta, I'd be happy to show you around.'

Margo smiled as she envisioned a new life forming in front of her. The possibilities of what could happen in a new city with a new guy were exciting. Austin was an unexpected development on her return to Lake Moss, but maybe this was just what she needed. After dinner they sat on the couch and had a few glasses of her dad's whiskey, a nice buzz warming her up. She felt flushed despite the air conditioning. She kept waiting for Austin to make a move, certain he was about to several times. But he didn't. In the end, Margo walked him to the door to say goodnight and decided to be brave and take her shot.

'You know, I had a big crush on you in high school. When we were lab partners. I hoped it would lead to something more . . . but I was too afraid to say anything,' Margo blurted out, looking to the side as her cheeks flushed with embarrassment. But then Austin laughed softly.

'I had a crush on you too. I can't believe we both felt the same but never said anything. I guess we really missed an opportunity to make high school more bearable back then, didn't we?'

Margo smiled at him and leaned against the door frame. 'I guess so.' They looked at each other for a moment and then Austin leaned in and kissed her. The air swept out of her lungs and her skin came alight with electricity. Margo felt it extend all the way to the tips of her fingers and toes. The kiss lasted for a minute, intensifying with each passing second. Finally, Austin pulled away. 'I'm sorry, I shouldn't have . . . I know you're going through a divorce and if it's too soon, I don't want to rush you into anything.'

'No, don't apologize,' Margo said softly, her lips still buzzing from his touch. 'It's been half a year since we split, and honestly, the love in our marriage was lost long before that. I think it was mostly just the hurt at his betrayal that lingered. But spending time with you, and the distraction of tagging along for the interviews, has given me a lot of clarity lately. You've been so nice, and it's just made it even clearer that he was never the right one for me. It took coming home to Lake Moss for me to see that.'

'OK, good,' Austin said with a smile, reaching forward to tuck a piece of hair behind her ear. 'I should . . . probably go, though. Early production meeting with my team in the morning. We should have a rough cut in a day or two, we've been working like crazy around the clock to see how all the footage strings together. We're planning a watch party when we get there, to see if there are any gaps we need to fill before we leave town, and of course celebrate the hard work. I volunteered my house since my parents are still traveling. Care to join us? You've helped so much, I thought you'd like to see how it's coming together. It won't be perfectly smooth and flashy yet, but you'll get an idea of how we're weaving together all the interviews and evidence, or lack thereof.'

Heat rose to Margo's cheeks. 'I'd love to come. Thanks for the invite.'

He leaned over and gave her one last peck. ''Night Margo.'

'Goodnight.'

She watched wistfully as he got into his car. Before he drove off, he waved, beaming at her. Margo waved back and then closed the door. She leaned back against it, unable to stop smiling. She glanced at the clock and was shocked to see that it was already one in the morning. She could still feel the lingering weight of his lips on hers, and she brushed her fingers against her bottom lip as she replayed it in her mind. She couldn't believe after everything that had happened in her life, that after fifteen years, she had finally confessed her feelings to Austin. It was like a childhood dream that had always played in her mind in black and white, bursting into full color as it finally came to life. After washing her face and brushing her teeth, she hopped into bed, quickly turning on the security system with the tap of a button. She'd clean the kitchen in the morning. With the whiskey coursing through her, she fell asleep quickly with Austin's smile floating around behind her closed eyes.

March 11, 2004

Dear Diary,

Today was one of the best days ever! Austin just keeps getting cuter and cuter and today, he actually asked ME to be his lab partner in Biology!! I couldn't believe it. Mr. Baskin told us to pair up and Austin asked me right away. I almost squealed I swear. I tried to play it cool, but I don't know. I hope he didn't notice how excited I was. But whatever- screw it! Let him know. Will Austin Hughes actually ask me out?? What if I tell him how I feel and he doesn't feel the same? I couldn't bear it. He's really the only friend I've had since Mom . . .

Anyway, it's best if I wait and see what he does first. I wonder what it'll be like if he kisses me? Will I be good at it? I wish Mom was here to give me advice on what to wear, how to do my hair, what to say . . . I miss her. I tried calling Dad multiple times but he didn't answer. It's so unlike him, he always answers my calls or at least calls me right back. He's at some basketball tournament for the traveling team he coaches when the high school team isn't in season, so maybe he's just busy, but still. He wanted me to go with him, but since I have a big project due on Monday, I convinced him that at seventeen, I can stay home alone for a couple of nights. I'm gonna keep trying Dad. Maybe he can tell me if Austin is really flirting with me or not from a boy's point of view. It's so frustrating when Dad doesn't answer his phone! Ugh!!

318

CHAPTER TWENTY-TWO

Thick hands clenched her throat tightly, so tightly. As Margo looked up, a drop of water landed on her cheek. And then another, until slowly the rain picked up pace and poured down on her. The man who was strangling her smiled at her pain, and all she could see hovering above her was the spread of sharp white teeth floating within a circle of black.

Margo lunged up from her bed, gripping her throat, gasping for air. A flash of white cloth flew up in front of her and she screamed as her arms flailed around. She quickly scanned the dark room, panting and shaking, a loud piercing alarm penetrating through her fear and confusion. The white was just her curtain flying up from the wind coming through the half-open window to the side of her bed, but why was the window ajar? Did she not properly check all the windows before falling asleep? She never slept with her window open, even when it was hot, preferring to sleep with the air conditioning on. She quickly pulled the window down and latched it shut, and then her tired mind registered what she was hearing. *The security system.* When her dad had upgraded the system per her request just before she left for college, he had a limited number of sensors. And since she was leaving, he hadn't put one on her bedroom window, so that couldn't have been what set off the system. Scrambling to silence it from her phone on the nightstand, she prayed it had just gone off by mistake, her dad had mentioned it had been finnicky. But in light of everything that had happened lately, a new layer of unease sunk in. If someone or something had set the alarm off, she hoped desperately the sound had scared them away.

Hitting the off button within the app, she remained perfectly still on her bed, straining her ears for any sound of movement in the quiet house. After a minute, her racing heart began to slow, the probability of the alarm going off accidentally seeming more likely. She couldn't decide if she was relieved or annoyed that her dad hadn't continued paying to keep it connected to the police. On the one hand, them following up for false alarms all the time would be embarrassing. On the other hand, if something had gone wrong, it would have been comforting to know they were ready to help.

Then, as she stood up and walked to look through the window for any signs of what may have set the alarm off, she was startled to hear a floorboard creak just outside her bedroom door. She spun around and stared at the door, almost daring it to open. The wood floors of their old house squeaked with every step, a symphony of disconcerting sounds betraying each movement like its own alarm system. Maybe it was her father? Had he come home from Frannie's in the middle of the night and accidentally set off the alarm himself, not used to her setting it each night? But she knew if it was him, he

320

would have come to let her know he was home and apologize for startling her. Her fear rose a notch and she felt like she was still locked in her nightmare. Another creak echoed in the silence and Margo jumped. She looked around her room for anything she could use as a weapon. She quietly crept over and grabbed her old baseball bat inside her open closet, trying not to make a peep. She was thankful for the carpet in her bedroom, muffling the sound of her movements.

Margo clutched the bat in her hand, ready to strike. She sidled up to her bedroom door, pressing the side of her face to the cool wooden surface and straining her ears once more. She heard a slight whoosh and another creak further down the hall. The wind whistled outside, a haunting soundtrack to her anxiety. Slowly, she clicked the door open and peered out. A shadow moved to the left, but as she watched it dance across the hallway, she realized it was the trees swaying on the other side of the hall window, its curtains partially parted in the center. She opened the door wider and slunk quietly down the hall, skirting around the wooden slats she knew squeaked the loudest. A rustling drew her attention to the entryway.

When she came to the end of the hall, she heard it again. In the mirror across from her, she saw a dark figure standing just around the corner of the wall she was hiding behind. She held her breath, her heart thumping in her ears, trying desperately not to scream as the urge built up deep in her belly. Margo pulled the bat back, her arms and shoulders aching from the tension, and inched around the side of the wall. She released her breath and let the bat fly toward the intruding figure with all the force she could muster.

The bat came into contact with a loud *thwack* before hitting the wall, her shriek finally exploding out of her. The figure was now on the floor, unmoving. Quickly, she flicked on the light with a trembling hand. There on the floor, was a man lying face down wearing a dark coat. Was this her stalker? Had she just attacked him? She inched around him and then blinked her eyes a few times before exhaling loudly. What she'd seen as a man was their coat rack lying on the ground, a jumble of jackets lying around it, resembling a long body, and one of her dad's baseball caps flung at the top like a displaced head. Margo ran a hand through her hair, now damp with cold sweat. She slammed her body back against the wall, trying to calm the adrenaline coursing through her.

After a few minutes, she walked over to the window next to the front door, her legs trembling like Jell-O. She noticed the alarm sensor on the side of the window frame had slid slightly out of place, the sticky strip most likely coming loose from the humidity. The system must have thought the window was open when it slid out of alignment. They were definitely going to need to screw those into the wood.

Margo shook her head, having a hard time releasing her body from its fight or flight mode. The house shook from another gust blowing outside and anger for the house betraying her so deeply swelled in Margo. She'd felt good about everything when she'd drifted off to sleep, focusing on Austin to drown out the paranoia creeping in after the mysteriously misplaced book, the dent in her pristine bedding, and the run-in with Charlie. Being deep in Jessie's murder investigation was playing tricks on her mind, and Austin was the perfect distraction. But the nightmares and noises came rushing back the minute she let down her defenses. She decided when she talked with Jazz, she'd tell her all about her mom's condition. There hadn't been time for it last time and Margo had still been trying to fully grasp what it meant on her own, but now it was important to get Jazz's opinion.

Margo moved the curtain to the side and peeked out. She scanned the area only lit up by the moon. As her eyes searched the area around the Avendales' house, she spotted a dark shape next to the trees bordering their front lawn. A chill shivered through her. She couldn't tell if the dark shadow was a person or just a hedge that looked human in the dark. She kept watching but the figure didn't move so she walked away from the window and crept into all the rooms with the bat still poised, opening closet doors and pushing shower curtains aside, just to be sure and quiet her uneasy mind. But the house was empty. It had to have just been the sensor. Relaxing the band of tension across her shoulders, she leaned the bat against the sofa and went around the house checking that all the windows and doors were closed and locked, even though she thought she remembered doing it earlier. Maybe that last glass of whiskey had really done a number on her usually foolproof routine. She hoped that was the case, because the other option was someone *had* been inside the house while she slept.

After she confirmed everything was locked securely, she went back to her room, pulling the curtain aside to check one last time, staring at the dark figure. Suddenly, the shape moved and darted into the trees. Margo's hand flew to her mouth and her breath hitched in her throat. She kept staring in that direction to see if the person came back. But was it a person? Maybe it was a bear. Margo shook her head, before dropping into bed, completely exhausted. She'd have to screw the sensor into

323

the window frame before she could use the alarm again, and she was for sure ordering an extra sensor for her bedroom. Margo tossed and turned, the dark figure refusing to leave her anxious mind, pulling the blankets on and off repeatedly as she tried to settle back in. But she was rattled. The old ticking clock in her bedroom sounded louder than usual as it ricocheted off the walls in the silence. Eventually Margo fell into a fitful sleep.

Hours later, sounds of cooking and cabinets opening and closing coming from the kitchen caused her to stir from her slumber. A glance at her clock showed it was already eleven. She couldn't believe she'd overslept; her dad and Frannie must have already arrived. She hopped out of bed, quickly ran a brush through her hair and threw on a bathrobe before wandering into the kitchen, snatching her cell phone off the nightstand and throwing it into her pocket at the last minute.

'There she is!' her dad exclaimed joyfully, sitting at the kitchen table with a cup of coffee in his hand. 'Someone was a sleepyhead this morning,' he said, shaking his head and laughing. Frannie was hovering over the stovetop making eggs and bacon; it was weird to see another woman standing in their kitchen, but the smell was incredible. 'Frannie, this is my daughter Margo. Margo, Frannie.'

Frannie turned and put her hand out with a warm smile. 'Margo, it's so nice to finally meet you! I've heard so much about you.'

'Same here. Sorry I slept so late,' Margo said as she shook her hand. 'I woke up around five and had a hard time falling back to sleep.' She sat down at the table across from her dad while Frannie turned back to flip the sizzling bacon.

'Everything OK? Another nightmare?' her dad leaned forward and asked quietly, looking concerned.

It was on the tip of her tongue to tell her dad about the open window and her subsequent freak out. But as she thought about it, she realized it was just that. A paranoid episode brought on by a bad dream and a loose sensor. She wasn't so sure this morning that she had closed and locked all the windows before going to bed after all, and there was no need to worry him further, especially when he seemed so happy.

'Everything's fine, Dad. The sensor on the window next to the door slipped and the alarm went off,' she said, giving him a smile.

'See! I told you!' he exclaimed.

'Yeah, yeah,' Margo said, rolling her eyes. 'We'll need to screw them into the frames so that doesn't happen again.'

Frannie brought the food out to the dining room as Margo set the table. While they ate, Frannie told Margo more about herself and how she came to be in Lake Moss. Her dad sat next to her, a smile plastered on his face. It was nice to see him happy again. Not that he'd spent her childhood being sad, but Margo had suspected it had been a brave face he put on for her after losing her mom. She'd heard him crying in his room sometimes, although he rarely did it openly in front of her. He'd always said Eloise was his soulmate, and he couldn't imagine loving someone like that ever again. But sitting at the dining room table, listening to Frannie talk about her childhood and her love of knitting, Margo felt such relief to see her dad so happy. And she realized that she was happy too. Not just for her dad, but for herself as well. She felt like she was on the verge of a new start, one that didn't involve constant worry about Mark leaving her. A new start that meant Margo needed to figure out who she was without him, what *she* really wanted out of life. It also meant getting control of her mind. And the first step to that was baring her soul to Jazz. While she'd been resistant at first to starting her sessions back up again, she was relieved that she had an appointment the following day.

Her phone vibrated and she pulled it out, rolling her eyes at the notification from her weather app about a storm on the horizon later in the week.

'What is it, sweetie?' her dad asked at her annoyed expression.

'This app is constantly warning me about incoming rain as if it's the apocalypse. Summer storms are nothing new for us here, I feel like I just need to turn off its notifications altogether. It was more helpful when I was on the coast during hurricane season than it is here.'

'Ah, yeah, I've muted pretty much everything that's possible to mute on my phone,' her dad said proudly.

He had recently joined the world of smartphones and liked to pretend that he was an expert. It made her smile, but her smile faltered when she noticed a missed notification bubble on her Facebook Messenger app. Thankfully, her father was distracted in conversation with Franny. Hesitantly, she clicked the icon and opened the app to see what was waiting for her.

She felt faint when she saw the message. Her stalker had struck again, sending a message in the night while she had been stumbling through the dark, scared someone had broken in. After staring at the message, she looked up at her dad for a long moment, as if she was trying to burn the image of him into her mind to block out what was taunting her from her phone screen.

Jumping up from the table she said, 'I just realized I'm going to be late to meet Austin, I've gotta get going. It was really nice meeting you, Frannie. And thanks for breakfast. I promise next time, I've got the cooking covered.'

'Anytime. Nice to finally meet you, Margo. Your dad has said so many nice things; he clearly loves you a lot.'

'The feeling is mutual,' Margo said, forcing a smile before rushing to her room to change, and firing off a quick text to Austin to see if he was home.

Margo rushed past Austin's car parked in the driveway, frantically knocking on the door of his parents' home. He had been in a long production meeting when she'd texted him, so she'd driven to a nearby lookout spot and waited anxiously until he texted that he had gotten home, unable to stay at her own house now that she'd told her father and Frannie she was leaving. She'd looked at that message for so long, she felt like it was tattooed on the inside of her eyelids. As it neared lunch time, she felt her stomach grumble but was too nauseous with nerves to eat. She hadn't filled Austin in yet on the message, wanting to show him in person. As she waited for him to answer the door, Margo could almost feel the phone burning her through the pocket on the back of her purse, a fiery landmine waiting to explode. The only question was who would be the collateral damage that it took down.

When Austin answered, the smile fell from his face as he took in Margo's furrowed brows and frantic expression.

'What's wrong? Has something happened?'

'Can I come in?' Margo asked, looking over her shoulder as if checking to see if she was being followed. She jumped as a dog barked in the distance.

'Yeah, absolutely,' he said as he opened the door wider and placed a soothing hand on her shoulder to guide her through the door. The warm weight of his touch dulled the anxiety bubbling within her. Deep down, she knew he'd be able to help her or at least do everything in his power to try. As Austin led her to sit on the couch in the living room, she continued to fidget and her eyes darted toward the windows. It didn't go unnoticed.

'Margo, it's OK. Just tell me what's going on.' He was alert, fully focused on her.

With a shaking hand, she pulled her phone out of her purse and quickly unlocked it before thrusting it toward his chest. She already had the Facebook Messenger app open. His eyes widened as they scanned over the screen in his hand. He placed the phone down on the coffee table and the images she received stared up at them. There, the latest taunts from the person stalking her from the shadows of the internet had taken things a step further. No longer just targeting her, but now the person who meant the most to her. The only person who had never left her side. Her dad. Glaring back at them was a photo of her dad exiting the police station with an officer after he'd been taken in for questioning. Paired with the photo was a message. 'Is everyone's favorite teacher about to get put in detention? Maybe Lake Moss should know who the subject of the police department's interest is these days.'

Directly below that was another photo of Margo on one of her evening jogs, a bold red target placed directly over her face. The message below the second photo read, 'I've got you both in my sights. This is your last warning. Don't force me to pull the trigger.'

Margo felt sick every time she looked at it.

'Is that your dad? Why is he at the police station?'

'Sorry, I should have told you about that. They came and picked him up a few days ago for an interview. When he came back, he said they just wanted a teacher's perspective of Jessie and her friends and since Jessie had several classes with my dad and went to all the basketball games, they brought him in. But it was nothing and now this person is trying to make it seem like my dad is a suspect!'

'We have to figure out who is doing this to you. That second photo is clearly a physical threat and I couldn't take it if something happened to you because of me. I feel like this is my fault,' Austin said, looking sadly at the pained expression on Margo's face as her eyes stayed glued to the screen.

'What?' she asked, finally pulling her eyes away from the images on her phone to look at him. 'How is this your fault?'

'I'm the one who pulled you into these interviews. I just thought . . . since you loved Jessie . . . that you'd want to see behind the curtain. And selfishly, I enjoyed your company. But it's obviously pissed someone off that you've been involved and now they're going after your dad too. And what if I've inadvertently put you in the killer's crosshairs?' he said, gesturing at the phone. 'I'm so sorry, Margo.'

'No,' Margo sniffled, shifting her weight to better look at him. 'Don't apologize. I did want to see what was going on with the investigation. I needed to know what was happening. And it's been nice reconnecting with you too, please don't apologize for that. I could have said no, I could have stopped when these messages started. But what happened to Jessie is too . . . enormous, too life altering, too . . . I don't know. But stopping was never an option. It's not your fault.'

He reached out and pulled her into a hug, and she felt the tension in her body release as tears flowed down her cheeks and she breathed in his warm, woodsy scent. The hug lingered, but as they pulled away, Margo sniffled and looked deep into his eyes. He nodded and reached forward, gently pushing away a stray hair that had fallen across her face. It sent a lightning jolt through her body, but she could feel the images still burning in her mind.

'OK,' Austin said at last. 'Your dad said that they were just interviewing him since he was her teacher, right? That they were going back and talking to anyone who had spent time around Jessie that wasn't interviewed initially for the case?' Margo nodded, wiping away a tear as it crossed over her lips. 'So, even if this person spreads this around, your dad doesn't have anything to hide. The truth will protect him in the end.'

Margo hesitated, wanting to believe what he was saying. 'You know how the people are around here, though. His reputation in this town could be torched if even one person suspected he was being questioned about Jessie's death. I can't let that happen to him, to our family. What can we do? We need to pull the mask off this person.'

'And what if we do, and it's her killer?' Austin said, the look on his face stuck somewhere between nervous and excited at the possibility.

'Then we hand them over to the police and you have a great story to add into the show,' Margo said with a half-smile, trying not to show the fear hovering just under the surface.

'Well,' Austin said puffing out his chest with a deep breath. 'OK, then. Send the photos to me and we'll blow them up on my big monitor. Our DIT showed me some tricks on how to clean up images.'

'DIT?' Margo asked, her forehead scrunched up.

'Sorry, our digital imaging technician. He helped me install a program and showed me how to use it. I'd planned on trying it out on the messages this person already sent you. Maybe we can find some sort of context clues in the background. There's got to be something in there we are missing that points to who is doing this. I doubt Lake Moss is turning out criminal masterminds.'

Margo snorted a short laugh, nodding in agreement. 'Thanks, Austin.' She snatched up her phone and sent him the images as they rose and walked to the room he was using as his office while he was in town. His monitors and sound equipment covered the long wooden desk, and he pulled up an extra chair next to his as he woke up his screens.

Margo sat down, snapping the hair band around her wrist nervously as he pulled the images up and enlarged them one by one. Austin's eyes drifted over at the sound, and he startled her as he set a hand on top of hers to steady it.

'Sorry,' she said sheepishly, clasping her hands in her lap as he pulled his own hand back.

'Why don't you start going back over the messages to look for any context clues while I scan over these two images. If I don't find anything, we can try the others.'

She nodded, grateful for something to do. After a few silent moments, her frustration mounting at the lack of new findings hiding in the messages, she sat back heavily in her seat and set her phone down. She looked at Austin who was leaning forward, squinting at something on the monitor.

'What is it?' she said, bending forward to get closer to him. He had the image of her father zoomed in so far that it almost didn't look like anything anymore, slowly panning across the pixels, but he had suddenly stopped moving the cursor.

'Do you see that?' he asked, pointing into the far corner of the window on the front of the police station. It looked like the vague outline of a person. He zoomed in further and ran a clean-up tool on the selected area. When it completed, they both gasped. There was a person's upper body reflected in the hazy window, a phone held up in front as they took a photo. Margo couldn't believe it. She recognized the person instantly.

CHAPTER TWENTY-THREE

Margo knocked on the door, the rhythm sounding like some frantic, secret pattern from the adrenaline surging through her. She could barely stand still, fidgeting as nervous energy ricocheted off her in every direction. She could feel the edge of Austin's arm brushing into hers as she shifted in place, and they locked eyes as they heard footsteps approaching the door. She couldn't believe they'd solved who was behind the messages. They were about to face the shadowy monster, bringing them out into the light of day. Margo couldn't help but wonder if they should have told someone before rushing over here in their excitement at solving the mystery. Should they have looped in the police? Amy? Anyone? But it was too late, she realized, as the door creaked open, the fading sunlight casting shadows across the crayon drawings scribbled on the wooden surface.

When the door fully opened, it revealed Claire, her eyebrows knitted in confusion, a dish towel draped over her shoulder. She wiped her hands off on its front edge as if to dry them.

'What are you two doing here?' she asked softly, looking back and forth between them.

'Is Tucker home?' Austin asked, trying to peek around her shoulder.

'He's out in the backyard with the kids,' Claire said, hovering in the doorway. 'Should I go grab him, then? What is it that you need to talk to him about?' She took a half-step back, starting to turn away, her voice betraying the annoyance she clearly felt at the intrusion.

'Actually,' Margo said, clearing her throat. 'We're here to see you, Claire.'

Claire froze, her eyes wide as her hand tightly gripped the door. She looked like she was trying to decide if she wanted to slam the door in their faces or not. 'Me? Why would you want to talk to me? I wasn't even that close with Jessie.'

'You know exactly why, Claire. We saw your reflection in the last picture you sent.'

The color drained from Claire's face, and she started shifting her weight looking like a caged animal trying to figure out how to escape. After a long, tense moment and a look back over her shoulder, she stepped out front and closed the door quietly behind her.

'Please, keep your voices down, I don't want Tucker to hear.'

'Oh, you don't want him to hear about how you've been stalking and threatening me?' Margo said, her voice rising slightly as her nerves were rapidly replaced with anger.

'I was never going to hurt you, Margo,' Claire said in an urgent but hushed voice, pulling the towel down off her shoulder and wringing it nervously in her hands. 'But you came bounding back into town like a hurricane trying to kick up dirt and ruin all of our lives, and I couldn't let you destroy my family.'

334

'And why would us looking into Jessie's murder destroy your family? Is there something you want to tell us about Tucker?' Austin asked softly, leaning in toward her.

'What? No, of course not. Tucker had nothing to do with Jessie's murder,' Claire snapped.

'Then why were you trying to stop us from investigating?' Margo fired back, needing desperately to know the truth and protect her own family.

'You both think I'm this naïve little housewife, don't you? That I'm clueless to the world around me and just live in a happy little bubble? I'm not stupid, Margo. I know about Tucker's affair. I've always known.'

'What?' Margo and Austin said at the same time, sharing a surprised look.

'Keep your voices down,' Claire hissed, straining her ears to make sure no one was coming around from the back of the house.

'You knew?' Margo asked, genuinely shocked. 'This entire time?'

'Of course I did.' She straightened up taller, as if she were trying to pull in every ounce of bravery she could muster. 'They thought they were being so sneaky, but it was obvious. And the backhanded remarks Jessie would make when we were all together just confirmed my suspicions. But I loved him. I mean, I *love* him.' She sighed deeply, looking for the right words, tears gathering on her lashes. 'After I got pregnant and we got back together, I overheard a phone call when Tucker thought I was asleep. He was in our bathroom talking in a hushed voice and it was clear he was talking to Cassidy. Then, I knew for sure, but I wasn't about to lose my family before it even started. Tucker doesn't know that I know, and I'd like to keep it that way.' Her lips started to quiver, tears leaving a trail as they gushed down her cheeks. 'We have a nice life now. Cassidy is far away, and we're *happy*. I didn't need you airing our dirty laundry to the world and blowing up my whole *life*. I will not let you do that to my innocent children.' She said it all in one fast breath, her justification for her actions exploding out of her, imploring understanding.

'So, all of these messages were to stop us from outing Tucker as a cheater over a decade ago?'

'I know he'll always have feelings for her. *Cassidy*.' The name rolled off her tongue dripping with disdain. 'The reason he keeps his distance from her is because he thinks he's protecting me from the truth, protecting our family's reputation. All I wanted my entire life was to be a mom. I have everything I've ever dreamed of with Tucker. You just can't tell the world about him and Cassidy. I will do whatever it takes to protect my children and our life.'

Margo shook her head, trying to wrap her brain around what was happening. This wasn't what she expected, at all. Sweet, innocent-seeming Claire, hiding behind a screen tormenting her to protect her husband's secret affair. As a woman who had been scorned by a cheating husband, she couldn't understand Claire's deep loyalty. But Margo wasn't a mother, and she knew those maternal instincts to protect must run deep.

'Why were all your threats directed at only me? It's not like it was my decision to reopen the case. Stopping me from running around with Austin, wouldn't have stopped *Into Thin Air* or the police from investigating and asking questions.'

Claire paused thoughtfully for a moment, her eyes bouncing back and forth between Austin and Margo. She

336

wiped the back of her hand across her nose and sniffled.

'Honestly?' She swallowed and dropped her arms heavily to her sides, the dish towel falling to the ground. 'You were an easier target. I knew you spooked easily and hoped I could scare you enough to at least get one person to back off. I was afraid if I went after Austin or the show, their researchers would just dive in even further and out me on camera or something. Plus, after looking around a bit online, it became clear that Austin is only on Facebook and he doesn't post much. I didn't even know if he would check his messages. You were more of a sure thing. I figured once I got you to back off, I could figure out a different plan to keep Tucker and our family out of the spotlight as far as the show and police were concerned. I hadn't really gotten that far yet.'

And there it was, the mask had been lifted. 'Were you the one who slashed my tire too? And has been skulking around outside my house?'

'What? No, oh no, I was only using social media. I took that photo of you and Austin a week ago, but that was the only time I was near your house. I haven't been lurking around there, I swear. I know what I've done makes me look suspicious, but I would never slash your tire or anything like that.' She glanced behind her before leaning in. 'I've tried my best to get Tuck to stop hanging out with Charlie, which thankfully he has for the most part. Because I know what he's capable of and I don't need that around my family, but the other night Tucker and I went to dinner and Charlie was sitting at the bar drinking. A lot. To be honest . . . we heard him bragging about slashing your tire. He feels like he's invincible in this town, so, I wouldn't put it past him to stalk you. He's always loved scaring you. I promise Margo, it wasn't me. You *have* to believe me,' Claire pled with her, nervous tears clinging to her bottom lashes. Her eyes darted down before quickly glancing back up.

Margo nodded solemnly, agreeing with her assessment of Charlie, and Austin rested a hand on her shoulder as if to say, 'It's over.' She wasn't sure why, but she believed Claire. She believed the desperation that was so evident in her words, she recognized it and understood. Claire just wanted to protect her family, but Margo knew she wasn't a threat . . . not anymore.

'What happens now? Are you going to turn me in?' Claire asked suddenly with a clear wave of panic taking over, her lips quivering.

After a long look, Margo and Austin turned back to her and Margo said, 'There's no point. It might get some good TV ratings,' Austin gave a small laugh and Margo continued, 'but it won't really change anything as far as the actual investigation goes. But you have to stop. Just leave me and my dad alone, and this goes away. If you come after us again . . .'

'I won't!' Claire said urgently, putting her hands out in front of her as if to physically stop that line of thinking. And then realizing her voice had risen, she glanced over her shoulder into the living room window before lowering her voice and saying, 'I promise. I'm sorry Margo, I just . . .' A squeal of delight erupted in the distance behind their home, and Claire scooped up the fallen towel and began to back away toward the door. 'I really am sorry. Can you please do your best to keep my family out of it?' She was talking faster now. 'I know you don't owe me anything after what I've done,' she tapered off.

'We never had any intention of blowing up your family,' Austin said. 'That was never the point of what the show

338

set out to do. Unless some other evidence comes up showing Tucker is connected to her murder . . .'

'That won't happen, I swear. He didn't do it,' Claire reiterated, reaching for the door.

'Then we're good.'

And with a final nod of understanding, Austin and Margo turned and walked back to Austin's car. By the time they climbed in, Claire was back inside. The door firmly closed behind her, keeping all her family's dirty secrets at bay on the outside. Margo couldn't help but wonder if Claire liked having a secret of her own, if it made her feel like she and Tucker were on a more even playing field. But it wasn't Margo's place to judge, as she wasn't exactly an expert on successful marriages.

'You OK?' Austin asked, looking over at Margo and placing a hand on her knee.

She gave him a sad smile. 'I will be.'

Margo walked into the kitchen the next morning, her mind still whirling from the events of the night before. Her dad was already up and having coffee, offering her a cup as she settled in at the table.

'You're up early,' she said as she took a long, grateful sip.

'I'm off for the day with Frannie, she wants to go into Asheville and see a new exhibit at the Asheville Art Museum so I very kindly offered to escort her,' he said with a wide smile.

Margo smiled back, 'That's great, Dad. I'm really happy for you, she seems nice.'

'She is, thanks, Margo. I know things haven't been easy, but I'm glad we are finally both moving forward with our lives.'

'Yeah, me too,' Margo said with another sip.

'So what are you up to today? Do you have your appointment with Jazz?'

'Yep, in a little bit. Austin is busy with work so I'm just going to take it easy here and look over my resumé, maybe start reaching out to some recruiters.'

'That sounds like a good plan.' Her dad's phone buzzed and he looked down. 'That's my ride, I'll see you later, kiddo.'

She gave him a smile as he made his way to the front door before she retreated to her room. After sending out her resumé and cover letter to a few postings and making sure her LinkedIn was up to date, she closed her laptop and pushed it back on the desk. Throwing on a pair of cut-off jean shorts and a t-shirt, she crossed the room and looked at the suspect board again. At this point, they weren't likely to uncover more evidence and there was still no clear killer. There was no point in leaving it up; she didn't see any gaps left in the investigation that could easily be filled. Margo pulled all the photos down and tossed them in the trash before wiping down the board of all her frantic red lines. She tucked a light cardigan in her handbag since she'd gotten a weather alert that a storm may roll in later. Her phone was sitting on her desk, so she reached for it to add it to her bag and noticed a voicemail notification. Picking it up, the message was from the unknown number yet again, but this time it was longer, almost a minute. With shaking hands, she hit the play button.

A loud sigh came over the line. 'Margo, this is Diana. Since you won't answer your phone, I guess I have to do this in a message instead. You need to leave Mark and I alone. I've been letting Mark handle this because I felt bad about how things went down, but I wanted you to hear

340

this from me. I'm sorry things happened the way they did. I really am. But you need to move on. No more messages, no more sitting in your car outside my house, no more phone calls. I mean it. I know you've been quiet the last few weeks, but I'm tired of living in fear that you're going to start up again when you hear the news . . .' She sighed again before continuing. 'Look, I hate to say this on your voicemail, but I'm pregnant. So please, I'm begging you, please stay away and just let us live in peace. If you start to harass us again, we are going to get a restraining order.'

She heard the click of Diana hanging up the phone. She sat in her bedroom in stunned silence. Margo had expected Mark and Diana to take the inevitable next step and start a family, but she hadn't expected it to come so soon. She wondered if that's why Mark had called her dad seemingly out of the blue, knowing that this announcement was on the horizon. Back during their heated argument after the dreaded break-up voicemail, Mark had shouted that he was in love with Diana. It had stung so badly she almost threw up. But now, she wasn't sure what she felt. Disappointment, maybe. But not sadness, and not jealousy. Her emotions were too hard to place but felt a lot less than she'd anticipated. Noticing the time, she grabbed her purse and rushed out to her car.

As she waited at a stoplight, her phone dinged with an incoming email. She opened it up and was surprised to find an email from her divorce lawyer. She almost laughed at the timing considering the message Diana had just left. The email was confirming her current address so her lawyer could send her the papers. They were near the end of the process, the end of their marriage. All that was left was to sign on the dotted line. Instead of the sadness she'd expected, she felt relief. She would apologize for her behavior and make sure they knew she would be leaving them alone. She wanted nothing to do with the past she'd left behind.

A car honked behind her, startling her. She glanced up and put her foot on the gas. When she got to Jazz's office, apprehension swelled inside her. She knew this would be a big session, filling Jazz in on so many things. Jazz greeted her warmly and ushered her in. She sat across from Margo and placed her clasped hands in her lap.

CHAPTER TWENTY-FOUR

'So how have things been since we last talked?' Jazz asked calmly, leaning forward.

'Things have been . . . OK. I'm still having the nightmares, just as bad as before. But I feel like my outlook on everything has improved. I'm thinking more about the future.'

'That's good progress. Did you do your homework assignment?'

Margo looked down, picking at a loose string on her denim shorts. 'Yes, I did. Looking back at my actions and Mark's reactions from that night I was late to his dinner, I think we were both too hard on me.' She paused, reflecting for a moment. 'When he laid into me, it was just so easy to beat myself up. But as I sat there on my bed after our last session, reliving that night, I realized there was no way that I did it on purpose. I really was backed up at work. I spaced out and just forgot about the dinner. You were right, Jazz. It was a simple mistake.'

'I'm glad to hear that.'

Margo spent the next half hour filling Jazz in on what her dad had told her about her mother. She also confessed to how she'd behaved toward Mark before coming to Lake Moss and how it had spilled over, embarrassed by her lack of self-control. And lastly, she filled her in on the stalking. The messages she'd received from Claire, her flat tire and suspicions about Charlie, now that she knew Claire wasn't behind *all* the tormenting. When she was done, she looked up at Jazz and was surprised by her silence.

'What are you thinking, Jazz?' Jazz was a straight shooter, and she was hoping for some direct insight to help clear the haze of muddled emotions she couldn't make sense of.

Jazz uncrossed her legs and leaned forward, 'I'm thinking that everything makes so much more sense now. I think it's pretty clear that you've experienced bouts of paranoia, of extreme fear that you're being followed or that something bad is going to happen to you. Granted, we know Claire really was sending you threatening messages and Charlie apparently did slash your tire, but it's quite possible you either inherited or learned some nervous behavior from your mother.'

Margo frowned. 'Are you saying I have the same disorder she had?' Margo pressed, fear swelling in her belly.

'No, that's not what I'm saying. You're not your mother, Margo.' Margo relaxed some of the tension she was holding in her shoulders. 'What *I am* saying is that it's something you should keep a close eye on. Take me for example. My mother was an alcoholic. I grew up thinking that drinking all the time, often to an extreme level, was normal. As an adult, I know that I have a higher predisposition to becoming an alcoholic myself. So I've made an effort every time I drink, to drink responsibly. Your mother had paranoid reactions about her own safety and then yours. She projected her fears outward. In this session, Margo, you've been more upfront with me about your own behaviors than you ever were before, and you're showing great improvement in your self-awareness. But now you need to accept what's in your family's past and try to be aware of how it could impact your future actions.'

Margo nodded, but refused to admit she may be as paranoid as her mother. 'I hadn't really known the extent of my mother's condition until my dad and I talked, and it really scared me. I don't want to live my life being ruled by fear like she did.'

'Your mother's concerns seem to have been centered on dangers in the world around her; her focus was on protecting you and herself. And while it may seem like your fear of being stalked is similar, yours feels different to me. Like it comes from a different place. Where do *you* think it comes from?'

Margo thought about it for a second. 'I don't know . . . loss maybe?'

'How so?' Jazz asked, looking thoughtful.

'I feel like I'm always losing people I care about. The only person I've cared about long term who never left me is my dad. Almost everyone else died or betrayed me. And I'm not sure how to get past that,' Margo said, crossing her ankles and looking at Jazz, wanting her to just give her all the answers, even though she knew that wasn't Jazz's style. Jazz liked to make her work for it.

Jazz nodded, agreeing with her assessment. 'Your mom left you at a young age and you had a hard time letting anyone in except your father for years. Then when you were finally reconnecting with Jessie and letting her back in, she left you too. And now, Mark left you for another woman. Your abandonment anxiety is natural given the circumstances. I think you are spot on with your statement that any paranoia within you stems from fear of loss.'

Margo straightened up, pleased that she seemed to be answering correctly. She couldn't help but want to impress Jazz, to show her progress and growth. Then, Margo thought more about when Mark started pulling away, well before his affair began. She had nurtured that fear every day without any tangible proof, and it ended up driving all her reactions and decisions. 'Yeah,' Margo said sadly, a heavy realization trying to take root.

'Margo, I don't want you to look at this as a bad thing. You have a clearer understanding of yourself and your motivations now. That's the first step in changing these behaviors, in being able to identify them when they occur. How are things between you and your dad?'

'Things are pretty good at home, we've been talking a lot more. He's dating someone, you know.'

Jazz returned her smile. 'I do know. Frannie and I are in a knitting club together. She's a lovely woman.'

'Yeah, he seems really happy.'

'Does that worry you? That you'll lose him? Like she'll take him away from you?'

Margo looked at Jazz for a minute, thinking about the question. 'To be honest, no. I thought it would, that was always such a fear of mine after my mom died. But I'm just happy that he's happy. And that he has someone to take care of him when I can't be here. I don't plan on staying in Lake Moss forever.'

'Well, there you go. The old Margo might have had a meltdown over this, maybe even pushed him away before he could do it to you. This is wonderful progress.'

'I keep thinking back to the moment he told me. My

gut reaction was to resist, to push this woman away and pull my dad closer. And then my second instinct was to avoid him. But those feelings slipped away as soon as they slunk in. I could see how happy he was and I realized my feelings were immature and pointless. I'm not a child, I can take care of myself and my dad isn't going anywhere. He loves me no matter what. It's ridiculous to even question that.'

'That's great Margo. I'm impressed with how much you've matured.'

Margo's cheeks flushed, not used to receiving so many compliments, especially in therapy. 'Everything that's been going on with the investigation and the threatening messages, talking more with my dad, and all the time I've been spending with Austin – I don't know, it's put some things in perspective. You know, I got an email from my divorce lawyer on the way over. He's ready to send the documents to sign. Pretty soon I'll be officially single again!' Margo laughed wryly.

'How does that make you feel?'

'Oddly relieved. I held so much anger inside me over what Mark did. But being angry is exhausting. I'm so tired, and in that moment, the reality of our marriage being over, I just felt relieved that I could stop being angry and move on with my life.'

'And what does moving on with your life look like to you?'

Margo briefly caught Jazz up on her developing relationship with Austin, how it had morphed from simply helping him with the interviews into something more.

'Does it feel too soon after the separation?' Jazz asked, her forehead scrunched up in concern.

'At first when these old feelings started to resurface, it

347

did feel too soon. I was still so hurt, how could I be having feelings for another man in the middle of all that? But over the last week or two, talking with you and with my dad, I've been able to see my relationship with Mark through a different lens; without all the resentment clouding my vision. It's like Austin's kindness held up a mirror to how, long ago, Mark and I actually fell out of love, and I never noticed it because I was focused on my fears about him cheating. And with that clarity, there were no lingering feelings for Mark at all. It was always about keeping him, not about how I actually felt about him. We just weren't right for one another. I think I'm finally OK with that.'

Jazz nodded and made some notes in her notebook. She glanced back up. 'I'd caution you not to move too quickly with Austin. You need to make sure your thoughts and actions are for the right reasons, and not reactions out of fear of being alone. Have you thought about your plans once your dad is fully recuperated?'

'I've been looking for jobs, considering a couple different cities and sending out resumes. And I know you are going to say this is too soon, but Austin mentioned showing me around Atlanta since that's where he lives, so I may take him up on that and see if I like it there. I'd actually already thrown my resumé into the ring for a few jobs there, and several other cities before Austin and I even reconnected. I don't have anything holding me to Wilmington, or to Lake Moss, really. Especially now that my dad is in good hands. I'm looking forward to exploring a new place. I've tried mountains, I've tried the beach. I'm thinking maybe it's time to try a city?' Margo shrugged. 'I need a fresh start and having a friendly face doesn't sound so bad.'

'I don't think it's too soon as long as you take things slowly. But again, I'd encourage you to look at your reasons for choosing Atlanta, if you decide to go there. Is it just for Austin? If it doesn't work out, you're stuck alone in a new city feeling resentful that you made this big leap for him. Make sure if you move there, that you are moving there for more than just him. I'd suggest you continue looking for jobs in multiple places, see what pans out. And if the best option ends up being Atlanta with all things considered, then you know you did your due diligence and can start out there with a clear conscious.'

'OK, I can do that.' Margo smiled, grateful for her level-headed advice.

'I know we don't have a lot of time left, but let's move on to the nightmares. I think they are tied specifically to your fears about someone stalking you. Do you think that's a fair assessment?'

Margo scrunched up her face, frowning slightly. 'Yes, that's fair.'

'Now that you know Claire was behind the threatening messages, do you still feel afraid? Do you believe there's still a threat to your safety?'

'I don't know, honestly. I know some of it has been explained away by Claire's confession, but I still have the lingering feelings from Charlie threatening me. Especially since now I know it was him who slashed my tire, I feel like he probably was creeping around my house trying to scare me. And after that encounter with him on the road, to me that's a real threat, and who knows if it's the last time he'll try something. But there's all these little things I heard or saw that scared me, like an impression on my bed, or seeing dark shapes outside at night . . . I wonder if those ambiguous moments were my paranoia rearing its head, imagining things that weren't really there. Maybe with the social stalking from Claire, and Charlie's actions, the combination made my mind see sinister things everywhere.'

'Well, it's reasonable to feel fear when your safety has legitimately been threatened. From what you've told me, it sounds like your worries about Charlie are logical fears, even if your reactions to them were a bit intense. But it's possible that coming back to your hometown caused old paranoid behaviors that you'd learned from your mother to seep into your life. From what you've told me in our sessions, you thought someone was watching you before the encounter with Charlie and messages from Claire began. And that the confrontation with him just intensified it. I wonder where that initial feeling stemmed from.'

There was silence as Jazz looked Margo in the eye. 'I don't have an answer for that, Jazz.'

Jazz looked at her for a beat. 'You told me that your fear and anxiety began after your first nightmare when you returned home. For me, that's telling. A lot of this still feels connected to your childhood trauma. While I feel like you *have* come to terms with your mother's death, you still have this uncertainty over whether it was an accident or intentional. I worry that your nightmares will never fully go away unless you confront that issue head on. Your mind is still trying to find answers and now that you've come back home and added the complex layer of your friend's body being discovered, it's intensified, manifesting in your dreams. The dreams could all be variations of searching for answers.'

'How can I move on from that though, if I'll never know the answer to that question?'

'By coming to terms with that reality. The question

350

you are so frantically trying to answer, will likely never be resolved. And what is it you think will happen if you do find the answer? What will it change for you? Come to terms with the worst possible case scenario and you take away the power of that question. Then it no longer *needs* to be answered. I'm hoping if you can accomplish that, the nightmares and anxiety will lessen over time.'

Margo barked a short laugh. 'And how exactly do I do that?'

'By confronting your trauma head-on, don't run away. Confront all your fears surrounding it. And then walk away from it, leave it at the site where it all began and move into your future. I'm not saying this will be a magic cure-all. You'll likely still have thoughts, but over time, when they come up, take yourself back to that moment of confrontation, relive that conversation with yourself. And then, ideally, you can walk away from those thoughts just like you are going to do now. Eventually, that mental muscle that you're working out will become stronger, making it easier to focus on the more wonderful areas of your life.'

'That's sounds way easier said than done,' Margo said, feeling nauseous at the thought.

'Oh, it will be very difficult. I'm not trying to make it sound easy. But you've been running away from these thoughts for over a decade, like touching a hot stove, your first instinct is to flinch back and avoid. If you stop running away and instead, confront them, then your dreams won't hold that responsibility. Each time you manage to face it directly, then you'll need to also force yourself to move on and not obsess. At first, it'll be hard and will take repeated conscious efforts, but as time goes on it should come more naturally.'

'I'll do my best.'

'Great. So . . . homework assignment,' Jazz said with a smile.

'Ah of course, homework!' Margo sighed dramatically, crossing her arms over her chest.

Jazz laughed. 'This will probably be our toughest assignment yet. You need to go back to the scene where it all began and ask yourself the hard questions, with your mom, with whomever you need to say it to. You have your journal, yes?' Margo nodded. 'Great. After visiting that spot and thinking about what's been haunting you, I want you to write one last entry in this journal and then dispose of it somehow. Set it on fire, drop it in the trash, whatever feels appropriate and final. All the thoughts and fears inside that journal need to be a thing of the past. By physically destroying it, you can metaphorically say to your brain, I'm putting it behind me. Then you can start a fresh, clean journal.'

Margo nodded again and glanced at the clock. 'That's the hour!' she said, stealing Jazz's famous ending line.

'Not so fast. I need you to say that you'll do this assignment before we meet next time. You know the rules,' she replied, cocking her head to the side and wagging a finger.

Margo stifled a laugh. 'OK, OK, I will complete this assignment before our next meeting. I promise.'

As Margo walked down the pathway to her car, thinking about the assignment that lay ahead, Austin texted her.

'Hey! Post-production on the episode went smoother than expected. We're doing the viewing of the rough cut later today. Can you make it? No specific time yet, they are just now setting everything up.'

'Sure, sounds fun! Just let me know when. ☺'

'☺ See you later!'

A warmth filled Margo up thinking about seeing Austin again. But first, she had something important to do. Jazz's latest homework assignment consumed Margo's head-space as she drove back home. The more she thought about what Jazz said, the more she realized Jazz was right in more ways than one. She needed to confront her past head-on instead of running away and acting like it never happened. Burying her feelings under layers of other problems had not made them go away, they'd only haunted her, forcing their way into her dreams and tanking her relationships. It was time for it to end. It had to end. She wouldn't be able to move on with Austin until she dealt with her past. Margo pulled her car up to her house and ran toward her front door. A foggy mist was rolling in, the humidity giving away mother nature's secret of incoming rain looming on the horizon. The air conditioning hit her like a brick wall as she opened the door. The house was empty, her dad still out with Frannie.

Good, Margo thought. She needed privacy to do this without her dad hovering around asking questions or worrying about her. She ran to her bedroom and pulled her journal out from under her mattress, still using the same hiding spot she had chosen years ago. On her way to the door, she stopped and plucked her engagement and wedding ring out of her jewelry box, tucking them into the pocket of her shorts. Heading through the back door into the thick damp air, she shoved the journal into her bag and rushed to the pond. Dropping to her knees at its edge, Margo reached under the gap in the rocks and grabbed her hidden metal box of memories. Holding it tightly in her lap, she sat on the edge of the rocks looking

353

into the water at her reflection. Visions of her mother and Jessie danced across the rippling surface, questions that might never be answered etched deeply on their faces.

Margo plunged her arm into the water elbow-deep and felt around, looking up at the darkening sky as she rummaged. After a moment, she pulled out the only rock from the bottom that had ever really meant anything beyond nostalgia for the days of hunting perfect rocks with her mom. It wasn't large, maybe the size of a grapefruit, and looked like any average rock. She took out her light cardigan and wrapped the rock inside, before placing it in her handbag along with the journal and the box. Then she went to the garage and grabbed a can of lighter fluid and a box of matches and headed back to her car.

Each step felt like a weight slowly being lifted. Margo was galvanized by a solid plan, a hope for moving forward. This was her chance to put it all behind her. She hopped in the car, a ball of frantic energy, and put her bag on the back seat before pulling out of the driveway once more. With determination, Margo turned left and drove down the main road leading out of town. She thought about what she might write in her final entry. Her mind kept trying to run away from the challenge ahead, but she heard Jazz's words and remained steadfast in her quest. As thoughts began flooding her brain unbidden, tears poured down Margo's face of their own accord, releasing years of pent-up distress.

Only a mile more to go. She slowed down as she came across the infamous tree with the wooden cross staked in the ground by her father some twenty years ago. The pink hues rolling into the sky ahead of the storm glinted off the plaque the town had anchored into the tree base. As she approached the memorial to the life of Eloise

354

Sutton, Margo brought the car to a stop. Someone had placed a bunch of daisies, her mom's favorite, against the cross. Most likely her father. He'd always wanted Margo to join him on these visits, but she never did. The few times she went by this spot she only wanted to run away as fast as she could. But this time, Margo let the thoughts come as she stared at the tree that had taken her mother's life. And finally, the thought that had always haunted her blazed to the forefront once more. *Did my mother kill herself?* She thought about it, and her mind drifted to the recent conversation about her mother's mental health. A switch clicked in her mind. Even if Eloise did kill herself, Margo could now see it was never about leaving her daughter and husband, it was about an unquiet mind that she just couldn't live with anymore. It was heartbreaking, but it didn't have anything to do with loving Margo or not. Perhaps she was even at peace now. That would have to be enough. Margo took one last look at the cross, wiped the tears from her cheeks, and switched her foot over to the gas pedal, pushing down with determination.

CHAPTER TWENTY-FIVE

As Margo drove away from memories of her mother, she mentally switched gears to what lay ahead. She followed the steeply inclined road up into the mountainside, clenching her jaw in determination as her car pulled her higher and higher.

Fledgling Hawks soar to peaking crests . . .

She kept going until she saw the familiar bank of trees on either side in the distance, overgrown and connecting above her, their limbs reaching out to touch one another like Michelangelo's Creation of David, moss weeping down like a waterfall.

Behind the canopy you'll find your quest . . .

She hung a right onto the unused, overgrown road. She drove for another mile before she saw *the* tree, its one thick limb stretching into the road, still zig-zagging above her just like she remembered it.

Jump the path at Lightning Tree . . .

She pulled the car to the side just past the tree and parked. That was as far as she could drive, the rest would have to be on foot. Taking a deep breath, she grabbed her bag and climbed out, entrenched in shadows from the dense foliage and dark clouds rolling in. The path was barely noticeable and if she hadn't done this before with the help of the riddle passed on to every rising senior, she might never have seen it. A slight indentation in the ground was all that marked it. She picked her way through drooping limbs, the decline quite steep in some parts, until she heard a hissing sound and scanned the area for the source. Sucking in a breath, Margo backed away from the tree next to her, a long limb reaching out with a snake wrapped around it, slithering in her direction. She yelped and ran away from the slinking creature, further down the path until she came out of the dense foliage. The creek was before her and to her right, three boulders stacked on top of one another, moss blanketing their surfaces. Whether someone had done it on purpose or if the boulders had fallen this way naturally, no one ever knew.

Journey west to rocks stacked three . . .

The creek at this junction was little more than a trickle. But as she walked further along the rocky shore, the creek filled up and the current gained momentum, creating a whooshing sound.

Travel along the whispering creek . . .

Margo was winded from the rough walk as she dodged large boulders and tree roots sticking out of the ground, feeling immensely out of shape despite all her jogging. She didn't remember it being this long of a walk before, but it had been ages since she'd taken this path. Finally, she came to the waterfall on the opposite side of the creek.

Pass the falls for what you seek . . .

The creek narrowed slightly when the trees pushed into its path, but on the other side the landscape opened up. And there it was. The swimming hole with the cove on

357

one side, the old rocky bridge towering way up above it. And jutting out high up over the water's glassy surface, the ledge within the rocks where they'd jumped the last day of junior year.

Hawks fly high for the final test. We'll pass the torch at Senior Nest.

The 'Nest' was the rock up top where someone had spray painted a red-tailed hawk, their school's mascot. Margo remembered standing up on that rock in her pink flowered underwear and white cotton bra next to Austin, hesitating at the edge. She'd been so scared to jump, not sure how deep she'd go once she hit the surface. She remembered being crushed, and she was sure Austin had been too, when despite making the jump, they hadn't been catapulted into the cool crowd like they'd hoped. They'd stayed for that torch-passing celebration but had never received invites to any of the parties held there in their senior year.

Margo climbed her way through the rocks until she came to the cove on the far side of the swimming hole. It looked pretty much the same as she remembered. Graffiti from generations of Hawks was scrawled all over the rocky walls that made the cove private. 'Hawks Rule' 'Jay Temperely is a jerk!' 'Hannah + Devin' jumped out at her as she scanned the walls. Empty beer cans and bottles littered the ground from a recent party. The small makeshift fire-pit assembled from nearby rocks placed in a circle was still there, the center filled with ash and the remnants of twigs. Margo sat down on the stone surface at the edge of the water and pulled out her journal. She opened its spine, flipping to the final entry she'd made in her youth, before Jazz had instructed her to pick it back up again a few weeks back. She ran her finger along the subtle, thin edge of ripped-out paper next to that entry, the only remaining evidence of the discarded page she'd carefully torn out years ago. She looked at that last page of ink, the one she'd written about boring takeout and a movie the night Jessie had disappeared before flipping slowly past her recent entries to the next clean page.

She clicked open her pen and lowered its tip to the crisp white surface but couldn't bring herself to write the words. She had to face her true feelings head-on. It was time to stop running. Setting her journal and pen down, she took a deep breath and looked into the water, allowing that day to play out on the reflective surface like she was watching a movie. A rustling sound caught her attention before her memory could take her very far. Looking over, she saw the journal's page had flipped back over to re-expose the thin, torn strip and she could see the missing page as if it was still there. She'd read that entry so many times before she'd torn it out, she had it memorized. The entry swam before her eyes, every detail of her scribbled ink gleaming fresh.

May 26, 2004

Dear Diary,

OMG it's FINALLY happening! I've wanted nothing more than to get my bestie back, and I knew if I spent time tutoring her that she'd come around. And my plan actually worked! It was like any other day coming home from school, grabbing the mail and dropping it on the entry table before going to the kitchen to make a snack. Dad, of course, wasn't home yet. He's been stuck

359

late at school all week grading his final projects or whatever.

After making a sandwich, I went back to the living room to watch The Real World episode I Tivo'd the night before, and THERE IT WAS! A small piece of paper curled up on the floor near the door. It must have fallen from the mail stack. It said, 'Behind the canopy you'll find your guest . . . 7pm. It's important!' I immediately recognized Jessie's handwriting of course. So, here I am, trusty journal, so excited I can barely hold my pen. Her note isn't about tutoring, or she would have just texted me. I was worried that she was pulling away again when she cancelled our session so close to finals. But no, she's invited me to the secret senior spot! My first official invite to the party cove!

I wonder what's so important that she wants to tell me without other people hanging around. Maybe it's about Charlie? Let's be honest, she deserves way better than that tool. Or what if it's a party, a REAL party and I'm actually invited this time! I can't wait, I really can't! Time is going by soooooo slowwwww. Anyway, the next time you hear from me, I'll be spilling about how lucky I am to have the most beautiful friend in the world.

XO

Flipping the journal back to the fresh page as the memory of the words dissipated into thin air, Margo clipped the pen over the pages to keep it open at the right spot until she was ready to write. Looking back at the water, Margo could see the scene as clear as if it was happening right now, the events that unfolded after she'd finished writing that entry.

She had been so excited to meet Jessie that when the time finally came, she drove over the speed limit, hoping she wouldn't get a ticket. There wasn't a whole lot of police presence in her town, and the force they did have was not very on the ball, so she thought it was worth the risk. She rushed through the woods and when she came to the clearing by the swimming hole, she spotted Jessie sitting inside the cove, her bright red cheerleading track suit a dazzling splash of color against the gray rocks. Margo made her way over to the cove, beaming ear-to-ear, but Jessie hadn't spotted her yet. She was busy looking at her phone.

When Margo lifted herself up to the cove platform, she said, 'Jessie! I was so happy to get your note. I can't wait to hear what's so important!'

Jessie's face scrunched up as she slowly rose and looked at Margo.

'Why are you here? I cancelled our tutoring session,' she said, snapping her phone shut and placing it in the small tight pocket on the back of her warmup pants.

A shot of embarrassment rumbled through Margo. Had she been mistaken? But how? 'Um, I got your note, so I came.'

Jessie's face turned to surprise, her eyes widening, her eyebrows arching up on her forehead as if they were reaching for her high ponytail. She sighed and said, 'Oh. Margo, that . . . wasn't for you.'

'What do you mean? It was in my mail.' Jessie fidgeted with the zipper on her track suit, biting her lip. She looked at the ground, avoiding Margo's eyes. 'Jessie what is it? Come on you can tell me anything, you know that.'

'I can't tell you this, Margo,' she said, an odd tone to her voice.

'Jessie, yes you can. We're best friends. Whatever it is, I'll help you figure it out,' Margo pled, hating the needy note she was hitting.

Jessie gave her a confused look. 'Best friends? You're . . . tutoring me.'

'Jessie don't be like that. I know we drifted apart after my mom died. That's probably my fault since I pulled away, but I'm here now.'

Jessie looked like a caged animal, her eyes darting around. She took a step toward Margo. 'Let's just forget about it, it wasn't important.'

'What do you mean? The note said it *was* important.'

Margo had never seen Jessie look so uncomfortable before. 'It's not. I was caught up in something, but I changed my mind and realized it's not a big deal. Let's just leave it at that.'

'Jessie, just tell me. I know things have been weird the past few years. But we've reconnected lately. It feels like our old friendship again, you know it does – come on!' Margo replied, her voice getting louder as she took a step closer to Jessie.

Jessie's face pinched in for a second and then morphed into a scowl, the corners of her lips turned down sharply. 'Margo, really? We were friends in elementary school. That was ages ago. I run in a different circle now. Do you really think I'd be best friends with . . . you?' she said, looking Margo up and down.

Margo flinched back. 'I don't understand. You've been confiding in me, we've been spending time together outside of tutoring. How could you say something like that?'

'I needed a tutor; you saw how badly I was doing. I had to pass the final in order to graduate. And yeah, we've chatted during our sessions but that was just to pass the time. School is *so* boring! But when I asked you to tutor me it wasn't an invitation into our group. We're out of your league, Margo. How can you not see that?' Jessie flicked her long blonde ponytail over her shoulder. 'Look, I've gotta go.' She took a step toward Margo.

Margo put a hand on her shoulder as Jessie stepped closer. 'Wait. How did that note find its way into my mail? If it wasn't for me?'

'It's none of your business Margo, let it go!' she said, her voice going up an octave.

'How is it not my business? It was in *my* house!' Margo felt her cheeks flushing, the heat rising in her confusion that was turning into anger. She couldn't understand why Jessie was getting upset with *her*.

Jessie paused for a second. 'Are you going to let me pass or not? Come on Margo, you really don't want to go there,' she said through gritted teeth. Margo didn't budge, holding her ground. Something was wrong here, but she didn't know what. Jessie exhaled loudly. 'Fine! You want to know about that note? It's not just *your* house, Margo!' she finally snapped, throwing her hands up in the air before letting them fall back to her sides.

For a second, Margo was confused. Then it clicked, and her stomach did a somersault. 'You left that note for my dad? Why? And why here?' she said, throwing her arms out wide. 'Why not just come by if you needed to talk to him?'

'Because he told me not to!' Jessie screamed, her emotions boiling over. 'I didn't realize I would need to spell it out for you. Yeah, I needed tutoring, but Cassidy could have easily helped me with that. She has straight As. I chose you because I wanted to get closer to your *dad*. And it worked! We slept together, OK? I love him,' she said, a proud smile on her face. 'I told him about this place, hoping we could make it our secret meeting spot when it wasn't being used for parties.'

Margo shook her head vehemently; she couldn't believe her ears. 'You're lying! My dad would never do that!'

Jessie laughed and Margo almost didn't recognize the person standing in front of her. 'God you're so naïve! Literally every girl in school is in love with him.' She shrugged one shoulder. 'I wanted to be the one who got him. And I finally managed it at that basketball tournament that Charlie played in for your dad in the off-season, when we were all staying at a hotel. The coaches had been celebrating after the team's big win, so your dad was a little drunk. I'd had a fight with Charlie and waited for your dad outside his room. I convinced him to let me in to talk, and well . . .' Margo's world was tilting on an axis around her, making her unsteady. 'But I didn't plan on falling in love, it just happened. So you need to come to terms with it, OK? We're going to be together after graduation.'

None of what Jessie said sounded like her dad. He rarely even drank. But since he didn't drink often, if he was drinking that night, he must have been too drunk . . . not thinking clearly. Jessie must have taken advantage of the opportunity to put her plan in motion and seduced him. She'd manipulated everyone, including Margo. Margo narrowed her eyes. 'This whole time you were just using me to get close to my dad? I thought we were friends!'

'You really thought *I'd* be friends with *you*? Come on Margo. After your mom died I felt sorry for you, but you became so whiny and pathetic, it was impossible to be around. You don't even *try* to make yourself look any better. You started dressing all tragic and mismatched. Do you even know makeup exists?' Jessie shook her head. 'We orbit in different universes now, Margo.'

'Don't say that,' Margo whispered, tears welling in her eyes, spilling over and trailing across her quivering lips. 'All I've ever done was try to help you! Try to be close to you again! I listened when you complained about Cassidy and Charlie, I made sure you got A's on all your assignments. All so we could be friends again. I knew the way you gossiped that you could be cruel, but I never thought you would turn on me. Not like this!'

Jessie sighed loudly. 'OK, we can be friends,' she said, putting up air quotes around the word friends, 'because I'm going to be in your life for a very long time. I may even be sleeping down the hall from you when you come home on college breaks.'

'You really think my dad is going to have a relationship with you? Obviously what he did was a huge mistake. And you called *me* naïve. He could get fired and maybe even go to jail if this gets out. Don't you understand that? You could ruin his life!' Margo's anger was rising with each second. She felt like steam was radiating from her face, the fire of betrayal raging so deeply. How had she worshiped such a monster?

'I'm eighteen, it's legal,' Jessie said with a shrug.

'Jessie, that doesn't matter! He was your teacher, there are laws about that. If you really care about him, you'll leave him alone.' Margo clenched her fists, an innate need to protect the only family she had left taking over.

'I can't do that,' Jessie said. 'You're too immature, you wouldn't understand.'

'Yes, you can. Just go to college and leave it alone!'

'I'm not going to college anymore. I can't.' Jessie looked up at her with a smile stretched across her face, enjoying the moment. 'I'm pregnant.' She put her hand on her stomach and looked down.

Margo couldn't breathe. 'Charlie's?'

Jessie looked back sharply at her. 'Of course it's not Charlie's! I told you we were having problems, that wasn't a lie. We haven't slept together in months, way before that night with your dad. After my night with Shane, I couldn't stop thinking about him. Obviously I had to break it off with Charlie.' Margo flinched hearing Jessie call her father by his first name. 'But Charlie and I never told anyone we split. He was embarrassed and pissed that he'd been dumped and I couldn't tell anyone because of your dad. Shane told me we can't be together and to stay away, but I'm sure he'll come around after I've graduated, especially with the baby and all . . . it'll be fine. It's the honorable thing for him to marry me.'

Margo shook her head, 'You're lying,' she seethed through clenched teeth.

Jessie laughed, 'Wanna bet? I have the pregnancy test in my pocket.'

'No, no, no! This cannot be happening!' Margo screamed, shaking her head and running her hands frantically through her hair. 'Jessie you can't keep this baby, it'll ruin everything!'

Jessie's laugh rang out again. 'I'd never give this baby up. It's *our* baby. So you'd better get used to it, Margo.

I'll probably be your stepmom someday. And when the baby comes, you'll be at college anyway, so what do you care? We'll start our own new family. Don't worry, I'm sure your dad will still include you . . . sometimes.'

Margo's mind flashed at a million miles a second, scenes playing at warp speed of Jessie's new baby taking her father away from her forever. Her last remaining family . . . gone. With a baby, would he even remember to call on her birthday? Would he be there when she called late at night crying about her mom? Would he still come visit her at college like he'd promised? Would Jessie let him see Margo ever again? Margo couldn't believe how expertly Jessie had orchestrated this whole thing. This was not the same girl Margo had played Barbies with and passed notes back and forth with in grade school. The one who'd told Margo they'd be best friends forever. She'd turned into a complete stranger.

Jessie tried to step past her again, but Margo stopped her by blocking her path. 'Jessie, you can't do this. Does he even know you're pregnant?'

'No, that's why I wanted to meet him here. To tell him, so we could start planning our future.' She paused and then smiled. 'Jessie Sutton, I like the sound of that. Now can you please get out of my way?'

'No, no, no! I can't let you ruin his life!'

'Me? *I'm* ruining his life? Please Margo,' she said with disdain. 'It must be awful to have you as a daughter. You're nothing and you will always be nothing.' Jessie inched closer, getting in Margo's face. Margo had never seen Jessie look so evil, her pretty face always so angelic. But now, she was ugly, her eyes dark and tight, her mouth smirking nastily. 'This baby is his second chance to have a real family. Not that psycho mother of yours. Everyone

367

knows she drove her car into that tree on purpose. And not a poor excuse for a daughter like you who's probably following right in her footsteps!' she spat out.

Margo's anger exploded out of her, taking control as she shoved Jessie to put some distance between her and her vile words. She wanted her to shut up, to stay away from her dad. Jessie stumbled back, tripping over the small fire-pit and falling back onto the ground, a loud crack echoing off the rocks. The sound seemed to go on forever. Margo waited for Jessie to get up, maybe even scream or push her back, prepared for the fight to continue. But she remained still.

The balloon of anger that had swelled within Margo began to deflate just enough to make room for other emotions.

'Jessie, look, I'm sorry. I didn't mean to push you so hard. Let's just talk about this,' she'd said, regret sweeping through her, but Jessie still hadn't moved.

Something was wrong. Dead wrong.

Margo's eyes popped open as she mentally sprinted away from the memories, bringing her back to the present. She wasn't sure she could relive what she'd done next. Her heartbeat was pounding in her ears. Stealing her last bit of reserve, she took a deep breath. What came next in her memories, she knew, was almost worse than the venom spat by the person she thought was her friend. It was what set her on a path she couldn't come back from. It was when a simple mistake, an accident, turned into a calculated decision. Releasing the binds holding her memories in check, her eyes drifting over the beautiful landscape in front of her, she let her mind wander where it needed to go. Here, with no one to bear witness to her ugly truth, she emptied out every last secret.

She closed her eyes and saw Jessie's body sprawled out in the cove, unmoving, as if Margo was standing over her that very night. She could feel her pulse racing, her blood running cold. Slowly, the rocky cove and water next to it came back into view in her mental frame, the rays from the setting sun streaming above her and illuminating the cove in a warm glow.

Margo was horrified by the scene in front of her. Jessie lying on her back, eyes frozen open, staring at her like a shocked porcelain doll. After what could have been seconds, or minutes, she frantically crouched down next to Jessie and jostled her. She shook Jessie's shoulders back and forth, but Jessie's head simply lolled to one side.

'Jessie, Jessie, wake up!' she blubbered, her anguished screams echoing. But no response came. Looking down, she saw a deep red pool of blood spreading out under Jessie's head. 'No, no, no, no!' She pushed her finger into the side of Jessie's neck, searching for the thump thump of a pulse. But there was none.

It had been a light shove just to make her stop. How could this have happened? Margo paced as thoughts of what to do flew by. She looked back at Jessie and kneeled down next to her body, frantically pushing up and down on her chest with her palms clasped on top of one another, hoping to restart her heart. Maybe there was still a chance. Tears streamed down her face and she whispered, 'Come on, come on Jessie!' After a minute, there was still no pulse. Margo knew then that it was futile, Jessie wasn't coming back.

She sat back on her heels and thought about what to do, her survival instincts starting to kick in. If she went to the police, she couldn't be sure they'd believe her that it was an accident. Jessie was the town's golden girl, the arm-candy of the most influential family in town's son. They'd be out for blood. Jessie was right, Margo thought, she was a nobody. No one would be on her side. She saw herself being led to a police car in handcuffs, an angry town pointing accusatory fingers at her, her classmates looking at her with horrified expressions, turning away in disgust. She saw twelve people pronouncing her guilty, dashing any hopes of a future. And then there was her dad. Surely, they'd be able to tell if Jessie was pregnant. Charlie would tell them he hadn't slept with Jessie in that time-frame. They'd be looking for the father. Her father. He'd be fired and possibly sent to jail, like she'd told Jessie. She couldn't let that happen. Her father was all she had left.

Quickly, she scanned the area, looking for a solution. Then she spotted it, sitting further inside the cove. The seniors had left a massive gray cooler so they could simply bring beer and ice in their backpacks and fill it up each time they came to party. Margo rushed further to it and opened the lid. A few bottles of Moss Creek Pilsners were still inside. She dragged it to the edge of the cove bordering the swimming hole. Grabbing several nearby rocks, she dropped them into the cooler, worried it would float unless weighted down since Jessie was so tiny.

Margo stopped her frantic movements and looked at Jessie's body. This was the part she was dreading. But she had no choice. Tears poured down her cheeks as she placed her hands under Jessie's still-warm body. Jessie only weighed about a hundred pounds, and thanks to Margo's considerable height, she lifted Jessie's body into the cooler with minimal struggle. But with Jessie's dead weight, it was awkward and sickening manipulating her body to fit inside. Jessie's vacant eyes stared up at her as her head fell back and rested on the lip of the cooler. Trying to avoid her glassy judgmental glare, Margo pulled Jessie's dangling arms in over the edge, crossing them across her stomach. She bent Jessie's legs at the knees so they folded tight up against her upper body, like she was in the fetal position on her back. With a shuddering breath, she pushed Jessie down to clear the opening for the lid. Her head tilted forward, chin to chest, as her body slid down into the cooler. Margo could barely look at what she was doing, and when she pulled her hands back, the tips of her trembling fingers were wet and sticky with blood. Nausea took over. She dropped to her knees and vomited into the swimming hole. Wiping her mouth once her body stopped heaving, she looked at the cooler. If Jessie had been even an inch taller, she may not have fit.

As her eyes lingered on Jessie's lifeless form, a loud sob burst from deep in her chest. 'I'm so sorry. I didn't mean it. Please forgive me.'

She pulled the lid down but it hit the top of Jessie's head and the toes of her white sneakers. Turning her feet inward toward one another, she pushed the lid down harder until she heard a sickening crack as the lid met the rim. Margo rested her upper body on top of the cooler as her legs threatened to give out, waves of nausea rolling over her again. Realizing through her panicked haze that she needed to move faster, Margo pulled the clasp down to lock the cooler, sweating and breathing in the warm air. With one last silent plea for forgiveness, she pushed the cooler with all her might. It scraped forward inch by inch, taking every bit of strength she could muster. At last, it tipped over the edge and gravity did the rest. The cooler bobbed along the top for a few seconds before sinking lower, the water finally pouring over the top.

When the cooler disappeared, the ripples in the surface pulsated toward the edges like a beating heart pumping blood out to the tips of fingers and toes. As the dark of night crept in, replacing the streaks of fading sunlight, the ripples lessened until stillness took over. Deep beneath the surface, Margo imagined the cooler settling into its final resting place on the sandy bottom. She stared into the murky depths, crying uncontrollably, as darkness settled both in and around her.

Suddenly she heard a twig snap and she whipped her head toward the tree line. She looked all around and spotted a deer darting away. She needed to get out of there. What if someone saw her? She looked around frantically, making sure she didn't leave anything behind. And that's when Margo spotted the pool of Jessie's blood with a small, average-looking rock resting in the center. The rock was topped with a pointed bloody edge. Jessie must have landed on it, the point piercing her skull. Margo tried to reassure herself that she likely died instantly, feeling no pain. It was the only piece of comfort to be found, and it wasn't much.

Margo picked up the rock and rinsed the blood off in the water, setting it aside. There was a discarded red Solo cup nearby, lying forgotten on its side. Margo grabbed it and began scooping water over the pool of blood on the cove floor, trying to keep her stomach from betraying her again. The blood was so thick it took more time than she'd expected to wash it all away. But she'd done a good job, the slight discoloration indiscernible from nearby dirty spots from who-knows-what. She glanced around one last time, searching for any other signs of her deadly deed. On the rocky floor of the cove, she saw lines etched in the dirt stretching to the edge of the water. It clearly betrayed something had been pushed to the edge. Margo swept her feet through the dirt, scattering it around until no obvious trail marks remained. Surely no one would know what had befallen here, that this was now Jessie's watery grave. The sleeves on her cardigan were drenched as she began trudging back up to her car, the deadly rock clutched in her trembling hands. She kept shooting looks all around, worried someone had seen what she'd done, guilt and paranoia chasing each other around her brain.

When she finally reached her car, Margo quickly started the engine and tore out from her spot in the gravel, anxious to get away from the nightmare she found herself trapped in. She drove for a few minutes and reached into her pocket, looking for her phone. It wasn't there! She slammed on the brakes, then did a U-turn to head back, worried it had fallen out somehow and was still at the swimming hole. Evidence she couldn't explain away if Jessie's body was ever found. After another minute of driving back in the direction of the swimming hole, she heard her phone ding. Abruptly, she stopped the car again, just off the side of the road. As she searched for the phone, her foot slipped off the brake and caused the car to pull forward a few yards. Panicking, she put the car in park and felt around under the driver's seat until her fingers brushed over the edge of her phone. It must have fallen out during her mad dash to the swimming hole. If only she had known what she was rushing toward.

Feeling relieved, she replied to the text from her dad. He said he'd be heading home soon, his work was almost done. She replied that she was watching a movie, about to order Chinese delivery and would save him some. She had to get home before her dad. She dialed Chow Funs, the only Chinese food in town, and quickly placed their regular order, trying to keep her voice steady. She would rent a movie on demand the minute she got home and fast forward so it looked like she'd been watching for an hour, so he wouldn't know she'd left to meet a friend. *Friend!*

She shoved the phone into her pocket and pulled another U-turn. Her hands were still shaking as she sped back to her house. She noticed blood on her sleeve and frantically tried to rub it out. But the red stain remained. As she approached her street, her mind darted to Mrs. Avendale, the nosiest person in her neighborhood. If she was going to pull this off, she'd need to stay out of Mrs. Avendale's view. Margo turned onto her street and clicked off her headlights. When she pulled up to her house, she was careful to position her car behind a tree, out of view. She turned off the car and watched the house across the street. The curtain in the Avendales' living room thankfully didn't flutter. Margo glanced at her driveway and was relieved to see her dad still wasn't home. Exiting the car, she closed the door slowly and carefully. But the click it made seemed deafening and she whipped her head toward the Avendales' house. Still nothing. She darted into her dark house, quickly shutting the door behind her.

She turned on the TV and ordered the first movie that came up, *What a Girl Wants,* and fast-forwarded a significant amount, before rushing to her room. She sat on her bed, her mind running wild while the sounds of the movie floated down the hallway. She looked at her hands and thought she could still see blood on them, even though they were clean. But there was the red stain on her sleeve. She went to the garage and pulled out the large trashcan her dad would be putting by the curb for pick up tomorrow. She opened the lid and buried the cardigan under piles of plastic packaging and lumps of used coffee grounds. Then Margo rushed back inside, peeled off her clothes and jumped in a hot shower, her mind replaying the night over and over, flashes of the swimming hole floating in and out of her subconscious as the steady stream beat down on her body on the hottest setting, turning her skin pink. She wasn't sure she would ever feel clean again.

Margo wracked her brain; was there anything that could tie her to Jessie that night? They'd had a tutoring session planned, but Jessie had cancelled. She had the text to prove it. But she'd written about meeting Jessie in her journal after finding the note. If she was ever a suspect, it would all be there, laid out for them to find. It was the only clue she could think of, so she turned off the water and leapt out of the shower, quickly drying off and rushing to her room where she threw on shorts and a tank top. Margo grabbed her journal from underneath her mattress and found the incriminating page. She folded the paper over near the binding and scored it with her fingernail. Delicately, she tore the page away, tearing it into small pieces. Then, after a long pause, she wrote a replacement entry. She chronicled a boring night for any potential inquisitive eyes in the future.

She put the journal back under her mattress and walked into the bathroom with the secret rolled up note from Jessie and the torn-up diary entry pieces clutched in her hand. She crumpled the note and flushed everything down the toilet. She watched that damned note that had caused all of this as it circled the drain and disappeared. There was only one thing left to tie her to Jessie. Picking up the rock that she'd carried away, unable to leave behind something that had changed the DNA of her life so drastically, Margo went out to the small pond in her backyard. As she sat on the edge looking at the water, she sobbed, struggling to suck in air. Her fingers grazed the sharp point that had taken Jessie's life as she held the rock to her chest and squeezed her eyes shut. Then she reached her arm into the water and pushed the rock into the bottom of the pond, wedging it between two other rocks. She wasn't sure why she'd kept the rock. Maybe it was panic at leaving the murder weapon behind. Margo flinched at the internal word, *murder*. But that's what it was, wasn't it? Maybe she wanted to punish herself with a constant reminder sitting there in her backyard, pointing a finger at her every time she looked outside. She felt she deserved it, even though it was an accident. But she had always been one to keep things that signified major moments in her life. And this night was one of the most defining moments she'd ever experienced.

The back door slammed shut and Margo jumped.

'Hey kiddo, are you OK? I was wondering why the back porch light was on. Thinking about your mom?' her dad said consolingly.

Margo's breath came quick and sharp as she struggled to keep her fear in check. She rose from the pond and ran to her dad, throwing her arms around him, sobbing. He rubbed her back and whispered comforting words before leading her inside. With one last glance back at the pond, Margo had followed her dad into the house, away from that accusatory rock.

Margo's phone buzzed in her pocket, the text notification pulling her out of the past and back to the present, dark skies threatening to burst open and drench her.

'Hey, what time can you get here? The rest of the crew is starting to arrive so I think we're gonna watch the rough cut soon,' the message from Austin read.

'I can be there in fifteen!' she replied, her fingers shaking as she tapped out the message.

How strange it felt to relive that night with Jessie and come back to the present now with Austin, her only other childhood friend. She now knew the true reason she'd never returned home at breaks. She knew that rock was waiting for her, threatening to unravel her carefully constructed mental defenses. She couldn't face what she'd done. She'd had to push it down deep in order to survive. Despite being in the exact spot where it had happened, she was miles away from that awful night. It felt like another lifetime, that it had happened to a different Margo. She picked up her journal and pen, pressing the tip against the page to complete her homework assignment once and for all.

Dear Diary,
It was only a push. One that forever stained my hands. And to try to forget would only be wishful, because sometimes the end is not really the end. You slipped between the folds of water, drifting down in an agonizing descent. I watched as the water swallowed my secrets, knowing I'd never see you again. Goodbye my friend. I never meant to hurt you. But this has to be the end.

Margo snapped the journal shut and placed it in the middle of the fire-pit, closing the book on some of most significant minutes of her life. Minutes that had haunted her every day and night for the last fifteen years. She

377

opened her memento box, removing the photos of her family, her mom's locket and the snow globe before dumping the remainder of its contents into the fire-pit as well. From her purse, she grabbed the box of matches and the bottle of lighter fluid. She doused the items, the overpowering smell of the fluid consuming her senses and making her cough. She struck a match, holding the warm flame in front of her before letting it fall from her fingers. It caught quickly, and the fire danced in the reflection of her eyes as she watched her secrets burn.

After it was all reduced to ash, she moved closer to the water's edge. First, she tossed in her wedding rings, wanting nothing left to remind her of past failures. Then, she unwrapped the rock. As she held it in her hand, she couldn't believe something so small had done so much damage. Margo looked into the dark water that had been Jessie's tomb for so long. Taking a deep breath, she tossed the rock into the deep dark depths. It was quickly swallowed up, ripples billowing out from the impact until finally, the water stilled once more.

Margo wasn't sure how long she stood there looking at the spot where she'd pushed the cooler that night. There was one more thing to get rid of. She took out her cell phone and navigated to the file she had emailed herself long ago. An old recording of a voicemail, transferred from phone to computer and then back to her new phone, expertly disguised but always within reach. She had tried to use audio enhancing software for years, just to make sure none of the new technology coming out would reveal her voice in the background as Jessie shouted. Thankfully, not even Austin had been able to uncover those hidden truths. She clicked the trash icon and an alert popped up, 'Delete WatercolorMemories.wav?' She clicked confirm and deleted the file, the last thing tying her to this place. Margo quickly dusted herself off and put her remaining personal items and cell phone back into her purse. She took one last glance around, knowing she'd never come back here again.

'It's over,' she whispered into the silence as she turned and walked away. She was anxious to see Austin, watch the final cut, and walk untethered into the future. Margo trudged back to where she'd left her car, feeling simultaneously drained and exhilarated. It had been hard to face the truth, but now that she had, it was like a suffocating weight had been lifted. Inserting herself into the *Into Thin Air* crew had been the perfect way to keep tabs on the investigation, to make sure they never got close to finding out her truth, and now, there was nothing even their tips could bring in to point at her. Margo took a deep breath and exhaled, feeling fully alive for the first time in weeks. She couldn't help but feel an electric buzz – a surprising thrill that she'd pulled it off. That even with the impressive investigative team on *Into Thin Air*, they were still spinning their wheels on the wrong people. Her family was safe at last. She could close the book on the most horrible chapter of her life, and for once, she was the one coming out on top.

She climbed into the driver's seat just as the clouds started rumbling ominously. Margo put the key in the ignition and turned as her phone rang out from inside her purse. Scrambling to grab it, she answered eagerly when she saw Austin's name on the screen. She quickly put it on speaker and laid it on the passenger seat face up.

'Hey, I'm on my way n—' but Austin cut her off, his excitement clear over the phone.

'Margo! You'll never believe it. My producer just sent

us a text that she's running late because the researchers unearthed a last-minute tip. She didn't tell me what exactly, something about the car the Buckleys saw the night Jessie disappeared. It'll mean a last-minute edit, but she's on her way now, you have to get over—'

Austin's words faded into a vibrating hum as the world spun around her. She snapped her hair band so rapidly against her wrist that it broke and flew off, landing somewhere out of reach.

'Margo? Are you there? Margo?'

She leaned forward and placed her forehead on the steering wheel, gripping it so tightly that her knuckles glowed white. A loud crack of thunder reverberated through her as the clouds above finally gave way, weeping thick tears onto her windshield as they splattered before her eyes. The raindrops covered the window in front of Margo, obscuring the very place she had driven away from all those years ago. A streak of lightning lit up the shadows around her, but she barely saw it through the darkness rolling in. She imagined what her dad would say. What Austin would say. What the world would say. She had thought it was done, that she had succeeded in burying the ugly truth, keeping it from ever seeing the light of day. But as Austin's voice buzzed in the background, she steeled her reserve and thought . . . *it's not over. Not yet. I might need a small miracle, but I've come this far. I have to see it through to the end, there's still work to be done*. Steadying her shaking hand, she picked up the phone and pulled it close to her ear.

'I'm on my way.'

INTO THIN AIR: Season 12 Episode 1210

'Whatever Happened to Jessie Germaine?
PART II'

Scheduled to Air: 10/13/2019

Jessie Germaine's remains were found folded up inside a cooler in a secret swimming hole known to the seniors of Lake Moss High on June 7th, 2019. During the filming of this episode, new evidence has come to light. Has the truth finally surfaced after all these years . . .?

If you have any information about the murder of Jessie Germaine, please call CrimeStoppers at the number below or log onto IntoThinAir. com/JessieGermaine

Acknowledgements

From Steph and Nicole:
We are so thankful to our editor at Avon Books, Lucy Frederick, who steered us along in this story and fearlessly encouraged more twists and turns. We can't thank you enough for all the time and dedication you've given to us and our novel. Thank you to everyone at Avon Books and HarperCollins for your support and enthusiasm as we've gone on this journey for our second book. We'd also like to thank Tilda McDonald, who helped us shape the plot and outline for this story in its early stages and taught us how to trust our gut instincts.

Jessica Battaglia, thank you for your wisdom on all things forensic. Educating us on how we'd find a body in very specific terrain and the condition that the remains would be found in was a jumping point for us to build the plot around. We thank you so much for your willingness to impart your knowledge for the sake of our book. Another big thank you goes out to Nicole's niece, Julia Seiber, for your help molding the opening riddle. We could not have crafted such a haunting and lyrical stanza to start from without your guidance and poetic finesse.

From Steph:

Thank you to my literary partner-in-crime, Nicole, for continuing to be my other half as I achieve something I've dreamed about my entire life. I am so grateful for your support, motivation, and encouragement throughout every stage of this journey. Your willingness to always listen to me vent or cry or celebrate, no matter what, is a relationship I truly cherish. Your ability to always shoulder burdens when I'm not able and turn over every rock until we find solutions to a plot hole or problem that arises is something I am forever thankful for. I can't wait to see what twisty stories our future holds.

To my husband, Danny, thank you for your support and encouragement as I work a full-time job and work on my second career as an author, all while trying to juggle our energetic puppy and everything else happening around us. I couldn't do it without your love and willingness to help around the house and bring me food and wine, and your kindness to never get offended when I answer calls or have to hop on the computer to tackle something. Thank you for always being my rock and grounding me when things get hard.

I am forever thankful for my family: Ann and Dave Durso, Katie and William Bagdorf, Chris and Kim Durso, Chris and Dave Johnson, Rosalie Gerace, the entire Mullin family, and everyone else in my circle who continues to support and love me every day. I'm so lucky to have family that has always encouraged me to go after my dreams.

Thank you as always to my dream team of beta readers: Lauren Totten, Megan Hilbert, and Jessie Kerr. Your feedback continues to be invaluable to the success of our stories, always giving us the notes we need (usually under insane deadlines). We couldn't do any of this without your support and selflessness and ability to point out things that we are too close to see.

And last but not least, thank you to my supporting and loving friends. Even when we can't see each other every day, your enthusiasm and encouragement keeps me going through the chaos. Thanks to the Tbooz (Lilli Winn, Darí Brooks Ahye, Amanda Mulligan, Lauren Totten, and Elisabeth Barker) for being the best squad a woman could ask for, and to Sara McCarthy and Megan Hilbert for being like sisters to me for over a decade and constantly cheering me on.

From Nicole:

Firstly, I'd like to thank my co-author Steph for continuing this journey with me. From the beginning of this book, we had no idea where it would go, but you were tireless in brainstorming to find the plot that was perfect for our concept. Your dedication to dropping everything and hopping on a call or zoom to hash out even the tiniest of details is always appreciated and a huge reason why we hit the finish line. Here's hoping we have endless dark and twisty novels in our co-authoring future.

As always, I could not have done this without my selfless beta readers, Sarah Sanchez, Deborah Kriger and Karen Chesley. Your ideas and notes have steered this story into what we were hoping for. You will never know how much your willingness to drop everything and read our very first draft has meant to us.

To the Murray Dog Park Crew, your unflinching support of my new career path has meant the world to me. You have become my family and I'm so thankful our dogs have brought us together.

And to my family, your love and support over the years has given me the courage to follow my dreams. Mom and Dad, you have always encouraged me, no matter how crazy my ideas might be, and I thank you for that. To my niece Julia, thank you for making me dinner every night while I was in the trenches writing this book. I didn't even have to ask, you just made me food so I wouldn't forget to eat. While it's a small thing, it meant the world to have you take care of me. I feel grateful every day to have such a wonderful family.

The DNA results are back – and there's a serial killer in the family tree…

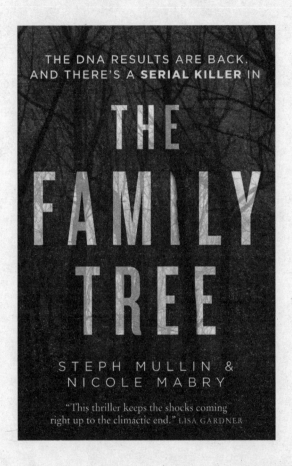
A gripping, original thriller for fans of a Netflix true crime documentary, and anyone who's ever wondered what their family tree might be hiding…

Available in paperback, eBook and audio now.